THE ISLAND WALKERS

THE

ISLAND

WALKERS

A NOVEL

JOHN BEMROSE

METROPOLITAN BOOKS

HENRY HOLT AND COMPANY

NEW YORK

Metropolitan Books
Henry Holt and Company, LLC
Publishers since 1866
115 West 18th Street
New York, New York 10011

Metropolitan Books™ is a registered
trademark of Henry Holt and Company, LLC.

Library of Congress Cataloging-in-Publication Data

Bemrose, John, 1947–
    The island walkers / John Bemrose.—1st American ed.
      p.   cm.
    ISBN 0-8050-7411-2
    1. Working class families—Fiction.   2. Textile industry—Fiction.   3. Textile workers—
Fiction.   4. Social classes—Fiction.   5. Labor unions—Fiction.   6. Ontario—Fiction.
I. Title.
PR9199.3.B3776I84   2004
813'.54—dc22

                                                                                              2003059954

Henry Holt books are available for special promotions and
premiums. For details contact: Director, Special Markets.

First American Edition 2004
Designed by Jo Anne Metsch

Printed in the United States of America

10   9   8   7   6   5   4   3   2   1

For Cathleen
and for Alix

THE ISLAND WALKERS

PROLOGUE

A TOWN OF two rivers, its plunging valley an anomaly in the tedious southwestern Ontario plain. Bridges. Water at dusk. The play of mist on the sloping face of a dam. High windows shot with gold, glimpsed among maples. Streets that beckon and disappear. The traveler, coming across this place, might be forgiven for imagining that life is better here.

In the deep center of town, the backs of the stores descend straight to the Shade River. From the Bridge Street bridge, you can savor the Old World atmosphere conjured by their wooden balconies perched randomly above the water, above the cut stone of foundations that seem to move upstream as the Shade brushes past through a flecking of shallow rapids. The cries of gulls.

Farther south, under the steep, wooded bulwark of Lookout Hill, you can make out the gap where the Attawan enters the Shade. Just now, a shaft of sun, playing from the hills to the west, lights up the vicinity of the forks. But even as you watch, the glow fades, saturating the air with the melancholy of an early dusk.

Look the other way, a hundred yards north of the bridge, and you'll see where a dam has stilled the river to a dark lake. Two tall stone abutments rise from the water, to support a rail trestle that disappears among the trees on the bank. Higher still, just visible among pines, the severe windows of the Bannerman mansion look down the valley with an air of confident, hard-earned plenty. Hidden behind it are the middle- and upper-class houses of the North End. There, a late sun pours its ripeness down leafy boulevards, across spacious lawns, into verandas shaded with striped awnings and trellises of Dutchman's pipe.

To the east, on the Flats, smaller houses huddle against the coming night. They seem not so much poor as crammed together and somehow hastily assembled, as though their builders did not make the same claim to permanence as those of the North End.

At the edge of this neighborhood, you will find a forest of sorts, sumacs and scrub maple forming a patch of wilderness in the heart of town. Much of this wasteland, curiously, has a cement floor, littered with broken liquor and wine bottles that glint in the dimming light, charred with the blackened remains of bonfires. You might make other interesting discoveries: rusted, nondescript bits of machinery, a few soot-stained bricks. It seems, almost, that by some scarcely imaginable act of violence, an entire building—a vast complex of buildings—has been torn up and carried away.

Nearby, the Attawan Historical Society has established a small park. Tidy beds of petunias and a couple of benches uphold an air of belea-guered propriety, under a solitary streetlight. An asphalt path leads to a metal plaque supported by a cement base.

BANNERMAN'S MILLS

On this site stood Bannerman's mills, in their time the largest knit-goods manufactory in the country. The mills were built by John Bannerman (1850–1932), a native of Boston, who arrived in Attawan in 1876, establishing his first mill on the Attawan River. In 1892, he built these larger premises to take advantage of the greater water-power potential of the Shade. At the height of its fortunes in the 1950s, Bannerman's Knitting employed over 900 people out of a total population of 5,200. The mills turned out socks, stockings, sweaters, T-shirts, and underwear, including the famous #99 long johns, popular in the hills and forestry camps of Canada's north. In 1966, the mills were destroyed by fire.

Little of importance is now made in Attawan. It has become a bed-room town, a place for strangers, where tour buses stop for half an hour and ladies with tinted hair take quick shots of the older houses, the pop-ular view from the bridge.

At Willard and Bridge, the little park continues to dream in a kind of bland, perpetual Sabbath. On its benches, a few old-timers linger. Some, no doubt, are veterans of the mills and the great work that went on inside. But you will find them reluctant to talk about the past. Ask about the fire, or the investigation that followed, and they will look at you, an outsider, with the rheumy farsightedness of the old and murmur that they really don't know about that, no, they can't remember. You would almost think they favored the argument suggested by the maples thick-ening each year toward the river: that Bannerman's mills had never been.

1

THE SMALLEST OF Attawan's working-class neighborhoods, the Island lay tucked behind the downtown Business Section, separated from it by an old millrace that formed a kind of watery shortcut across a bend of the Attawan River. This sluggish canal was shaded by black willows and bordered by a narrow trail that ran past vine-freighted fences and decaying sheds. The Island contained about two dozen houses, crowded along its two intersecting streets, Water and West. For several generations, the people of the Island—mostly mill workers and their families—had considered themselves quite separate from the town's other residents: a state of mind most pronounced among the children, who conducted ongoing crab-apple and hockey wars with their enemies on the Flats or in the North End.

The Walker house sat at the bottom of West, overlooking a cul-de-sac where the street met an earthen flood dike. Nearly a hundred years old, the house had walls of plastered lath work, with shuttered windows and a front door of solid oak boards. The unstable ground of the area—which was still, in some sense, the province of the river, still prone on occasion to floods that topped the dikes—had over the years skewed the frame of the house and tilted its floors. But it was a well-kept place, the walls cleanly whitewashed, the shutters and doors painted a deep forest green.

One Saturday in the summer of 1965, Joe and Alf Walker climbed onto the roof and spent the better part of the morning stripping the old shingles. By eleven they were busy nailing down the new ones. Joe, who had turned eighteen that July, worked on the slope that overlooked the backyard. He sat shirtless and hammered sullenly between his legs, aware of the sun-baked expanse of tarpaper stretching up the slope behind him. From the other side of the peak, his father's hammer thundered without rest. It seemed crazy to try to keep up.

He shifted his weight, placed the next shingle, and looked across the yard with its picnic table and apple tree, its narrow lawn and rows of vegetables, beyond the flood dike blooming cheerfully with his mother's flowers, to the Atta, flowing through the shadow of Lookout Hill. Under its far bank, the water looked cool and inviting: another world. He was laboring under protest, under a sense of injustice that drove him on in angry spurts and then dragged him into a sloth so deep it was like a spell. Why were they doing this today? Today—as he'd mentioned to his father last Wednesday, he was sure—he and Smiley were planning to go hunting with Smiley's new .22. His friend had gone on without him. A few minutes ago he'd heard a shot echo down the valley.

He dipped into the bag beside him, and the sharp nails bit his fingers. For weeks the shingles had sat beside the house in their paper wrappings, under a paint-spotted tarp. A dozen times at least his mother had said, "Alf, I am getting so tired of that *heap* out there. You'd think we were living in the Ozarks." His mother's idea of the Ozarks came from television, but she used the phrase to convey a sense of social embarrassment, of appearances that were not up to the mark. He always thought it sounded funny in her English accent. His parents had met during the war. Hearing the words *war bride* as a young boy, he had imagined his mother striding off to battle in skirts and helmet. The vision had made him slightly wary of her, as if she could lay claim to secret, irresistible powers. Yet there had been nothing but weary exasperation in her complaints about the roof, the mechanical recitation of an old war cry that no longer frightened anybody: an act for tourists. She had grown up in a finer house than this; she'd told him many times about the books, the grand piano, the holidays in Normandy. "Your father's uniform fooled me completely." This was another of her stories. "For all I knew he was a millionaire's son." It had become a family joke, told, at the right time, at parties; her coming down in the world was a mistake, based on her inability to read his father's status by his accent or his clothes. Not until after she'd arrived in Attawan in the spring of 1946 did she realize what she'd done. She hadn't given up, though. Getting the roof shingled was only the most recent in an endless series of assaults on their rough edges—on their house, which by her standards was too small and, despite their relentless improvements, still too shabby, not to mention situated in the wrong part of town. Again, Joe looked at the river. Such thoughts were troubling, leading to shadows, sadness. Better to hunker down like his father and pretend he wasn't affected.

Yet his father wasn't impervious. His wife's complaints might seem to sink in him without a trace, snow into dark water, but they could achieve a critical mass. This morning he had roused Joe early and announced that today they were shingling the roof. But why today, Joe wondered, the hottest so far of the whole summer? At breakfast, over a trembling forkful of fried egg, he dared to question the decision; maybe they should wait till it was cooler, he said, thinking the whole time of Smiley's gun, of the wafer of silver light at the end of the scope and even of the word *scope* itself, so pleasing and final, like a bullet smacking into mud. "It's going to rain," his father said, and when Joe said, "It's rained before," meaning *and you never bothered then,* his father had said quietly, looking at him with those ice-blue eyes the color of Lake Erie in spring, "No arguments."

He thought there was something fanatic in his father that came from a place of silence and brooding Joe couldn't reach: something extreme and overbearing and violent that thank God was not there all the time, but which could spring up like a blade you hadn't been careful with and nip you. Now it was his arbitrariness that bothered Joe most. What gave his father the right to decide? Why did he have to obey? Why didn't he just throw down his hammer and leave the roof? Joe suspected that, if he did, he would have to leave the house as well. He had absorbed some notion that work was something you did for everybody, without complaint. He had worked for as long as he could remember, washing floors, washing the car, digging gardens, stacking cans in the A&P; this summer he was at Bannerman's. He expected to work, but this morning some remnant of an ancient grievance had surfaced. The need for unquestioning obedience was an injustice, and so was the loss of his day.

The hammering from the other side had stopped. A moment later he heard his father's heavy, braced steps come down the slope behind him. A pack of shingles slammed into the roofboards like a body. Then the labor of his father's breathing as he surveyed Joe's work.

"Good," his father said curtly, and Joe knew he was disappointed. "Pete's coming after lunch. We should be through by three or four."

The footsteps retreated up the roof. It was then, as a breeze touched the trees across the river, that a voice called his father's name. Joe looked around but could see no one. The voice had seemed to sound from the blue sky or his own head: a husky baritone he did not know, calling *Alf Walker?* on a cheerful interrogative note.

His father stood at the peak, against the burning sky. His graying hair had fallen from its place over his ears and was hanging down stiffly, like drooping pennons. He was staring into the front yard, at someone not visible to Joe.

"Malachi Doyle," the voice barked, and for a moment Joe thought he heard a foreign tongue or a code. Then he realized the man had spoken his name.

"I'm from the UKW," said the voice, which had the trace of a lilt: "United—"

"I know who they are," Joe's father said.

"Like to have a word or two. Only take a few minutes."

Joe's father did not reply but went on gazing into the yard, as if all that had sounded was an echo.

To Joe, his father's silence was excruciating. He had never gotten used to his habit of saying nothing, so that you wondered if he had even heard your remark, or if (meeting the candid stare of those pale blue eyes) he had found it too stupid or trivial to merit a response. His father dealt in silences. When he spoke, he seemed to rise out of silence as a fish might rise from the water, its natural element, soon to return to it. Even though Joe had heard him tell stories in his droll way, and laugh and talk as any ordinary man might, such moments seemed exceptional. His father existed at a distance, and the distance was reinforced by silence, as though there were simply too great a space for a voice to carry over: only a fool would stand there shouting what could not be heard.

Now his father's gaze seemed to lift, over the rooftops of the Island. Joe licked his lips. Mere seconds passed, but to him they seemed like minutes. He was expecting something even more embarrassing to happen. For the last two weeks, at the mill, a rumor had been circulating that a union organizer was in town. Joe had heard the other workers talk about him during break, joking about his alleged presence with a skittish indirectness, as though it had something to do with sex. His father, who was head fixer in Number Six knitting mill, had made no comment on the subject until one evening, walking home after work, Art Johnson began to chat about the organizer. Art had fallen silent, as if sensing disapproval. After a few seconds Joe heard his father say, "The bastard better not show his face at my place."

Well, here the bastard was, apparently. Joe watched his father briefly touch the back pocket of his trousers, the bulge of his wallet. Then he climbed over the peak and began to sink out of sight: the soiled factory greens, the heavy shoulders in their filthy undershirt, the head with its drooping strands of hair, its bald spot.

When Joe heard the ladder rattle, he got up and climbed swiftly to the peak. Down the steeply sloping roof, he saw the top of the ladder shake a little. But on the sidewalk that ran past the house, and on the small front lawn burned the color of straw, he could see no one.

2

THE ORGANIZER WAS waiting at the foot of the ladder: a short, thickly built fellow, perhaps ten years older than Alf, with grizzled fly-away hair and a face so red Alf assumed he was a drinker. He wore a madras sport shirt, darkened with sweat over the massive chest, and shapeless trousers of an indeterminate color. He watched Alf descend with an ironic but not unfriendly glint in his small eyes, as though he sensed some hostility but wasn't offended. It was part of the game.

"Doyle," he said, holding out a large hand.

"Maybe we could go for a walk," Alf said, aware of Margaret, somewhere in the house behind him. Across the street, a sprawled cat twitched its tail; a dark window looked out with self-effacing curiosity. The whole world was watching while pretending not to.

He took Doyle down the sidewalk toward the dike at the end of the cul-de-sac. They passed the organizer's dark green Edsel—a '58, Alf thought—its horse-collar grill and protruding headlights circled in rust. Alf chuckled gloomily to himself. There was something fitting about Doyle driving this unholy relic of a car, a car so bad Ford had stopped building it after three years. "The UK-whatever-it-was can't be up to much," Alf thought, "sending him out in a junker like that." Despite his acknowledgment on the roof, he hadn't heard of Doyle's outfit. He supposed it was one of those small bottom-feeding unions that lived off what the larger ones had missed.

Doyle was chatting away gruffly at his side, as if he were used to being smuggled out of sight like some disreputable relative. "Had a helluva time finding you," he was saying. "Went to one place across town there; they told me I had the wrong Walkers. 'You got the Flats Walkers,' they tell me. 'You want the Island Walkers.' The Island Walkers," Doyle repeated. "A name like that, I thought I was back in Ireland. Everyone had their queer little monikers. The backstreet Kellys, the sidehill Corcorans. I sort of miss it."

Alf gestured ahead of him, indicating the path that saddled the dike. Doyle jogged ahead with a burst of energy, his heavy haunches churning through goldenrod. They descended to a foreshore of loose, clattering rock where puddles of stagnant water lay, frowsy with scum. A few stunted willow bushes watched them like dogs. Doyle walked on a few steps and stood with his thick arms akimbo, gazing at the river.

"Grew up on water like this," the organizer said. He seemed pleased to remember.

"In Ireland," Alf said wearily. He felt he was taking up a role.

"A salmon river. The fish that used to come up it, as long as your feckin' arm."

"Well, there's nothing like that here," Alf said. Downstream, a fisherman was casting into the tunnel under the Shade Street bridge. Alf hoped the man—it was Del Featherstone—wouldn't turn and see them.

"I remember my dad and I went out this one time, early morning." Doyle's red face shone. There was something of the child in him, an astonishingly ugly eight-year-old. "We took our bikes. Oh, it must have been three or more miles we went, to a new river. At least it was new to me. Dim. Dyne. Something like that. We fished for two hours and got nothing. Then my daddy made one last cast—you'd have thought all creation had erupted. I mean, the thing was like a bar of silver. . . ."

A kindred memory—fishing, a river coppered by dusk—slipped through Alf's mind. He let it go.

"Well," the organizer said. Groping at his breast pocket, he plucked out a sorry-looking pack of Macdonald's. Alf waved the cigarettes away and waited while the man hunted for his matches, scraped up flame.

"You're not going to get anywhere here," Alf said.

"You mean with you?"

"With anybody," Alf said. "We aren't in the union way here."

"And why would that be?" Doyle said, blowing a leisurely plume. He looked, Alf thought with despair, as if he were in a bar somewhere, with a pint at hand and a small one at the side, preparing to enjoy his companion's story.

Alf frowned. He wished he were back on his roof.

"Let's just say we've been through it before."

"Ah, yes, the famous strike of 'forty-nine," Doyle said, taking another drag.

"Bugger the fame," Alf said, with real heat. "It tore this place apart." There had been a wildcat strike, entirely unsuccessful. The fledgling union had been crushed; wounds had opened that still hadn't healed. The only way people tolerated them was to keep silent.

"Tell me about it," Doyle said. Alf shook his head in disbelief. He

didn't want to think about the strike—the habit of years—let alone talk
about it with this stranger. He looked away, to the edge of the river,
where the corpse of a big carp had been picked over by gulls. Only flies
were moving now.

"I take it you went out," Doyle said quietly.

Alf glanced at the other man. How did he know? He supposed he'd
been talking to people in town. He supposed that he, Alf, still had a reputation as a troublemaker, even though he'd left the strike weeks before
it ended. Even though the whole thing was over sixteen years ago. They
didn't forget in a place the size of Attawan. They didn't change their
minds about you either, he thought with bitterness, at least not easily.
That was how it was in a town where everyone knew everyone else. Or
thought they did.

"More fool I," Alf said.

Doyle went on watching him as he smoked. He seemed comfortable
with the silence, as Alf was not. Alf was torn between saying more and
simply walking away. But he felt he had to warn Doyle off. It was why he
had brought him to the river.

"Look," he said. "No one—I mean no one of any account—is going to
be interested in your project. You might get a few of the malcontents;
there's always some of those. But the great majority—you start pushing
them, and they'll run you out on a rail."

Doyle's big chest and shoulders heaved, as if he relished the idea.

"Actually, Alf, there's more than a few." The organizer spoke quietly,
confidentially, as if sorry to have to contradict him. "Wrote me quite a
letter," he said. Leaning forward, he tapped his nicotine-stained fingers
on his chest pocket, where apparently the letter lay, nested with his cigarettes.

"Don't even start," Alf said, shaking his head. "You won't believe the
trouble you'll cause." He stopped. There was so much more he might
say, so much more he wanted to say, pressing its dark weight on his
mind. He stared off toward the dead carp, and the legacy of 1949 was
there, as real and palpable as the rotting carcass under its boiling cloud of
flies. But he did not know how to put it into words.

"I've got to get back to my roof," he said.

Suddenly Doyle snapped away his butt. His eyes had narrowed on Alf, through smoke, and there was a sudden sense of attack.

"And Intertex," he said sharply. "How do you feel about them?"

THE FIRST TIME Alf had heard the name, he hadn't quite taken it in. It seemed more properly the name of a machine or a process than a company. It was Johnny Carruthers, Bannerman's assistant general manager, who'd told him one evening in May—this was in the parking lot of the beer store—that Intertex had picked up Bannerman's. Not only did the name put him off balance, there was the phrase, *picked up*. What had happened? "They've bought us," Johnny explained, in an overly loud voice, as if speaking to a child. "International Textile, big firm out of Montreal. Picked us up last week." Alf had an image of the new company plucking Bannerman's from the ground, like the big hand in the insurance ad. "Picked us up for a song," Johnny said, shutting his trunk. There was a cockiness in his manner, as though he dealt in this kind of high-stakes activity every day, nothing a real businessman couldn't handle. "They're into industrial wovens: car seat coverings, commercial drapes, that sort of thing. But recently they've been picking up knitting mills, mostly in Quebec."

Alf experienced a faint vertigo, as if the ground had shifted, for hadn't he been picked up as well? Later, he sat at the picnic table in his back-yard, under falling apple blossoms, and read about the sale in the *Attawan Star*. Under the lead line BANNERMAN'S SOLD was a head-and-shoulders shot of a bald, handsome, heavy-jawed man in a suit, his shoulders slightly tilted, as though he were leaning out, a bit mischievously, from behind a tree. The caption identified him as R. J. Prince, an Intertex vice president. The article revealed that Intertex owned plants in Canada, the United States, Britain, Italy, and France and quoted R. J. Prince as saying how proud Intertex was to acquire such a venerable company as Bannerman's—"a real slice of our national history." He looked forward, he said, "to working with all the good people who made Bannerman's such a success in the past." Alf lowered the paper to the picnic table. A petal, like a tiny silk hat, fell onto Prince's head. Alf brushed it off and studied the man's face with its suggestion of penetrating frankness. On the whole, he approved.

The next day on the fire escape outside the sixth-floor knitting room, where the knitters and fixers took their breaks, all talk was of the sale. Alf sat sipping from his plastic thermos cup and listened to the eruption of speculations, rumor, and fear along the long iron balcony. Some of the workers remained quiet, like himself, but most agreed the sale was a bad thing. It might mean layoffs, Pat Kenner said. He'd heard from his brother-in-law in Quebec that Intertex were "real sons of bitches. They'll take an ax to the place."

In the millyard below, a pigeon glided on taut wings, fleeing from sunlight to shade.

Alf said, "Come on. You'd think the mills had never been sold before."

He spoke so infrequently that everyone turned to look at him.

"When John Bannerman was an old man, back in the twenties, they were sold then," he said. "Everybody was worried then too, but it turned out to be the best thing that could have happened. The next thirty years were the best we ever had."

There was silence after that—he'd given them something to think about—and a minute later, as they trooped back in to work, someone clapped him on the back. But he was uncomfortable. He had his own worries about Intertex. Two weeks before the announcement of the sale, a notice had appeared on the knitting room bulletin board, asking for applicants for the position of foreman. He'd applied, feeling the indignity the whole time. He'd been in the knitting mill for eighteen years, worked his way up from knitter to head fixer, and had come in recent years, as everyone said, to pretty much run the place. Increasingly it was he, and not the foreman, Matt Honnegger (who was due to retire that winter), who made out the knitting schedules, hunted down lost orders, and expedited rush ones. He was more than a foreman-in-waiting, he felt; in some sense he was the foreman already, and any suggestion that he had to ask for what was his infuriated him.

The notice had asked the applicants to submit ideas on how operations in Number Six knitting rooms might be improved. Alf had delayed
for days but finally filled several sheets of paper with drafts of possible
answers. In the end, he'd presented Joe with two paragraphs of tight
script and stood by, as thin-skinned as any adolescent, while Joe read it
over. When Joe had suggested changes, Alf barely managed to keep civil.
It was hard to be reminded that he, Alf, had dropped out of high school
at sixteen and that his son would soon be in his final year, on his way to
the distant planet of university. But he accepted most of Joe's suggestions (and worried later he should have accepted the rest), and Joe typed
up his proposal. The next day, handing the letter to May Watson, the
receptionist at General Office, Alf felt a piece of his life pass out of his
hands, as though he were releasing into the sea a bottle with a note for
help inside. It seemed impossible that so tenuous and haphazard a signal
could find its way to the right place.

Spring became summer, the flood dikes turned pink and blue with
dame's rocket, and there was no response. On the fire escape, the talk
turned to softball and the summer holidays. Bannerman's had changed
hands, but the mills, it seemed, were entirely unaffected. The steam
whistle above the boiler plant continued to howl up the dawns, calling
the workers from sleep. The tall machines continued to pour out their
rivers of soft, fragrant cloth. It's like the phony war, Alf thought, remembering the fall of '39. Canada had declared war on Germany, but when
he'd looked up at the sky, suddenly thrilled and frightened by the
thought of being at war, the white clouds had moved on with unruffled
stateliness, declaring all earthly business an illusion.

On the bulletin board the notice faded under its blue-headed tacks.
Every morning as Alf climbed the stairs to the sixth floor, he looked in
trepidation. The notice's continuing existence seemed a judgment, an
unfavorable one, that said, We've considered your application and found
it wanting. We continue to search.

"Everything's up in the air with this Intertex business," Matt Honnegger told him one day, his fleshy face expressionless. "It'll be a while
before they get around to the likes of you and me." Matt's resigned air

put Alf off even more. He wanted to be made use of. He imagined his letter waiting under a mountain of others while men he did not know, in offices he would never see, ignored his fate. What did it matter? he thought bitterly. Wasn't he a fool to put his faith in something like this, over which he had no control, rely on it to the point of sleeplessness?

Then in mid-July an earnest young man in a yellow hard hat appeared in front of Alf carrying a clipboard and demanding answers in a shouting voice to such questions as "When you go to the yarn room, how many bobbins do you bring back, on average?" Alf looked into the evasive eyes swimming behind thick glasses. "I'm a fixer," he said. "I don't go into the yarn room." This was not, strictly speaking, true, but he couldn't resist a poke at the automaton. He was rewarded with a brief flutter of panic— something human—but the young man quickly found another question on his board. "How many times a day, on average, do you go to the washroom?"

The place was crawling with them—young men whose excruciatingly detailed questions and bright helmets spawned bitter hilarity among the workers. Hard hats in a knitting mill! What were they afraid of, falling threads? The hard hats measured, watched, timed, noted down, disappeared, came back for more measurements, and then disappeared for good. Weeks later the layoffs began. Twenty from the night shift, an additional sixteen from day. Three from Alf's floor alone, including his young friend Rick Stevenson, who had two kids to support and a wife going crazy with migraines. Those who were left were working harder; Alf often wasn't home till eight o'clock. The discussions on the fire escape intensified. Time to look at a union again, a few workers said, breaching a taboo. But most, perhaps remembering 1949, argued No: at this stage a union would be a red flag; it would bring on more firings. Better to hunker down, ride out the bad times, and (though this was never expressed) hope it was your neighbor who got hit, not you.

Alf said little. The firings troubled him a great deal. He lent money to Rick Stevenson and voiced his concerns to Matt Honnegger, hoping Matt would pass them up the line, up the chain of command that led to the holy-of-holies where someone with half a heart might be listening. At the same time, he tried to grasp the rationale behind the turmoil—tried, as a foreman-in-waiting, to see things from management's point of view. He felt that, as foreman, he would bring a special understanding to the situation; somehow he could bridge the gap between what the workers needed and what the company had to do. How he would manage this remained unclear, but now his letter seemed more urgent than ever. The new men, whoever they were, needed him.

"INTERTEX IS DOING what they have to," Alf said, stubbornly defensive. He had lost his taste for argument. The sun seemed to be tightening an iron hoop around his head.

"You like what they're doing here?" Doyle said, not bothering to hide his sarcasm.

"Of course I don't like the layoffs; I know these people. But the place was slipping. Something had to be done."

"Place was still making a profit, though." The organizer had pounced gleefully on *profit,* evidence that refuted all arguments. His black eyes gleamed.

Alf faced the stark slope of his roof, floating tentlike above the dike. His son was there, a slim, tanned figure standing on the peak. The boy seemed impossibly distant, like youth itself. A panel of shingles hung from his hand like a broken wing.

3

THE FAMILY SAT for lunch at the picnic table, in the flickering mesh of light spread by the dwarf MacIntosh that leaned from the base of the dike. Twenty feet away, in full sun, Red, their malamute, lay on his side in the dirt, panting heavily, his lolling tongue speckled with dirt.

Margaret had asked Jamie to say grace. The eight-year-old was peeking over his clasped hands as he listed the things on the table. His thick sun-bleached hair stood up here and there in tufts.

"Thank you for our milk, and our water, and our pickles—Don't!" he cried suddenly, jabbing his elbow at his sister.

"I didn't touch him," Penny complained to Alf. Her eyes—pale blue like his—were huge with protest. Under her pink T-shirt, her shoulders jerked up, declaring her innocence.

"Come on," Joe urged, "the sandwiches are getting stale." Alf's older son had put on a shirt, at Margaret's insistence. Beside his place was a paperback, turned face down. Another book about the war, Alf noted wearily, glancing at the flaming swastika on the cover, the Moloch head of a tank swiveling among ruins: *The Anvil of Stalingrad.*

"I don't like tuna fish," Jamie said to his mother. "Do I have to—?"

"There's peanut butter for you," Margaret said coolly, sounding very English. She was wearing her seersucker housedress, the one that left her slender arms bare. Her dark hair, still damp from washing, clung to the side of her head, leaving the tips of her ears exposed and, to Alf's eyes, oddly vulnerable. She was singing at a wedding that afternoon at the church. "And anyway, you don't have to thank God for individual items."

Penny snorted, which brought another murderous glance from Jamie. But he went on with his great enumeration. High overhead, a cicada drilled through the heat of noon. Alf looked over at his wife. Her closed eyelids were trembling, as though animated by a subtle electric current. Her face with its pale forehead and fine brows was lifted slightly, as she listened to Jamie's prayer.

"Make us truly thankful, inChristsnameweaskit—"

"Thank you," Joe said dryly, reaching for a sandwich.

"Wait!" Jamie's brown eyes, copies of his mother's, struck out at his brother. "I'm not done."

"I don't believe it!" Penny cried.

"Penny," Margaret warned. The girl looked at her father, always her court of last appeal. Alf had always felt they shared secret, unspoken

things about the family that were rarely made specific. He looked tactfully away.

They waited again with bowed heads, stoically. The cicadas whined,
and in Lion's Park across the river the merry-go-round screeched with a
sound of metal on metal.

"Amen," Jamie said finally.

"I think I'm going to kill him," Joe said.

"He did very well," Margaret said, as she drew the platter of sandwiches toward Jamie. On her own plate was a lone scoop of cottage
cheese and a slab of beefsteak tomato, red as blood. Another of her diets,
Alf thought ruefully. She was thin enough, he felt, hardly heavier than
when he'd first met her twenty-three years ago, at a servicemen's dance
in Henley-under-Downs. Her slimness was a thing people remarked on.
"If only I knew Margaret's secret! I think she's made a deal with the
devil!" Her skin seemed nearly as clear as it had been in 1942. Her hair,
which she continued to wear in the same style, brushed in waves away
from a central part, was as dark and vigorous. All the same, he knew she
had changed. There was a hint of sallowness in her face. In her eyes, he
glimpsed what he feared was disappointment.

Yet that week she'd been bubbling around the house, in a much better
mood than usual. Jack Ramsay, he thought. Jack Ramsay was the new
minister at the Anglican church. Jack was from England, like her, a tall
young man of thirty or so, with a brightly boyish face and an affable
manner Alf found a bit glib. He had a fine tenor voice, though. That
afternoon he was not only going to officiate at the wedding, he was going
to sing with Margaret. Alf had heard Margaret rehearsing her part, the
words of the duet wafting through the house in her clear soprano.

> The sparrow hath found her an house
> And the swallow a nest
> Where she may lay her young:
> Even thine altars
> O Lord of Hosts.

Alf supposed she was in love, after a fashion, with Jack Ramsay. He was used to her falling in love—with men and women both, or with singers or authors or symphony orchestras. It never lasted for more than a few days or a few weeks, and while it was happening she was effervescent and pleased with everything. He tried to be philosophical about Jack Ramsay—after all, nothing but high spirits came from these infatuations, and her high spirits were a good deal easier on them than the grim patches she fell into at other times.

"I think you're an atheist at heart," Joe was saying to his brother.

"No I'm not."

"You don't even know what an atheist is."

"Yes I do."

"What is it then?"

"He doesn't know," Penny said, with the scornful certainty of a ten-year-old, biting a pickle.

"I do," Jamie insisted, his eyes bulging at his sister. They had been at each other all morning.

"Tell him then," she sang. Jamie stared hard at Joe, as if by ferocious willpower he could force the answer to appear in Joe's face. Jamie had the clear, open face of a believer, it seemed to Alf. The boy worshiped his brother and considered him a source of impeccable truth.

"It's somebody who doesn't go to church."

"Close but no cigar."

"Perhaps you could just tell him what an atheist is," Margaret said impatiently. She was sawing at her tomato, eyes burning. A couple of weeks before, Joe had announced he would no longer go to church. Alf knew his withdrawal had hurt her.

"An atheist—" Penny began.

"I want him to tell me," Jamie insisted, pointing to Joe. Alf noticed that Bob Horsfall had appeared in his garden next door. It never failed. Whenever they ate in the yard, Horsfall or his wife would come out and hang around, pretending to be busy, like children hoping to be asked to play. Horsfall—a small man in baggy shorts—scowled at Alf (his face was set in a permanent scowl anyway, it only needed to darken a little) and gestured violently to something in his garden—some tomato that had rotted, no doubt, or a broken stem, more evidence that the world was going to hell. Alf ignored him. Both Horsfall and his wife were deaf. They could speak only after a fashion, in grunts that scarcely resembled human speech.

"—is somebody who doesn't believe in God."

Jamie's eyes slowly grew bright. He looked at his sister, his quarrel with her forgotten. He looked at his father.

"I believe in God," he said, almost in a whisper.

"Of course you do," Margaret said, trying to hurry him past this crisis. "We all do."

"I don't," Joe said flippantly. He was staring at his book.

"You don't?" said Jamie.

"Some nice big guy in the sky," Joe said.

"That's enough," Alf said.

"The great white father who thinks it's fine if people die of cancer, or starve to death—"

"I said that's enough!" Alf couldn't stand his older son's moralizing, the narrow, superior tone he used sometimes, telling them all what was good for them.

They ate in silence, in a heat pierced by the whine of cicadas. Jamie's shocked gaze kept returning to Alf. Alf winked and the boy's face twitched but he was unappeased. Alf sensed he was hoping for some reassurance in the strange, bleak sense of aftermath that had settled on the table. It wasn't just that he had yelled at Joe; it was what Joe had said, about not believing in God. But what do I know about God? Alf thought. He went to church, but this was mainly a social thing, seconding Margaret's great involvement there. Occasionally he prayed. But to whom, what power? Waist deep in his tomato plants, Bob Horsfall grunted, his face twisted with emotions he couldn't speak. Alf concentrated on his plate. He couldn't imagine Horsfall's life of total enveloping silence, like a life underwater. Sometimes he heard Horsfall's wife, shrieking in the house like an animal in pain.

A large ant crawled up Red's tongue. He gulped wetly: gone.

Margaret said, "Joe tells me you had a visitor?"

Her tone was casually interested, but Alf knew her too well. He heard criticism, alarm.

His eyes met his wife's. Some recognition was there, some quickening, beyond the scope of their daily lives. It could not be sustained, though. He frowned at Joe, who had kept reading his book. Why had he told his mother about Doyle's visit? Surely the boy had some notion of the trouble he would cause.

"From a union?" Margaret persisted, on a note of cheerful innocence.

"Just doing his rounds," Alf said, reaching for another sandwich. "He'll be on to some other town by now."

As he said this, he realized it was probably not true; the man would not retreat so easily. Still, he wanted to placate her.

"I'm surprised you talked to him."

"You'd prefer me to throw my hammer at him?" Alf said, and was gratified to hear Jamie laugh.

"Well, no," she said, as if he actually might have. "I just thought, with the foreman's job still up in the air . . ."

"I think that's why Dad took him down to the river," Joe said. Alf glanced at his son, not his usual ally in these quarrels.

"To keep him out of sight," Joe added.

Margaret cut into her tomato.

"I just think we have to be careful," she said.

"I was careful, Margaret," Alf said in a soft voice, suppressing his anger. She did not meet his stare. He looked down at his plate, smeared with crumbs and pickle juice. The cicadas drilled through his brain. Some large emotion seemed in the offing, but distantly, immured in ice, shining like a sea he could not reach. He was sorry he'd told his wife about applying for the foreman's job. It clearly meant as much to her as it did to him, perhaps more. Sensing he was being watched, he raised his head and saw Penny gazing at him with infinite seriousness. Her eyes locked on his. She might have been reading his mind, reading some obscure current of thought he could hardly make out himself.

SICKENED BY THE hatred and violence boiling through the town (one worker had died of a heart attack after his family had been threatened), Alf had left the strike a few weeks before it finally limped to its ignominious conclusion. Margaret had inherited a few thousand dollars from an aunt, and she urged him to use it to start the carpentry business he'd been talking about for years—in fact, since the first weeks of their courtship, in England. Walking with her on the downs above her house (the air trembling with the drone of bombers setting out for Germany), he had discovered his calling. "I'm going to build houses," he told her, in a rush of excitement. In Attawan before the war he had worked for the town's finest builder, Bute Erikson. He'd learned how to put up houses from scratch; he could do carpentry, electrical work, plumbing, cement. But it was not until he met Margaret that he glimpsed his future whole. "I'll build you a house," he promised her. "We'll pick out the best lot in the North End. Whatever your little old heart desires."

In France, sitting with his back to some ruined wall, with black smoke threatening on the the horizon, he had amused himself by sketching various versions of their future house, tucking the sheets into letters he sent to England. Margaret made drawings, too, and mailed them on. The house became part of their mutual dream, a shield against the war.

Back in Canada, he found there wasn't enough money to set up on his own, not right away. Bute Erikson was dead, so he went to work in the mills. To save money, he and Margaret lived with Alf's parents, in their brick cottage on the east side of the Island. But Margaret and Moira—both of them English, but from different classes—got along like oil and water. His nerves already strained by the war, Alf thought he would go mad with their bickering. He and Margaret soon moved out to a rented place around the corner—the house they were still in, which recently they had managed to buy. In 1948 he got involved in the movement to bring a union to Bannerman's, enticed by Cary Winner, the organizer from Montreal who charmed him into thinking that socialism was the only way forward. Yes, he'd bought it hook, line, and sinker—the vision

of a world where all were equal, all shared. But after months of prepara-
tions, the strike had faltered in just a few weeks. ("Nothing worse than a
strike gone bad," Cary had told Alf, not long before the organizer
washed his hands of the whole business.) Margaret's money arrived in
the nick of time.

Alf bought secondhand tools and a Ford pickup truck, with a stake box
he sanded and varnished to make look like new. On the doors, he stenciled ALF WALKER AND SON, BUILDERS (Joe was just an infant at the time,
but Alf included him as if he were creating not just a business but a
dynasty). He papered the town with advertisements. But the business
had not come. His part in the strike had sabotaged him, he believed; his
reputation as a troublemaker ensured that no one with money to build a
house would hire him. After two years he'd built only one—and had
been left holding the bills for more than five thousand dollars when his
client skipped town. The bank took his truck and most of his larger tools.
He managed to keep back a few screwdrivers and saws, which still hung
in their neat graded rows above his basement workbench, a reminder of
his failure. There were other reminders, like the plans for the Cape Cod
he'd never built for Margaret. They'd had them drawn up by an architect
in Johnsonville in the first heady days of the business. He'd noticed them
the other day, rolled in oilcloth and stuck in the cellar joists with his
father's old fishing rods. He hadn't had the heart to take them down.

A manager at Bannerman's—a fishing crony of his father's—had wan-
gled Alf's old job back for him, and he climbed again to the sixth-floor
knitting room where the tall machines waited in familiar, mocking stillness. For all his efforts, it seemed, nothing had changed.

Thirteen years passed. The previous summer, his mother had died of
cancer. They had buried her, a stick woman with an expression of long-
set unhappiness the undertakers had not been able to soften entirely,
under the red granite stone where twelve years earlier they had buried
his father. George Walker had drowned in 1952, while fishing from Bannerman's dam. There were no buffers, now, between Alf and the place
where time, his time, simply stopped, like a field that ends in the distance, its sheer edge cutting the blue of the sea. He could see that sea's

blue haze, getting steadily brighter. Where had his life gone? It had gone up in war, in anger, in hope, in the years of raising children, in the churn of knitting machines, in the lick of water on stone. And now he was forty-seven, with a sore back, less than half his hair, and only one chance left, maybe, to prove to himself and to Margaret that he was more— better—than a fixer in Bannerman's mills.

PETE ARRIVED WHILE they were eating dessert. Alf heard the throb of the Sarasota and watched the big two-toned Chrysler swing into the drive behind his Biscayne. The car had fins like the Batmobile in Jamie's comics, so tall they looked on the verge of flapping. The Sarasota was eight years old and secondhand. Pete preferred to drive the more expensive cars, even if he had to wait five years to be able to afford them. His friend strode across the yard, a case of Carling's Red Cap under his sinewy, tattooed forearm.

"I see the party's under way," he sang out. With a courtly, ironic nod, he darted a wary glance from under the peak of his ball cap. "Margaret."

"Pete," she said, putting down her glass.

"I guess you guys have been busy."

"Well, you can take over now," Alf said, glad of his old friend's arrival. With Pete there would be jokes, stories; he would forget.

Margaret stood up.

"Don't get so drunk you fall off the roof," she said dryly, reaching for Alf's plate.

"Don't worry. I'll keep an eye on him," Pete said, shooting Jamie a wink. The boy's face swam with pleasure. To him and Penny, Uncle Pete was the closest thing they knew to a relative.

Margaret did not deign to reply. She only tolerated Pete for *his* sake, Alf felt. Years ago, she had asked Alf why he considered Pete Moon his best friend. "I just think you might do better," she'd said. "I wouldn't say he was my *best* friend," Alf had said, wounded and defensive. Yet he knew what she meant. There was something of the lost soul about Pete, with his broken teeth and fixed stare, his eighth-grade education.

Margaret lingered with a stack of dirty plates in her hand, asking after Pete's wife, May.

"Oh, jeez, she's not fit to live with, these days." Pete's eyes with their look of innocent candor had settled on Alf, even though he was technically answering Margaret. "I can't do anything right. I put my glass down, she says, *Don't put it down there!*"

Jamie laughed at Pete's mocking falsetto. But Penny was watching him soberly, as if unaware of any joke. On her plate was an apple with a slice cut off its side, the white flesh turning brown.

"Well, I'm sure she has her reasons," Margaret said. "Penny, you haven't eaten your dessert. Bring it in with you, you can help me with the dishes." Moving as if hypnotized, Penny swung her legs over the bench but sat, seemingly absorbed by the grass.

"You heard about Timmy Morton?" Pete said to Alf.

Alf murmured that he hadn't and looked away, hoping to dislodge his friend's gaze, hoping Pete might address Margaret, who in the past had complained that Pete ignored her. "Is it just me," she'd asked, "or does he do it with everybody? Sometimes I get the feeling he's afraid of women." Alf assured her Pete was like this with everybody, at least when Alf was around. And it was true: Pete always directed his attention to Alf, as though that were the only comfortable place he could look. They had been friends since childhood.

"Guess he got so lubricated he went home to the wrong house," Pete said, still fixing on Alf. "You know those houses on Gold Street, they all look the same? Timmy pulls in the drive, thinks it's his place, but he's actually next door!" Pete grinned around at Joe and Jamie, but quickly returned to Alf. "Sly Callum's place. Timmy goes right inside like he's in his own kitchen."

It was a good story. Pete was always up on the latest scandal—which he usually dramatized with a few twists of his own—but Alf was distracted by Margaret's departure. She and Penny had gone off across the grass, picking their way over the scattered reefs of old shingles to the back steps. A few moments later, Alf saw his wife's dark hair reappear at the window, as she clattered the dishes in the sink.

"So he's in the wrong bedroom," Pete was saying. "He's taking off his clothes in the wrong bedroom! So then Sly wakes up and says, 'Who in hell's that?' And Timmy thinks, That don't sound like Jean. So then Sly jumps on him, starts pounding him out—"

"Sly's just a little guy!" Joe said, relishing the story.

"Yah," Pete says; his eyes growing huge. "But don't cross him, eh? So I guess Mary finally turns on the lights and they get it sorted out." Pete was focused on Alf again, his eyes wide with amazed disbelief, as if Alf and only Alf might have the answer to the wonder of human behavior he was expounding. "Jean was so mad at Timmy when she found out—made him spend the night in the car!"

Hearing the laughter of his sons, Alf grinned. But he was somewhere else, thinking of the woman moving through the dim house behind him.

4

SANDY CLIMBED INTO the Biscayne. Her new Catwoman eyes met Joe's.

"Wow," he deadpanned. Eyeliner. Mascara. He wasn't sure he liked it.

"If you don't like it, I can take it off."

"Take it off?" His gaze slipped to the tops of her breasts, white above the dipping edge of her halter top. A thin silver chain fell out of sight. At its weighted end, he knew, down there between her breasts, hung Christ in his agony.

"Dirty mind," she said, lifting her chin to the windshield.

West Street lay deserted. They drove off the Island, past small plaster houses and small frame houses, past Bannerman's old hosiery mill with its decapitated bell tower, and up the broken asphalt road wedged into the hillside. At the hump of the level crossing he glanced left and saw heat shimmering in the distances beyond the town, over the oily bed of the empty tracks: the emptiness of Sunday.

She took a small spade-shaped bottle from her purse, removed the top with its little brush, and with great concentration began to paint her nails. Irritated, he watched how she curled her tongue over her upper lip and held her hand away to examine her work, an artist enslaved by perfection. It was his notion of her that she was too absorbed in trivial things.

"Why do you do that?"

"Do what?"

"Paint yourself like that?" He had nearly said, Tart yourself up. Sometimes, and especially now, in the daylight, he was ashamed of their connection.

She frowned at her hand. The bright red polish suggested to him cheap carnival gaiety, a violence.

"You don't like it?"

"It just seems . . . I don't know."

"I could take it off if you don't like it."

"No, no," he said, and, a moment later, "Anyway, once we get in the water, it's not likely to last, is it?"

"The nail polish?"

"The stuff on your eyes."

She adjusted the mirror and studied herself, worriedly. In profile, her face was almost flat. It had been her father who, years ago, had begun to call her Monkey.

"It's just for fun," she said, pulling down the skin of her cheekbone. "Look at me."

There *was* something attractive in her makeup, almost primitive, like a mask that made her new. Behind its drama she might be anyone.

"It's growing on me," he said.

She was a year younger than he—his best friend Smiley's little sister, or at least that was how he'd thought of her until a school dance in May, when in the heat of the spring evening, among bodies turning to the pulsation of the speakers, she had tugged him onto the gym floor for a Ladies' Choice. And in the maelstrom of couples, with Paul McCartney wailing, they had drifted into a swaying intimacy so easy and natural he felt he had been preparing for it all his life.

They had been steadies all summer. She wore his school ring, taped to make it fit. His mother disapproved. He'd overheard her responding on the phone, to a friend who had apparently seen him and Sandy together in the Biscayne, "It's only one of those summer things, quite temporary. I mean, they've grown up together—hardly a seedbed for romance." Then his mother's friend said something, and his mother had replied, in a tone of infinite knowing and scorn, "Yes, exactly. She's not really up to his mark at all."

Later, Joe had upbraided her. "She's a wonderful girl," he said angrily, wanting to hurt her, "and it's not temporary." In fact, he knew it was— his mother's judgment of Sandy and his own were uncomfortably close—but he hated it when his mother anticipated his thoughts; it made him feel she had stolen a piece of his future.

Sandy slid over, burrowing a place for herself under his arm. Her hair yielded to the pressure of his body. In its teased, complex, slightly sticky depths was mostly air. Her breasts pressed together. Under the seat he had brought a flashlight. Later, after they'd swum at the bridge, after they'd eaten a hot dog at the Rendezvous, they'd drive out to their parking place above Coles Rapids. He was planning to leave the flashlight on, someplace in the car where it would shed an indirect glow, softer than the overhead light, easier on the battery. For him, Coles Rapids was the focus of their date, the exciting end point of a journey without which the journey would hardly be worth making.

At the Fairgrounds, he accelerated. They crested the new bridge, with its fleeting view of the gravel pits that surrounded the town—turquoise spring-fed craters, too cold for swimming—and, farther away, the conveyor belts leading like little elevated roads across a sad, desert landscape littered with boulders and rusted equipment. Finally, they came out among the farms; the old houses flashed behind windbreaks of poplar and spruce while the great weathered barns held their course like ancient galleons riding the seas of green and bronze crops.

BY FOUR-THIRTY THEY had had their fill of swimming and retreated to the flat limestone of Turtle Rock. They lay on their stomachs on Sandy's pink beach towel, facing upstream toward the old iron-bridge. Chunks of collapsing roadbed hung beneath it like the innards of a disintegrating mattress, suspended by strands of rusted steel. The bridge had long been closed to cars. Only the pedestrian walkway remained open.

In the pool below, there was only one swimmer now. Her head moved slowly upstream, edging toward a little rapid flickering under the bridge. From deep in the recesses among the trees on the bank, over the cooling sand littered with the remains of fires and picnics past, voices could be heard. A bottle popped as it broke on a rock. There were almost twenty people on the river this afternoon, but except for the cars ranged along the sand flats on the opposite bank, there was little sign of them. They had retired to escape the heat, to neck, to drink. By now their activities were all but enveloped in a drowse of silence.

Sandy rolled to her back, wriggled against him. Her hair had collapsed into a stringy mass. Most of her eye makeup was gone, save for a blotch at the corner of her right eye, as if she had been weeping tar. He licked his finger and cleaned it off. Her mouth was wide and thin-lipped and supple. But what took him aback just now were her eyes, gazing at him with such unguarded affection he had to look away.

"Think we'll get married?" she said.

"Married?" he said, suddenly grinning.

"I don't mean now, but maybe"—her finger traced something on his bare arm—"you know, someday."

"I've got university," he said.

"I could work, help put you through. Lots of gals do that for their guys."

Gals bothered him. As her makeup bothered him, her too-bright clothes. Sandy might live on the Island too, but their families couldn't be more different. He thought of her house: the ugly wallpaper, the mess of clothes that never seemed to get picked up, the absence of books, of decent music.

"How do you know lots of girls do that?"

"I read about it," she said, sulking. "I do read, you know." She gave him a little shove. But what she read mostly were romances with titles like *April's Summer* and *Ann Masterson's Only Choice*. He had tried to get her to read something more serious—James Joyce's *Dubliners,* Churchill's history of World War II—but she hadn't gotten very far. "Not really my style," she'd said, handing his volumes back. "I'm not as smart as you." She said it happily, as if her lesser intelligence were a relief.

"I don't know," he said, after a while, referring to marriage. In fact, he'd known as soon as she raised the subject that he wasn't going to marry her, if he got married at all. But he was being vague to avoid hurting her. It was the one thing he could give her to make up, a little, for the imbalance in their feelings: the solicitous tenderness of the guilty.

"We'd have our own place," she said. Her fingertips were moving up and down his arm, brushing the blond hairs against his skin. "Our own bedroom."

"Oh, yeah?"

"Where we could . . . you know."

Her eyelids dropped, and he glimpsed possibilities—a silky intimacy—that was more than they had known. They had not made love, not fully, not in the way he craved, and now, in the webbed crotch of his suit, flattened against the warm rock, things were beginning to happen.

"Tell me more," he said, looking at her.

"Well, you know." She blushed. He had run up against her modesty. When they made out in the Biscayne, she kept her eyes closed.

"You make it sound pretty good."

"It would be good." There was play in her gaze now; he had not known her to be so openly seductive.

"Why don't you kiss me?"

Her mouth had never yielded such softness. All he could think of was what her kiss promised for later, at the Rapids. He kissed her again.

"So what do you say?" she said cozily, as if the matter were all but decided. He was amazed at how tenaciously she hung on to her idea.

"Will you show me tonight?" he said. "What being married to you will be like?"

"Bad boy!" she said, slapping at his arm.

"But will you?"

"Bad boy," she said, pushing at him.

He hung his head; he liked being a bad boy.

"Seriously now," she said. "What do you think: a possibility?"

"I never thought about it," he said truthfully.

"So you just think we'll go on like this?"

"It's kind of nice."

"But it's enough for you?"

The swimmer—it was Marilyn Truscott—reached the shallows and stood up, water pouring off her shoulders. For a few seconds, as she fiddled behind her neck with the tie of her swimsuit, she was all the girls he hadn't known yet.

"Yeah," he said. "It is enough for me."

"You!" Sandy said. Now she pushed at his arm dismissively, with a show of good humor, but he knew she was hurt. She lay back and closed her eyes, lifting her chin, as if she had found a superior lover in the sun.

A flat, headachy light was coming off the river. "Think I'll take another dunk," he said. After a few minutes he got up slowly and padded with a show of indifference to the edge of Turtle Rock.

HE SURFACED TO hear Smiley call out, "Ship ahoy!" His friend stood in his plaid swim trunks at the edge of the willows, his pale, hairy gut spilling over the elastic waist of the suit, the iodine glint of a beer bottle clamped in his hand. Across the river, a large sky-blue car was descending through the pasture toward the sand flats. Slowly, almost hesitantly, it eased over white outcrops of bedrock, brushing weeds and disappearing behind a cluster of wild fruit trees to reemerge with glare masking its windshield: a Lincoln, and brand-new by the look of it. Joe had no idea whose it was.

"Jesus," Sid Kovacs said. Sid had just entered the shallows from among the parked cars a few yards to Joe's right. He was standing in his slouchy little trunks and black horn-rims, his hair swept up by his last

dive like a merganser's crown. His mouth gaped in an expression somewhere between amazement and moronic self-forgetfulness.

"Well, it's Sunday," Smiley said drolly. "It might be him."

Treading water, Joe watched the great flat-sided car nose down the
slope. Its engine was audible now, a low throbbing hum, a little ominous, as though it were connected to powers and purposes he could not
read. In that moment many of the kids on the river felt like trespassers.
They didn't know who owned this place by the water; perhaps they were
about to find out. Then, as the Lincoln approached the long ramp leading to the ruined bridge—"Maybe he'll try to drive over," Smiley
quipped hopefully—Joe caught a glimpse of Sally McVey in the driver's
seat, her chinless face lifted like a turtle's. Beside her sat her older sister,
Liz, and in the backseat a third person, at once lit and obscured by the
sunlight flooding the car.

Sid said, "What the fuck are *they* doing here?" and it seemed he spoke
for everyone on the river. They were all watching now, from the woods
and the water's edge, as the big car crept toward their parked cars, its
steering singing and weeping, its engine complaining at having to go so
slowly. Why *were* the McVeys here? They never came, kids from the
North End just didn't; they swam mainly at the country club, in a pool
Joe had never been in, though driving past at night he had glimpsed its
turquoise glow on the hillside and had heard the excited voices of swimmers across the dark fairway.

The Lincoln crept forward, among the loose ranks of Chevys and
Fords and Plymouths with their rust spots and reddish primed panels
where some home-repair job had gotten stalled halfway. It passed the
Walkers' old beige Biscayne and went on, like a visiting dignitary
inspecting the tatty honor guard of some third world country, stopping
at last behind Smiley's pickup, loaded with the furniture he was supposed to be delivering to his uncle. Then the sky-blue car fell silent. In
the pause that followed, a gull, anguishing, fell away down the sky. The
doors of the car opened and shut and three figures emerged to walk
swiftly out onto the sand flats toward the bridge. Sally led the way, in her
Bermuda shorts and golf hat, followed by her sister Liz, with her slightly

rounded shoulders, her ponytail jiggling. A few steps behind came a girl Joe did not recognize, tallish, also in Bermudas, who wore her blond hair in a Dutch bob: a blond helmet whose front edges curved up slightly over her cheeks. She seemed aware, as the McVeys did not, of the people watching from the river. Twice she looked over at them, at Sid Kovacs, gaping back at her from the shallows, and at Joe, treading water in the deepest part of the pool. There was curiosity in her glance, he thought, and a sense that she knew her situation was absurd.

The McVeys forged on as if they were on an important expedition, Sally with her usual air of good-natured, slightly goofy self-confidence, her face up, and Liz hurrying after her with her head down. And finally the third girl, taller than either of them and walking more slowly as she followed them up the earthen ramp and onto the pedestrian walkway.

At first, it seemed as if Sally was planning to lead her little group across the river and into the woods on the far shore. But about two thirds of the way over, she turned to the rail. Her sister stopped beside her. The third girl paused a few feet to their left and leaned over the rail to look down into the little rapid. The movement lent a curve to her wide-set shoulders, bare in their sleeveless blouse, and in the water, Joe was suddenly aware of the nakedness of his feet, bicycling slowly.

It was an odd moment, the three girls on the bridge and the others in the water and at the edge of the woods looking at one another wordlessly, as if until that moment they had not suspected the world contained any but themselves. The only sound was the plash of the little rapid and, briefly, the faint tearing roar of a high jet as it trailed to the west.

The moment continued for several seconds, an eon. The sun burned orange on the top girders. The river gleamed distantly, as it descended between the green fields upstream. The distilled, shadowy air held them all in suspension. Joe could not take his eyes off the third girl. There seemed to be something on her right cheek, a whiteness, like a dusting of flour, but when she moved her head a little (or perhaps he himself had moved, carried almost imperceptibly away by the current) he could not be sure he had seen anything.

It was Smiley who finally broke the spell, calling up to the bridge for the girls to come swimming, the water was great.

Liz McVey, who in class sounded so icily sure of herself, replied in a voice that seemed oddly quavery—an old woman's voice—that they didn't have their suits.

"Not really necessary," Smiley said in his normal speaking voice, to Joe.

"What?" Liz called, her voice gaining strength. "Can't hear you!"

"What?" Smiley roared, to the bridge.

"What?" Liz called. "What did you say?"

"I mean, she can always borrow mine," Smiley said quietly, to Joe.

"Ah, let up," Joe said.

"What! What did I do?" Smiley held out his hands, his beer, in a plea of innocence.

"Stop teasing them."

"Teasing!" Smiley practically shouted. "I'm not teasing! Why would I be teasing?"

Joe knew they had to have heard, on the bridge, and that this was Smiley's intent.

On the bridge, the two sisters drew together to confer. The third girl continued to look over the water. At the edge of the woods, someone growled, "What the fuck are *they* doing here?" It was Marty Cain. Joe watched him step out from behind a tree, his thick body pale and unhealthy in the shadows. From his hand drooped a pint of rye.

Someone else said, "We should make 'em go swimming."

"Ah, come on," Joe said again, but he was not sure anyone heard. In truth, he didn't give a damn about the McVeys. It was the other girl he was worried about. She seemed out of place with the McVeys, better and, in some inexplicable way, vulnerable. In the space of two or three minutes, he'd become her protector.

But of course there was nothing he could do but watch, in a state of extreme attention, slowly moving his arms and feet to keep his place in the current.

The McVeys looked down the river and over at their car, clearly uncertain. Beneath, the little rapid hushed and splashed.

"Fuck the lot of them," Marty Cain growled, taking a swig from his bottle.

"We're waiting!" Smiley shouted, to the bridge.

"Shut up!" Joe said.

"What's eating you?"

"Just leave them alone."

Smiley looked at him, mischief glinting in his deep-set eyes.

"Hey, you in love again?"

Joe turned in the water, furious. On Turtle Rock, Sandy had sat up and was watching intently. She sent him a smile of amusement: wasn't this fun?

On the other side of the river, Sid Kovacs shouted up to the bridge, "Who's your friend? The good-looking one?"

"Asshole," Joe seethed, across the water.

"Use your eyes, man," Sid squealed back, making no attempt to keep his voice down. "Look at the body on her!"

"Take off your clothes and join us!" Sid called joyfully to the bridge. "We can have an orgy!" And he let out a whoop and threw himself backward in the water. His spluttering head reappeared a moment later, minus his horn-rims. "My glasses!"

The sisters were no longer in doubt. They began to walk back along the walkway, with as much casualness and dignity as they could muster. As they reached the third girl, Sally murmured something to her and touched her arm, but instead of following the sisters, the girl turned and looked down over the opposite rail, on the upstream side of the walkway, through the torn roadbed. Joe knew what she was seeing: the speeding water visible through the hole in the concrete, that made you feel the bridge itself was racing upstream. Finally she began to follow the McVeys.

Sally McVey reached the sand flats and Marty Cain, tilting back his big head, bellowed, "Rich bitches out!" with a viciousness that broke from him like a torrent of poison. "All fucking whores back to Snob Hill!" Even then the situation might have been salvaged, for at first only a shocked silence answered Marty, as if the others felt he had gone too far.

Then Liz McVey began to run, spurting forward suddenly, and in a moment her sister was running too. From the edge of the woods, pandemonium erupted: catcalls, boos, the pack gone wild.

Under a willow, someone beat jubilantly on an oil drum with a stick. The sisters passed the parked cars, Sally leading as they headed for the safety of the Lincoln. Joe smashed at the water and yelled at the others to stop but soon realized he was only adding to the din. Appalled, he watched the third girl walk calmly across the sand flats. She neither hurried nor looked as if she wanted to. The abuse from across the river might have been only a breeze.

Then she did something extraordinary. She stopped. She looked, first, at Sid Kovacs, tilting her head a little as if she were wondering what kind of odd beast this was, sitting up to his chest in water and braying like a five-year-old. Sid fell silent. Then she looked at Joe. He said "Sorry" to her but, with the din still going behind him, was not sure she heard. He saw there *was* something on her cheek, at once whitish and pinkish and in the dimming light oddly elusive, changeable: a dusting of snow, the imprint of a tiny hand.

The others too had fallen silent. It was odd, as if they were expecting her to make a speech or lead them toward some other, more interesting activity. Someone, a girl, laughed sharply, perhaps in embarrassment. The mad tattoo on the oil drum had stopped.

Down the shore, the Lincoln gunned into life. As Joe turned in the water to watch, the girl walked calmly toward it, her white tennis shoes lifting and falling on the packed sand.

IT WAS LATE when they got back to town, and raining gently. They came down West, past the crouched, jammed-together houses of the mill workers. Beyond, the Atta and its valley made an unfathomed darkness, stretching for miles into a countryside that was a misery to think of: wet woods and mud and huddling animals. Sandy sat next to him, her hand with his school ring resting on his thigh. It was how she always rode, but something had changed. There was a sense of distance, disjunction, a sadness that seemed to flow from some irrevocable and inexpressible failure. At the same time, a new idea was coursing through him, with an excitement that made him blow suddenly through his teeth.

"You okay?" Her voice was small.

"Fine. How about you?"

"Fine." She did not sound fine. Expansively—and to forestall any serious talk—he swept his arm around her shoulder, gave her a squeeze. The black road shone like a pelt.

Stopping in front of her house, he watched as she got out and went up the drive. When she turned on the porch to wave, he had already started to pull away. As he swung east onto Water, the whitewashed, foreshortened facade of his own house dropped behind as, with deepening anticipation, he accelerated through the rain-sweetened air. The Biscayne charged up the long hill past King's Park and Central School and the railway station, flying over the hump of the bridge into the North End. For a moment, as if a spotlight had found him, questioning his right to exist, he was aware of the condition of the car: the rust eating its way around the fenders, the old-car smell, the dust on the dash. His shirt prickled at his back, another flaw; it was a hand-me-down from his father.

The rain had stopped. He prowled the streets in a hush of tires, passing under ancient trees where solitary streetlights burned in nests of wet, shining leaves. Across vast lawns, the big houses peered darkly from their porches. Every object—those paired wooden rockers, glazed with rain—seemed about to disclose some secret. He turned onto Robert and the McVeys' house reared up among its maples: a neo-Georgian place with banks of shuttered windows and a wide front door, framed in a glass transom. All the lights were out save one on the second floor, glowing between slitted drapes. Slowing as much as he dared, he glanced up the drive and saw the Lincoln nested in shadow, its big low-slung body alive and, it seemed to him, ambiguous, its properties only to be guessed at.

5

MOST MORNINGS, ALF walked to work. And most mornings, when he reached the corner of West and Water, he glanced left, to see Pete striding off the footbridge from Lion's Park, lunchpail swinging. Pete lived on the other side of the park, in a small clapboard bungalow he had built with Alf's help in the early fifties, under the wooded flank of Lookout Hill. Pete worked in Bannerman's dyehouse, which explained why his hands and arms were often stained with streaks of Persian red or navy blue and why even his clothes sometimes looked (Alf thought) as if he'd been painting a barn with a shovel. He wore a baseball cap, tilted well back off his narrow forehead.

This morning they met as usual. Pete's thin face lit up as he saw Alf, his eyebrows rising in humorous acknowledgment as though the two of them shared an ongoing joke they need not explain.

They fell in together, striding at a good clip along Water. Fifty paces ahead, Joe scraped along in his jeans and T-shirt, armored, it seemed to Alf, in the trappings of a secret life. What was the boy thinking about? Alf had no idea. Six-forty-five. A torrent of light swept the trees on Lookout Hill. Birds sang like mad from maples shrouding the small front yards. They passed the brick cottage where Alf had grown up—the same ragged cedar hedge, the same balding lawn—under the maroon leaves of the maple Alf's father had planted after Alf and his brother had gone off to war. He always sensed a presence here, as if his parents were alive still, peering out from the curtained windows, waiting for them to come back. But he gave the house scarcely a glance. He didn't want memories now, any more than he wanted talk. Enough to be awake in the flooding light. Mercifully, Pete was quiet.

The main street still lay in shadow. Others were traveling with them, on the opposite sidewalk, or gliding past in cars: all headed for the mills, all wrapped in the solitariness of their recent sleep. They passed the white pillars of the war memorial. Without looking, Alf was aware of it, of the names carved in its stone, a chorus breathing with a nearly inaudible hush. Then past the hardware store with its display of powerful lawn-mowers, the tiny office of the *Attawan Star,* where the show window featured a large aerial photo of the town, the forking rivers a dark inverted Y. High overhead, the eastern face of the post office clock met the assaulting light.

Pete tugged down his visor, to shield his eyes from the sun streaming down Bridge Street. Bannerman's whistle gave a warning howl. I better get that old Jacquard going, Alf thought, and felt the sudden shock of cool air as they advanced over the Shade.

Pete gave a tap to the bridge rail, as though for luck. "Alf—"

Something in his friend's tone alerted him. Far ahead, Joe reached the end of the bridge and abruptly pivoted toward the path that ran along the dike. His sudden movement startled Alf, as if the boy had simply flung himself away.

"You might have heard. There's this organizer in town—"

Overhead, gulls screamed.

"A bunch of us have been meeting with him. Nothing's settled, like. We're just checking out our options."

"Doyle," Alf said, half to himself. He hadn't heard anything of the man for a couple of weeks. He'd begun to believe, to hope, that he'd left town.

Pete gave a little laugh that to Alf sounded guilty. "I guess maybe he's talked to you."

"I think maybe you know he's talked to me."

"Yeah, yeah. Well, actually—"

"Well, actually, what?"

"I said I'd speak to you."

"About what?" Alf said grimly. Of course he knew. He glanced sharply at his friend and Pete's nervous eyes shifted under his visor.

"Like I said, we're just checking out our options."

"You don't have any."

Pete fell silent. Alf knew he was being remorseless, unusually so. And still he had anger to burn; he tried to put it into walking, as if he could simply leave Pete's news behind. Up ahead, Joe had already disappeared from the dike. There was a stink of decaying river weed. And the screaming gulls.

They were not used to major disagreements. They might argue about who was the better hockey player, Pulford or Baun, but their friendship was built on an easy amiability, an understanding they would avoid anything that roused strong emotion. It was no preparation for this, the air bright with danger.

Pete tried again, on a placating note. "A union can do things, Alf. These layoffs—if we had a union, there'd be seniority, like."

"You always said you were antiunion."

"I mean they wouldn't be able to treat people like they do. There'd be protocols."

"Protocols," Alf mocked. He was sure Pete had got the word from Doyle. His friend, after all, had barely graduated from eighth grade, and he had never cared about current events or political matters, as far as Alf knew. He never read a newspaper. "You know what happened the last time we tried this?"

"I know, it was bad. But we gotta move on."

Gotta move on. He suspected that was Doyle's argument, too.

"You don't know," Alf said grimly, "You weren't here." Meaning, You were still in the navy in '49. You have no right to speak about what happened.

"Different circumstances, Alf."

Alf threw up his hands in anger and despair. They had nearly reached the end of the bridge. Pete had to hustle to keep up.

"Malachi's a good guy, Alf."

"A good guy." Alf seethed. The very mention of Doyle made him want to hit something. He felt as if Doyle and Pete had been conspiring behind his back. He spoke with angry sarcasm. "So Malachi's a good guy. A nice guy to have a beer with. Is that any reason to follow him? Hell, good guys have been screwing up the world since it began."

He swung onto the dike-top path. Pete kept right behind him, down the dirt incline that led onto the playing fields behind the arena. Two hundred yards away, sunlight pierced the upper stories of the mills. At the lip of the stack, a rag of smoke flapped.

Pete said, "I mean, hell, if you think a union's such a bad idea, why don't you come out to one of our meetings and tell us why?"

Alf stopped. Pete's eyes met his frankly, from under his visor. There was a plaintiveness there, beseeching. But at the same time, over a nervous smile, Pere was challenging him, and this was new. Alf was shocked.

"You're a fool," Alf said. "You follow this guy, and we'll all live to rue it. Honestly, Pete, you're a bigger ass than I thought."

Something changed in Pete's gaze, something went bright yet seemed to burn up at the same time. It was as if he disappeared. His face was still there, grinning as if he believed Alf was only joking, but Pete had gone away, sunk beneath his features like a drowning man under the surface of a pool. Alf turned away, joining the crowd streaming into the deep canyons between the mills.

THE STAIRS OF the knitting mill were a mass of people, a steady thunder of shoes climbing the filthy treads. He put his head down and trudged. He had done this for eighteen years, all told. The thousands of mornings seemed to have become one morning, this morning: an eternity he was condemned to spend watching, a few inches from his face, the wide laboring bum and knotted calves of Millie Jennings.

He was still furious. How many of these people had talked to Doyle? Who was taking the organizer seriously? What he could see told him nothing. Yet everything he looked at—Millie's ugly legs, a discarded gum wrapper—seemed a clue. Every face in its bland, dreaming thickness had turned treacherous.

The knitting room was on the top floor, the sixth. He walked toward the bench where his tools were kept, noting with disgust that someone had failed to put one of his wrenches away. A faint, chortling murmur made him look around. Sun slanted among the rows of tall machines, each bearing its circular rack of bobbins. Against the far wall, the knitters sat on their long bench, looking back at him with blank, unreadable faces. He was swept with distaste at their sullen immobility. Just then, the buzzer gave out its nasal command: seven o'clock. It was time to work but the knitters did not stir. Their tardiness—it would last only a few seconds—was meant to declare that they were their own masters, even here.

Hearing the sound again, he looked up. Under the high ceiling, a drive belt hummed, awaiting the moment when its power would be channeled to the machines below. Inches above it, on a sprinkler pipe, sat a trapped pigeon. Alf could clearly make out its slender head, cocked sideways to look down on him with its tiny, burning eye.

THE NEXT MORNING, when Pete didn't show up on the Lion's Park bridge, Alf went on by himself. It was the same the next morning, and the next. Pete was driving to Bannerman's now. Each day, arriving at the mills, Alf saw the Sarasota's towering taillights parked in the dead-end lane beside the dyehouse. But he never managed to run into Pete himself.

He felt he should call his friend. Pete was prone to these withdrawals. Once, years ago, he'd criticized him for something, and Pete had vanished from Alf's life for nearly a month. Then he'd just showed up again, acting as if nothing had happened. Alf supposed that's how it would go now. One morning Pete would come striding off the Lion's Park bridge, grinning his gap-toothed grin, telling some funny story, and they would go on as before, without mention of their quarrel. He was worried, though, and sorry—yes, definitely sorry—for some of the harsher things he'd said.

Twice he picked up the phone to call Pete. Twice he put the receiver back down, with a sense of confusion and defeat. He couldn't sort out apologizing from admitting he was wrong.

One hot afternoon during this standoff, he was sitting on the floor of the knitting room, among the parts of a machine he'd spread on newspapers, when the freight elevator floated into its bay. Alf caught a flicker of bodies moving behind the safety gates. Then the gates were flung back, and a group of men stepped out. Their dress shirts, turned back crisply at the cuffs, broadcast a shock of white into the room. There was a young woman with them: tall, in an extremely short skirt, her long legs stalking forward in black mesh stockings. A bald, tanned, handsome man touched her back and leaned over to whisper something into the teased cloud of her hair. She put back her head and opened her mouth in a silent, cheerless laugh, showing a wealth of teeth.

Twenty feet away, Alf instinctively drew up his legs, a man exposed in the bath. They had stopped outside the elevator. The bald man, who stood well over six feet, seemed oddly familiar. But the only figure Alf recognized was Gordie Henderson, assistant manager of the sweater mill, looking around anxiously as if searching for shelter in a thunderstorm.

Spotting Alf, Gordie hurried over.

"Alf, I need Matt."

"Think he went down to the dyehouse," Alf said, glancing up. Tufts of black hair blocked Gordie's big nostrils. In truth, Alf had no idea where Matt Honnegger was. The soon-to-be-retired foreman was just as likely to be in the can, relaxing.

"These people are from Intertex," Gordie said, in a tense undertone. "Top guns. They want a tour."

"I'll see if I can find Matt."

"Maybe you could take us around."

Gordie had already decided for him. As he waved the others over, Alf struggled to his feet. Unable to find a rag, he hurriedly wiped his hands on his trousers.

"Alf, this is Mr. Prince—"

"Bob Prince," the bald man said in a low rich voice. Alf remembered where he'd seen him—that photo in the *Star*, the previous spring. It was a bit like meeting someone whose fame had preceded him, a little whirlpool of excitement. Alf was on edge, aware that these men were perched high on a ladder he wanted to climb.

"Mr. Prince is vice president of—ah—" Gordie faltered.

"New acquisitions," Prince said. He put out his hand.

"I'm a little dirty," Alf said, dragging his hand again across his shirt front. The others were watching blankly.

"Honest dirt," Prince said. The hand remained in place; it had become an order. Alf took it. For a lingering moment the other man's glowing eyes—they were a pale, icy blue, almost the same color as Alf's—reached into his with a searchlight's candor. Alf experienced an obscure shame.

"Alf's our head fixer," he heard Gordie say. "There isn't anything he doesn't know about this place." Alf wondered if Gordie was about to leave him with this bunch.

Prince introduced the others. Their names and faces flashed by him. Jacobson. Martin. Raleigh. Macrimmon. Each one leaned forward, following the boss's example, to take his hand. A thin man with rimless glasses looked at him more directly than the others; then the green eyes fled.

"And this is Shirley," Prince concluded, with a hint of affectionate condescension. He offered no last name, as if, like a child or a mascot, the young woman at his side did not need one. Shirley preened, smiling at a place beside Alf's head.

To Alf's relief, Gordie stayed to conduct the tour. The assistant manager led them into the first aisle of humming machines. Unsure why he was wanted but relieved at no longer being the center of attention, Alf tagged along.

They stopped by the first machine, a Richardson. In a circular drum, hundreds of latch needles made a soft hushing sound as they worked in rapid synchronization, while above them blue bobbins swept round and round on a carousel, wafting a faint breeze over their sweating faces.

"If you could stand up here by me, Alf."

His mouth suddenly dry, Alf took his place beside Gordie. To his relief, the assistant manager seemed determined to do all the talking. Alf thrust his hand in his pockets. His fingers found a key, the teeth of which he raked absently with his thumb. A bit of lint drifted across the floor; on a distant window ledge, sun glinted on a pigeon's neck. Gordie's high, frantic voice fluttered on the close air. He was explaining how the mill was organized: knitting at the top, cutting just below, all the stages stacked one below the other so that at the end the finished sweaters could flow out the door. Alf cast a glimpse at Shirley's bodice, the artfully undone button.

Out of nowhere, his father's drowned body rose. He saw the pale head laid back on the metal table in McArthur's Funeral Home, saw the deep, nearly bloodless gash crossing the shoulder and chest like a bandolier. The wound had not killed him, Rick McArthur told Alf. He had drowned first and then sustained his injury while turning in the currents under the dam. "The old timbers down there," Rick told him, "they're thick with spikes." He had never forgotten that phrase, *thick with spikes*. He thought of it as he crossed the Bridge Street bridge and happened to glance upstream at the dam, foaming benignly across the river. *Thick with spikes*, as if some monster were down there, bristling with spines.

Momentarily, he felt adrift in space, a ghost among the machines. Wiping the sweat from his brow, he looked up. Prince was listening to Gordie in a fume of impatience. The executive's heavy jaw worked at a piece of gum, while he cast hard glances around the room. The other men seemed to have caught their boss's unhappiness: their frowning faces fed off it like scavengers with a half-eaten kill. Only Shirley seemed unaffected. She seemed hypnotized by the machine working in front of her, by the streaming threads that raced from the bobbins into the drum of pullulating needles. But what mainly appeared to fascinate her was the place below the drum, where the tube of patterned cloth appeared as if out of nowhere, inching down between the machine's iron legs like something newborn.

THE PARTY MOVED deeper into the room, down the aisles of tall machines, under the drive belts thrumming near the high ceiling. Most of the models here were older than the Richardsons; with their stationary racks and dark metal they had been churning along since Alf's father had started as a fixer, back in the twenties. The knitters took care to keep clear of the visitors. Occasionally, a hand reached up to place a loaded bobbin on a spike, or a face was glimpsed briefly in a distant aisle. But the executives from Intertex might well have had the impression that the machines were running themselves.

Gordie was not doing well. Sweat poured from his high, bony forehead, dripped off his nose onto his plaid tie with its red-ensign clip. He had been all right describing the mills' overall operations, but when it came to specific machines and routines, he was out of his depth, and Prince knew it. The executive was watching him coldly, snapping questions at him like pucks. When Gordie managed to send back a coherent answer, Prince fired another question, mercilessly. Gordie—the only one of the party wearing a jacket—mopped compulsively at his face and repeated "Right, right," over and over.

The tour had become a display of cruelty on Prince's part, for by now the executive wasn't even giving Gordie time to answer. The other men stirred uneasily, averting their eyes.

Finally a question came that Gordie seemed not to hear. The little man stood with an odd half smile on his wet face, gazing at a place below him as if at his own doom. He almost seemed to welcome it.

"Sorry," he said at last, looking up.

Alf said quietly, "Mr. Prince wants to know how we handle rush orders."

Prince said, "Maybe you could tell us, Alf. I think it's time we heard from the man on the floor." Prince's attention, in all its remorselessly shining insistence, had swung to him. The others too turned to Alf, perhaps with a touch of hope, like a crowd looking at a new challenger, a new victim.

Alf explained about rush orders. Remembering how irritated Prince had seemed with Gordie's meandering, he kept his answer short and to the point, and when he had finished, Prince had another question ready and he answered that too, returning it as efficiently as he could. Prince glowed. He cast a knowing glance at the others, as if to say, There, that's what we want, as if he were taking credit for having created Alf's answer and maybe creating Alf too, shaping him out of the chaos of this hot, almost-wasted afternoon. They went on down the aisle, stopping at another machine. Alf tried to turn Prince's next question back to Gordie, but Prince said, "No, no, you've got the ball now," so of course there was no choice. He was leading the tour.

He expected that at any minute a question would come that he could not answer, or that Prince would throw him more questions than anyone could answer, but the attack never came. Prince had turned genial, interested, as he listened to Alf with a proprietorial enthusiasm. It was as if another man altogether had appeared in the white shirt and faultless tan trousers. He even began to make jokes. The others responded with exaggerated, relieved hilarity, and after a while Alf relaxed too. He realized that Prince had no intention of humiliating him. He was on home ground. He'd tended these machines for years, taken them apart and fitted them back together, and he knew them as well as the heavy Lee-Enfield he had once lugged around Europe, the parts of which he could have assembled blindfolded. But he had never put his knowledge into words before, not to such an extent, and now he saw his years of experience transformed, almost effortlessly, into the currency of language, and it was exciting to him, liberating.

Prince stopped abruptly. Everyone else stopped too, as the boss gazed around with a self-satisfied smile. "Shirley," he said, "I've been thinking," and it was evident his words were meant not just for her but the whole party. His voice held an invitation to prepare the tribute of their laughter. "Don't you think it'd be a good idea to get one of these things for your apartment?" He indicated the tall machine beside him, disgorging its river of soft white cloth. "Save you all that shopping."

Even Gordie laughed. Alf saw him at the rear, grinning like a kid desperate to be one of the gang.

BEFORE HE LEFT with his party, Prince paid Alf a compliment that made Alf's face burn. "This is the salt-of-the-earth sort," the executive said, looking around, "that keeps a company going. Without the Alf Walkers you might as well call it quits." The tour had cost him an hour he could hardly afford, but he was cheerful enough about having to stay late. The future was suddenly looking awfully rosy. It was nearly eight before he left the mill and made his way along Bridge, stopping by the plate-glass windows of Bud Mackie's Motors.

In the showroom, a navy blue Impala rotated slowly. One door was open, revealing the instrument panel, seats swathed in creamy leather. What clean lines the car had, compared to his old Biscayne! Yes, fins were definitely out; even the snug horizontal fins of the Biscayne seemed clumsy and old-fashioned now. He gazed at the flawless flowing surfaces, the deep blue panels disappearing and reappearing endlessly, as in a dream.

6

"I SUPPOSE HE'S always buttering people up like that. Saves having to pay them more."

"Don't be so modest," Margaret told him. "You deserve it, Alf."

She was sitting opposite him, while he shook HP sauce on his dry chop and tried to suppress the tide of his excitement. He hadn't meant to tell her about Prince's compliment, he felt too much like a schoolboy bringing home news of some minor triumph, but it had just popped out.

Through the screens came the distant cries of children at play, in the park across the river. Margaret leaned forward in her chair, her elbows on the table, her forearms crossed, her hands spread on her shoulders in a way that made her seem young, eager.

"I'll be happier when I see it lead to something definite."

"I don't know why it wouldn't."

"It all depends whether Prince remembers me. I mean, when they get around to deciding on the job. If he has anything to do with it—"

"Honestly, love, I should think you'd get it with or without his help. If they want the best."

It seemed to be tempting fate, to be talking like this, but he was pleased at her support. How long had it been since she'd looked at him as if he were her beau, his head full of plans? He frowned, although he was irrepressibly buoyant. When he'd finished eating, he went out to the garden. The sharp, earthy scent of tomato was on the air. He cupped his hand under one of the great lobed beefsteaks, hefting its coolness, and to his surprise it released itself into his palm.

Later, in bed, he listened to the thin cry of his wife's zipper from the walk-in closet where she undressed. Slipping from under the covers, he crossed the floor and peered around the door. She was just bending to step out of her half slip. He gazed at her wide back, cut by the stark white statement of her bra.

"Would you like a cuddle?" It was their word for making love. They had not made love for weeks; there hadn't seemed time or energy for it.

She hesitated, and he seemed to hover over an emptiness. The worst of it was, he felt he was asking her for his reward for bringing her good news.

"Well, I was counting on it," she said, giving him a smile over her bare shoulder. He wasn't sure he believed her, but he crept back to bed, satisfied.

He waited for her under the sheet, already hard, waited as she went down the hall to the bathroom, waited as she turned on the taps and flushed the toilet and squatted with a sound of cracking knees to put in her diaphragm, waited as she came back up the hall, detouring to check on Jamie and Penny, waited as she closed the door and slipped out of her dressing gown in the dimness that allowed him a brief, thrilling glimpse of her small breasts, waited as she slid under the sheet beside him, her hair dark on the pillow as he reared on one elbow to begin his courtship, waited another moment or two to let her settle, in the near-dark, where she waited, as always, with a stillness that moved him.

A curtain blew from the window as he bent to kiss her. Her lips picked softly at his. His hand crept over her stomach, where the skin was extraordinarily soft, slack, discolored, he knew, with marbled streaks. It was what having children had done.

She grasped his wrist.

"You know I don't like that."

"Right. Sorry."

He moved his hand to the bottom of her rib cage, under her breasts.

There was a tension in her that seemed to evaluate his every move. He had noticed it the first time he ever touched her, dancing together that night of the servicemen's party in Henley-under-Downs: a pulse that seemed to push him away as he struggled to lead her. They had fought each other around the floor.

But he had loved her that first night: the clear, vibrant openness of her face and wide-set eyes, which seemed to look toward the future, toward him, with an adventuring gladness ready for anything. And her air of refinement—her trim high-shouldered dress, cinched at the waist, the sharp plunge of her bodice over a chest of pale unimaginable smoothness. She seemed so much better than any of the other girls in the crowded hall. So he learned to put up with her physical wariness. In a way, he felt he had been stalking her, courting her, ever since, still trying to come close.

Her lips tempted his with a searching delicacy. She had learned how to hold him, her slender fingers firm. He found her exciting, and her physical aloofness part of this, an infinite tease.

When he was in her, he moved slowly, postponing his own climax in the hopes he might help her to her own. He wasn't actually sure she *could* come, though she insisted she did, or at least that she had pleasure enough. Beneath him, her long body trembled with her high-strung alertness. He sensed she was pushing herself harder than usual, hungering perhaps for some kind of breakthrough, and he stayed with her. Finally she told him she was getting sore. "You finish, dear," she whispered. "Are you sure?" "Yes, yes." But he was so numb himself he had to work a good while longer before he finally crested and passed quickly, too quickly, through that place where he had never been able to stop.

7

JAMIE WATCHED ANDY Wilson slide his bike into the stand and walk away through the crowded Boys' Yard, throwing back his orange mop of hair with a jerk of his head. Moving in closer, Jamie touched the racing tires thin as snakes, the cherry-red frame, not a scratch. Andy Wilson lived in the North End. Snob Hill, some of the boys called it, the ones who lived lower in the town, where the brown and misty rivers were that smelled of mud and rotting things. His mother had bawled him out when he'd said, "Snob Hill." She said she was sure people up there wouldn't like it. She said they were no more or less snobby, no better and no worse, than anybody else. Maybe, but they were different. When the Grade Three boys from the North End played tag, they didn't ask anybody else to play with them. They ran back and forth between the fences of the Boys' Yard, shouting one another's nicknames, Pud and Clumbs and Schooner and Drums. It was like a private party, a party where everyone pretended to have a good time. There was a lot of pretending about the boys from the Hill, he felt. They were always together, talking loud, getting something organized.

His own bike—he didn't ride it to school—had a banged-up maroon frame and no fenders, which meant you got sprayed when you rode through a puddle. Andy Wilson's bike had silver hand brakes and swept-under handlebars that reminded him of the horns of the mountain sheep in *Animals of the World*. Just looking at the racer made him happy, like looking in the windows of Eaton's that time his family had gone to Toronto, all the little elves working in Santa's shop and the electric train chugging through the tunnels in the mountains, a happiness for looking only; you couldn't touch.

He drifted away from the bike stand, lingering in the yard for a while to watch some Grade Six boys play conkers. One chestnut struck another chestnut, hanging on a string. There was a loud crack and a cry from the boys, as the nut swung crazily in an arc. When it settled, they saw that a bit of its shell had come off, revealing the yellowish meat inside. "Mick's gonna have a ten-kinger," a boy said.

Jamie went over to the chain-link fence that surrounded the yard and stood with his back to it, hooking his fingers in the wire and leaning forward. Behind him, on the other side of the fence, an enormous elm tree rose, its great branches drooping over the yard "like a giant umbrella," his new teacher, Miss Wayne, had said. She had shown the class the leaves of the elm, pointed like spearheads. He gazed around the milling yard, where boys ran or gathered in groups. Some were trading or flipping cards, or roughhousing, or talking in bragging, shouting voices. A few stood alone, like him, but these boys were too old or too young to be friends. Last year, in Grade Two, Johnny Simms had been his friend. But Johnny's dad had been laid off at the mill, and in August the whole family had driven away, Johnny's mother and sister in the car, and Johnny and his dad in the cab of the truck with all their furniture, and Jamie's heart had gone *no no no* under his T-shirt because he'd heard his dad say that they, the Walkers, would probably never see the Simmses again.

He looked up into the elm arching over him and remembered what Joe had said about not believing in God. At the time, Jamie had sensed something move with extraordinary speed—*whoosh!*—like the wings of ducks flying up from the river. Everything looked the same as before—the backyard, the picnic table, his daddy's face—but something had left; he'd gone empty inside.

I believe in God, the voice said.

Jamie looked around, half expecting to see somebody. He never did, though. Whoever spoke in that voice—a voice so close to him, it seemed to have slipped into his own head—was gone. Gone or invisible, like the Invisible Man.

Once, driving in the country after supper, he and his family had gotten lost. On both sides of the road, green water shone among trees. An old man on a horse had come by, sauntering beside the car with a slow *clop-clop*. He wore a slouchy hat, bronzed like his face in the thickening light, and he drew to a halt as the car stopped, and pointed back up the shadowy road to show where they should go. Sometimes, in the early morning, Jamie woke to a sound he did not understand: a faraway cooing that filled him with sadness as well as a happiness that was even deeper, like a lower note. Looking out the window, he could never see exactly where the sound was coming from; it seemed to come out of the hill and the trees and the river, and yet from none of these things. Once, looking for its source, he had seen the old man in his slouchy hat standing under a tree across the river. The man had nodded to Jamie, and Jamie had nodded back. Later he wondered if the old man had been God. Or perhaps he was an angel, and God was nearby.

You can't see God, the voice said. *He's shy.*

"Hey, stupid, where d'ya get those pants?"

Tommy Leach, from the Flats. Tommy had a large face from which his bony nose stuck out like a fin. He was in Grade Five, two grades above Jamie, and was several inches taller, a fleshy boy with pale white skin like the belly of a carp. Jamie followed Tommy's sneering gaze to his pants, which had once belonged to Joe. On one pocket was stenciled a picture of a bear, rearing up on its hind legs, its big head roaring. On the other pocket was Davy Crockett in his buckskins and coonskin hat, aiming Old Betsy at the bear. Down the outsides of the legs ran a brown plastic fringe.

It was the first time he'd worn them.

"They're not stupid."

"Sure they are. You look stupid. What's that stuff sticking out?"

Tommy's upper lip had curled, showing two big teeth. Jamie had noticed that Tommy was one of the boys in the Yard who had no friends. He had watched him hang around other boys who ignored him. Lately, he'd taken to carrying a little horseshoe magnet. He'd stick it to the fence, then look up with a smirk to see if anyone was interested.

Tommy reached out and began to pull at the fringe.

"Hey, don't!"

"Gimme a piece of your pants!" Tommy cackled.

"No!"

"Just a little piece!" Tommy was snorting with laughter. Little pearls of snot appeared under his nose.

Jamie's hand slapped at Tommy's, where it was tugging at the fringe.

"Hey, you hit me!" Tommy cried. His eyes lit up, as if he thought this was a good thing, good and funny.

"Just leave me alone," Jamie told him. His heart was knocking.

Tommy shoved him back into the fence and held him there with one hand while his other hand tore off bits of fringe, sprinkling them around like grass. "Look! His pants are coming apart!" he called over his shoulder. No one was even looking.

His nose. Grab his nose, the voice said.

Startled, Jamie looked and saw Tommy's big thin nose. He seized it.

"Hey!" Tommy shouted. Now he sounded like a duck.

Tommy's mouth was open, showing those big teeth, and he flailed at Jamie, striking his head, his shoulder, but Jamie hung on for dear life. He was in an odd state, almost calm, knowing only that he had to hang on to the slippery thing between his fingers. Tommy lashed out with his foot, in its high black running shoe. Jamie dodged and kept tugging on his nose, this way and that, like the string of his kite when he made it dance. Tommy sank to the ground. Still Jamie wouldn't let go, even though white stuff was seeping from the nose, and Tommy was starting to sob with a hiccup sound. Others had gathered, laughing and yelling: "He's got him by the nose!"

Tommy tried to get up, but Jamie put him down with another jerk of his nose and sat on him. Finally a big boy from Grade Eight said, "I think you've beaten him, you better let him go."

When Jamie released his grip, Tommy lay blinking at him. On his upper lip was a mustache of bloody white stuff. Jamie barely had time to stand before the others had picked him up, lifting him into the air. At first Jamie thought he had to fight them too. But then he realized they were cheering. The big boys from Grade Seven and Eight were calling his name as they carried him, chanting "Jamie Walker! Jamie Walker!" and other boys were running over to see. Soon there was a great gang moving through the yard, with Jamie perched awkwardly on their shoulders, clutching at someone's head, worried he was wiping Tommy's bloody snot in the boy's hair, feeling he was going to slip at any minute. Then he looked toward the bicycle stand and saw Billy Boileau. Even at that distance he knew Billy was following him with his black eyes around the yard, and fear went through him like cold water, because he knew what Billy was thinking and what he, Jamie, was going to have to do.

AT RECESS, HE went to the boys' washroom. He was standing in front of the urinal, which was taller than he was, watching his pee flow over the cracked porcelain into the sick-smelling drain, when he heard someone behind him. Zipping up, he turned. Billy's eyes fixed on Jamie's nose.

"So I guess you think you're the best fighter now."

"No."

"I guess you're gonna have to prove it."

"I don't think I'm the best fighter. You're the best fighter." Jamie believed this. He'd once seen Billy fight a boy a foot taller than himself. He'd leaped on him, biting and scratching like a wildcat, until the boy, Dickie Collins, had run bawling into the school.

Billy's eyes were still on his nose. Jamie wanted to hide his nose, put his hand over it. Because he'd twisted Tommy's nose, it was as if his had to get twisted too. Billy didn't really seem to see him at all, only his nose, which suddenly felt as big as his face.

"I don't want to fight you," he said.

In a cubicle, someone farted, a real good one. Jamie grinned, thinking he and Billy might share the joke, but Billy didn't smile back.

"After school," he said.

On Friday afternoons, they always had art. It was Jamie's favorite class: the smell of paints and glue, the rattle of the big sheets of paper, white as new snow, where you could do anything, whatever you could think of. The previous week, he'd started a picture of Indians attacking a covered wagon train. The wagons were racing along the prairie, and the Indians, mounted on their spotted ponies, were shooting flaming arrows. Their camp was up in the hills: lots of tepees (easy to draw), and a fire for dancing around, and lines going up and down like waves for the hills. Ever since Joe had told him about Geronimo and Crazy Horse, he'd always been on the Indians' side. When he took his bow up the river, he pretended he was Crazy Horse, spying on the people who'd built their homes on his land. He took secret paths, so no one could see him.

But today, thinking of Billy, art wasn't much fun. He drew in a few more Indians on their horses. Out the window, the great frowsy head of the elm filled the sky. Once, he'd seen it in a storm, gray and tossing and lit by lightning: a huge living head, tossing its wild hair. Was that God? Silently, he said to the tree, *Please help me,* but the tree went on hanging, like a great sad old umbrella with holes in it. Maybe there would be rain and he wouldn't have to fight. He'd never seen anybody fight in the rain. He thought Billy might, though.

Billy was his age, but he was in the special class for slow learners, along with the retarded kids like Dougie French—Dougie with his big slobbery lips and happy eyes. Billy wasn't retarded—the previous year he'd been in Jamie's class—but he was always in trouble. Once he'd gotten the strap for sassing Miss Bell. The dark leather strap, thicker than a belt, had smacked down on his hand four, five times and Billy had laughed a strange gurgling laugh, while Miss Bell, her face getting redder, had hit him three times more. When Billy came back down the aisle to his desk, his cheeks were shiny with crying but he hadn't made crying sounds; he was grinning, as if it were all a joke.

When the bell went, Jamie stayed behind and asked Miss Wayne—he *loved* Miss Wayne, with her broad, happy face and kind voice—if he could help her clean up. But she said, "No, thank you, dear," and smoothed down his hair a bit. He went out into the hall, with his rolled drawing in his hand. From the landing, he could see out the window above the door, see clear through the empty Boys' Yard, all the way to the gate and the park across the road. Billy was there, sitting on the curb, poking a stick at something in the gutter as if, maybe, he was torturing an ant. Jamie felt alone, maybe more alone than he'd ever felt before. Billy was alone too. The two of them were more alone, it seemed, than if there had been only one of them.

Jamie went to the washroom and tried to pee. But there wasn't any pee to come out, so he went to the fountain and let its clear water bubble up like little silver balls for a while before he drank. When he came out, Mr. Small, the janitor, walking with quick steps behind his wide broom, said he shouldn't be there.

He left. Walking across the Boys' Yard toward the gate, he thought of a plan. When he got to the gate, he'd tear away like blazes down the hill and hope he could make it home before Billy jumped him. But for some reason he didn't run. He walked past the elm to the gate while Billy dropped his stick and stood up. Jamie had a strange feeling that all this had happened before, and there was nothing he could do about it. He didn't feel afraid anymore, just lonely, like that time when he was little and his mom had forgotten to pick him up at the baby-sitter's.

"Come over here," Billy said.

Jamie hesitated. Somewhere nearby, a whisper in the trees, the voice said, *It's all right.*

Clutching his drawing, Jamie crossed the road.

"What's that?" Billy said, scowling at the tube.

"My drawing. Indians."

Billy looked at him. Not at his nose this time but at him.

"Show it to me."

Jamie unrolled his drawing on the grass. Billy got down beside him, on his knees. There was heat coming off him, as if he'd been running.

"The Indians are attacking the wagons," Jamie said. "It's because the white people are taking their land away. This one with the red feather, that's Crazy Horse."

"Crazy Horse," Billy said. The name sounded hard and queer, stuck somehow in his throat.

"He was the greatest Indian leader. He was a friend of Geronimo. They used to live around here, a long time ago."

Neither of them spoke as they looked at the picture.

"I'm an Indian," Billy said.

Jamie went on staring at the picture, but he wasn't seeing it anymore.

"My mother's Indian. She don't like me to tell anybody."

"I won't tell."

They looked at the picture.

"This is a good drawing," Billy said.

"I'm gonna put more Indians in."

"Scalps?"

"Yeah. I could show them scalping somebody."

Jamie rolled up the drawing and they got to their feet. Now he saw the black hair that came down in a mop almost to the black eyes, and the skin that looked brown, tanned maybe, and maybe a bit dirty. Jamie's heart was going again, under his T-shirt, but it wasn't because he was afraid. It was because this was all new. He was somewhere he'd never been. He was with an Indian.

8

A TUESDAY: BURNT grass under a cloudless sky. The Grade Thirteen boys plucked lacrosse sticks from a cardboard drum and played a game—shirts versus skins—between the towering white H's guarding the ends of the football field. In the distance, across waves of goldenrod and the low darkness of a marsh, rose the faultless green of the golf course. Joe flung a long pass to Bobby Merchant and remembered he'd forgotten to study for his French test. Later, he skipped his shower and walked quickly through the crowded halls to Mr. Kay's room. He'd bone up before the others arrived.

The first-floor classroom held thirty desks of blond wood. Along the

walls hung framed posters depicting the Place Pigalle, the Eiffel Tower,
and the ruins of the Roman theater at Orange. At the front, Mr. Kay
stood with his back to the blackboard, talking to someone sitting at the
desk before him. The teacher was speaking French, pushing out the
sounds with an exaggerated earnestness in a big, hollow voice. He wore
a short-sleeved nylon shirt, a narrow wool tie, and black horn-rims
whose bridge he kept nudging up his nose with the middle finger of his
right hand.

She sat in the first desk of the window row: a girl in a pale green
sleeveless dress, her slender right arm lying on the desktop, motionless
except for a small stroking movement of her fingers on the wood. As Joe
flung his gym bag under his seat, the teacher offered a bland hello and
the girl turned to glance at him. The shock hit him before he knew what
the shock was for, as if his body had recognized her before he did, recognized the face whose details he had pretty much forgotten, under the
thick bangs.

He opened his book and stared into it, seeing nothing. At the front of
the room, the conversation ran on. Joe looked up again and saw, on her
cheek, the pale dusted whiteness, a burn or a birthmark: the brand of the
evening on the river.

She too was speaking French. He thought she sounded French, the way
she rounded the sounds, savoring them before she sped them on their
way with protruding lips. Mr. Kay's wide, grinning face had reddened.

Joe turned a page, but it was all a charade. He might have been an
actor pretending to read while he waited to say his next lines. He was
aware of her dress, cut in a low square at the back, exposing smooth
tanned skin; of the thin silver bangle she toyed with at her wrist. Her
light voice had a trace of something low in it, an impure note that
thrilled and obscurely frightened him. He listened to her with a dry
mouth, half resenting her arrival. He had been happy with his life.

What was she talking about? Though he'd always done well in
French, he was lost before the effortless flow of her talk. It was something about France, he thought, or was it Switzerland? Something about
picnics and cheese and the price of coffee—or was it cafés? In the street,

Vern Melling's truck rumbled by, carrying a small mountain of fly-circled trash.

The rest of the class began to arrive, a hubbub of voices and flung gym bags and books slapped down on desks. The girl in the pale green dress watched, curiously. She did not see how in the aisle behind her Elaine Brown hugged her books to her chest and directed a tolerant smile at the interloper who had stolen her desk.

"*Bien!*" Mr. Kay said loudly, their signal to quiet down. "*Alors, mes amis,*" he said. A book dropped, and through the open window a bee floated in, drifting up toward the fluorescent lights.

The teacher discovered Elaine, waiting.

"*Oh, Elaine! Ton banc!*"

"*C'est votre banc?*" the girl said. Silence spread through the room. The girl started to rise, but Elaine said she was happy to sit at the back. "You're sure?" the girl said. In her voice was a hint of laughter, as if she were secretly enjoying this bit of confusion. Still hugging her books, Elaine walked to the back.

Speaking in French, Mr. Kay introduced the new girl: Anna Macrimmon. The name sounded odd to Joe, a patch of rocky land in the smooth lawns of the French. She had turned to the class, and Joe could now drink in every detail of her face: the birthmark on her cheek, the faint Asiatic slope of the eyes, a pale, unusual green under her dark and well defined brows. Her bobbed hair with its thick bangs gave her a tomboyish look, he thought.

"*Bonjour,*" she said, to the whole class.

One or two ragged *bonjours* answered back.

"*Non, non,*" Mr. Kay admonished. "*Encore! Plus fort!*"

They managed it better the second time. Joe was chagrined, on her behalf. Their welcome must have seemed childish to her, he thought, like something in grade school.

Mr. Kay handed out scrap paper. The test was about to begin. The teacher's brogues squeaked as he paced slowly at the front of the room, reading out, *en anglais,* the sentences they were to translate. *He will have come. You ought to stay. She will have been there.* Pens scratched and tapped in the pauses. Anna Macrimmon tilted her head to the side as she studied what she had written. One wing of her hair fell forward, and she tucked it back behind her ear. He saw that her ear stuck out a little, a flaw of sorts. Above, the bee followed the lights and then abruptly glided down to touch the poster of the Roman theater at Orange, the golden ruins under a blue, savage sky.

IN SMALL GROUPS, the students of 13A walked along a sidewalk white as bone and straight as a runway, between the carports and burnt lawns of the new housing development known as the Shade Survey. Every year, Mr. Mann invited his senior history class to lunch at his home. Joe trudged beside Smiley, who was telling some story about how he and Freddie Farmer had been nearly killed that weekend. They'd been driving on the Johnsonville highway, going almost 90, Smiley said, and it wasn't only dark, it was foggy, and suddenly they'd noticed the road curving away to the right and they were headed to the left, into God only knew what. "Shit, man," Smiley said, a great happiness shining in his deep-set eyes, "I thought we'd bought it."

But a lane had appeared in the headlights. They'd run over a gate and smashed the grill on Freddie Farmer's dad's car, but otherwise no damage done.

Thirty yards ahead, Anna Macrimmon was walking between Liz McVey and Elaine Brown. Joe caught the back of her head, vanishing and reappearing among intervening bodies. Even when he lost sight of her or looked elsewhere, he could sense her presence, a magnetic darkness in the blazing sun. He had failed his French test and had an intimation that worse lay ahead. His lack of a shower left him sweating, a disaster when he considered that he was also wearing his red-and-white checked sport shirt. The cloth was cheap and stank as his sweat reacted with the dye.

They went up a narrow drive between high cedar hedges, past the plaque that told them that Abraham Shade, founder of Attawan, had built this house in 1823. The house itself appeared, a long low cottage with unshuttered windows, surrounded by tall locusts. Patches of sun trembled on its whitewashed plaster walls. The blue door stood open.

They sat on the parched front lawn, under the huge arthritic trees, while Archibald Mann talked to them. The teacher—Joe's mentor and favorite—was a slim, rather short man, his heavy eyelids pouched with melancholy, his thinning white hair combed forward in points like Julius Caesar. He spoke more quietly than any of their other teachers, and on the whole said less. Yet there was something in his slow, abraded speech that held them, a kind of casual sincerity, as though it would be impossible for him to say anything but what he actually thought. He was retiring at the end of the year.

Mann spoke of Abraham Shade and his house. Behind him, the valley floated in late summer sun. Details were visible, miniaturized by distance: the dark, high webbing of the CN trestle and, glimpsed through its stone legs, the brown water of the river, easing toward the sheer line of the dam's edge. But what predominated was the vast ecstatic light, a presence that heralded the still-hidden reaches of autumn.

"Try to imagine," Mann said, "another day like this. One hundred, five hundred years ago. Some things don't change, at least not very quickly. This kind of light. The crickets. This has always been a good place to be. There are springs in the hillside, hardwood trees for timber and shade and fuel, good soil. A view of the valley so you can see your friends or enemies approach.

"Of course, other people knew this place before Shade did—Indian people. I've found arrowheads on the hillside, bits of pottery. We call our town Attawan, after these people, but in fact we have no idea what they called themselves. It was the Hurons who called them the Attawan, or rather the Attawandaeron, quite a mouthful. The word means 'People who speak a slightly different language,' and it tells us that the people who lived around here spoke an Iroquoian dialect, not too different from the Hurons' own. Anyway, the Attawandaeron disappeared about four hundred years ago. Disappeared completely," Mann added, and paused. A cricket went on turning its squeaky wheel. Faintly, mournfully, a diesel horn sounded beyond the town. With Mann's word *disappeared,* a profound absence had been summoned. They all felt it and were held by it.

"What happened to them?" someone said finally, breaking the tension. There was a stir among the others, a deepening of attention.

Mann shrugged and shook his head. "We don't really know. They may have been wiped out by disease, or by Iroquois raiders coming up from the south. Maybe they made some bad political choice—you know, allied themselves with the wrong power. Maybe they didn't keep up technologically—were too slow to get guns or other things made of iron. In any case, they're gone, and we've inherited these late-summer days of theirs, which they must have found as lovely as we do."

Mann paused, frowning, as if slightly chagrined at his outburst of poetic sentiment. His audience remained still. He went on. "When Abraham Shade came here, in the early 1820s, he fell for this place immediately. We have his diaries' word on that. He always said it felt haunted. He and his family were the first whites to settle here, and he claimed he could sense the people who had lived here before, even though they'd been gone for—oh, two centuries or more at that point. It was his brother John—a bit of a scholar, in an amateur nineteenth-century way—who told him what we know of the Indian people in this region. Shade decided to call the town after them. A lot of people didn't like it, at the time. There was quite a debate. But the name stuck. . . ."

By moving his head slightly, Joe could see Anna Macrimmon. She was sitting on the ground, under an oak tree, with her hands clasped around her shins, her chin lifted a little as she listened.

THEY CROWDED INTO the long living room lined with books and comfortable-looking couches and chairs. Over the massive fieldstone fireplace hung a small framed painting of mountains falling sheer to a glacial lake. In a corner sat a spinning wheel like some strange upended wooden bicycle.

It was the first time Joe had been in Mann's house, the first time he'd looked into the teacher's private life, and he was alive to every object. At the same time he felt uncomfortable and rushed, aware of his stinking shirt and of the others who, with no idea how important this all was, crowded around Mann like cattle. He hated having to share Mann's house with them, hated that Anna Macrimmon had come on this day of all days, when he wasn't ready for her. He could sense her, somewhere in the hot press of bodies.

Mann said, "If you take note of the floor."

Miserably, Joe surveyed the wide, darkly gleaming boards. A drop of his sweat fell.

"Usually, you'd expect pine floors in a pioneer house like this. But this is oak, two-inch oak laid across oak beams. In fact, unusually, almost all the wood in the house is oak. Can anybody tell me why that might be?"

Silence met his question. The brown eyes in the expressionless face swept slowly over them, challenging. While the pendulum clock ticked from the mantelpiece, a faint nervous pressure spread. The students knew Mann was capable of waiting minutes for an answer.

Joe put up his hand. Mann nodded at someone else.

Brad Long spoke up in his deep, pleasant voice, easily filling the room with his habitual hint of happy scorn; surely it was all so obvious. "There was lots of oak around here—it was handy. And being the kind of guy he was, he wanted to be number one, so he put in the best."

"Good," Mann said.

Joe burned at the lost compliment; he knew as much. But Brad wasn't through.

"I guess he wanted us to stand here one day and admire him." Brad raised his large hands and looked toward the ceiling, as if addressing a gallery of ancestors, looking down appreciatively on the scene from heaven. "Great floors, Abe!"

The class laughed. Joe thought he heard Anna Macrimmon's voice behind him, silver among the rest.

THEY ATE LUNCH outside. Joe took a sandwich and paper plate from the long table Mann had set out under the locusts and retreated to a shady spot near a concrete birdbath. Anna Macrimmon was still moving through the line. With her were Liz McVey and Sheila Benson, a pretty sharp-featured girl with bouffant hair and a hard, snorting laugh. They carried their plates to a little knoll under a tree and sat on the ground, tugging their skirts over their knees. A few minutes later, Joe watched Brad Long join them. He lowered his rangy frame onto the dry grass at their feet, stretching himself out with all the ease in the world before the prim statuary of their folded legs.

Brad raised an arm, gesturing lazily to make some point, and Joe saw how the cuff of his pale blue shirt was turned back, with a pleasing yet casual exactness, turned back once and kept there by some magical gravity-defying power, unlike the cuffs of his own sad shirts, which fell down constantly unless they were rolled up several times. Now Brad's laugh came, tolerant, self-enjoying, warm. Joe saw Anna Macrimmon shake her head in disbelief or denial, saw the heavy silk of her hair move like something alive. But she was smiling too, or fighting back a smile, as if to say, Go on with you.

A little way off, a group of Brad's friends—boys from the North End—were watching him with barely suppressed merriment, as if he were doing what they hadn't the nerve to try themselves.

Joe picked at his tuna-fish sandwich. Ever since he'd seen Anna Macrimmon that first evening on the river, she had seemed to exist for him only. Now she had become the property of everybody who cared to look at her, including Brad Long, who had no idea what she was, what her true value was, not really.

"Yugga."

Smiley. He sat down cross-legged beside Joe, his plate loaded with booty.

"Food." He grunted, playing the caveman. Joe looked away.

Mayonnaise leaked from Smiley's mouth. "That new girl," he said. "I keep thinking I've seen her somewhere."

"How could that be?" Joe said coldly.

Smiley ate with hunched, predatory enjoyment. "I dunno. It's weird. She's pretty good looking."

Joe said nothing. Smiley looked up with staring frankness.

"Don't you think she's good-looking?"

"She's all right. I haven't really noticed."

"You should. She's right over there."

To Joe's horror, Smiley pointed.

Wretchedly, Joe studied the trembling islands of shade and sun across the lawn. He wanted to start the day—his life—over again.

"Not there. There."

"For Christ's sake, I know where she is. Stop pointing."

After a moment Smiley said, "I wonder what that thing is on her face—you see that?"

"No."

"Look at it. It's like some kind of burn."

Joe lurched to his feet and started to walk quickly toward the house, picking his way through groups of students. Just then Mann emerged, carrying a pitcher of ice water. Normally Joe was happy to see the teacher. He liked to stop after class to talk with him, finding in his power of listening something that made his own thoughts rise and come clear. But he wasn't ready for Mann now. He asked where the washroom was.

Mann put down his pitcher and led Joe through the house, which sprawled to the rear through a series of additions. The teacher moved swiftly, his small feet in their worn, pointed shoes pattering on the tiles. The bathroom was behind the kitchen. "The old summer kitchen," Mann said, and as he stepped back to let Joe pass the teacher touched him lightly on the back.

Joe closed the door, fit the bolt, stripped off his shirt, and began to wash his face and chest, sloshing water almost wildly. In the mirror, his face seemed an assembly of imperfections. Under his right eye, a pimple raised its minaret of shame. Padding himself dry, he studied a framed photo hanging beside the window. Two young men, both wearing shorts and white shirts, their arms draped loosely over each other's shoulders, grinned back at him with large smiles of pure happiness. Behind them soared the white tentlike summit of a distant mountain. He saw with a start that one of the men was Mann, his hair dark and curly, his eyes less pouched, Mann in the bright disguise of youth. The other man had the kind of smooth, almost feminine face Joe remembered from a painting he'd seen in a book: the unearthly face of an angel by Raphael. This is crazy, he thought, breaking suddenly from the image with a sense of alarm. I'll speak to her. I have to speak to her.

He passed through the house with a feeling that he was living under a sentence, that he was being dragged forward in a kind of dream state. Yet the whole time he told himself he was free; maybe he'd speak to her, maybe he wouldn't. He was afraid of his own cowardice while half looking forward to its intervention. When he reached the front step he glanced across the lawn and saw with a thudding heart that she had gotten up; she was moving away from the others with a paper cup in her hand, following the hedge that ran from Mann's yard into the adjacent property.

Then Mann was by his side. The teacher held up an old-fashioned camera, with an accordion chamber of black fabric, and asked if he could take Joe's picture. He'd taken every graduating class for years now, he said, candid shots; it had become a tradition. He positioned Joe against the door, softly gripping his biceps to move him back a little. As Mann frowned into his viewfinder, Joe watched Anna Macrimmon drift down the line of hedge, her head raised and tilted a bit to one side, as if skeptically.

"There we go. Handsomest fellow in the class," Mann said with a grin. A moment later, laconically: "I see we have a new girl."

"Yes." Joe evaded the teacher's eyes.

"Why don't you introduce me to her?"

"I don't really know her. She just came."

"Then we'll introduce each other."

Walking with Mann under the locusts, he was under sentence again, marching out to his execution. They passed Smiley, who looked up from his sandwich. "Yugga," his friend said quietly, as if he knew.

She was now walking toward a belvedere on the brow of the hill, past an untended garden where the surviving flowers fought silently with the weeds. It belonged to the Bannerman estate, which had been turned into a retirement home.

Mann was going on about the arrowheads and other artifacts he had found in the hill. Someone from the museum in Toronto was coming down to have a look. Joe nodded automatically, scarcely hearing.

She was in the belvedere, kneeling with one knee on the narrow wooden bench, looking into the valley. As they approached, she turned. Each time Joe saw her face it seemed new to him, a revelation. Again he saw a dart of amusement in her eyes, as if their arrival were the beginning of an adventure she had half expected. But there was also a candor that chilled him. He wondered if she remembered him from the river.

Mann introduced himself and shook her hand. "This is Joe Walker, one of your classmates."

"Yes," she said, putting out her hand.

Joe took it and was conscious of its firmness in his, and of the coldness of his own.

She looked back to Mann. "I was just thinking about what you said. About how Shade fell in love with this place. Do you think certain places call to us?"

"I suppose it depends to some degree on individual psychology," Mann said, "and of course there's the general human need for shelter. But there's also something else—people, at least most of them, don't like to pitch their tents just anywhere."

She was watching the teacher with her head still a little on the side, ignoring Joe. He stood like a servant, miserable and grateful.

"You take this place," Mann said, gesturing to the valley behind her. "There's something about it that satisfies a need."

"Beauty," she suggested.

"Yes, maybe it's as simple as that," the teacher said, his eyebrows going up.

"Or as complicated." She was looking at Mann with a kind of fencing irony, clearly enjoying herself.

"Indeed. I mean, I wasn't born here, not like Joe," Mann said. Her gaze flicked over Joe and returned to the teacher. "But when I came— well, I was rather like Shade—I felt I belonged here."

"It reminds me a little of Europe," she said.

"Oh, yes? What places?"

"Oh. . . ." She trailed another idle look over Joe. He had never in his life heard people discuss beauty as a thing in itself, as though it were possible to meet Beauty walking down Bridge Street. "The Dordogne, maybe; bits of Italy. You know, limestone and bridges."

"Yes!" Mann said, with a sudden outburst of enthusiasm. When he smiled, which he did rarely, his face was radiant. "I've often felt that myself. The feeling of lives that have gone before. Of course, the spirit is different here and I'm afraid the food isn't as good."

"I don't suppose," she said.

"Where are you from?" Mann said. He glanced at Joe, as if inviting him to participate.

She gave a short laugh at that, as if this were at once the most simple and most complex question in the world; really, it had no answer. "I was born in Montreal," she said, with an arch emphasis, as if getting born were a kind of joke, "but my father's worked all over the place. Abroad, mostly. I've lived almost as much in Europe as here. My mother's French."

"Aha," Mann said. He looked again at Joe, with a kind of shining blankness. But Joe had never been to Europe, a mythical land to him, a land of wars and towers. He felt completely out of his depth. He shifted and smiled vaguely as they talked, and hoped she couldn't smell his shirt.

"So what brings you to Attawan?" Mann said.

"My father's working here now. He's an accountant. His company's just bought some mills here."

"Bannerman's," Mann said. "Joe's father works there too."

"Really," she said, sounding not at all interested. But at least she looked at him again.

"He's in the sweater mill," Joe said, his face heating. He wished Mann had never mentioned his father. He wanted no past just now; he just wanted to stand here, as new as she was.

There was a pause, excruciating to Joe, who felt he should keep the conversation going. He grinned but could think of nothing to say.

"Say, listen," Mann said, rousing himself. "I'm taking a picture of everyone here, it's a tradition with my graduating classes. If you wouldn't mind—"

Anna Macrimmon stood with her back against the dilapidated belvedere. Her playfulness had suddenly evaporated, replaced by a kind of moody tolerance of the process, as she squinted against the sun, turning away the cheek with the birthmark. When it was over, Mann said, with inexplicably blushing face, "Well. Good. I'm sure Joe would like to show you around." He left within seconds.

Anna Macrimmon looked at Joe.

"I've seen you before," she said flatly.

He thought of denying it, but with a nod his admission escaped him.

"Where?" she said, rather grimly.

"That—"

"No, no, let me guess!" She went on studying him, as if his face were a painting. He knew he was was blushing; knew the pimple under his eye was getting bigger, knew his smell must soon reach her, if it hadn't already.

"The bridge," she said, "That time with the McVeys—"

"I didn't yell anything," he said.

"You were in the water," she said, squinting at him.

"I was telling them to stop—"

"Were you?" she cried skeptically.

"Scout's honor," he said, raising two fingers.

She was looking at him mischievously now. "You know, the McVeys were quite upset."

There was a hint of accusation here. He nodded.

"So why were you doing it? Why were they doing it?"

He shook his head, as if to say, Stupid kid stuff, Who can explain it? But she was not going to let him off so easily.

"Walk with me," she said. "Tell me."

They went down the wide, grassy path. The back of her hand brushed his.

"I'm waiting," she said.

He knew perfectly well why the others had taunted the McVeys. They disliked them for their wealth, their snobbery, for the fact that Doc McVey was landlord to several of their families, for the fact that they'd come down to the river to gawk.

"There's too much history to it," he said.

"It sounds fascinating."

"It's sort of a neighborhood thing. Stupid, really."

"You mean like a class thing?"

He thought she meant *class* as in school.

"Most of those kids weren't in their class, the McVeys' class."

"That's what I mean," she said, misunderstanding. "They're—what, working class?"

He was sure he was going to burn up in front of her. He never used the term *working class*, though he knew perfectly well what she was getting at. Working class was lower than middle class. His father was working class; his mother was, or had been, middle class. What did that make him, a kind of mongrel?

"It's stupid, really," he said. "It's because Doc McVey owns a lot of houses. Some of those people pay rent to him. They think he charges too much."

"Aha," she said. "And does he?"

"I have no idea. We own our own house."

She studied him as they walked.

"I'm sorry, I'm embarrassing you. We'll talk of something else."

"I'm not embarrassed," he lied. But he was relieved when she turned her attention to the outbuildings of the Bannerman estate. They moved toward the great house, its high-pitched slate roofs looming over the treetops, passing by an assortment of sheds and the gardener's stone cottage. She peered in the windows, where glass shelves held African violets and knickknacks, into the gloomy little rooms beyond. Her forwardness amazed him. He knew they were trespassing but did not say so. In her curiosity she seemed unconscious of such concerns, and he felt he should be too, as if she were teaching him about some wider form of freedom.

THAT EVENING AFTER supper, he climbed over the dike and stood watching the river. Upstream, a small rapid turned its liquid body between rocks: a flashing of white in the dimness. Everything had changed. Because of the half hour he had spent with Anna Macrimmon, everything he looked at—the little rapid, the hill lifting in darkness, the ghostly band of children traipsing noisily over the footbridge to Lion's Park—bore her sign.

She was not in class the next day. Taking attendance on his clipboard, Mr. Kay glanced over his horn-rims at her empty desk and hiked his eyebrows slightly—a mere twitch of surprise before his round face subsided into the stoic blandness behind which adults lived their remote lives. To Joe, it was as if the teacher had passed nonchalantly by a burning building.

The morning was saturated with her absence: a deserted classroom, the red jumpers of the girls' phys ed class as they flowed across a sun-beaten field, the tribal echo of laughter from a washroom, an absence that still contained the promise of her, for it seemed possible she might materialize unexpectedly, as she had the first time, and the second too. He wondered if she had decided not to come back at all. Her powers in this matter seemed absolute; she was everywhere and nowhere, as fluid and invisible as his mood. In biology he sliced his finger on a scalpel. The blood, a small red sac at his knuckle, surprised him, because it was him. It was a shock to remember that he had his own body, his own separate life.

At noon, Sandy waited for him in the little park across from the school: a waif in a shapeless plaid dress, coming forward with a hopeful half smile from under the caved shadow of a maple. He was appalled by her ordinariness, by her very existence, so small and finite and limited. Her powers touched nothing beyond her, not a single blade of grass.

He fell silent as they trudged along Shade Street, past mansions pre-
siding with humorless reserve over long sloping lawns. He felt his real
life had reached out to claim him. He had become someone else with
Anna Macrimmon; now he was his old humdrum self again, sweating
and disconsolate in his best shirt, a dark green corduroy that was too hot
for the day and not nearly good enough for his purposes. This was his
life: the armhole of Sandy's sleeveless dress, where the band of her
sweat-stained bra showed; her bright chattering voice saying nothing he
cared about.

They passed the mouth of Senator's Lane. Boys were flinging sticks into
a tree. Clumps of leaves fell, chestnuts in their spiky rinds like the heads of
medieval war clubs. She said, "I guess I was expecting you last night?"

Her very gentleness, her care for his mood, irritated him.

"What for?"

Her flat face lifted to him, an offering. "My essay?"

"What essay?" He scowled, trying to evade his rising guilt. It reached
him anyway. "I'm sorry. I forgot. I was busy." A moment later, more gently, "Did you finish it?"

She shook her head, like a child, he thought.

"It's not due till next Monday."

"Maybe we can do it on the weekend," he said. Immediately, the
thought of even a few more days with her oppressed him.

ANNA MACRIMMON RETURNED the next morning. Joe was sitting
at his desk in Mr. Kay's room, waiting for the class to begin, when on
some instinct he turned to see her making her way among the students
who had not yet taken their seats, threading a course with her books
held, in that way girls had, to her chest.

Her face restored itself to him in a heart's leap of glad recognition; of
course, that's what she looked like! In the intervening day, so many par-
ticulars had slipped from memory: the neat helmet of her ash-blond
hair, her dark brows, and of course the mark on her cheek, that appeared
just now like the image of a small, pale, half-ruined flower.

Yet she was different. It was her clothes. The green sheath had been replaced by a crisp white blouse with sleeves that ended partway down her forearms, a full skirt in some rich shade of green, threaded with hints of other colors, a broad belt. He watched in astonishment as she came closer. Her change in appearance seemed like the evidence of some mysterious fecundity, like the flowering of day lilies in his mother's garden, each morning new blossoms in new places, lifting their trumpets on the still air.

After the class, he caught up to her in the hall.

"Hi there," he said casually, falling in beside her.

There was something unsurprised and wholly accepting in her glance, as if his arrival were nothing special. He was put off balance.

"Hi there," she said, with an irony he could not grasp.

"Were you sick, or . . ."

She was searching his face with a simple calm.

"Or what?"

"I missed you," he said, and blanched at his mistake.

"Thank you," she said quietly.

It was hard to keep beside her among the jostling, streaming bodies. A locker clattered shut, and someone nearby growled in an undertone, "Eat your nose!"

They went into the biology lab, with its black desks and deep sinks. A smell of formaldehyde penetrated everywhere, from vats at the front of the room. The class was dissecting cats. Joe pulled out his stool, aware that Anna Macrimmon had stopped several desks behind him. He kept playing and replaying his appalling gaffe. He felt like pounding his head on the desk.

Smiley had fetched their cat. Lying stiffly on its side, on a metal tray, it looked drowned, the eyes crimped shut, its soaked, matted fur standing up in points. Joe turned the page of his notebook, looking bleakly over his drawings. The previous week they had cut up frogs: the yellow skin of the bellies, pulled back like waistcoats; the gum-wad hearts, turned gray by the preserving chemical. Such knowledge had nothing to do with Anna Macrimmon, it seemed. She was behind him now and somehow, in her power, she had withdrawn meaning from everything, from his carefully drawn pictures, from Smiley, bent with his knife to the cat.

He let Smiley do most of the dissecting, while he halfheartedly made notes and diagrams. Mr. Brunt patrolled the aisle, an intense little man with an oversized head, like a baby bird's. He chewed a pencil and shouted instructions in an almost incomprehensible, chastising way. It was like being harassed by a yipping dog. Outside, the burnt playing fields stretched toward the huddled ranch-style houses of the Shade Survey. A black cat was slinking across a lawn.

From the back of the room, over a low murmur of voices, a girl's voice spoke up clearly, saying she couldn't do this, she wouldn't do this. Anna Macrimmon.

He saw her addressing Mr. Brunt. Her face had colored, filled with an expression of disbelief sharpened by anger. She was demanding that the teacher give an accounting of himself.

"This is disgusting," she said for the second time. "Where did you get these cats?"

Mr. Brunt removed the pencil from his mouth, gave a hollow chuckle. "You going to faint?" he said. He seemed hopeful she might.

"That's not the point! I can't do this, not to her!"

She was holding up her hand—a scalpel was in one—and looking down at the gray, soaked form in front of her. Everyone watched in amazement. She had spoken to the teacher as if he were an equal, or even an inferior. It was unthinkable.

"Lie down if you're going to faint," Mr. Brunt said. His face had grown tomato-red.

Anna Macrimmon shook her head. She bent down behind her desk— Joe wondered if she had fainted—and a moment later popped up with her books and went swiftly from the room, leaving the door ajar. Liz McVey hurried after her, a silent helper.

"Meatheads," Mr. Brunt said. It was his favorite phrase of disapproval. He put his pencil back in his mouth, like a stopper into the vial of his fury. "There's always one," he mumbled, forcing a grin. No one laughed. No one understood what had happened, but the breaching of the usual boundaries of obedience and decorum had touched them deeply, as if they had witnessed an act of violence. Only they did not quite know, as they turned back to their trays, where exactly the violence lay.

THAT NIGHT JOE dreamed of a cat. It lay on its side, in a clear shimmering bath of formaldehyde, not moving. There was a sound of quick, shallow breathing, as if someone were laboring in a high fever. It was not the cat, which was still, or almost still, under the warping shine of the chemical. The nightmare did not change focus or show him anything else. It was extraordinarily oppressive, like being shut in a brightly lit room scarcely bigger than he was.

ANNA MACRIMMON WAS excused from dissection and allowed to learn anatomy from her textbook. The next day she sat at the back of the lab by herself, working at her books with a peculiar, private intensity that made him sad and wistful. She wore a thick black ribbon bound around her hair. The change seemed to Joe to have something to do with the events of the previous day, as if she were in mourning for the cats, though at the same time there was something sharp and aggressive in the new look. She did not smile, not that he noticed. It was clear he scarcely existed for her.

One morning—it was a week after the cat incident—he was walking by himself through the North End, on his way to school, when he saw her coming toward him on Senator's Lane: down the deep sun-splotched cut between two big Victorian houses. She was wearing a sand-colored dress with a shallow V-neck and was walking with her head bowed, her books cradled loosely in her arms. She was quite close before she broke from her daydream and saw him, saying his name in a friendly enough way, but with that hint of flatness that had so discomfited him before.

He had picked up a chestnut in his nervousness and now stood rolling it in his fingers.

"What's that?"

He gave the nut to her, and she examined it with obvious pleasure, at one point putting it to her face to smell it. "It's like mahogany. And what's this?" She was pointing to the bits of sticky white stuff that clung to it. He noticed that the skin around her nail was shiny and red.

"I'm not sure. All the new ones have it, when they come out of the shell."

He helped her find a couple of others, which she put into the pocket of her dress. "This is one of the best trees for them," he said, and watched her intently—her throat, her hair—as she gazed up into the foliage.

"Do you live near here?" he said.

"Over on Banting. I haven't walked this way before."

He nearly said, I'm glad you did, but managed to hold back. They walked together up Shade.

"Too bad," he said, "about that cat business."

She did not immediately respond, and he wondered if he'd made a misstep. He did not seem able to be natural with her. She said, "I'm probably too sensitive about some things. It just occurred to me that the cat hadn't died of old age."

"He gets them from farms," Joe said. "Barncats."

"Barncats?"

"They live half wild in the barns. They keep down the mice."

"A good and useful life," she said. "I don't know why they have to die. It's not as if we don't already know about cat anatomy."

"No," he said, with a nervous laugh. There was a quickness in her, tart, opinionated, a little intimidating.

"Does he kill them himself?"

"I don't know."

"I'll bet he does. That man gives me the creeps."

A bee skimmed across the road, passing them at knee level. A red Studebaker swished down the tree-shaded street, and a woman in one of the large houses on the embankment to the east paused in the sweeping of her porch to look at them.

Anna had stopped to fumble in her binder. She extracted a paper, shaking out its folds with one hand and offering it to him. "I wrote a poem about it."

He took the page in the glare of light. What did he know about poetry? Tennyson's "Ulysses"—he liked that one—Wordsworth on daffodils, bits of Hamlet's soliloquies, they knocked around in his head and sometimes, at odd moments, they'd pop out. *To be or not to be. Now, fair Hippolyta, our nuptial hour draws on apace.* He looked at the page with its column of typescript and suddenly, the slight touch of a breeze, he sensed her vulnerability as she waited for his reaction.

> The cat is not dead.
> That is only the illusion of her wet, spiked fur,
> Her stillness
> Her buttoned-down eyes
> Her last, desperate run stiffened into an emblem
> Of former cat.
> The cat is not here.
> What you see in these packed organs
> This gray waste of cells
> Is only a trace of cat—
> Cat tracks
> Printing the snow of our notebooks.
>
> The cat has gone elsewhere.
> Once again
> The cat has eluded us:
> A whisper in dry grasses,
> A howl of dismay
> From the country of her other lives.

Reaching the last line, he felt something. He wasn't sure whether it was his nervousness around Anna Macrimmon or the poem itself, its strangeness, like a bullet cutting water.

"It's good," he said, and colored at the appalling inadequacy of his remark. "It's very good—wonderful! That last line." He shook his head, stymied by his amazement.

She took the page back from him, and they went on without speaking. Just knowing her the little he did, he had been pitched into new territory, and it was stranger than he had realized. There were shadowy regions, tricky paths. He was lost, and he didn't like it. He felt he was failing her, in his silence.

"You're a poet," he said, to the space in front of him. "I mean, I don't know much about poetry. But that!"

He glanced at her suddenly and found her looking at him; there was something alert in her eyes, searching, that he couldn't decipher.

"Do you have more?"

"A few," she said.

"I'd like to see them sometime. I mean, if you—"

He thought she was blushing.

"I'm sorry, Anna, if you don't want to . . ."

"No, I'll show you sometime. I want to."

"Good."

"Good," she said, a dull echo. He felt she was slipping away. Desperate, before his advantage disappeared entirely, he said, "There's a dance next week, Friday. Maybe not the greatest dance in the world, but I wonder if you'd like to go with me."

She looked up the street. "I don't think so, Joe."

Her voice sounded muffled. Not for the first time, he felt she was older than he.

"Or we could go to a movie, or . . ."

"Don't take this the wrong way, but I'm just not up for that sort of thing."

"What sort of thing are you up for then?"

She smile faintly, shaking her head a little, as if she found him incorrigible and a bit amusing. She did not answer.

———

HE FELT AS if she had taken him very gently and put him aside. She was friendly enough afterward, so he wondered if she had dismissed him after all. But no, it was done. He licked his wounds for a day or two and then—he could scarcely help himself—began to shadow her again. He contrived meetings in the hall, and a couple of times ran into her on the way to school. He was careful not to force anything, to pretend to be at his ease, camouflaging his true feelings. Once or twice he tried to push things farther, but she rebuffed him. He understood it was a matter of trust. If he did not chase her, then from time to time, for a little while, they could be together. Watching her, laughing at some joke she'd made, pretending she was only one of a dozen girls he liked, he drank her in secret, deeply and gratefully.

She was often alone—it seemed to him her natural state—but when she wasn't she was with Liz McVey and Diane Cochrane and Sheila Benson and Carol Jeunesse—the reigning clique of girls had closed around her like a herd welcoming their own kind. To his eyes, they were her inferiors. Walking with her down the halls, holding their books to their chests or under their arms, in their plaid skirts and neat blouses, their cardigans and blazers and cropped or bouffanted hair, they seemed her attendants only, ladies to her queen.

Brad Long was clearly in the picture. Brad Long with his easy ways and fine clothes—those always-new-looking shirts, their tab collars left so deftly open, the soft cardigans, the neatly creased khakis, the choco-late Hushpuppies—Brad was paying a lot of attention to Anna Macrim-mon. His locker was beside Anna's—damnable luck—but Joe thought there was more than coincidence in the number of times he saw Brad leaning there, bending over her as she reached to select something from the narrow cupboard or simply listened to him, held in the protective space his tall body made, held by his low voice that surrounded her with a chuckling casualness, easy and smooth and carrying them on together like two idling lovers in a canoe.

Once he saw them walk away together after school up Angle Street, which was telling; Anna Macrimmon lived in that direction, but Brad didn't. He wondered if she'd asked him to her house. He followed at a distance, and saw them turn up Cairn, but after that, wary of being seen, he lost them. They could have gone into a house (he didn't know which one) or turned down another street. He was too upset, too aware of his own pathetic absurdity to follow further, but that night he was sure he had certainly lost her, friendship was surely the most he could expect. Yet he was angry with her for being with Brad Long; he felt he was better than Brad, and better for her too, and it seemed a major flaw, the first he'd discovered, that she could not see this.

Soon afterward, he and Anna Macrimmon met at the fountain in the hall. She bent to the silver knob—it seemed alive, under its quivering beads of water—holding back her hair with the tips of her fingers.

"So good," she said, wiping her mouth with her hand as she turned to him. "Cold."

"It's from springs outside of town," Joe told her. "They get it before it even comes out of the ground." Remembering dimly something from their first conversation, at Mann's house, he added, "From the limestone."

Something sparked in her green eyes; he felt quickened by their sudden watchfulness. "I love the word *limestone*," she said. "It's so odd. There's lime trees, and the color lime and the lime they used to throw on dead people."

"Quicklime!" he said happily.

"Yes! And then there's the stone," she said. "All those things shouldn't go together, but they do, because of the word. The word fuses them, somehow."

She seemed excited by their wordplay; he felt challenged.

"It makes me think of secret things, deep in the earth," he said, still held by her gaze. He felt half drunk, beyond the reach of his usual nervousness. His mind was dancing. "Underground rivers. Caverns."

"Caves," she said ominously.

"I know a cave near here," he told her. "It's not very deep, really, but it's made of limestone."

She looked at him brightly; she liked the sound of that.

"What's this?" Brad Long said.

He had approached them from behind, grinning.

"Oh, Brad," she said, glancing back to Joe with an air of complicity. "We were making poetry. You wouldn't understand."

"I love poetry," Brad protested, in his joking way.

"I know you do, poor boy," she said, patting Brad's cheek. Joe, who had been feeling wonderful about his exchange with her, was appalled at their familiarity.

The three of them went into English together. Ahead of Joe, Brad brought up his hand behind Anna, to the place where her blouse met her skirt. Joe couldn't tell if Brad was actually touching her or simply coming close, in a gesture of protection and ownership meant as much for his eyes as for her.

9

WHEN THE PHONE shrilled, Alf had his hands in the innards of a knitting machine. Quarter to nine. The lights were on in the deserted mill. In a nearby window, a yellow sky hovered behind the reflections of the machines. He had often complained to Margaret about having to work late, but the truth was he liked the quiet and isolation of the mill at this hour, when the knitting machines stood silently in their rows and he could concentrate on one thing at a time. He ignored the ringing and it stopped abruptly. Two minutes later it started again. Wiping his hands on a rag he hurried up the aisle, into the stark cubicle that was Matt Honegger's office. It was Margaret, gasping out his name as if she'd just been running. Jamie hadn't come home, she said. He'd gone out after supper by himself and now he was an hour late. Joe had already searched the Island and the park.

The fear he experienced seemed small and faraway, as if a fish had jumped, out in the center of a calm lake. "He'll be along," he told her. "He's just traipsing around with one of the other boys. Probably out in the woods."

"All the other boys are home."

Hesitating, he thought of the night outside, the long shadows of woodlots edging across fields, the cold remorseless fret of water as it undermined banks, frothed over stone. He intuited all this in a flash—the wild lands to the northwest of town—and it woke him to a sudden plunging loneliness, as if it were he himself who was lost.

When he swung into the driveway, the headlights of the Biscayne caught Margaret and Penny, turning on the top of the dike to look at him. Behind them, Lookout Hill loomed darkly. His daughter's white socks flashed and crisscrossed as she ran suddenly toward her mother. Below, Red's tawny eyes glowed. A few minutes later Joe appeared, and the family stood by the picnic table while Alf tried to calm them and make a plan. They were all looking to him for a solution; he could feel the pressure even from Joe, as if in this hour of crisis some instinct to turn to the oldest, strongest man had pushed aside all the usual subtle and not-so-subtle challenges to his authority. But Margaret gave him this authority provisionally, he knew, sensing an impatience that verged on fury. "We'll go up the river," he told them. "We should check that fort he made with Johnny Simms."

"He's always talking about going out to Devil's Cave," Joe said.

They turned their guesswork into a kind of certainty. But Alf knew the boy might be wandering anywhere. He might (he pushed the thought away, but its essence remained) be miles from town. If someone had taken him, missing him by thirty seconds was as bad as missing him by a day. It might already be too late. In the light from the house, Penny lifted her face to his. He could hardly stand the way her big eyes took in his every movement, his every word, as if she could conjure up Jamie out of his body. Alf swept her hot cheek with his fingertips. "Hey there, girl. He's going to walk in here and wonder what all the fuss is about."

"This will teach you not to tease him," Margaret said to her.

"I never," Penny said, and burst into tears.

Alf shot a glance at his wife. "This isn't the time for a Sunday school lesson."

"Well, I'm just saying, this will teach us all," Margaret said defensively. She could change directions as swiftly as a politician.

Alf nearly said, That's not what you meant. But this was not a time for that game. He could never beat her anyway.

"What about Red?" Joe said. "Maybe he could find Jamie."

The big dog had been trotting up and down the yard, in a frenzy of activity, whining and yelping, his ears pricking forward, then lying back.

"More likely to find a skunk," Alf said. "Better tie him up."

He went into the house for his flashlight. When he came back out, Margaret urged him to call some of the neighbors. At first, Alf resisted. The prospect of a search party seemed melodramatic. He didn't want to look like a fool in front of the Island men. "At least call Pete," Margaret said.

"We're losing time," he said, still irritated with her.

"Alf, there's so much ground to cover out there."

"Call him," Penny said. Everyone looked at her, startled by something in her voice. She was staring with perfect calm at Alf, and for that moment she had more authority than anyone else in the family.

Alf went in to phone Pete. They hadn't spoken since their quarrel.

"Pete," he said, starting right in, "we've lost Jamie. I think he might be up the river."

"I'll be right over."

They gathered in the backyard. Their neighbor Bill Olmstead had arrived too, drawn by Margaret's calling Jamie's name from the dike; and Bill's oldest son, Dick. Alf disliked both of them, fleshy, talkative men, the son a taller copy of the father. They were brimming with high spirits and gave the impression that hunting for Jamie was some kind of adventure. Pete, though, was subdued. He had brought a rope.

Margaret and Penny came with them as far as the footbridge. They were going to stay at the house, in case Jamie showed up. "Or if someone calls," Alf said. He wouldn't let himself think too clearly about who might call, or for what reason. He knew the police wouldn't call, they would arrive at the door.

"We'll find him," Alf said, and for a moment met his wife's eyes. It was too dark to see them clearly, but something in her face seemed to reach out to him, and in an instant the hostility he felt for her evaporated.

At the edge of Wiley's farm, the men split up. Alf took the low trail that followed the bends of the Atta through the woods. Over the high pasture to his left, the sky carried a last faint streak of iodine. He lashed his beam at the shrubs on the bank and out over the river, unable to resist the call of his fear. Of course, he wasn't going to see Jamie floating down the middle of the Atta (he told himself), but it was the river that worried him. A night in the woods wouldn't hurt the boy, but the water was an unknown factor, hurrying on with a purpose of its own. High in the south, a chalky flat-sided moon had escaped the clouds.

He could hear the others shouting out Jamie's name from the hills of the farm. He resisted calling, though the word *Jamie* kept rising in his throat. To shout seemed an act of desperation, and he was fighting desperation as though, once set loose, it might generate what he feared most. Then he heard Pete call again, and almost as an echo he shouted too; the word *Jamie* broke from him, sounding hoarser than he'd intended. He shouted again, as his flashlight penetrated the saplings at the edge of the dam. There was no response, or at least none audible over the steady bass hush of the water. For a few minutes he explored the area around the dam, playing his light over the wide sweep of concrete, shiny with the water that skimmed down its steep face and into the mildly boiling pool at its base. He found the dam disheartening, and he was glad to continue on up the trail. In a grove of dead saplings he darted his light at a sudden gleam and saw the metal basket of an abandoned shopping cart.

He had walked on these paths all his life. He had played out here, fished, swum, he had even worked for a couple of summers for old man Wiley, at a dollar a day, weeding turnips and mucking out barns. Yet tonight the place seemed new to him, as if he had never seen its true aspect, the malevolence lurking in a darkness that closed around his beam with a catlike swiftness. He wasn't even sure what he was looking for. If Jamie was conscious, he would surely hear their cries and call back. And if he wasn't? Alf's beam leaped between the trees and combed the undergrowth of tangled weeds, looking for a small huddled body. Perhaps Jamie had knocked himself out, trying to climb a tree. Perhaps he had fainted with the pain of a broken leg. Alf tried to make orderly sweeps with the flashlight, but the darkness and density of the woods made a mockery of his system. He trekked through ferns—their brown, dying fronds flattened to the earth—and climbed the little hill to the swinging vines. There were footprints here, made by several feet. Some seemed about the right size for Jamie, but he couldn't be sure. He tried to force himself, unsuccessfully, to remember the pattern on the soles of his son's shoes. The tracks seemed fairly fresh, made in the last day or so. A little encouraged, he went on, under tall, leaning oaks. They had been giants when he was a boy. To his left the fields of Wiley's farm had turned gray in the moonlight.

Again his light swept over the river. Jamie could swim, but Alf's father too had been able to swim. It came back to him, despite all his efforts to keep the memory at bay: the Sunday afternoon in June 1952, when he'd looked out the front window and seen Gerry Milton, the Town Yard foreman, pacing on the sidewalk as if he were undecided or lost, his rubber boots leaving faint wet tracks on the concrete. They met at the front door. When Gerry told him, his face plaintive, his eyes boring into Alf's as if he, Alf, might save him from this distress, it seemed to Alf that he had always known that his father was dead. Gerry was not giving him news but only forcing his gaze to the side, toward a blackness that had always existed.

He had had to tell his mother. He led her to a chair while she cried What? What? and he understood that she too already knew. Perhaps it was the war that had given her foreknowledge; she had already lost Joe, Alf's brother. Now she knew that her husband too was dead. He had been dead through all the forty-six years she'd known him, dead through their courtship on these same paths where he, Alf, was walking now, playing his feeble beam ahead of him, dead from the first moment he had taken breath. Dead was inscribed in the bone, in the minuscule pushing seed, in the whirling atom.

When he told her, her right arm flailed with a life of its own, as if she might push the knowledge away. He had hated life at that moment, and he felt the same hate now, as he stopped and looked up through the tree-tops, where a few faint stars pulsed, to calm himself. This was what it came down to: the fear, entirely justified, that somewhere out there your own death and the deaths of those you loved were waiting for you.

He followed the trail along the edge of the woods. He felt ice-cold now, determined to pluck his son from the trap. He would find the boy if he had to die doing it. The trail descended to the bottomlands of the Atta. The area had changed since his boyhood. Then cows had grazed here, and kept the land clean and open. Now it was thick with wild fruit trees.

"Jamie!" a voice cried distantly, and hope flared in him. Had they found him?

Silence. The little trees, like rough bouquets, seemed to stand in his beam as if expecting something, stupidly. Then the brush exploded beside him, and he whirled to meet the attack, his heart slamming. The flashlight caught a fleeing deer, its white tail uplifted, bold as a placard, as it bounded into the trees.

"Christ," he said, and regretted swearing. He felt he had to keep him-self pure or Jamie would not appear. He went on, aware he no longer had a plan. He was simply following his instinct, tracing the paths to the north, searching in the mud for more running-shoe marks (he found none). He could no longer hear anyone calling. Perhaps they had found him? "Jamie!" he cried, and his own voice came back to him, a much smaller cry from the wall of the valley.

Again he reached the river. The water, in his beam, seemed sinister, furtive, scheming. The air smelled of autumn, of decay, a chilling emptiness.

Upstream, a rapid surfed along, a scrap of whiteness moving errati-cally in the dark. Alf shone his light and it stopped. Jamie was there, in his white T-shirt and shorts, his eyes glassy, blinking in the light like an animal caught drinking. In a moment he would vanish.

"Jamie!"

"Dad!"

"Stay there! Jamie, don't move! I'll come to you!"

He moved around the edge of the black inlet that separated them, stumbling through thickets and water, his light darting back to Jamie continually. Then they were together, the boy in his arms.

His beam swept over a second pair of legs, also in shorts, standing about twenty feet away. There was a boy there, a dark-haired boy about Jamie's age, his arm raised against the light. His little body in its red T-shirt was pulling slowly back, as if he meant to run away.

"Who's that?" Alf said. He had let Jamie slip to the ground. The other boy had put a start of fear in Alf, as if he were somehow a danger to Jamie and was a threat still. He turned the light back to his son, who was waving the other boy over.

Jamie! Jamie! voices cried from the hill.

"I got him!" Alf yelled.

A silence, then: "He's got him! He's got him!"

"Is that the Boileau boy?" Alf said.

"Billy," Jamie said, "it's all right. It's my dad." The Boileau boy was peering to see past the light, his eyes fiercely suspicious. Alf was surprised to find the two of them together. The Boileaus were tough, poor. The boy's uncle—or was it his cousin?—had been in jail. "He lost his dog," Jamie said. "We tried to get it. We went up past the cave. We got lost."

"Come here, son. It's all right."

The Boileau boy grinned woodenly and took a step toward him.

The searchers returned in a group, jubilant under the lopsided moon. Jamie rode for a while on Alf's shoulders. Pete offered to give Billy a ride, but the boy shook his head and moved away, walking at a distance from the others and saying nothing, though from time to time he offered his painful automatic grin, as though he thought it was required of him.

Beside Alf, Bill Olmstead was going on about how he'd never had any doubt they'd find the boy. He branched into other stories about lost children and lost dogs and the time he'd gotten lost himself, in the bush behind some cottage up north. Not one of those episodes had turned out badly, Bill declared, as if good fortune were only a matter of having a positive attitude.

Ahead, Pete was walking with his head down, the unused rope swinging in a coil from his hand. The sight moved Alf; his friend had come through for him, without a moment's hesitation. Well, of course, he'd have done the same. Catching up, Alf put his hand on his shoulder. "Pete—thanks."

"Okay, buddy," Pete said, avoiding Alf's eyes and blurting out the words, as if they sprang from an emotion too powerful to be safely acknowledged.

Alf drove Billy home. The boy sat alertly on the edge of the Biscayne's front seat, grunting *yep* or *nope* to Alf's questions and watching every turn of the road. His small hard voice sounded trapped in his throat. There was something of a queer little man about him.

The Boileaus lived on the Flats on the east side of town, in a plaster-and-lath cottage overshadowed by the rail embankment. One of the supports for the front porch had been replaced by the trunk of a birch tree. Pulling up at the curb, Alf looked at the curtainless front window and saw the flickering of a small televison, the top of a couch, and a hole in the wall that showed the laths beneath. He wondered if Billy had even been missed. But then he saw Lucille Boileau, trudging along the street from the direction of the river. When she spotted the car, she stopped. Getting out, Alf shouted, "It's all right, I've got him!" and watched as she buckled, as if struck in the stomach. She was still weeping when she came up to him.

She crushed Billy's head against her. Then thrust him back abruptly, giving him a sharp slap on the side of the head. "You had me worried sick!"

"Don't be too hard on him," Alf said. "He was with my boy. They got lost up the Atta."

"You never told me you were going up there! Where's Fuzz, eh? You lost him again?"

"The rope broke."

"The rope broke," Lucille said to Alf, with heavy sarcasm.

"They were doing their best to get back," Alf said.

"You get inside," Lucille said.

Billy shot up the walk.

She turned back to Alf. She was about thirty-five, Alf guessed, beautiful in a severe, threatening way, her long black hair escaping its pins in wisps and collapsing waves, her high cheekbones shiny with tears. The smile she offered him was shy, he thought, with a hint of something evasive and cunning. For years—he saw her often at Bannerman's, where she worked in the sewing department—her mouth had fascinated him, it was so wide, the lips so large and mobile, a freakish mouth, like some odd sea creature come to live on her face.

"I'd die if I lost him," she told him, her eyes fixing blindly on his shirtfront.

She lunged up at him, catching the back of his neck with one hand and putting her mouth on his. It was more than a kiss, it was as if she had leaned up to take a large soft bite out of his face. Driving back over the bridge, he was still thinking about it, an electric excitement flaring across his chest where she had pressed against him. He felt twenty again, everything vivid: the damp, rancid air over the river, his hands tingling on the wheel, and there, past the traffic light, past the Baptist Church and the library, the high, lonely, crumpled moon.

10

THE LIGHT IN the bathroom had a greenish tinge. Jamie's mother made him sit on the toilet with the seat down, while she perched on the edge of the tub, one knee in its brown stocking touching his. In Jarrod's Shoe Store was a machine you put your feet into. Then you looked into a viewfinder and saw the bones in your feet, all pale and strange like little ghosts. He felt she was looking at his bones.

"What were you doing with that boy?"

"Nothing."

"You weren't doing nothing."

She tapped his leg with a rubber spatula. It was what she used to spank him. Her anger was huge—it shone off the tiles behind her head—but he didn't know what he'd done to provoke her. He watched the flat rubber touch his knee and looked into her eyes. Usually there was help there, but now there was none.

"We were just playing."

"I don't want you playing with that boy again."

"Billy?"

"I don't want you to have anything to do with that Boileau boy. Do you understand me?"

The spatula tapped again on his knee.

"Why?"

"His family are not our kind of people. Do you understand?"

He looked at the faucet in the tub, where a big drop was swelling, getting ready to fall.

"We were just having fun."

"Jamie!"

"We tried to get back!"

He was crying now, and when he cried his thoughts started to slide around; he couldn't keep track. What was our kind of people? Kind was good, wasn't it? His teacher, Miss Wayne, was kind, and his mother was, usually. Now she was not kind—was she not his kind of people?

"Look at me!"

He tried to meet her dark eyes, looking at his bones.

"Dad wasn't mad," he whimpered.

"He doesn't want you playing with that boy either. Promise me you won't play with him again."

"Mom!"

"Promise me!"

The spatula tapped. He was crying, he hardly knew why, except that something was not fair. What had he done wrong? When you did something wrong you were punished, but why was he being punished for just doing what he thought was right? He had tried to help Billy find his dog, and he had tried to get home as fast as he could. Only he hadn't been able to find the trail.

"Jamie!"

"I promise! But Mom, why aren't the Boileaus our kind of—"

"Why are they not our kind of people? Because, they're just not nice good people. They've been in trouble with the law."

"What trouble?"

"That doesn't matter. The point is, we're done with them. Right?"

"Yes."

"That's my boy."

She gave him another tap with the spatula and stood up; the matter was clearly finished, as far as she was concerned. He watched her peer at herself in the glass. She put a finger to a place on her cheek and pulled the skin down. Inside the pouch under her eye it was red, like the inside of a fish's gill.

ON MONDAY AND Tuesday he stayed home from school with a touch of the flu, his mother said, feeling his cheeks. He sat in bed sipping ginger ale and looking at his books, especially the *Tim* stories, and at his Superman and Donald Duck comics. On Wednesday his mother announced he was well enough to go back. He went up the hill and found Billy waiting for him at the gate to the Boys' Yard, grinning so widely—so clearly glad to see him—that Jamie felt sick to his stomach.

"Hi."

"Hi."

"Look what I got!" Billy said. He looked over his shoulder, then put his hand in his jacket pocket and pulled out a little cardboard tube, with a brass cap on one end. It rolled in his palm.

"A bullet," Billy said, in his throat-gurgling voice.

"For real?"

"Shotgun."

"Where's the point?"

"They don't have points. You put in gunpowder. Then you put in other stuff, like marbles or rocks or BBs. We can make gunpowder after school. Okay?"

"I don't know. I promised I'd help my mother."

Liar, the voice inside him said. Jamie blinked.

"You grind up coal and put other things in."

"I don't know."

"We can go to my house," Billy said.

Liar, liar, pants on fire.

"Shut up," Jamie said to the voice, and felt his face burn. "Not you," he said to Billy.

Billy put the bullet back in his pocket. Some Grade Five boys went by with their heads back, howling like wolves. Jamie walked off abruptly toward a group of boys who were playing conkers. Billy came with him. Jamie stood pretending to watch the nuts as they swung and smashed, but all he could think about, really, was Billy, who pushed another boy out of the way and stood beside him. He walked away again. Billy followed. He stopped and Billy stopped.

He tried one more time, walking over to the wall where Fattie Lonsdale and Mike Harms were down on their knees, tossing cards into a corner with quick flicks of their wrists: baseball cards and hockey cards and flags of the world and car cards, covering the asphalt in the corner like leaves. Billy joined him. He grinned at Jamie with his brown-edged teeth; this was fun!

The monitor shook her bell and the boys in the yard began to drift toward the school. Billy fell in beside Jamie, in the line going into the south door.

"You better get to your door," Jamie said.

"Oh, yah!" Billy said, and he clapped his hand over his head and pulled a face, as if to say what a goof I am, and Jamie laughed in spite of himself. Then Billy started off, but he came back almost immediately and told Jamie to hold out his hand.

"What for?"

"C'mon, just hold it out."

He put out his hand. Billy laid the empty shotgun bullet in it.

"It's a present," Billy said, and ran off.

During spelling, Jamie felt a little queasy, and then, just as he was putting his speller away under his desk, vomit shot out of his mouth. It slapped onto the hardwood and lay there in a big brown pool with flecks of yellow in it. He couldn't believe it. He'd seen other kids throw up in school, seen them taken off to the nurse's room while Mr. Small, the janitor, came in and spread sawdust on it and scraped it up and washed the floor, though for a long time afterward no one would step there, on the vomit-smelling place that made you feel like vomiting too. Now he was the kid who had done this stupid, smelly thing. They were all looking at him, up and down the rows, some of the boys grinning or craning to see, or saying Wow and staring at him like they didn't know him anymore, just like they had Hel Grimm, the German boy who couldn't speak English and who had come to school one day wearing leather shorts.

11

BEHIND HER DESK in General Office, the receptionist, May Watson, lifted her sagging alcoholic's face. "They want you in the boardroom," she droned, her heavy-lidded eyes fixed on Alf's chest.

"Did they say what it was about?"

They: like a creature with twenty heads.

May's right shoulder twitched, a faint shrug.

He went through the office, up the carpeted stairs, and on through a murmur of voices and the machine-gunning of typewriters, conscious of the stains on his factory greens. The last door on his right bore a small brass sign: BOARDROOM. He paused, imagining a dozen men waiting for him on the other side, their heads turning as he knocked. But the room was empty. He went in, leaving the door ajar. Chairs of yellow oak surrounded a long table of the same wood. On a corner of the table, someone had left a napkin and a half eaten Digestive Biscuit.

He sat but after a few seconds got up again. On the wall by the door, the grave features of former Bannerman's executives, in photographs and paintings, gazed past him with a serenity that seemed fixed on some distant, finer place. On the opposite wall hung several historical photos. He paced with his hands in his pockets, glancing at women in long-sleeved high-necked blouses with elaborately piled hair, looking up from their sewing machines, men posed stoically by trolleys and drive belts. He recognized several of his parents' friends. They looked younger than he was now: Mary Plumstead, Vickie Short, Johnny Bickersteth, Al Partridge, so many of them English. Yes, when he was growing up, Midlands accents had been as common in town as Canadian ones. His mother had come out in 1910 on the *Empress of Ireland,* a girl of twenty-three with a ten-pound note pinned inside her blouse and her mother's best silver teapot riding in her trunk, knowing no one. He searched for her in a large photo of the 1927 Bannerman's staff picnic. He might have been there himself that year; he would have been what, eight? A great mass of people in summer whites stared from a bleacher. Their unsmiling faces seemed to squint into the glare of an immense imposition.

He moved on to the next photograph: The Bannerman Stingers, Ontario Senior "B" Champions, 1938. He had a smaller version of the same picture at home. All the same, he had to look for Joe, had to make sure his brother was in it, as if Joe, the wild one, the one who always did the unexpected, might have slipped from the frame when no one was watching.

There he was, in his place in the first row, kneeling with the other players in his striped Stinger uniform, his curved stick slanting toward the enormous silver cup that stood in front of them. He wore his blond hair slicked straight back, suggesting—even in repose—speed, his genius for attack.

"Found someone you know?"

The rich, genial voice startled him. His entry masked by the drone of the air conditioner, Bob Prince had materialized across the table. He held a manila file folder against the breast of his light beige suit. His deeply tanned bald head gave him an oddly foreign look—Italian or even Arab.

"My brother," Alf said, glad to see the executive. No matter what this meeting was about, he felt he had an ally.

"Oh, yes? Let's see."

As Prince rounded the table and leaned to examine the photo, the air was suddenly brisk with his aftershave. In profile, his heavy jaw jutted out a little, with an exaggerated aggressiveness. "A hockey player!"

"He was pretty good. Best player on that team, anyway."

"Ontario Champions," Prince noted approvingly.

"After that series, the Leafs scouted him."

"Did he go to the pros?"

"No, uh—"

"He had better things to do," Prince said, with friendly condescension.

"I guess you could say that. When the war came he signed up right away. My mother didn't want him to go, but we couldn't keep him out of it."

The pale blue eyes were watching him guardedly now. A note of respect entered Prince's voice. "And after that, did he—"

"He was killed," Alf said, turning away. He felt ashamed, but of what? Of the hollow place, the silence, when he said the words *He was killed?* Or of the emotion trapped behind the words, like an animal in a too-small cage?

He knew he had struck a blow at Prince, and that he had used his brother's death to do it, like a stick he had found in the street.

"I'm sorry," Prince said, in that beautiful voice. The air conditioner rattled. Behind smeared glass, sumacs drooped in the heat. "We left behind some of the best, didn't we?"

The executive shook his head, letting a beat go by.

"I was air force, myself," he said. "Not that I saw much flying. I wanted to be a pilot, but I kept getting airsick, so they shunted me over to intelligence. We went ahead of the Spitfires, in France, looking for new airfields as the front moved forward." Prince rounded the table, gesturing at a chair for Alf. "Bert Hatch tells me you were army."

"Yes, did the walking tour."

As he took his seat, Alf glanced at the file folder lying before Prince. He couldn't read the tab.

"Well, I got to ride in a jeep," Prince said. "It's funny, I always felt I'd missed something, like I hadn't really done my part. I mean, no one ever shot at me."

"It's not all it's cracked up to be," Alf said.

Prince released his brilliant grin. "I don't suppose," he said, and in an instant the smile was gone. "So," he announced, frowning at the file folder: a change of mood, direction. The war, Spitfires, Joe's death, were swept aside. "I called you over to talk about a problem I have. I think the thing to do is give you a bit of background first." Prince leaned back in his chair, a big man trying to make himself comfortable, his jacket open, his rich-looking brown tie with its gold clip buckling over his white shirt. Alf glanced at the shut door behind him—apparently no one else was expected.

"We're determined to get Bannerman's back on its feet," Prince said. "New lines, new machines, new accounting—we're planning to put a computerized order system in. All this costs a lot of money, of course— more, really, than Bannerman's is earning. But we're willing to invest it, providing we don't think we're going to get any nasty surprises."

The executive frowned and tapped his fingertips together, fixing his gaze on Alf as if he might have something to do with nasty surprises. There was a weight about the man, a sense of grave and important responsibilities. Alf was flattered at being taken into his confidence. He was also mystified. Surely it wasn't Prince's job to tell him he'd been made foreman? But what else could this be about?

"You've probably heard, Alf, that there's been a union sniffing around."

"I've gathered," Alf said, shifting in his chair.

"Well, I've nothing against unions in the abstract. But the thing is, with all the investments we're making here, we really can't afford one."

"No," Alf said.

Prince said, shooting him a meaningful glance, "I mean we *really* can't afford one."

"No," Alf repeated, his face heating.

"If I can share a confidence with you, Alf. If Head Office—I'm talking about my bosses now—thinks there's going to be labor troubles here, they could pull out just like that. I mean, they feel it's a gamble coming in here anyway. They're nervous."

The executive winced as he put his hand into the breast of his suit coat. He might have been feeling for a pen or touching a sore.

"Have you seen any sign of the union yourself?" he asked. Alf understood why he had been summoned. Prince felt he could trust him; he needed information.

Alf sat forward in his chair. There was danger here; he felt it would only increase if he wasn't candid. "Actually, an organizer came around to my place. I sent him packing."

Prince did not return his smile. "Ugly bugger with a red face?"

"That's right."

"Doyle," Prince said.

"That was the name," Alf said, nodding.

"We've had a lot of trouble with his outfit in our plants down east," Prince said. "He doesn't look like much, but he's dangerous. What did he say?"

Alf shrugged, eager to dismiss Doyle as inconsequential. "The usual. Sign on the dotted line and your worries will be over." He glanced at Prince, who was clearly waiting for something more substantial. "He said Intertex had such deep pockets it was a crime they didn't pay people at Bannerman's more."

"These socialists," Prince said, shaking his head. "They're all alike. They think we're walking treasure chests. They have no idea what it takes to run a company, to keep it running. No idea where wealth comes from—"

"No," Alf said.

"That's all he said to you? Did you get any sense he was making progress?"

"He wasn't with me."

"You said that," Prince said, with a touch of impatience. "I mean with others. How many has he signed up?"

"He didn't say," Alf said. "But I wouldn't think he's got more than a few, if that."

"Why is that?" Prince said, leaning back in his chair, his look remorseless and searching.

"Well, we tried the union route before: 1949. People got burned, badly. I don't think there's many who'd like to try it again. Truth is, they don't even like talking about it."

"Yes, I've heard that," Prince said. Behind the tanned, handsome exterior Alf sensed a pressure, as if some emotion had been so long contained there it had solidified. "Let's hope you're right. I gather you went out yourself."

Alf's face was fairly burning up now. He could not stop glancing at the manila folder. He knew what was in it now. His whole life was in it.

"I was young and foolish," he managed.

"Tell me about it."

"Oh." His mouth had gone dry; he had never explained these things to anyone and doubted he could. He was half afraid of condemning himself. "I'd seen things, in the war. I guess you'd say I had a chip on my shoulder. If it hadn't been the strike, it would have been something else. I guess life seemed simpler then."

"What did you see, in the war?"

Alf shook his head; it was indescribable, really. "Lives thrown away. My brother. I guess I had it in for authority. Some of that left-wing stuff sounded pretty good to me. Get rid of the bosses and do it ourselves, if that's what they were saying. I was never very good on the theory."

"I had some of the same feelings myself," Prince said.

Alf looked at him in surprise.

"The fuck-ups you saw come out of headquarters; they were enough to make you sick. But anyway, we won," Prince said grimly. "I guess that's the bottom line."

There was a pause. Prince looked at the palm of his own hand. The air conditioner clattered, and a bird thumped against the window and was gone.

"Alf, look, I want you to help me. This is something you can do now, before you're made foreman. Oh, I should've mentioned that," Prince said, showing his smile. "We're so behind on some of the housekeeping stuff. We won't have the new promotions figured out till November, but I think I can reassure you that you're in."

Alf nodded, and a small airplane did a loop in his stomach.

"Oh, yes, you're definitely in," Prince murmured. "But before then, I want you to have a look at this union. Go to their meetings, if they're having any. See if this Doyle fellow's making any progress. I don't need to tell you, Alf, that a lot depends on this. Will you do that for me?"

Prince was looking at him keenly, with just a hint of a brotherly smile, a neediness. Alf said, "You mean, just take the lay of the land."

"Go to a few meetings. Make some notes. You can report directly to me." Prince took a card from his jacket and scrawled something on it before handing it to Alf. "That's my phone number at the Executive Motel, over in Johnsonville. Call me as soon as you've got anything." Prince nodded at the card. " 'Fraid I'm living out of a suitcase these days. My wife's not too happy about it." They shook hands. "I know I can count on you, Alf." The pale blue eyes held Alf's in a glow of sincerity. Alf was the first to look away.

1 2

"YOU MENTIONED A bunch of you guys were meeting with an organizer."

Silence came back to him, down the line. To Alf it sounded conspiratorial, as if the others were with Pete even now, listening in. Out the kitchen window he could see Margaret's dark head, the hissing spray of silver as she watered her garden.

"I'm not saying I'm on board. But I'd like to—see how the land lies." He was trying, scrupulously, not to tell a lie.

Someone was coming down the stairs. He seized gladly on the interruption. "Look, it's kind of difficult to talk here."

"This is good news, Alf."

Alf peered around the corner into the hall, and saw Penny in her shorts and halter top. His daughter was trailing one hand along the wall, singing softly, tunelessly, to herself.

"So when can I—"

"I've gotta check with Malachi first," Pete said. "If it was just me, Alf—but we're worried G.O.'s found out. We have to be careful."

Alf thought, Anybody could have seen me go over to General Office. Maybe Pete knows I was there.

Already he regretted calling. This mutual suspicion was giving him a terrible sense of déjà vu. It was the atmosphere they had breathed in '49. Then, though, he had been excited by the cloak-and-dagger games. Now this maneuvering seemed juvenile, poisonous.

Penny entered the kitchen, crossed to the sink, her sandals scuffing the linoleum. In the weak light the whites of her eyes shone.

"Tell me at work, will you? It's a bit difficult just now."

"I'm really glad to hear this, Alf. Malachi was saying just the other day how much he'd like to have you aboard."

"I'm not saying I'm—"

"I was telling him what you and Skinny Jones did during the strike. Putting that flag up. We had a good laugh."

With a fresh pang of regret, Alf remembered the bedsheet, dyed red, they had raised over the post office clock. He said thickly, "We didn't know what we were doing."

When he had hung up, Penny turned to him, her large eyes watching as she drank. She lowered the glass with a little explosion of breath. "What didn't you know what you were doing?"

"Oh, nothing. Something a long time ago."

"When you were a boy?"

"A little older than that."

"Tell me." Anticipation lit her face, at the promise of a story she hadn't heard. He felt almost compelled to tell her. He could talk to her more easily than anyone else, even Margaret; it was like talking to himself.

"Did you do something bad?"

"No, just kind of stupid."

"Tell me."

"Some other time."

She continued to wait. Like a calm sea, open and clear and blank, she seemed capable of waiting forever—for what, he couldn't be sure—

waiting with a simple, troubling absence of judgment. Deep in the house a pipe whined as Margaret turned off the outside tap.

"You said we could skip stones," Penny said. The previous summer, the summer of his mother's death, his daughter had been diagnosed with diabetes. Every morning she gave herself a needle. Alf found it hard to watch, less out of squeamishness than because it—the diabetes—was something he hadn't been able to protect her from. Alf's great-uncle John had died of diabetes as a boy, so the disease, the doctor said, had most likely come to Penny through him.

They went down the brick path through the dripping tomato plants, over the dike to the river. The flat water in the bend gave off a dim light of its own. Mechanically, he began to hunt for a stone. He felt detached from all activity, detached from himself. In the thickening dusk, the substance of things was washing away.

Penny handed him a piece of slate. It seemed unreal in his hand and he had to toss it a bit, press his thumb on its sharp edge to make it come alive. It seemed she was posing a test—he knew this was pure superstition, and ridiculous—a test he felt he'd already disqualified himself for.

He sent the stone down the gleaming river, a path of little white nicks erupting in the dimness.

"Seven!" Penny cried.

She handed him another.

TWO DAYS LATER, Pete phoned back. "Tonight at eight. My house."

At a quarter after eight Alf crossed the footbridge to the Lion's Park and made his way past the deserted swings and empty bandstand, climbing the embankment toward Pete's ranch-style bungalow, tucked into the wooded hillside. A dozen cars were parked in the drive and on the shoulder of the road that descended darkly from the flank of Lookout Hill. With a start he recognized Doyle's heavy Edsel, abandoned on a tilt, two wheels in the ditch.

Pete's wife, May, met him at the front door, a tall woman in slacks and a sleeveless blouse with an anxious, searching quality in her prominent eyes. She and Alf had been lovers for a few weeks in the thirties. Ever since, he'd felt her yearning, as if she were still waiting for him to do something, say something, that would assuage the churn of unfinished business. Slipping her gaze, he kissed her on the cheek, and for a moment their intimacy came back to him: her cries in the hotel room in Johnsonville, under ugly wallpaper with purple roses as big as cabbages. From the back of the house, he heard a tribal bray of laughter. "I better get in there," he said. But she caught his arm. "Alf, I'm worried about this union business. If G.O. finds out . . ."

"It'll be all right," he said, assuming more responsibility than he'd meant.

He went down the hall to the kitchen. Beyond, the porch was a cave of shadows lit only by the light from the kitchen door. Around the perimeter, in the murk and glow of cigarettes, a dozen or more people raised their ghostly faces.

"Alfie!" he heard Pete say. Others caught up the welcome. They seemed glad to see him; he heard his name tossed out by several voices, male and female, heard "Hey, buddy, good to see you" and "Here's Blue-eyes!" and "Sit here, Alf." He was taken aback. For a moment it was 1949 again, when they had called each other brother and sister without self-consciousness.

Christ, don't get sentimental, he thought. But he was shaken. Something old and forgotten had touched him in his isolation.

May brought him a chair and he sat near the kitchen door. Near the far end of the porch, in the faint light from the yard, Doyle's pitted face glowed like bronze.

"Glad you could make it," the organizer growled. A note of irony? "We're just going through the mills, one department at a time. Trying to get an idea of who's likely to support us."

"Who's solid and who's kind of wishy-washy," Ed Berry said, from his chair beside Alf. The tiny planet of his cigarette reddened under his downward-tilting face.

At first, Alf had trouble concentrating. He was preoccupied with the emotion that had taken him unawares, the uncanny sense that this was not 1965 but 1949. Sitting across from him was a little owl-faced woman, Margo Love. She'd been one of the most violent of the strikers then. He remembered how she'd followed every vehicle that broached the lines, pounding on the hood and screaming obscenities. When the police had tried to drag her away, she'd lain on her back kicking in the air so that her underwear showed, threatening to impale all comers with a hatpin. She looked a little heavier now, but it was the same Margo, quick to take offense and challenging the other speakers so often Doyle had to tell her to wait her turn. Rebuked, she scowled at the wall over Alf's head.

Yes, sixteen years ago there had been an excitement in the air, a sense that they were not just making a union, they were reshaping the world. This lot seemed depressed by comparison. They seemed remote from one another, as if they hadn't fully made up their minds to be here at all; they were slow to offer suggestions, letting two or three people carry the ball, while Doyle, smoking and cajoling and glowering at his clipboard, seemed to get more irritated by the minute. Already—a secret sigh of relief—Alf saw himself reporting back to Prince: *You've got nothing to worry about. This bunch isn't going anywhere.*

The discussion turned to Number Six knitting. The organizer's gravelly voice came down the porch. "All right Alf, you see any possibilities there?"

Before he could answer, Woody Marr broke in. "You can put down Sid Queen and Ellie Snider right off the top," the knitter said, raising his bulldog face and stabbing with a thick finger. Woody had always been resentful of him, Alf felt, for reasons that were never clear. Perhaps it was simply that Woody was resentful of everyone, angry, bitter, with no discernible cause. Woody had gone out in '49 and gotten fired for it. Like Alf, he had returned to Bannerman's after an absence of a few years.

Doyle tapped the bottom of his pencil on his clipboard. "You agree with Woody, Alf?"

"I'm not so sure about Ellie Snider," he said.

"Why not?" Doyle said sharply.

"Hell, she's solid," Woody growled, as he watched them both.

"What are your reasons, Alf?" Doyle said.

"Well, she might be sympathetic, which I doubt. But she's got three kids to look after, and no husband."

"This is bullshit," Woody said.

Doyle made a note. "Anyone else?" he said, looking straight at Alf. He shook his head.

The porch fell silent, though there was a covert restlessness, as if people were disappointed by his response. "Hell," Doyle said suddenly, "it's like a bloody dungeon in here. Could we have some light?"

The weak overhead bulb flooded the porch with a sickly glare. Eighteen washed-out faces blinked and avoided each other's eyes as if they had been exposed in a private, vaguely shameful act. The woods up the hill had disappeared. Alf was startled to see Lucille Boileau in the corner behind Doyle. His heart leaped, for she was leaning out to look at him.

"The overall picture," Doyle was saying, "ain't very good, brothers and sisters. In fact, it stinks. The for-sures don't add up to more than ten percent of the total. We're really gonna have to do some persuading. Really go after those maybes."

"So is there any hope or what?" someone said.

"There's always hope," Doyle said abruptly, as if hope were a weak ally it was best not to depend on. "The thing is, we have to build, get thirty or forty percent of the place signed up before the suits find out. And they will find out, believe me. Then the bloody horse race starts. We might have to sign the last ten percent, to take us up to fifty-five, in a weekend."

"So is it worth going on?" Rob Cole asked, a young shipper Alf knew. He had a wife, and God knew how many kids. "I mean, I don't mind takin' the chance if there's decent odds."

The porch went still. No one wanted to get fired for trying to start a union; everyone knew there was a risk. Doyle stared at Rob as if he hadn't heard him, his pencil twitching in his fist like a little orange tail.

"What this company's doing to you here isn't right," Doyle said at last, and his voice was low and threatening, as if coming from the back of a cave. "It isn't just. It may be legal, at least as the world stands presently, but that's a different matter. Slavery was once legal too.

"These layoffs. I know many of you are worried it's going to happen to you. Some of you are running twice as many machines as before. You know in your hearts this isn't right. It's no way to treat people. It's just a backdoor way of cutting your pay. There's signs they're going to cut your benefits too, such as they are. Without a contract, you have no protection against that."

Doyle paused—melodramatically, Alf thought—to light another cigarette. Everyone watched as the flame lit his pitted face.

"What you're asking for—to make a union—is only what's yours by law," the organizer continued, under a spreading cloud of smoke. "You understand that, which is why you're here. All we have to do is bring some of the others to the same place of understanding. Then they'll act, they'll join us. I remember a mill in eastern Ontario, Dempster's Mills, we started off with a smaller group than this. There were ten of us, a band of ten. By the time we'd finished, we'd organized a two-hundred-man shop. Two hundred and seventeen. Nineteen fifty-nine. And still going strong."

Doyle's tiny eyes nearly closed for a moment, as he took another draw and sent the smoke on its way. He had presence, Alf gave him that. What he did seemed important. What he said, in that raw, earthy voice, seemed worth listening to, and true, or at least truer than the common run of talk. If I hadn't been through it once already, Alf thought, I'd be half ready to sign up myself.

"This isn't just about money," Doyle said. "We're making something here that has to do with justice, security, decency. This is a rich country. Ordinary people worked hard to make it that way. Why shouldn't they have a fair share of what they've made? Why should the rich get to keep their jobs and their privileges, while all the cost saving is taken out on you? It's the same question people were asking in the Depression, and it hasn't gone away. If there's enough for all, why are some forced to make do with so little?

"The rich think they have the right to forget the rest of us. They think they have the right to take and take, even if it means pushing us down. They don't call it pushing us down, they call it the laws of economics. They call it freedom. They call it the market. They say that the best way for the market to work is for them to get as rich as Croesus and some-how, magically, we'll all be taken care of. Well, it ain't true, brothers and sisters. They're playing a game with the rules rigged their way. And no matter what they call it, it isn't right."

AFTERWARD, MAY SERVED cookies and fresh coffee. Alf found himself standing next to Ed Berry.

"Thought you were dead set against this union stuff."

"Not me," Ed said, struggling to raise his head. Years of working over flatbed knitting machines had left him preposterously stooped, his face nearly parallel to the floor. Alf wondered how old he was—sixty-three, -four?—not far from his pension anyway. And putting it at risk by being here.

"I mean, you didn't go out in 'forty-nine."

"I wanted to," Ed said. "My wife said she'd leave me if I did. Regretted it ever since."

"You could take that more ways than one," Alf said with a laugh. Ed didn't smile, so he switched to a more sober tack. "So even after what happened the first time, you're willing to try again?"

"I want another chance," Ed said softly, with great dignity, his gray eyes—a young man's eyes—suddenly vivid.

"So your wife has changed her mind, has she?"

"Edna's no longer with me."

Chagrined, Alf remembered the car accident: the newspaper photo of Edna Berry's crushed car.

"Ed, I'm sorry. I forgot." They stood uneasily, nibbling at their cookies. Then Lucille Boileau was there, smiling up at Alf. She seemed extraordinarily pleased to see him, as if their encounter the night he'd brought Billy home had ignited some sense of loyalty or friendship or simple liking out of all proportion to what he'd done. "Wasn't that some speech?" she said. Choking on a piece of peanut-butter cookie, Alf couldn't answer.

"He's overcome by your beauty," Ed said to Lucille.

"Go home with you!" Lucille said.

"Only if you'll come with me," Ed said, heaving a little.

"You liked that speech, did you?" Alf said, when he'd recovered.

He was watching her sharply, and for a moment an acknowledgment, a fear, passed between them.

"You didn't?"

"Well, these old lefties," he said. "They know all the tricks."

"You don't sound very keen," she said, perplexed.

"Oh, Alf's keen," Ed said, "Back in 'forty-nine he was one of the keenest."

"He helped my father," Lucille said. She had recovered from her moment of doubt and was glowing at him again. He saw the gap in the side of her teeth, which gave her a hint of the hag, and was aware of how the white cotton of her blouse swelled over the faint V of her bra.

"That wasn't really the strike," Alf said, a bit embarrassed. He'd forgotten all about the incident.

"A bunch of guys started pushing Dad around in the hotel," Lucille told Ed. "Alf stepped in and stopped them."

"He'd do that," Ed said, nodding.

It was another half hour before he could get away. Catching him in the kitchen, Pete slapped him generously on the back and drew him into a conversation with two women from sewing. Alf kept glancing at the clock over the stove. The sense of his own fraudulence was overwhelming. He felt he was in a bubble, with his oxygen slowly running out and no real connection to anyone.

1 3

OVER THE NEXT week, Alf slid Prince's card from his wallet so many times it was soon covered with gray smudges from his fingerprints. But each time he picked up the phone, something stopped him: the memory of the faces at Pete's house. If he did what Prince wanted, he'd be putting those people in danger, no question. And he was resentful that he had to do anything, let alone something distasteful, to get the foreman's job. Of course, Prince hadn't said that one thing was dependent on the other, but the implication had been there: a smiling understanding, a nod toward the manila folder where his past sins lay entombed, the suggestion he might move on, move up, if he atoned.

Days later, the phone shrilled through the kitchen where Alf and his family were eating supper. A few minutes earlier, he had quarreled with Margaret. She had asked him, innocently enough, if he'd heard the rumors about a union organizer living at the Vimy House. "I wonder if it's the same one who came here?" He tried to avoid a direct answer, and when she pressed him, he snapped back at her that, hell, he couldn't go around checking every bloody rumor that came through town. In truth, he suspected her of suspecting him, though of what exactly he wasn't sure. He felt he had done nothing wrong, not yet, and yet a vague pressure of guilt, a foreknowledge of what he was going to do or might do, made him see criticism everywhere.

His outburst had spread a bruised, isolating silence in the room, which the phone now interrupted. Penny answered.

"Daddy, it's for you."

As he crossed the room, she kept her eyes fixed on his.

"Alf. Bob Prince here."

The *Bob* took him unawares, postponing for a moment his understanding of *Prince*. Whom was he talking to? Then he lurched forward, obscurely thrilled, into the intimacy offered by that rich, confiding voice, as if, already, he were being offered membership in those places where the powerful met in affable familiarity: on the greens of private golf courses; in elevators flashing up towers of light and steel.

"Have you got any news for me on that matter we discussed?"

"Uh, yes. Yes, I think so."

The silence over the line demanded more.

"It's difficult for me to talk now. Could I see you at G.O. tomorrow?"

"I'm not sure that's a good idea, Alf. Too many curious eyes. Could you come over tonight? I'm at the Executive. Room two-twenty-six."

When Alf hung up, his family was staring at him: four faces backlit in the receding light, watching him with the stillness of grazing animals interrupted in a field. "Is there something wrong?" Margaret asked.

"No, no," he said, touched by her note of concern. "Mr. Prince wants to see me—company business." As soon as he'd spoken the phrase *company business*, he felt reassured. It was as if he'd cited *state secrets* at a time of national emergency. Company business was not always nice business, though it was necessary. The awards, the beaming honors, would come later.

IT WAS A twenty-minute drive to the outskirts of Johnsonville. In fields sprinkled with garbage, the hulks of closed and decaying factories drifted by in the sunset. Smaller businesses still clung to the edge of the highway. The Biscayne passed an auto-glass outlet, several fast-food restaurants, and a sprawling store that sold wooden lawn furniture, the unpainted rockers and lounges crowding right up to the shoulder.

The Executive Motor Lodge formed a square **C**, two stories high, around a central courtyard where a swimming pool gave off a clinical glow. He parked near Reception and climbed metal stairs to a long exterior balcony that ran past a series of identical doors and picture windows. A pretty young woman in a short dress marched crisply toward him, her high heels ringing on the metal gangway. Like a disapproving restaurant hostess, she coldly assessed his canary-yellow polo shirt (one of Bannerman's, four years old), his too-short, synthetic, navy-blue slacks, his black church shoes. He had put on the wrong clothes, he saw that now, though he didn't suppose there was anything better in his closet. Margaret had picked them out for him, discarding nearly everything she unearthed with an impatient brusqueness, kneeling to sponge vigorously at an ancient mustard spot on the trousers, as though she had guessed how much was riding on tonight and was angry with him and with herself for not being ready.

The drapes in the window of 226 had been drawn. The lining behind one of them hung down like a discarded undergarment. Beyond the door, a man's nasal voice climbed in excitement: "He's going for it! Look out! Oh!" The TV, Alf realized, a football game. He had to knock twice before the door opened and Prince's brown rectangular face loomed.

"Alf. Good to see you. Come in."

Prince offered him a chair near the window and padded away in bare feet to stand by one of the twin beds, arrested by a collision on the screen. "Toronto and Hamilton," he said, mesmerized. In his large hand, a glass contained ice, a smear of amber. Alf smelled again the atmosphere of his aftershave, at once brisk and suffocating, saw the heavy, slightly protruding jaw open in a smile that tightened into a wince.

"You a football fan?" Prince had not taken his eyes from the screen.

"You bet," Alf said. In truth, he never watched it. The repetitions of chaos along the line of scrimmage, the frequent stops, bored him. He was a hockey man.

"I got ten bucks riding on this with my son."

"You've got kids?" Alf caught hopefully at the domestic detail, a hint of normalcy, of something he had in common with Prince. He was trying to relax, to adopt the air of someone who'd dropped by a friend's place, for wasn't Prince's casualness with him—the bare feet, the game—a signal they'd moved onto a more intimate plane?

"You don't mind if we watch for a while?"

"No, no, great."

Still riveted to the screen, the executive climbed onto the near bed. He was wearing faultless tan slacks and a white sport shirt with buttoned pockets, open at the throat to reveal a fine gold chain that disappeared into the first shadowy hint of chest hair. Alf crossed his legs and surreptitiously eyed the spot on his trousers. It had dried, but the mustard stain had survived Margaret's attack: a rude little splotch.

To the screen, Prince said, "You want a drink? I got a scotch going here."

Prince poured his drink on the little table between the beds.

"Ice?"

"That'd be great."

Alf sat with the heavy glass, trying to lose himself in the game. Bodies streamed together, collapsed in a writhing heap. The referee ran up in his stripes, waving furiously. "Ho-ho," Alf said with enthusiasm. "He really ran into it that time."

"Patterson didn't give Clarkson his block," Prince said with disapproval. "He'd have been away." Alf realized Prince was pulling for the Argos and adjusted his comments accordingly, for in truth he hardly cared who won. Sitting with his knees up, the executive picked absently at a corn. The ballcarrier dodged under the uprights, raising both arms.

Alf looked around the room. Prince's suitcase lay on the far bed, opened like a giant clam to reveal a mass of neatly packed clothes. There was a shiny gold package in it, beside the rolled socks: a gold brick, with a frilly bow.

On the shag carpet, just past the TV and inside the closet door, sat another suitcase: small, square, powder-blue. A woman's, Alf realized, a makeup case. Did Prince have his wife with him or—what was her name—Sharon? Shirley. Those long legs. He looked at the closed bathroom door and bleakness went through him like a cold wind. He sipped his scotch and stared at the far wall at a painting of sailboats: vague impressions in yellow and pink, leaning in the curve of a tropical bay. Prince roared his approval at a play. Alf had the feeling he'd been here before, exactly like this: waiting for someone who scarcely knew he was there. He wondered if Shirley, or his wife, or whoever she was waited too, behind the closed bathroom door, maybe, or downstairs in the bar with its neon palm in the window.

"Yes!" Prince cried suddenly, with shocking fierceness. There was a huge fund of energy in the man, of willpower. He wasn't just watching the game, he was trying to make things turn out the way he wanted.

Half an hour went by before the game finished and Prince got up with a tired groan to turn off the TV. "Guess I owe the kid ten bucks," he said, and flashed Alf a brilliant smile. There was something so open, so boyishly charming in it—the thought, perhaps, of his son—that Alf instantly felt better.

His ankles cracking, Prince padded over to the closet and reached inside a hanging suit jacket. As Alf watched, the executive looked down and discovered the makeup case; his bare foot nudged it discreetly out of sight. Then he sat on the edge of the farther bed, facing Alf. In his hands was a small spiral notebook and a fountain pen, which he pulled apart, fitting the cap over the other end with surgical fastidiousness.

"Okay, tell me what you got."

Alf had tried to imagine this moment. He was still not sure what he would say.

He chose his words carefully. "I don't think you've got a thing to worry about. This union—Doyle's not going anywhere. There's only a small band that's interested—and they tend to be people no one would follow. Malcontents, I'd call them. They're a pretty sad lot."

The word *malcontents* pleased him. He had been saving it.

"Who are they?" Prince said flatly.

Alf rubbed his shoe on the turquoise grass.

"I mean"—and he cleared his throat as he prepared his lie—"their own leader, this Doyle fellow, told me he wasn't at all pleased at the prospects."

"They may be malcontents," Prince said, "but that's how it usually starts, with malcontentism." He delivered the word with cheerless irony.

"I went to a meeting," Alf said.

"Where? Whose house?"

Prince made a sharp stroke in his notebook.

"Not a house, not anybody's house," Alf said. "It was—ah, out in the country. By the river. They had a fire," he added absurdly. He was describing a meeting he'd been to in the fall of '48, when they were just starting the union. They had roasted wieners, and it had been a happy time, an exuberant time, beyond Prince's reach.

Prince looked at him with bemusement. Alf felt his lie was obvious.

"All right," Prince said. "A fire. Who was there?"

"Only a few. Doyle. A few others."

"How many?"

Alf shrugged: "Half a dozen or so."

"You didn't count?"

"Six," Alf said, "not including myself."

The tip of the pen made a small mark in the notebook.

"So who were they?"

"You have to understand," Alf said. "Some of these people I've known for years. They may be misguided, but they're—"

"This will be confidential."

"It's not that. I've grown up with these people."

For a few seconds Prince's eyes met his. They seemed to contain no emotion at all, just a long chilling evaluation. Alf might have been only a post, or a piece of paper. Then the executive began to speak. He was all concerned seriousness now, confiding and almost gentle. "Alf. You've been picked out as one of the people who has a future in this company. But if you're going to succeed, you're going to have make up your mind about which side you're on."

"I'm with you," Alf said.

"Once we have confidence in someone—well, the possibilities of moving up in Intertex are excellent. We pride ourselves on being a meritocracy. There are executives in this company who began as office boys, as ordinary workers. We gave them a chance, and—well, they knew what to make of it." Prince paused, letting Alf take that in. When he spoke again, it was on a whole new level of intimacy. He seemed, almost, to be confessing. He seemed weary and more human. "Look, I sympathize with what concerns you. You're loyal to these people, and that's a fine thing. I'm loyal myself. I mean hell, I come from a poor family. My father worked in a mattress factory all his life. Never made foreman, though he deserved to. There were seven of us to feed, including my mother, God rest her. I know what it's like, Alf. I know what it's like to wear hand-me-downs and sleep under an old overcoat because there aren't enough blankets. I have every sympathy for the workingman. But the only way the workingman's going to be taken care of, the only way things are going to improve for him, is if the company he works for does well. That's the only place the wealth is going to come from. It doesn't come from the sky. It doesn't come from good intentions."

Prince took a sip of his drink and frowned at the floor before going on. "Textiles isn't steel. It isn't General Motors. The margins aren't big, the competition is ferocious, every penny counts. Every quarter penny counts. We can be good guys and sign a nice fat contract, and three, five years from now, we wake up and realize we can't compete anymore because we've been too generous—I put that word in quotes—in fact, we've priced ourselves right out of the market. So the company goes under, and where's your workingman then?"

Prince leaned forward. "I don't want to hurt these people, Alf. They're my people too: I haven't forgotten that. I'll do everything I can to avoid hurting them. But better a little blood now than a lot of red ink down the line."

The silence lasted for several seconds. Now Alf felt patronized—he knew these arguments and had even used some of them himself. But he'd slipped back, he knew, from a point of understanding he'd reached before. *All right,* he thought.

"If I give you their names," he said, "what will you do with them?"

"Bring them over to G.O., one by one. Give them a good scare, frankly. Tell them we know what they're up to and imply—this is not something we can come out and say, in any case—that they better get back on the straight and narrow or risk losing their jobs."

"So you won't fire them?"

"I find that's rarely a good tactic. As far as it lies within my power, no."

"As far as it lies within your power."

"I'm not here to split hairs with you, Alf."

Alf got up and turned to the window, parting the curtains a little. Across the highway, the spotlit image of a beautiful blonde gazed from a billboard. She was expelling smoke from her cigarette, her heavily lidded eyes smiling with carnal suggestiveness over the frail thrust of headlights.

"Woody Marr," he said, turning back to Prince.

Prince hesitated, then wrote.

Alf experienced a plummeting absence. It was like being at a memorial service. All that is read out is a name, and yet somehow the whole life is there, its dark parade.

"Next."

Alf said nothing. He was staring at the bed with its flowered spread, its rumpled pattern of twining brown vegetation, huge pink flowers, a nightmare jungle repeated in a million rented rooms like this.

"I have to go," he said.

Prince's grin flashed.

"You've only given me one name."

"I shouldn't have. I'm not on the union side, but this is—I know these people."

"Alf, as I've said—"

"When I'm foreman, then I'm on your side. But I can't do it this way."

"So you're putting the gears to me."

"This has nothing to do with you. It's them."

Prince fixed him with a disbelieving smile. Oh, come on, it said, you and I know what's going on here. I can't believe you'd be such a fool.

Outside, the pool lights had been turned off. Above, along the rails of the balconies, a heaven of small white lights had come on, twinkling around the courtyard.

THE NEXT DAY he watched Woody climb the stairs to the knitting room with a start of dread and relief. Relief that he was still here, and dread that he, Alf, had hung the other man's life over an abyss. All that morning he kept glancing over at the knitter. The powerful little man with the straight back and the pug's face moved quickly around his machines, tying up threads or replacing bobbins with brusque, angry gestures, just as he always did: a man perpetually pissed off and apparently liking it that way. Just before noon Alf walked down the aisle to Woody's stand.

"So how's old number six going?" Alf had fixed the machine two days earlier.

"Hey, buddy," Woody said, his ugly face lighting up. He had never called Alf *buddy* before; evidently he suspected nothing. "She's goin' like the hoor from hell."

That afternoon when Alf took his break on the fire escape, Woody sat where he had rarely sat before, beside him. There was something deliberate, almost ceremonial, about the way the knitter poured coffee into his thermos cup, his breathing coming with a slow, labored huffing. He sat erect, his back not touching the warm brick, and put one big scarred hand on his knee. Then he raised his cup in a way that seemed extraordinarily dignified, like a stout Japanese warrior.

Along the balcony the other knitters smoked, talked, and drank coffee or tea as they gazed out through the bars of the railing, over the deep millyard. Through a distant gap between buildings, goldenrod gilded the face of the dike.

"Best season of the year," Woody growled. His blunt face was raised scowling to the sun; even his praise was defiant. "My old man used to go deer hunting up on Manitoulin with the Indians. Had a bit of Indian blood himself."

Alf didn't suppose Woody could actually remember his father, who had been killed in the Great War. He kept silent. He didn't want to encourage Woody, didn't want to know any more about him. Yet Woody was determined to talk. He told Alf about Manitoulin Island: a hunt camp on an inland lake, a story about his father's prowess with a rifle. "Went up there myself a few times. They remembered him in Wicky."

Six floors below, a cart rumbled across the asphalt floor of the yard. Woody took out a package of Macdonald's and offered them to Alf, who felt compelled to pluck one out, though he had stayed away from cigarettes for the last ten years. But now he bent to the flame dancing in the chapel of Woody's hands and dragged smoke into his lungs, sitting back to expel it with the sense it no longer mattered what he did, watching the smoke's pale body twist and disintegrate on the blue air.

THREE DAYS LATER, Alf crossed Willard to the flat-topped building that held General Office. May Watson's chair was empty, which was just as well; he didn't have an appointment. He went swiftly up the stairs and down the carpeted hall, past the boardroom where he'd had his first meeting with Prince, searching for Prince's office. But his name appeared on none of the brass nameplates marking the doors. Just as he was about to retreat, he heard a toilet flush. A few seconds later, Judy Stackhouse, Prince's secretary, stepped into the hall, smiling warmly as she saw him.

He stood behind her in her office as she leaned into an inner room. The brief factual rumble of Prince's voice answered her. "Send him in."

Prince was standing with his back to him—pointedly, Alf thought—by the window behind his desk, one hand in the pocket of his trousers as he surveyed a thicket of reddening sumacs. Without turning he told Alf to sit. Alf slipped warily into an armchair covered in green leather. On Prince's blotter was a paper napkin and a half-eaten Digestive Biscuit.

Prince took his own chair. "So," he said, dusting at some invisible particles at the edge of his blotter. When he finally looked at Alf, his face was expressionless, as if Alf were no longer worth even minimal courtesy.

"I think we've gotten off on the wrong foot somehow," Alf said, his voice suddenly parched, breaking. "Somehow you've ended up teed off with me, and maybe I'm a bit teed off myself. But the thing is, I'm loyal to this place—"

"You have the names then."

Prince brushed again at his desk, at the last few grains of the time he had to spare.

"Well, no. That's not why I—"

"Then why are you here?"

"I—I thought we might start over, you and me."

"And how would you propose that we do that, you and I?"

"I want to bury the hatchet. It's just that—"

"I hadn't realized the hatchet was out."

Alf stared back at the man now regarding him, it seemed, with utter frankness. Had he misjudged something? Was Prince offering more leeway than he'd imagined? Encouraged, he went on. "The thing is, that name I gave you, I've had it on my conscience. I'd just like to say he's a good man, a good worker, and I'd hate to feel I'd put him in danger in any way. Especially since, like I said, this union business is going nowhere."

Prince swept once more at his blotter. "I know you like to tell yourself that, Alf. But it's actually not the case. We have evidence that it *is* going somewhere. Those names you have are critical."

Alf had a cutting sense of letting the side down. What was the matter with him? And yet his chance still lay before him. He was still in Prince's motel room. All he had to do was say a few names and he would instantly be back in Prince's good graces. He would resume his progress along the upward-climbing road, the road that led, by degrees, out of the world of sore backs and time clocks. He stared at the rich wood of Prince's desk.

"Alf, I fear you may be a little too sentimental for this business."

Prince's voice seemed to arrive across a great distance, as his father's once had, calling him out of a daydream.

"Business, Alf, is war, really. I mean, played within the law, more or less, and people try to be gentlemen about it, even buddies. And that's all necessary—oil for the wheels. But to be frank, it takes a certain bloody-mindedness. You can't worry about other people too much." The cajoling drone of Prince's voice went on. Remotely, Alf heard separate words and phrases, floating sedately by on its tide. Past the smooth head in front of him was the jungle of sumacs behind the office. What he saw was a wine cellar in France: shadows and blood. In September of 1944 he had killed a German soldier who had ambushed him. The fellow had leaped over some barrels and Alf had whirled just in time to take his weight on the barrel of his gun and fire. A few moments later one of Alf's mates had flung back a door and light had flooded the body at his feet. It was a boy, not more than more than fourteen or fifteen. Above his gray army uniform the startled eyes had already fixed on nothing. His mouth was open in a small rabbity smile, as though he'd intended only a joke. In his hand was a broken wine bottle.

Feeling light-headed, he left immediately. In the outer office, Judy Stackhouse looked up brightly. "Alf—are you all right?" She stood as he leaned there for a moment, planting his hand on the edge of her desk. "Would you like a cookie?" Smiling helpfully, Judy nudged the package of Digestives toward him, across her scarlet blotter.

14

SMILEY PHONED. DID Joe want to go hunting?

"Come up to my place," Smiley said, and hung up.

For weeks Joe had avoided his friend's house, because he was avoiding Smiley's sister. He had broken off with Sandy, but seeing her was painful: his guilt was provoked by the way she clung to him still, by how she looked at him, as if there were a debt he owed her, though of course she would never say that. She gave the impression of being willing to go on waiting, patiently, willing to do whatever he wanted, even if it was going to be years before he asked her. One morning he had walked to school, knowing she was following a block behind. He had refused to turn and wait. Then at the rail overpass he had looked back, in remorse, to discover she was no longer there.

Now he followed the path along the top of the dike, with its view over the Island yards where people were raking leaves toward spindling fires. The smoke rolled past him, flattening over the dark water of the Atta.

Sandy's father was kneeling on the back porch, prodding with a screwdriver at a small electric motor. His round face with its shiny cheeks glanced up at Joe.

"Joe," he said flatly, looking back at his task. Almost casually, a judgment had fallen.

Joe lingered, watching, held by the hope of reprieve, by the chance

Charlie Richards would say something that would allow them to go on as before.

"What's that for?" he said.

Charlie Richards worked on without answering, he who for years had treated Joe with such friendliness. During the summer, waiting for Sandy to come home from her waitress's job at the Oasis, Joe would sit with him on the patio under the Manitoba maple, sharing a lemonade while he talked about the war with an air of humorous disbelief—so unlike Joe's father—as if the whole thing were a bit of rollicking bad luck he'd been fortunate to have escaped—like that time in Italy, when a sniper had kept him pinned against a rock for an entire day. . . .

Then Sandy would arrive, swinging around the corner of the house in her beige Oasis uniform, her eyes going straight to Joe's, her lips suppressing a smile that emerged anyway; they had thought their happiness a secret, though he saw now it must have been plain to everyone. All that was gone, a summer, an eon, ago. Watching her father's prodding screwdriver, he was filled with regret.

"I found it in the cellar," Charlie Richards said. "It's a good little engine. Seemed a shame to throw it out."

SMILEY CARRIED THE .22, its barrel pointing toward the ground as if it were scenting a trail. They left Lion's Park and entered the cleft in the cedar bush. Then they bordered the fields, weaving in and out of the light, past an old haymow rusting in a heap of rocks spotted with golden lichens. He wondered if his father had ridden it. His father had worked on Wiley's farm as a boy, and its fields were saturated with the stories he had told Joe: unharnessing the draft horses, King and Maud, riding them bareback into the river in a time before time when actions seemed grand, so powerfully etched they could almost be happening still, just out of sight—his father and Pete Moon still racing the heavy-shanked horses through the shallows. He had a sense that little had happened in his own life by comparison. His father, in a way, owned the land he was walking on, just as he owned the Depression and the War, all the great adventures of the past, and now nothing was left to Joe but a kind of ordinariness.

Across the sloping field, stubbled with the pale chewed-off stalks of corn, lay small heaps of earth—groundhog mounds—as if someone had dug random postholes. Joe and Smiley watched them keenly, hoping for something to kill. A blue jay flew toward a pine, and Smiley followed it in the scope, his heavy face grimacing against the stock.

"Pow," he said softly, and the jay both died and lived.

They settled into a hollow, on dry pressed-down grass, looking back over the field they had just skirted. Distantly, across the river, they could see the heights of the North End, above the severe gash made by the CN tracks. Joe scanned the backs of the big houses, their roofs and second stories visible above the edge of the precipice. It was possible Anna Macrimmon lived just there, behind the green awning, or there, where a huge beech had shed half its gold.

"Give me the gun," he said.

The tunnel of the scope took him closer. He planted its thin cross on the naked limbs of the beech, on a dilapidated gazebo where an orange towel hung from a railing.

Swiftly he lowered the .22 and sighted into the field. His shot raised a puff of yellow dust that drifted away.

"Hey!" Smiley said.

"I thought I saw one," Joe said, lying. He had had to fire. He handed back the gun with trembling hands.

After an hour they had seen no groundhogs so they went on, following the trail where it descended through trees into the bottomlands of the Atta. They came to a sandy beach by the river and sat on a great silvered log, looking out at the beer-colored water where it spread toward a rapids.

"So," Smiley said.

Joe waited for the blow; he was sure his friend was going to lay into him about Sandy.

"So I guess I'm dropping out," Smiley said.

"Dropping—you mean, out of *school*?"

Smiley's attention was fixed on the water. There had been no hint of this.

"Smiley?"

His friend shrugged, as if the whole matter were beyond explanation and even comprehension; it was just something that had happened. Joe was on the verge of laughing. Surely Smiley was joking, in his deadpan way. He was one of the best two or three math students in the class. He had talked of university.

"I thought you were going on. I mean, what are you going to do, go into the mill?"

Smiley sat with his head down, twisting a bit of stick.

"With your abilities, you could be a teacher. Some kind of scientist—"

"Thought maybe I'd join the marines."

"The marines?"

"See the world," Smiley said, with a bleak smirk.

"Tell me why you won't go on. Seriously."

Smiley twisted the stick in his hands. "It just seems pointless."

"What does? Getting up in the world? Not having to work with your hands?"

"I sort of like using my hands."

"So you're going to join the marines and"—Joe gestured angrily at the river—"kill people."

"I wouldn't do it for long. Just for a year or two, for the fun of it."

"They shave your head and call you an asshole. You call that fun?"

Joe could get no more out of him. He looked at his friend: at the snug nose plastered with coppery freckles, at his eyes flicking back and forth over the sand, his smile secretive and angry, as though he were enjoying the destruction of his life. Joe moved toward the water, picked up a stone, and flung it hard.

"I love Anna Macrimmon," Smiley said.

Joe turned back. What Smiley had said seemed so preposterous, so impossible, that it was unfathomable.

"The new girl," Smiley said in a choked voice, looking at him miserably. "I love her."

It was impossible. Smiley never spoke like this, never revealed his feelings, straight out, about anything. There was always a joke.

But Smiley was exuding such desolation he knew it was true.

"You're friends with her," Smiley said. "Maybe you could speak to her for me."

"Speak—what would I say?" He was just starting to feel outrage at what he felt was a trespass.

"I don't know. Find out how she feels about me."

"She's not your type!"

"How do you know? What's my type?" The small eyes flicked at Joe, hostile.

"She's a poet. You don't like poetry," Joe said, grasping at straws. He couldn't come right out and say, She'd never love you. You're a slob. It's unthinkable.

Smiley looked back at the river, unmoved.

"I mean, hell," Joe said, returning to the log. "She's—you know, the way she is, the way she dresses, she's—"

"What, better than me?"

"I wouldn't say that exactly."

"It's what you meant." And to the river: "You're saying she's too good for me." After a moment he added, "I know she is. I know I won't ever get her. But when she—all I have to do is see her, and I know she's the only one I'll ever want."

"You'll want others," Joe said.

"Fuck off," Smiley said.

"Oh, come off it."

Smiley exploded from the log. Joe had no time to react before his friend was shoving him backward with a cold fury.

"For fuck's sake, what are you doing?" Joe yelled, shoving back. In a way, he was not surprised. What was coming out of Smiley now—he'd always known it was there, resentment that had become more tightly packed with every year, awaiting a spark like this. He was frightened, not so much by any physical danger as by the sense of vast emotion running amok. With pounding heart, a little desperate, guilty too (he knew he'd spoken in a superior way to Smiley, knew he'd always felt secretly superior and now was reaping his punishment), he pushed back. They were slapping at each other, on the verge of punching, when Smiley strode back to the log and picked up the .22. He turned and aimed it at Joe's forehead. The eye Joe could see was closed, while Smiley's other eye was buried behind the glass porthole of the scope. Smiley's finger held motionless on the trigger, and still Joe didn't believe he'd pull it.

He stood watching, alert but not really afraid as Smiley sighted the gun at his chest.

"Pow," Smiley said.

15

BILLY WAS WAITING for Jamie under the elm. Yellow leaves were falling, one, two, three at a time, twirling and wafting and setting down, soundlessly, on the asphalt of the empty Boys' Yard. Every day Billy's class for slow learners was dismissed fifteen minutes earlier than the other grades, and every day when Jamie's class got out, Billy was waiting. Several times, Jamie tried hanging back inside the school, but Billy went on waiting, sitting under the elm. Jamie always had to leave eventually, driven out by a teacher or the janitor, and always he told the same lie to Billy. "I have to go home and help my mother." Billy usually walked back with him, though his own house was in the other direction, on the Flats. Jamie would say, "Don't you have to go home?" and Billy would say, "My mom ain't back from work yet," and keep shuffling along beside him, grinning his brown-toothed grin as if there was nothing better in the world than scuffing in the leaves whispering and swishing around their knees, in air that smelled of bonfires. The first time, he had come right up to Jamie's back door and would have come in too, if Jamie hadn't blocked the way. "I have to help my mom," Jamie told him again, while Billy peered past him into the kitchen. Jamie was afraid his mother would see them together. Then there would be the spatula to deal with, the bone-searching in her eyes.

The worst thing was that sometimes Billy would wait outside the house, even for a long time. Jamie would look out and there he'd be, sitting on the curb, poking at something with a stick. Once his mother had seen Billy waiting. "Is that the Boileau boy out there?" she'd asked. Jamie had shrugged and said he didn't know, and his mother said, "Just wait in here till he goes away." When he was finally allowed out, Billy had gone, and there was nobody to play with. The sad, lonely feeling he got was not just in him then. It was in Lookout Hill, rising yellow across the river, and in the river, the color of old metal, chopping at its scummy rocks. He'd floated sticks and bombed them with stones until he was called for supper.

Now Billy stood and crossed the yard, smiling a blazing smile that made Jamie feel bad, knowing he was going to lie again, lie and disappoint him and—after they'd walked down the hill together—leave him standing on West Street while he went indoors.

"I know," Billy said in his flat voice, with the hint of a sneer, "you have to go home and help your mother."

"No, I don't," Jamie said.

Billy was walking beside him now, toward the gate. "No I don't" had just popped out. He was sick of making the same excuse, but now that he'd said something else, said the truth, he felt like he didn't know where he was anymore. He didn't know what to say next.

Across the road a black dog with a white streak between its eyes was lifting its leg to pee.

"We could go to the Indian Trail," Billy said, after a moment.

"All right," Jamie said. But he felt like running away.

It's all right.

He looked up, startled.

"Really?" he said, questioning the voice. He had stopped at the gate. The dog was by another tree: a squirt of yellow and it trotted on.

Sure, the voice said. *Go ahead.*

"What?" Billy said.

Praise the Lord and pass the ammunition!

Jamie laughed. The voice had tickled him.

"What?" Billy said, dancing around him.

"Praise the Lord and pass the ammunition!"

"We could make gunpowder!" Billy cried. He was dancing from foot to foot and holding his crotch like he had to go to the bathroom.

They crossed the park and went down the road that led to the Indian Trail. The trail ran through woods on a steep bank, so that you could look down and see a road and rooftops, far below, or look up and see the fences straggling at the end of people's yards. But the trail itself (which was really many trails, interwoven) was a secret place, and they jogged hidden from view, with sticks for spears, a raiding party that had snuck into town to burn and steal things and kill people. They were on horses now, little Indian ponies that neighed and stamped and sidestepped down a slope to a clearing. On the far side of the clearing was a smooth, rounded rock, like the half-buried shell of an enormous turtle.

"My grandfather's buried there," Billy said. "Underneath the rock."

"For real?"

"He was a chief."

Jamie had forgotten the spatula and his mother's eyes. The motionless yellow trees around the stone (they were standing on it now, as on an island in a rising flood) seemed to know the boys were there.

16

TALK OF LIZ McVey broke out one day after gym, when the boys of 13A were dressing in the locker room. Dick Osborne said he'd heard that Liz had broken up with her boyfriend, Bobby Tanner, a salesman three or four years older than she. Bobby, someone else said, had been banging her. This set off a spirited discussion about who might get to bang her next, a happy prospect since Liz was generally agreed to be one of the best-looking girls in the class. That's when Brad Long—idly drying himself in the doorway of the shower—shamed them all into silence by announcing, with an air of melancholy authority, that Liz was a "classy lady." His reputation as a ladies' man took the ground from beneath their feet, for if Brad, who was generally thought to be doing it, spoke up for a girl, it reminded them of their own pitiful lack of experience. The classy lady was out of range of most of them, anyway, because of her looks and because she was the daughter of the town's richest man.

When Liz stopped Joe in the hall, all this was in his mind. You couldn't hear that a girl had been doing it and then forget what you knew as she stood not two feet away, gazing at you with large, beautiful, yet somehow frozen eyes. She wore her curly hair cropped short, and her full mouth was crimped a bit on either side, pushing out the underside of her top lip. It was a babyish kind of mouth, with a look of having just been pulled off the bottle. Joe was attracted to her, yet didn't care for her affectations, especially her air of langorous boredom. She was a star actress in the Drama Club. A year before, he had watched her play the lead in *Deirdre's Island,* a murder mystery about a vengeful society lady and her guests. An entirely different Liz had emerged: taut and feline and astonishingly mature. The critic from the Johnsonville *Gleaner* had gone off his head about her, but at the same time she had given Joe the willies; there was something repulsive about the controlled hysteria she had conveyed.

Now she was asking him to a party at her place the following Saturday night. This was so unexpected—he was not a member of the North End gang—that he hesitated. She seemed provoked by this; staring at him with her too-bright eyes, she purred, "People will be disappointed if you don't come," with such an insinuating emphasis on "people" that he'd received some as-yet-undeciphered message and said sure, he'd be glad to come. After she'd gone, he stood dissecting that cryptic "people," coming almost instantly to the conclusion that she was referring to Anna Macrimmon.

In the next class, English, he watched Anna reading her copy of *Macbeth.* For weeks now he had been aware of a deepening connection between them. Their conversations seemed to carry a complex load of emotion. Their glances, he felt, increasingly hinted at the possibility of a mutual future. He was almost sure this was real, but he didn't speak of it in case he was fooling himself. She read with a quality of concentration, of absolute self-containment, that she seemed able to summon at any time. He had seen it during assembly, while a comic skit was being performed on stage. He had observed her—amid an entire gymnasium roaring with laughter—simply looking, neither amused nor disapproving nor oblivious. There was a force of calm in her, of mindfulness, that he admired and was in awe of, for he had never seen such a thing in anyone, except perhaps in Archibald Mann, though in Mann's attention there was always something stern, as if he were dissecting or even judging what he saw. But there was no judgment in Anna Macrimmon; she was simply looking, her head a little lowered, and in that looking, he felt, was more seeing than he could himself imagine. What was she thinking? Did she think them all fools? At this point she seemed superior not just to all the other girls but to himself as well. This was daunting. What could he possibly do to deserve her? Yet he pressed on in his secret way, pursuing her.

He let two classes go by before he contrived to meet her in the hall. She seemed no more friendly than usual, chatting as they moved through the crowd, though when he asked if she was going to Liz's party, she sent him a brief sideways smile, past the pale wing of her hair, and said, in a whimsical, singsong voice, "Oh, I think so." This was flirtatious, he thought, touched with shyness, at once hiding and disclosing something deeper.

LIZ'S INVITATION TIPPED him toward buying the coat. He had been eyeing it for weeks, fearful it might disappear from Art Blostein's display window: a windbreaker-style jacket with a body of rich chocolate suede and beige knitted arms. Propped in front of the headless torso that wore the jacket was a little card carrying the silhouette of a rabbit's head and the message AS ADVERTISED IN PLAYBOY. The coat, when he tried it on, seemed too large for him, but Art Blostein assured him that was the style, and as he gazed at his three selves in Art's triple mirror he seemed to have changed; he looked bigger, more relaxed, more in the know. "It's

you!" Art said happily, and his rubbery clown's face sent a laughing smile
of approval over Joe's shoulder.

He crossed Shade Street to the bank. At the teller's window, he
couldn't help looking around, worried his mother might come in. He
had never taken money out of his savings account before, not since
he and his mother had opened it ten years earlier. Wearing her best coat,
a heavy English tweed, she had announced to the teller, and anyone else
who cared to listen (the whole bank had seemed to be listening), just
how well Joe was doing in school, how someday he'd go to university;
that's what this account was for, to save up all allowances and gifts and
income from small jobs. Afterward, she'd practically made a ceremony
of handing him the little book with its stiff red cover. "This is your
future," she'd said. "Take good care of it." He'd carried his future
through the streets of Attawan, his hand sweating, it had felt so important. When they got home she'd relieved him of the book and put it in
her dresser drawer.

According to the book—which he now kept in the battered blue
dresser wedged beside his desk—the account now contained over a
thousand dollars, most of which he'd earned himself, working summers
in the mill and filling shelves at the A&P after school. The teller handed
him four new twenties and a ten, which he took back to the store. Art
folded the jacket into a box, turning two wings of tissue paper over it
with the tenderness of someone burying a baby.

That evening, after he got home from the A&P, he smuggled the box
up to his bedroom and hid it in the back of the closet. It was critical that
his family not see the coat, which was like a new skin to him, tender and
vulnerable. After supper, he felt he had to look at his purchase again. His
parents were watching television—the rumble of canned laughter
floated up the stairs—so he opened the box, slipped on the coat, and
went swiftly down the hall to his parents' bedroom, where a full-length
mirror hung on the closet door. In its icy rectangle, the coat looked fine,
too fine, with bulky arms like knitted chain mail. It outshone everything
else: his green slacks with their shiny, shapeless knees, his tired desert
boots, even his face. Yes, the coat was perfect, but his mouth was too thin

and his ears stuck out. He examined himself suspiciously and disapprovingly, as if he had run into a disreputable cousin.

Leaving the room, he met his father in the hall. As they passed, his father threw out his hip in a friendly body check. He didn't seem to have noticed the coat at all.

"Say, Joe," his father said. Reluctantly, Joe turned back to him.

His father looked tired these days, hollow-eyed—Joe's mother had mentioned he wasn't sleeping well—and now he drew back his lips in a kind of wince, as if his words had to be tugged from his flesh, like a sliver.

"You're going on to university."

The coat suddenly felt huge on him, almost clownish.

"That's right."

"I was wondering," his father said, as he drew his hand over his balding head. "Are you doing it for the money? I mean, is money your main purpose for going on—to make a lot of money?"

"Not really," Joe said, bewildered. In truth, he had never thought about money per se. What he thought about, in that line, was a different way of life: a house with a library, maybe. But even *that* wasn't the whole story.

His father's eyes rested on him. "It's history, I guess, that attracts you?"

"That's right."

His father motioned with his hand, as if tossing away a fistful of sand.

"You love it, I guess."

"Uh-huh."

They were both uneasy now, at this mention of love. Joe was reminded of the time, years ago, when his father had tried to tell him about sex. They had both been mortally embarrassed by his account— "and you put your body inside the woman's"—delivered with grimly set jaw and averted gaze. Joe had already known that.

Now his father looked at him directly, and for a moment the blue eyes embraced him with strength and glad discovery.

"Good," his father said. "That's good." And he nodded and nodded, in awkward, fond approval. "You keep on, then."

Joe went back to his room and stripped off the jacket. He did not understand what had just happened, but he felt like weeping. He felt like a fraud. His jacket was a fraud, and he was a fraud for thinking it might make a difference. His dad loved him. He hated to be reminded of it. The knowledge flooded through him like a weakness, dissolving everything that a moment before he had been reasonably certain of. Who was he? What in hell was he doing? He stared at the new coat with remorse and hatred.

Two days later he went back to Art Blostein's and bought tan slacks, a pale-blue button-down shirt with faint pinstriping (just like the shirts Brad Long wore, he noted with satisfaction), and a soft navy-blue cardigan. At Jarrod's, down the street, he bought a new pair of Hushpuppies in chocolate suede. He hid these items in his closet, and on the evening of the party smuggled the new jacket, still wrapped in its box, into the trunk of the Biscayne. Then he went back to his room to change.

At nine o'clock, he was ready. Wearing his old poplin windbreaker over the new sweater, he crept down the stairs. But his mother must have been listening. She came down the hall in a fluster of excitement, to see him off. A week before, when he'd told her he was going to the McVeys', she'd barely been able to contain her pleasure. A day later, she'd announced that she'd washed his best slacks and shirt; she'd even cleaned his church shoes.

Now she would see what he had done. He stood in the little entrance hall and watched her eyes—her wide-set eyes in which he could read every shift of her inner weather—watched them brighten as she took in the new slacks. And the cardigan, peeking out below his jacket.

"Joe, what are you wearing? Let me see!"

He was ready to do battle, to tell her, It's my money, I earned every penny, but she was delighted.

"Oh, Joe, open the jacket! Let me see!" She stood back, glowing. "Yes, that's wonderful, you've got wonderful taste. Where did you get them?"

He told her the story. She stood close to him—too close, really, for comfort—gazing at him in a fever of admiration and picking microscopic bits of lint off his sweater, pushing his hair off his forehead. "I got a new jacket too," he told her sheepishly. She made him fetch it from the car. She seemed less delighted with the coat—he thought her face darkened when he told her the price—but the tide of her enthusiasm could not be stopped. Suddenly leaning up, she planted a kiss on his cheek. For a moment, smelling her familiar smell, feeling her lips brush his skin, he sensed the vanished world of her girlhood. His mother too might have been eighteen.

THE STREETS OF the town were lit with bonfires, where householders had raked leaves to the curb. Some of the piles flared as he drove by in the Biscayne; others smoldered, till the gust from the car fanned them, sending bright sparks tumbling across the road. Occasionally, a heating chestnut popped. Smoke rose in pale columns, and the smell of it at his open window was the joy of the world burning, life-giving and sharp. He parked on Robert and walked past a dozen other cars toward the McVeys', glancing at the open garage where the windshield of the Lincoln gazed out with imperial calm. The car was one of the chief shrines of the many he had created wherever Anna Macrimmon had sat, walked, spoken to him. In his chest, another fire burned.

The glass transom gave a view into a large hall covered with an Indian rug. He saw the flowing, curving base of stairs, carpeted in deep green, and a long paneled hall leading toward the arctic glow of an empty kitchen. Music pulsed distantly—he thought he heard Diana Ross's voice cake-walking to heaven—but no one answered the rap of the heavy knocker. He was wondering if he should try the back of the house, when the door opened and Doc McVey stood before him in a silky black and red dressing gown, worn—Joe found this odd—over his shirt and trousers. At his throat was a dark blue ascot; in his hand a glass filled to the brim with ice.

"A late reveler," Doc said, in his mild, slightly fey voice, as he peered with cheerful irony through his round glasses. He was a tall man with a babyish face and a habitual look of playful bemusement, slightly scornful. He was a doctor, and though he no longer practiced, he kept his old office downtown, at the head of steep stairs over Maggie's Beauty Parlor. He had inherited money—Joe had this from his father—and made a great deal more investing it in the stock market, as well buying and selling properties in the area. For several years—this was an open secret in the town—he had been having an affair with a woman called Babs Wilcocks, who worked as a secretary in Bannerman's General Office.

"Aren't you Alf Walker's boy?" Doc McVey said, ushering Joe in.

Suddenly his past, his family, seemed all too vividly present, as if they had trudged in behind him. The music was much louder now, but he could see no signs of a party.

"Your dad and I went to school together. He was very fast on the track, your dad. He gave me a lot of trouble in the hundred."

"Is that right?"

"Oh, yes, he was fast," Doc McVey said suggestively, as though some scandal were associated with his father's speed. His large eyes—magnified, it seemed, by his glasses—fixed Joe with a look of amused watchfulness. Joe had the sense he was being tested, as though Doc McVey were waiting to see if this interesting creature, Alf Walker's son, might perform a trick or two. From down the hall Sally, Liz's younger sister, was approaching with a bowl of popcorn. She acknowledged Joe with a shy smile and, sticking her neck out awkwardly as if to facilitate her escape, started up the stairs, followed by a fluffy white cat. Doc McVey was still focused on Joe. "Down there, through the kitchen," he drawled, gesturing with the ice.

As Joe reached the kitchen, Liz McVey climbed from a dark room sunk beyond it, from a babble of voices and the wail of Dion complaining, once more, about Runaround Sue.

"Joe! I was afraid you weren't going to make it!" She came toward him with that overly intense look of hers, almost tragic, and leaned up to kiss him on the cheek. He caught a whiff of something musky, arousing. Taking his jacket, she tossed it over several others on a chair; as she moved away, the pile toppled to the floor. "Can I get you a drink?"

While she rummaged in the fridge, he restored the coats to the chair, hanging his own over the back, and turned to the doorway that led, he saw, to a large room packed with shadowy bodies. The only light came from the kitchen and from the outdoor lamps shining through the patio doors. He could not see Anna Macrimmon.

He lingered in the kitchen. Liz stood with her back to the counter, with one arm planted on her hip, the other stretched along the counter. It was a bold pose, and it suited her. Below her knee-length skirt, maroon stockings complimented the deep cherry red of her blouse. She wore more eye makeup than usual, a touch of Cleopatra. He found her alluring, in a provocative, almost vulgar way.

"I liked what you said yesterday in Mann's class, about war not being good for anybody. Very beautifully put."

He muttered his thanks. He'd been rather embarrassed by his comments, his argument with Brad Long in front of the whole class, in front of Anna, about the benefits of war. Brad had boasted that his father, an officer on a destroyer, had gone away a boy and come back—this had raised a laugh—"a real cool guy."

"War must be so horrible," Liz said, looking at him with distress, "don't you think?"

He said, "Did your dad go overseas?"

"Oh, heavens, no!" Her hand with its three rings splayed over her chest. "They would never have had him, not with his eyes. My God, he couldn't have said which end of a gun was which. Oh, no, he missed it all, thank God. Or I think, thank God," she added ominously. He was aware of the dark door to his right. He was expecting Anna to appear at any minute. Someone turned up the music. In the cupboards, glassware was beginning to dance. Liz said, "Why don't we go somewhere where we can actually hear each other?"

Reluctantly, yet half glad of the distraction, he let himself be led through the dining room, where a vast table gleamed in the dimness. Then into a large living room, past a long couch with carved, shapely legs, upholstered in some striped fabric. Two identical moss-green wing chairs faced a fireplace with a marble mantel. There were Indian rugs scattered over the broadloom, while oil paintings glinted under little tubular brass shades: bright, ornately framed landscapes showing winding autumnal rivers, a red northern sky stamped by a V of geese. He had never been in such richly decorated rooms before. From this moment on, he would never think his own house anything but shabby and second-rate.

But the living room was apparently not to Liz's taste. She led him on, through the hall where he'd first entered and through a heavy door into a large den. This room looked more lived-in. Photographs in gilt frames hung over a carved desk where a stack of papers was pinned with a rock of raw glass. There was a small television and a wide couch covered in a beige material, with throw cushions in green and blue. Liz curled up at one end of it, drawing up her legs in their maroon stockings. He sat at the other end but had difficulty finding the right posture. To match hers would have committed him to a directness and intimacy he did not feel. He sat at an angle to her, his attention diverted by a large book resting on the coffee table. On its cover, a racing yacht tilted under full sail.

"So," Liz said, as if they were two old friends who at long last had found time to talk.

"Your dad likes sailing?"

"Oh, yes," she said, a bit impatiently. "He's already got one boat, up at the cottage. But he's threatening to get one he can go around the world in."

"Really?"

"I hear you broke up with Sandy," she said, ignoring his question. "Or do I have that wrong?"

"No, you've got it right," he said, a bit surprised. He looked into her face, all sympathy and concern now, though in her eyes the brightness danced: wasn't life hard and wasn't it fun?

"A very pretty girl," Liz said. "I hope it wasn't too painful."

"Well," he said, shrugging. It had been painful, but not in the way she perhaps meant.

"When Bobby and I broke up—this was over a month ago—well, it's not something you want to go through every day."

"No," he said. It occurred to him she might be vetting him for Anna, who would have to know whether he was free. "No," he repeated, more strongly. "Not every day."

Behind him, though the closed door, he heard someone come into the house. He looked around.

"Just ignore them," Liz said. "They can find their own way."

"Is Anna here?" he said.

"She was," Liz said, without missing a beat. "She and Brad got here first. They went off about twenty minutes ago."

"Oh, they're here together?" he said, feigning a mild interest.

"Together?" she cried. "The original Bobbsey Twins! We were running out of beer and Brad said he could get some from a friend, although of course knowing Brad they probably went by way of the gravel pit." She spoke with a straight-on innocence. The abandoned gravel pit to the east of town was a favorite parking spot. There were nights when the spring-fed lake at its center was completely ringed with cars.

LATER, SHE DREW him onto the dance floor for a slow number. Her hand was cool in his, and as she snuggled in, her pelvis brushed his thigh. His own excitement—the stirring in his trousers—seemed a distant thing, a nuisance, really, and he pushed her back a little. It was clear now that Liz had never been fronting for Anna, she was fronting only for herself, and though he found this flattering, he could not stop thinking about Anna, out there in the night somewhere, Anna with Brad Long. He rejected Liz's view of them as inseparable, because it didn't square with what he knew. It was true, Anna and Brad had gone out together, at least once, but to Joe's mind she was more at ease, more content, with him. He didn't trust Liz. All he needed was to have Anna find him wrapped up with Liz and he could kiss his chances goodbye—which, maybe, was Liz's plan.

After three dances he left her, on the excuse he needed a washroom. The one off the kitchen was in use, so Liz directed him to the second floor. Returning downstairs, the sound of a cabinet door squeaking in the den tempted him to look in. Anna Macrimmon was there, leaning forward to peer into a tall bookcase. She wore a rather short pleated skirt of green plaid, which he'd never seen before, green stockings, and a tight-fitting white blouse with long sleeves.

"Anna," he said, going right up to her. Beer had given him confidence. "I thought you weren't coming. I was heartbroken."

"Go on!" she cried, catching his bantering tone. She put her arm through his and drew him to the books. He was suddenly giddy, and at the same time, stone-cold sober. She had never been so physical with him. His right arm felt weightless.

"Look at this," she said. "They've got Shelley's poems—"

"Jeez, do you think we better tell him?"

"Oh, you're as bad as Brad," she said, giving his arm a squeeze.

"Don't say that," he said, keeping up the levity. But her reference to Brad had stung. "I'm far worse."

"Then I'm really in trouble!"

She squeezed his arm again before releasing it. He watched her take down the ancient-looking volume in its faded leather cover. He was drunk on her now: her smell that was scarcely a smell but a freshness, her shoulder brushing his as they leaned over the musty-smelling book. He read:

> The awful shadow of some unseen Power
> Floats though unseen among us. . . .

Her attention to the brittle page was all-consuming; it drew the whole room toward Shelley's words: the furniture, the photographs, the other books, all found their center in the packed lines of verse. But he couldn't concentrate on the poetry. He kept looking up at her, at the way her lips moved slightly as she read, at the way her hair fell across her birthmark, white burned below brown.

She uncovered a picture of the poet. Under a tissue overlay, Shelley's huge eyes searched upward in anxiety and exaltation. "I've been in his house," she said, "on the Gulf of Spezia—the Casa Magni. You can feel him there. He was only thirty when he drowned."

"How did he drown?" he said, for something to say. His eyes went on roaming her face, her hair.

"He was sailing, and—he put out in a storm he shouldn't have gone out in. Maybe he thought it was time."

She spoke with a meaning Joe could not decipher: a probing serious-ness and, far away, a hint of gaiety, of cold bright gaiety, sun on a cold sea.

"I wonder what year this is," she said suddenly, turning back to the book.

She found the date on the last page, and they struggled with the roman numerals.

"I'm no good with these things."

"Eighteen fifty-six," he said at last. "The year the Crimean War ended."

"You love it too, don't you?" she said. And, when he looked puzzled: "The past."

"Sometimes I feel like it's still going on," he said. He had once tried to tell this to Smiley, who had mocked him mercilessly. He had not told anyone since.

"Yes!" she cried. "You think that when you turn a corner, you'll run into women with long dresses. You'll run into Shelley!"

"You've been in his house," he said, wondering.

"I went there with—a friend. It was hard to find. But the people around there all call it Shelley's house. There's not a plaque up or any-thing. They just remember. You get a feeling they're proud to."

"Where is it again?"

"In Italy, near Leghorn. It's on the sea. You know, the last anyone saw of Shelley, he was laughing as he went out to meet the storm."

For a moment, their gazes remained locked. She was the first to look away. He saw color flood her neck, saw it change the mark on her cheek, the white becoming pink.

"Let's go out," he said.

"Where? Out in the cold?"

She had her head down, evading him.

"I mean let's go out on a date. Let's go for a walk."

"I can't, Joe."

"Why can't you? You go out with Brad."

"I like Brad," she said, lifting her face in defiance.

"You don't like me?"

"You know that's not what I mean. I like you very much."

She was riffling quickly through the Shelley now. She put the book back on the shelf.

He touched her hair, tried to tuck it behind her ear, as he had seen her do, so many times. She pulled away.

"Just go for a walk with me sometime," he pleaded.

"Of course I will—a walk."

She had turned her back on him, and her voice sounded muffled, miserable.

"Anna," he said.

Liz came in.

"There you are," she said, "We've been looking all over for you!"

Brad towered behind her, grinning.

17

THE GREEN RIBBON in the Oldsmobile's speedometer grew longer, extending to 75, 80, as Brad sped them past a string of slower cars. He steered with one hand, his arm straight to the wheel, and kept glancing over his shoulder at Joe, chatting with his happy, boasting mixture of enthusiasm and disbelief, as if the world were full of marvels he could scarcely credit.

"Too fast," Anna said, from the seat beside him. Her dark glasses gave her the air of a convalescent. She had a headache, and for the last half hour had kept mostly silent. They were on their way to Niagara Falls. The trip had been Liz's idea: Anna, unlike the rest of them, had never seen the Falls, and wouldn't it be nice for all four to go down together? So here they were, on the day after the party, in Brad's father's black 98, watching the oncoming lane where a tractor and wagon had just pulled into their path.

"Brad," Joe warned, from the backseat.

"I got it," Brad said, and at the last second tucked the Olds behind a station wagon.

"You see," Brad said cheerfully, "if we'd been going any slower we'd be dead." In the filthy window of the station wagon a child was waving frantically.

"If you'd been going any slower, we wouldn't have been out there," Anna said dryly, and Joe, sitting directly behind her, thought, How can you go out with him?

Through gaps in the trees, Lake Ontario gleamed dully, like flat metal. Their near miss filled the car with silence. The bitter, devouring land fled past in its post-harvest brownness. A dog ran down a hedged drive, its bark small and faraway. On a porch, a carved pumpkin scowled. After the exchange over Shelley, Joe had not had a chance to talk with Anna alone. He felt there was unfinished business between them, that she had been at the edge of a response that would have led into new territory. He clung to a conviction that they were bound together at a level she must eventually acknowledge. The center of his awareness was the soft helmet of her hair, not two feet away, and her face, looking straight ahead, alive with expressions he could not see. He felt he was alone with her—the others in the car were no more important than strangers—and that she felt this way too.

They came down through the city of Niagara Falls, past the empty motels and cavernous eating joints, past the low hall with its shadowy bumper cars, huddled together for the winter, past a ten-foot-high picture of a bearded fat lady: Rasputin with breasts.

"God, isn't this awful?" Brad said happily. No one answered him. A Sunday grimness had settled in; it seemed a mistake to have come.

Just ahead, across an area of parkland, the tops of the two great falls came into view: sheets of shredding whiteness, unreal amid the clouds of mist rising from the gorge and filling the air with moisture. Brad set the wipers going.

"Stop!" Anna cried suddenly.

"There's no parking here," Brad said, grinning across at her.

"Stop, stop!" she ordered. Sitting forward, she was pounding her hand on the dash like a child in full tantrum.

"Brad, stop!" Joe shouted. He thought she was going to be sick. When Brad pulled over to the curb, Anna got out immediately. Joe followed.

"Joe, please, I have to do this alone."

"Are you all right?"

"Yes. Please—I have to see the falls alone."

She hurried across the road without looking back, the collar of her camel-hair coat up, and passed through a series of shrubs wrapped head to toe in burlap. On the far side of the park, she crossed another road and disappeared behind a tour bus.

Her sudden desertion left them stunned. "We should wait for her," Joe said, but when after several minutes she had not come back, or even reappeared, Brad suggested they go and park. They drove on, behind the dolorous thump of the wipers, to the public lot near the Canadian Falls.

A few minutes later, Joe stood looking down the length of the stone safety wall, which snaked along the rim of the gorge through the mist. He could see tourists, gathered here and there on the wet pavement, peering over the railing that topped the wall, but there was no sign of Anna. Turning to the rail, he watched the shallow water of the Niagara race to the brink. The river at this crucial juncture was green, an extraordinary livid green, and it seemed to slow as it rounded over the brink, the muscled, glowing water cleansing his mind of all but itself. Far below, on the shifting foam-marbled surface of the basin, the *Maid of the Mist* looked like a toy, its decks crammed with yellow-suited ants.

Desultorily, they debated whether they should look for Anna. Where the wide river descended toward the falls through rapids, a rusting barge had stuck on a reef, a pivot for circling gulls. In Anna's absence, the Niagara seemed cold and desolate. They had come here to show her the sights; without her, the falls seemed to lose their meaning.

"If she wants to trek around out here, that's fine," Liz said peevishly. She hadn't bothered to look into the gorge, and she appeared miserable, her hands buried in the pockets of her fur jacket. The mist and cold and thundering water seemed an affront to her, an unnatural habitat compared to the comforts of more sheltered places. "I'm going into the restaurant."

"I'll go have a look for her," Brad said.

"She hasn't had enough time," Joe said, meeting Brad's eyes.

"Oh, really?" Brad said, bemused. Joe found his superior manner maddening.

"She's never seen the falls," Joe said. "This is important to her, seeing them for the first time. She doesn't want to be disturbed."

"I'm not going to stop her looking!" Brad laughed.

"She's a poet," Joe said, with real anger. "She can't look at something if you're there jabbering beside her."

"Who says I jabber?" There was a knifing seriousness in Brad's tone—he didn't always play the joker.

"Come on, boys," Liz pleaded, a bit wearily. She took Joe's arm and tried to draw him toward the restaurant. He broke away.

Joe was prepared to do anything to keep Brad from going after Anna. He knew he was being ridiculous and knew he couldn't really stop Brad, but he hung on stubbornly, with his hands jammed in the pockets of his new coat, glaring at everything that moved.

"Joe, please," Liz begged softly.

"You don't know the concentration it takes, to make a poem," Joe said, and felt color flood his face, to find himself defending poetry. "She has to really look at the falls. She's told me about it," he added, half lying. She had told him about looking exercises she did, when she'd stare for minutes at a time at a leaf or an insect, to train herself to see what was really there. But exactly how this connected to the creation of poems was a mystery to him. "It's important that she be alone, because even to have another person around distracts her."

"Okay, okay," Brad said, raising his hands in sarcastic surrender. "I'll tell you what. I'll walk along here—is that okay? I'll walk along here, and when I see her I won't go up to her. I'll hang back, okay?"

When Brad trailed off along the wall, Joe was tempted to go after him. For a furious moment, he wanted to grab him, start a fight, throw his joking, lanky body into the gorge. But Liz was tugging at his arm again, and this time he allowed himself to be led into the restaurant. They sat at a linen-covered table behind tinted glass, which made the falls outside seem doubly gloomy, like an old photograph. A waiter brought them water. Liz ordered coffee and a sandwich. Joe, who was not hungry, and who was still conscious enough of his surroundings to be appalled by the prices, ordered soup. He was furious with himself for revealing the depth of his feelings for Anna, exposing himself to the mockery dancing in Brad's eyes.

"Anna's a strange girl," Liz said, in a neutral tone.

Joe mucked with his spoon in his bowl.

"I guess you've seen her poetry," she said, trying again. "She never shows it to me. Is it good?"

"It's better than good," he said. "She's a poet; it's what she wants to do. It's what she does do," he added defiantly, pushing bits of cracker around. Anna had told him one afternoon, when they were together in the school library, that she hoped to publish books one day. "I think my life would be well spent if, at the end, there were a hundred pages of poems that people still wanted to read when I was gone," she said. He remembered the iron wistfulness of her voice, the sun falling across their scattered books, how the inside of his foot had accidentally brushed hers. A wave of sadness had washed over him as she declared her ambition, as if giving your life to poetry were a heroic but ultimately doomed act, like setting off to cross the Atlantic in a boat too small. He had experienced the same feeling while defending her to Brad. Her task seemed hopeless, and yet it made him want to protect her all the more. Her ambition was her place of vulnerability, and there, somehow, he felt he could help her.

"So tell me about it—this poetry of hers."

He met Liz's frank violet gaze. She had made poetry sound like a childish indulgence.

"You can't tell somebody about poetry," he said. He was quoting Anna: If you could say what it was about, there'd be no need to write it. Outside, the sepia falls roared dully. He felt half drugged by the warm restaurant and half furious with frustration. His body needed to act, to work off its seething energies. He kept tearing open packets of crackers and crumbling them in his soup, while Liz watched.

"You like her, don't you?"

He blew out dismissively and looked past her to the falls.

"Because I'll be straight with you, Joe. She's in love with Brad. And anyway, I don't think she's really for you. You're too much like her. Too moody. She needs someone like Brad, to keep her spirits up."

He looked into Liz's cool, almost beautiful face, and hated her. He felt she had put long cold fingers inside him and grasped some essential organ and squeezed it. But he sat perfectly still, not speaking while she ate her sandwich and sipped her coffee. Dreariness overcame him, exhaustion. The world was not as it should be, and yet the world was here, as unchangeable and formidable as bedrock. He went on watching the shredding water, sitting in the restaurant chair. It was as if he and Liz had been together for years: she, his wife, calmly eating, accustomed to his sullen refusal to talk, his wandering eye.

A few minutes later, Brad and Anna came in, their faces pink with activity and excitement.

"She wants to go everywhere now," Brad announced triumphantly. "*The Maid of the Mist*, the whirlpool—"

"I'm drunk on this place!" Anna said, stripping off her coat as Joe, suddenly self-conscious, grinned at the tabletop. "It's cured my headache."

Later, they drove to the whirlpool, where the Niagara coiled against itself in a great elbow of the gorge, about a mile downstream from the falls. A steep forested path descended through a break in the gorge wall. At the edge of the water, Anna stood on a low rock and looked out over the wide green pool, where whitecaps charged in all directions and chewed-up logs circled, unable to escape the whirlpool's sucking power. She remained absolutely motionless, with her head a little down, her sunglasses pushed back onto her hair, her hands in the pockets of her coat, confronting the whirlpool. Joe could feel the force of her concentration. Once, she reached up to keep her glasses from falling, but otherwise she was still. She had forgotten her friends completely, she had forgotten him. Her deep gaze seemed to travel out, across the surging river, the shifting slabs of water, the eruptions of liquid bedrock, and at the same time in, as if taking the whirlpool inside her. Perhaps sensing his attention, she turned to him, though he was not at all sure she actually saw him. Her eyes, he thought, seemed oddly blind.

18

ANNA FELT ILL again—her headache coming back—and on the way home she lay in the backseat with her head in Liz's lap and Joe's new coat pulled up to her chin. From the front seat, Joe could sometimes hear her let out a long sigh or a whimper of pain. Mostly, though, she was silent, and this silence suggested an act of concentration, as if she were trying to accomplish some delicate, difficult task, like threading a needle in the dark. He had never witnessed such a severe reaction to a headache before; his mother simply took an aspirin and turned grim. For all her calm, Anna Macrimmon appeared to harbor an extraordinary vulnerability. In some way Joe could not fathom, her headache seemed connected to her excitement in the gorge, to the way she had looked so steadily at the river. It was as if she had stared too long at the sun.

The headlights of the 98 plowed up the highway, briefly illuminating the windows of anonymous villages. Everyone had fallen silent, out of respect for—and perhaps oppressed by—the suffering in the backseat. Joe felt his outburst at Brad had somehow corrupted their time together, trapping him in an isolation and jealousy he was unable to escape. Only one thought consoled him: his new coat on her body, as if he were secretly holding her. When Brad let him out at the end of Water Street, he left it in the car.

SHE WAS NOT in school the next day, Monday, or the day after. Again, her absence had a palpable quality, as though it were part of her. In phys ed he stopped on the playing field to watch some sparrows blow down-wind, the whole flock pulsing along almost merrily, their tiny lives somehow at home in the vast stone-colored sky. In a few seconds they were gone, vaporized by the distances over the empty fields. Her absence was there too: in the brown earth stretching toward a stand of pines; in the dreamlike progress of a white truck making its way out Golf Links Road. All this purified him, in a lonely way, of his sense of failure. Away from Anna, he gradually felt ready to meet her again. Each time he saw her she was new, but so was he.

On Wednesday, she was back. She seemed under the weather, Joe thought, pale and a little remote, but warm enough as she smiled at him and touched his arm. In English class, Mrs. Fraser asked her to read her essay on the Romantics, which the teacher said was the most remarkable work she'd seen in years. Joe watched as Anna stood hesitating beside her desk, frowning at the loose sheets of paper in her hand. Two rows over, Elaine Brown lifted her small head and gazed stoically into space. Until Anna Macrimmon's arrival, she was considered the best English student. Now, with every essay returned to them, with every answer Anna made in class—though she never volunteered one and always had to be asked by Mrs. Fraser—Elaine seemed to be mourning her fall into second place.

"Aspects of Romanticism," Anna Macrimmon read, in a voice that to Joe was touched with doubt. "Among people who read poetry, the Romantics have apparently fallen out of favor. Where once young men and women read Wordsworth or Shelley or Keats, now we prefer 'tougher' or more 'modern' writers such as T. S. Eliot or W. H. Auden or Dylan Thomas. It may be true that those more recent poets speak directly to our troubled times, when two world wars have shattered some of the certainties society once rested on. We are in error, though, if we think that Wordsworth and Shelley and their company have little or nothing to say to us. In fact, they understand the modern world as well or better than many of the writers who followed, for they were there at its birth, when the first factories and industrial towns were creeping across the English countryside, and science was beginning its long undermining of the Christian church. While they still looked to the future with confidence, there is a shadow aspect to their work that presages, profoundly, our own skepticism about the phenomenon of so-called progress. I believe that their analysis is the deepest we have, and that in a way we have yet to catch up to them.

"Take Wordsworth, for example. In his sonnet that begins, 'The world is too much with us. . . .' "

She read on. They listened, they who for the most part did not read poetry, for whom Wordsworth was only the author of "I Wandered Lonely as a Cloud," which they had had to memorize, they listened with a quietness that was rare for them. Perhaps it was her voice that held them, more than her ideas: light, almost a woman's, yet breaking at times like an adolescent boy's in little patches of roughness. A few of the students seemed to listen to every word. Others slipped into daydream, staring at the bare trees outside the classroom windows.

When she sat down the silence continued. A radiator clanked in solitary appreciation. Then applause rippled briefly through the class.

AFTER SCHOOL, JOE turned past the trophy case and saw her in her brown cloak and tam, pushing open the glass doors to the street. In seconds he was beside her.

"Your essay was wonderful."

Immediately, he felt the poverty of the word. She used language so well that when he tried to speak he felt hopelessly inarticulate. Yet the irony was that around her, or even just thinking of her, he seemed about to say everything he had always wanted to say, to relieve the pressure of all the confused ideas and feelings he carried with him that no one else wanted to hear—not his parents, who never had patience or time, or Smiley, who had made fun of him for trying. He had fallen into the habit of silence, and into the deeper habit of not paying attention to his intuitions about beauty and ugliness and truth and the strangeness of things. Instinctively, he knew she was his chance to speak.

She was walking quickly, as if fleeing something, her face cast down, sheltering behind the erect collar of her cloak. She thanked him for his compliment but in the same breath added, "I couldn't help thinking how simpleminded it was."

"Oh, no—"

"By the time I was through, I even doubted I agreed with it, with most of it."

She seemed genuinely dismayed. He did not know what to say. If he had written such an essay, he would have strutted for weeks afterward. But to her it seemed a defeat.

"I mean, how can I say that life has got more regimented than it was then? I wasn't alive then—and I don't have that much experience now. It was all wrong."

A car went by, full of students, honking as if coming from a wedding. Davy McElroy thrust his freckled face toward them and screamed. Joe watched Anna jump back and glance quickly at the car, and in that moment he saw, again, her vulnerability. He had once thought of her as remote and superior and unblemished, as she had appeared that first evening on the river. But he had since seen a great deal more: her headaches, the red places on her ink-stained fingers where she'd torn her cuticles, her fearful reaction now to the kids in the passing car. He saw she was immersed in the thousand particular details of life—all that misery he knew himself.

Suddenly he was swept with tenderness for her. His fear and self-consciousness had vanished. "Factory life. I liked what you said about that."

"I've never worked in a factory," she said. There was derisive laughter in her voice. "What do I know about factory work? It's ridiculous that I stand up there and tell people about it. Half of them probably know more about it than I do."

"But you still got it right," he said.

She looked at him.

"I've worked in a factory: at Bannerman's." He could feel his face flush with this admission. He had always tried to hide his background from her. Now he was willing to risk exposure. "It's no fun," he said, "watching machines go around all day. Putting socks in boxes. It almost drives you crazy. You go numb. Nobody likes it. I mean, people write things on the walls, in the washrooms, about how much they hate it. The management keeps painting them over and putting up signs, but the writing always comes back."

"What work did you do?"

"Lots of things. For a while I was a knitter."

"A knitter!"

"Sure, I sat in a rocking chair and knitted," he said, joking. "There was a whole roomful of us." When she laughed, it was sunlight on a wave. He walked her home. She lived on Banting Street, in a large house of weathered brick with a small white porch supported by four pillars. For a while they stood at the curb, in the drifting smell of bonfires, talking. She seemed in a better mood now, holding her books to her chest, smiling at the stories he told her about life in the mill. But he wasn't simply telling stories. He was watching her, calculating when to make his next move. He couldn't help himself.

Stepping up on the curb—a sudden hot rush of courage—he said, "So when are we going on our walk?"

She looked at him. "Did I promise to go for a walk?"

"At Liz's party. I wanted to take you out to Devil's Cave. It's a cave in the limestone, you'd love it, what the river does there. It sort of slides in, you know, with these little whirlpools in it—they pop up and spin away."

"It sounds fascinating," she said, still looking at him; he felt he had moved her. But then she added, "Maybe Liz and Brad would like to go along."

"I was thinking, just the two of us."

"Oh, Joe," she said quietly, a note of alarm.

"I don't think they'd mind. Heck, we don't need to tell them." He half hated himself for pressuring her—surely he was being boorish and insensitive. She was looking askance now, into the road.

"If I tell you something," she said, "do you promise to keep it to yourself?"

"Yes, of course." Unexpectedly, she was presenting him with two of his most fervent desires: opening herself to him and asking something of him.

"And not ask me for more than I want to tell you?"

"Not a word," he said. He was watching her eagerly now, loving her eyes, her face.

"I—this sounds so melodramatic. I made a promise to myself. A couple of years ago, I—well, something happened. I had a pretty bad time. And after, I promised myself I'd—I'd take things easier. I'd live a more ordinary life."

"Ordinary." He did not see how anything about her could be ordinary.

"I just wanted to be—I don't know, like most people my age. I wanted to do my schoolwork, have fun, have a boyfriend, and not get too serious—just ordinary things." She was deeply flushed now, watching him, and her eyes seemed to be begging an understanding for what she could not express. "So I guess what I'm saying is, let's just be friends. You're very special, Joe, but I can't—I guess what I'm saying is, I need some room."

"I'll give you room," he said. He couldn't help from adding, "I'll give you anything you want."

She let out a little explosion of breath. Abruptly, she turned from him and hurried up the walk.

That evening after supper, he crossed the dim yard and climbed the garden steps to the top of the dike. She had pushed him gently away and at the same time had given him a secret, or at least a piece of one. How could having a bad time make her want to be ordinary? Had she told her secret to Brad? Did Brad know he was part of the ordinary life she wanted, or in this ordinary life was there no room for the telling of her secret? Did Brad know—how had she put it—that she wanted to have a boyfriend and not get too serious? Where did that leave him, Joe? She had said he was special. Did being special disqualify him for the ordinary life she wanted? He walked along the path on the top of the dike. Someone was riding a bicycle across the footbridge to the park. He could see the spokes flash, behind the wire mesh fence, and hear the planks rumble, each one speaking out in turn as the wheels fled over it.

19

MID-NOVEMBER. LOOKOUT HILL a gray cloud looming over the Business Section and the Island. Alf was walking home from work when Pete's Sarasota drew up beside him.

"Hey-yo," Alf said, stooping to peer inside. Pete held his cigarette like a pencil in his crimped fingers, turning from the wheel to look unhappily at Alf. His hand, Alf saw, was stained red with dye.

"You get it too?"

"What?"

"I just got laid off."

Sudden nausea swept him, from the smell of stale smoke and sour, ancient seat covers. And Pete: Pete went on looking at him—accusingly, it seemed to Alf—with the butt smoking in his fingers. It had been a couple of months since Alf had given Woody Marr's name to Prince, months of worrying what the outcome would be. But nothing had happened, to Woody or to anyone else. He had begun to think he was home free.

"They didn't lay you off?" Pete said. Still his eyes held Alf's, with their look of pain and accusation and, under it, something of his old plaintiveness, his old hopefulness, hanging in gamely.

"No. Pete, this is terrible."

"The scumbags said there wasn't enough work. Complete bullshit. Somebody squealed on us."

"How do you know?"

"Everybody's who's been let go was at my place that night."

"There's more?"

"Eight I know of. I'm going to phone Doyle," Pete said, finally releasing Alf from his gaze. He ground out his cigarette with a sharp twist.

"Who else?" Alf managed.

"Get in," Pete said. Alf got in and shut the door. Ahead, a few snowflakes drifted across Water Street. He felt he had passed a subtle border into another world. Everything looked the same, and yet he knew it wasn't. The sign hanging outside the Royal Hotel, the orange cloud of willows above the millrace—they seemed hollowed out from the inside, less themselves. Pete put the car in gear and they made their way down Water.

"You're sure it's just union people?" Alf said, rousing himself.

"Every one of them was at my place."

"Who?"

"Terry, Lucille, Ed—" Pete ran through eight or nine names. Alf found it awful, the darting of his wounded eyes. He felt Pete suspected him. What else could he think, given that he, Alf, still had his job?

"How about Woody?" Alf said, as casually as he could. He had worked it all out before, tossing in bed, imagining the worst. Woody Marr was the key. He had given Woody's name to Prince. If Woody had been fired or laid off as well, it meant Woody had not talked. But if Woody still had his job, it might well mean he had given Prince some names to save himself. And if Woody was the only person to keep his job, other than himself, it meant he had talked for sure. In that case, though Alf hadn't given up the names directly, he might as well have. He had knocked over the first domino, which toppled the rest.

"Well?"

"What?"

"Was Woody laid off?"

"I don't know," Pete said dully, as if something had just collapsed inside him. "There's a few I ain't heard about."

When they got to Alf's place, Alf insisted that Pete come in and have a beer. Mercifully, Margaret and the children were out, but all the same

Alf immediately regretted having Pete there, regretted his thin figure hunched at the table peering bleakly through the smoke of his cigarette, gesturing with his red hands, bad-mouthing his foreman and everyone else in management he could think of. Alf wanted to get on the phone to Woody—no, not to Woody, that would give the whole business away, but to somebody—and find out if the knitter had been laid off. He was smoking now too. Blue uplands of smoke hung in the kitchen, drifting in the snowy light from the window. Ever since he'd taken Woody's cigarette on the fire escape, he'd been smoking on the sly and hiding the fact from Margaret. Now he no longer cared.

That evening he was unable to use the phone; someone was always in the kitchen. At eight o'clock he put on his coat and drove over to the Flats, passing Woody's stucco bungalow. Woody's brown Ford sat in the drive. A minute later, approaching the arena, he saw the jammed parking lot and remembered the hockey game. Someone there would know. He parked the Biscayne on the edge of the baseball field, near a grove of oaks. Ahead, a muffled chanting sounded in the pale, round hill of the arena.

He slipped down a corridor and emerged in the open space at the end of the stands. Woody was there, standing by himself near the corner boards, watching the game through the wire mesh. This is stupid, Alf thought, all you have to do is see if he's at work tomorrow. But he couldn't help himself. The image of a pheasant was emblazoned on the back of Woody's sweater coat. The bird was beating up on sharp wings, its head like a hood pierced by a red eye.

He stood beside Woody. Just then, the puck caromed into the corner, and in a moment several players thudded into the boards. Sweating faces grimaced through the mesh as they battled for the puck. A whistle blew and they skated calmly away.

"So," Alf said. His heart was slamming. "You still have your job or what?"

For several seconds Woody went on watching the ice, where the green and white uniforms milled. It was as if Alf didn't exist, as if he were a ghost making sounds the living could not hear.

The cold air smelled of rotting wood, of winter.

"Yeah, I still have my job," Woody said at last. "Can you think of any reason why I wouldn't?"

Alf met Woody's flinty eyes, like tiny flashes of metal, pure hatred in the pudgy face. Around them, the crowd bayed.

20

WITHIN ANOTHER DAY, he had the full picture. Everybody who'd been at Pete's that night had been laid off, fourteen people in all. Only Alf and Woody were unscathed.

It seemed to Alf his involvement must be obvious to everyone, at least to everyone who had been at the meeting, though by now, surely, word had spread. He couldn't go out without the sense of being watched—watched and commented on, as if his guilt were indicated by a mark on his face or by one of those signs the mill workers sometimes stuck on a fellow's backside, for a joke: PLEASE KICK HERE. Hell, he told himself, he'd only given up one name, and that man still had his job. He couldn't really be blamed for the others, could he?

But he was unpersuaded by his own arguments. He traipsed down Shade Street, avoiding people's eyes. Entering the A&P, he tripped on the step. A moment later he pushed through swinging doors into the odor of fresh-ground coffee.

His cart had a squeaky wheel. He pushed it past one aisle—too many people—and turned it, squeaking faithfully, down another. Joe was there, in a long white apron, putting up cans of peas.

They made small talk, awkwardly.

"I was thinking I could get some tickets for the Gardens," Alf said. He felt an urgent need to give his son something, to fill his own sense of emptiness. The boy's cheeks flushed.

"That a good idea?" Alf asked.

"Sure."

"Great."

"Good."

Over Joe's shoulder, Alf caught sight of Dick Forsyte, his small face grimacing as he studied the label on a can. Dick was one of those laid off. The sight of him—so casually looking up from the can to the shelves— momentarily paralyzed Alf. Dick's presence seemed huge; he might have been famous. Alf shifted a step, concealing himself behind his son. "For- got to go to the bank," he said, swinging his cart away. In the street it was snowing: large, slow flakes falling peacefully out of the darkness.

The bank was overheated. He waited in line, in the hushed churchlike atmosphere, on gray tiles tracked with slush. Ahead of him, a woman with her hair in a fraying bun—it was Matilda Squires, the Presbyterian minister's wife—moved forward a step. By the heel of her shoe lay a quarter. Alf shuffled past it.

"Say, is this yours?"

He knew the voice—its compressed, slightly muffled quality, as if coming from underground—and turned to meet Lucille Boileau. She was holding up the dirty quarter between thumb and forefinger.

"Oh, jeez, Alf, I didn't recognize you."

Her smile with its missing tooth lit her face.

"I'd say it was yours," he said dryly.

She slid the coin into the pocket of her jeans. There was a childlike deliberateness in her movement that he found pathetic: as if she thought the quarter was really going to make a difference. She was wearing a black leather motorcycle jacket with silver studs on the shoulders, black jeans, and cowboy boots with pointy toes.

"I'm sorry about what happened," he said.

"Well, what can you do, eh?"

"What they did, it was illegal."

He felt he was about to burn up, in his buttoned coat.

"I guess you got off, eh?" she said, glancing shyly.

"For now, anyway."

"Oh, they won't lay you off. Not a good man like you."

He waited for her in the street. She came down the steps counting a handful of bills and scarcely seemed surprised to see him. Snow fell silently around them, appearing and disappearing on her black hair, the black leather. He had a curious sense of their absolute isolation, as if they were meeting in a forest.

"Look, Lucille, I want to help you out." He held out a small wad of twenties. "You can pay me back when you get another job."

He was conscious of her wide mouth, the inflated lips. Years ago, he had heard a rumor that Lucille Boileau took in men for money.

"You keep that," she said, pushing back his hand. "But tell you what. You can buy me a drink."

They crossed the street to the Vimy House, passing through its low arching porch and stubby pillars of orange marble into the dim lobby, where a fuzzy gray cat lay curled on the desk. A leather couch leaked hanks of matted wool. He had not been in the Vimy House for years. His distaste for the place was underlaid by a feeling of inevitability, as though the intervening time had been a kind of illusion. This was what had been waiting for him, this was real: the smell of smoke and stale beer and longing, the dregs of happiness that hadn't lasted a single night.

He traipsed after her black jacket into LADIES AND ESCORTS, letting her choose a way among the small round tables. She stopped near a large window entirely covered by shapeless drapes. Beside it, in an ornate frame, hung a photograph of the old king and queen, taken during their brief stop in town before the war. The famous couple were standing on the platform at the rear of their rail car, the king in a double-breasted suit, the queen in a cavalier hat and white fur stole, waving over a mass of roses. The pale photo was like a reflection of distant sunlight, a lost afternoon.

"I was there," he said, pointing, and knew again the smell of the oily railbed in the heat, the town band playing "God Save the King."

"So was I," Lucille Boileau said. "We walked up the West River Road, all the school kids. They gave us little flags. I was so happy: I was going to see the king and queen. But the train stopped too far down the tracks and the crowd got in the way. I never saw them."

"You didn't miss much," he said. But he could still remember the thrill of seeing those royal faces, so familiar from photographs, smiling over those in the crowd who had run down the tracks to catch up to them. When the train finally drew away, sliding into the heat-warped distance, it was as if some magic had fled their lives.

In a distant corner the only other customer, Bessie Kinnaird, touched her wineglass. Behind the bar, Rick Taylor, in a white shirt rolled to the elbows, was working something out with a pencil. The room was quiet, a cave shelter from the snow. Alf was relieved to be here.

Rick brought them four draft beers, setting each one on the yellow arborite with a sharp rap. Alf supposed Rick was wondering what he was doing here with Lucille Boileau—he knew tongues would wag later—but for the moment he felt armored in indifference.

Lucille raised her glass. "To all us poor sods who lost our jobs," she said. "No, that's too sad. To the future!"

He threw back the bitter beer, swept by a wave of disgust. He couldn't understand why she wasn't accusing him, or at least acting suspicious. Did she really trust him so much? At her distant table, Bessie Kinnaird lifted her glass in a trembling hand and took a brief, wondering sip, like a girl.

"So, are you looking for work?" he said sharply.

"Oh, yeah, making the rounds."

Her vagueness irritated him.

"Where've you been? Up to Samuelson's?"

"Sure."

He didn't believe her.

She shrugged, and he saw the passive drift of her life. Indians. They were all the same, weren't they? Drifting through things, never helping themselves.

"Have you been over to Johnsonville?"

"I don't really like Johnsonville."

"Why not," he said, "if you can get a job there?"

Again she shrugged.

"What's the matter with Johnsonville?" he persisted. "I would think that'd be a good place for you."

She was staring unhappily into her beer.

"Isn't it?" He thrust his question home, wanting to provoke her, wanting her to see he wasn't the man she thought he was.

"Why? Because there's Indians in Johnsonville?" she said finally, to her beer. "Everybody hates Indians there," she said, tossing her head. "Anyways, I got to be home for Billy."

"Well, were you home for him before, when you were at Bannerman's?"

She was silent; her wide face, open and trusting, was trained unhappily on the table now. He pitied her and yet he kept the pressure on: he was waiting, half elated by his own cruelty, for her to attack him. "There must be somebody who could look after him."

"Not anybody I trust," she said.

They drank, for a while, and smoked. She took his cigarettes sullenly, and their smoke rose, mingling under the high pressed-tin ceiling. They had nothing more to say, it seemed, and yet he felt bound to her, responsible. Behind the heavy drapes, cars swept the snowy street.

Alf shifted in his chair and noticed something at his feet: a stuffed animal, a little brown horse with a red wool mane.

"What have we here?" he said. When he tried to stand it up on the table it fell soundlessly into a puddle of beer.

"Cute," she said. "Rick's little boy."

He spoke in an undertone. "Can you imagine bringing up a kid in here?"

"Sure," she said, as she ground out her butt. "It's warm."

She left to go to the john. Her bitter reprimand lingered in the smoke. What did he know about keeping warm? Compared to her, he supposed, he was rich. He saw her coat, with its torn scarlet lining, crushed at the back of her chair, and wondered if he could slip the bills into her pocket.

Amazingly, she came back laughing. She told him she hadn't noticed the toilet seat was up; she'd nearly fallen in. He lit another cigarette for her. Her head descended to his flame like someone drinking light and for a moment he loved her: her broad, foreshortened face with its black eyes shining like pools of oil, the little sickle scar on her forehead. Settling, she told him a story about ice fishing with her father, years ago on Lake Erie. "I fell in," she said, laughing again. "I mean, I was up to my neck in slush. Just like a bottle of Coke." Her father had pulled her out and carried her, wrapped in his coat, to the nearest house.

"The people wouldn't let us in," she said. "So he had to run to the next house; it was another mile over, just about killed him. Just about killed me. They put me on the stove, eh? They had this platform for drying boots. I got good and baked."

"What do you mean," he said, "they wouldn't let you in?"

Her pink tongue skimmed her lower lip, and he understood what she meant, in the same moment that he understood he had shamed her.

HE COULDN'T STOP thinking about Bob Prince. Whatever his own guilt in the affair, Prince was the force behind the layoffs, he had no doubt—the liar who'd told him he'd only give the union supporters a good talking to. He was in a fury with the man, with whatever fury he wasn't directing at himself. In a dream, he saw the executive's dark blue Cadillac Fleetwood patrolling behind him. He ran into the woods, but the car was soon there, above him, descending through the treetops with a thwacking sound, like helicopter blades. Its underside was composed of creamy flesh. In this belly a slit—some sort of mouth—pulsed open and shut, briefly revealing a toothless cavity.

The snow did not stay; the town reverted to the dour emptiness of late autumn. One Saturday, emerging from Tugg's Hardware, Alf saw the Fleetwood moving down Shade. It was definitely Prince, his tanned head and handsome face lifted a little, with a kind of offhand nobility. The car crossed the Shade bridge and climbed toward the upper town, accelerating so smoothly it seemed to be powered not by an engine so much as a magnetism, a wish. Backing the Biscayne into the traffic, Alf began to follow. He had no plan. He was simply drawn to the other man, half in anger, half in the hope that something might yet be done about the layoffs—that he still had some purchase in the places of power. About a mile from town on the Johnsonville highway, the Fleetwood turned down a secondary road. At a rail crossing, he lost it behind the monotonous lumbering of boxcars, and when the caboose finally rattled by and the clanging and blinking at the barrier finally stopped, there was no sign of the dark blue car in the wasteland of gravel pits and cold gray lakes beyond. But a mile down the road, with the countryside swathed again in the brown tangle of autumn, he saw the car between the stone posts that marked the entrance to the Langside Golf Club (MEMBERS ONLY), parked among several others.

He left the Biscayne and walked into the clubhouse, through an empty locker room, up some stairs onto a red carpet that led down a paneled corridor. A young waiter in a short jacket asked if he could help. Alf brushed past without a word, instinctively heading for the smell of food, the clatter of dishes. The dining room was mostly empty: a scattering of white linen squares across a large space. Prince was at a window table, in a gray tweed jacket, tieless, just pouring beer into a tall glass. As Alf approached, he looked up without expression. He might have been expecting him.

"Have a seat, Alf."

That voice again: freakishly unruffled, the soul of civility. Alf had an urge to throw a chair through the window. He remained standing, in his jeans and windbreaker.

"You said this wasn't going to cost anybody their jobs."

"Would you like a drink?"

"You said this wasn't going to cost anybody their jobs."

"So you said."

"Don't get clever with me!"

The young man in the short jacket and bow tie hovered.

"Is everything all right, Mr. Prince?"

"Just fine, Danny. Bring Mr. Walker a—"

"I don't want anything," Alf told Prince. With a gesture from the executive, the young man turned reluctantly away. Prince spoke to the table-top, gravely.

"As I remember, I was speaking only of the people whose names you gave to me. Or were going to give to me. There—well, I believe I kept my word. The man whose name you gave me wasn't laid off."

It seemed a snake's argument.

"What are you saying? That if I'd given you all the names they'd have kept their jobs?"

The other man winced, as if at a digestive pang. "As it happened," he said, frowning at the bubbles that rose in his Pilsner glass, "I had no intention of laying off those people. But I have my own bosses, Alf. I don't have the free hand everyone imagines I do. There are people above me who are determined to play rough."

Prince looked up frankly now, coldly, a warning that he was barely tolerating this interruption and it had better not go on much longer. Alf fumed, moved his feet. In a company where the line of command stretched out of sight, you could always say it was someone else's fault.

"I hold you responsible," he said.

"So do they," Prince said wearily. "I'm the meat in the sandwich."

"Take those people back," Alf said. "Go to your bosses and beg. Like I'm begging you now. Hell, do you know what it's like for them? With Christmas coming on? Take them back. I'll stake my job on their not starting a union. If they do, fire me."

Prince touched the neatly folded napkin beside his cutlery: the peace he was not being allowed to enjoy. The young waiter came back with a salad. Alf watched in a trance of blankness as he set it down, left.

"Take back Pete Moon," Alf said.

Prince played with the Pilsner glass, making the surface of the beer tilt rapidly.

"As I understand it, he was one of the leaders."

"He didn't lead anything. All he did was have the meeting at his house."

"Oh, really?" Prince said, and his eyes flashed. "I believe you told me the meeting was by the river. There was a fire?"

He spoke with riveting irony. It was clear he had known all along that Alf had lied to him.

Out the window, a groundsman was trundling a wheelbarrow past the putting green. Beyond, the fairways rolled toward a distant palisade of woods.

The waiter reappeared with Prince's sandwich. Alf went on watching the groundsman as he put down the barrow and began collecting the small flags from the holes of the green. Alf thought how much better it would be to be out there, in the cold air, with his hands on honest metal, honest wood. He was nauseated, his rage turning sour. Prince pushed the sandwich away from him, as if in distaste. The executive spoke directly now, with grim self-containment.

"Alf, I can't give anyone his job back. But I can tell you this. As far as I'm concerned, that foreman's job is still open for you. We've had our disagreements, you and I, but I still consider you the best man for—"

"You can shove your fucking job," Alf said.

Driving back, he pulled up to the shore of one of the lakes in the gravel pit and turned off the engine. His hands were trembling. He tucked them into his armpits and watched the gray water. It was ominously still, as though it had come to the very point of freezing.

21

ALF SAT AT his cellar workbench, trying to ignore the commotion of an arrival overhead: the cheerful soprano of Margaret's greeting, the drag of chairs. In his hands was a bit of pine he was struggling to carve into the likeness of a pike. His model was an old Lands and Forests poster pinned on the tool board behind the bench. Caught in the glow of the hanging lamp, the freshwater fish of Ontario swam in an ordered school. Rock bass. Yellow perch. Pickerel. The pike was the most sinister: a flexible torpedo of pure appetite, its splotched body narrowing to a flattened, evil head. To be that efficient, beyond all feelings but hunger and satiety—it seemed to Alf an ideal state.

He had taken up carving during the war, as a distraction. He could remember sitting on the bank of a canal, its surface broken by pieces of machinery and the bloated belly and stiff legs of a dead cow. In his hands he held a little piece of wood, its dirtiness nicking white with each stroke of his pocketknife. He had carved farm animals and given them away to children.

There had been a boy about Jamie's age with huge, ravenous eyes. Alf had given him a tin of rations, but the boy's face had lit up only when Alf offered him the little horse he had not quite finished, its tail still of a piece with its hind legs. *Un cheval. Pour vous.* Fumbling in his high-school French.

He stirred at the memory, come up after all these years: the boy in his cloth cap, a smell of burning oil and rotting flesh. Alf brought the piece of wood to his nose. Someone else had been there too, a soldier, a shadow without a face, though he could see the man's boots dangling beside his own over the putrid water. He was sure the man, whoever he was, had not lived out the day.

Margaret came down the stairs and stood beside him.

"It's May," she said in an undertone, touching his back. "She's terribly worried about Pete."

He toyed with the fish in his hand.

"Alf, I wish you'd tell me what's wrong."

"Nothing's wrong," he said tersely.

Nearby, the furnace blower came on with a soft roar. They had known each other for twenty-three years, and silence between them could never merely be silence; it was night broken by the flight of coded messages, the riffling of dog-eared files. He slid her a hard glance and saw her face rapt with a pained earnestness, offering him the balm of listening and talk. She loved him, he knew. Often he tried to tell himself it was otherwise, that they had been going their separate ways for years—she with her church interests, her music; he with his work, his fishing, his sports. They had the family in common, but otherwise they might just as well have been living apart. It was convenient to believe this; it set him free and justified his unhappiness. But it was not true.

He pushed past her and trudged up the stairs. May sat at the kitchen table. In her haggard face he saw the shadow of his own malaise.

"I'm worried sick, Alf."

"Hey, it can't be that bad." His voice sounded magnified and unreal to him, like when he'd acted in a play for the Couples' Club. He had played a gardener, a role with only three lines, and yet he'd felt as false as at any time in his life. "Pete's had rough times before."

"Not like this."

Alf pulled out a chair. Behind him, Margaret filled a kettle at the sink, then turned to the stove. The soft explosion of little blue flames gave the promise of powerful, saving domesticity. For a moment he believed that together they might help May.

He said, "You know, when he got out of the navy, he had a hard time then? He was really down. But he got through it, eh? A few weeks?"

May was watching him hungrily, her eyes glittering with unspilt tears.

"Or that time you lost the baby?"

"Yes." Her voice small.

"You know, he's got too much of the devil in him, that guy. He'll bounce back."

Margaret had swept noiselessly from the room. He noted her departure with a slight start of panic. He did not feel up to comforting May alone.

"How long has it been since you've seen him?" she said.

He shrugged, pulling a face. "I don't know. A few days, maybe." He was lying; it had been at least two weeks. He found it unbearable to be with his friend. He had to move with such careful, guilty deference that he seemed to be holding his breath. "I lent him tools," he said, eager to put in a good word for himself. "He was going to start work on the rec room. He seemed fine." He went on pouring words into the silence. "Practically his old self. In fact, he struck me as pretty hopeful." Manic was more like it. Alf had seen his friend in this state before, though never so bad: half crazy with plans, talking a mile a minute, and still, unbelievably, going on about the union. Talking about Malachi Doyle as if the Irishman were Jesus Christ himself, as if he were going to save them all yet. Malachi this, Malachi that. Malachi thinks we should lay low for a while. Malachi says that when the union goes in, we'll get our jobs back. Alf hadn't had the heart to contradict him.

"He was looking for work," Alf said. He knew his friend had been out every day, covering the county in the Sarasota, filling out forms. "Had some good leads too. Up at Samuelson's. . . ."

He found himself talking about the places where Pete was likely to find a job, as if he had caught his friend's desperate optimism and was drawing on it to fill the space above the table. But May was shaking her head.

"It's different now. He's given up."

"Not for long," Alf said quickly, and saw, again, the boots of the other soldier, hanging above the canal.

"He just sits in his chair all day, watching TV. He's drinking."

Margaret returned with a box of Kleenex. May was looking at Alf through her tears with a strange, frantic smile, as though everything she was telling him about Pete was in fact the source of some secret happiness.

"He hit me," she said, in a high, pleading voice. "It's the first time he's ever. . . ."

Margaret leaned over, sliding her arm along May's back.

"I can't blame him," May was saying. "Not really. I was nagging him to get out, to see his friends. I told him it wasn't the end of the world, people had lost their jobs before, and he started to swear at me, and then he—he's not himself, Alf."

Tears swam down her face. He watched in dull horror. You did one thing, and it made other things happen, like a scattering of billiard balls. Then there was a woman you had known all your life, an innocent woman, weeping at your kitchen table.

ALF TRUDGED ACROSS the Lion's Park footbridge. The Atta churned toward him through shallow rapids: a waste of yellow water he wished he could go on following indefinitely, along the muddy trails that accompanied it out of town.

He had to knock twice before Pete's eye and part of his face appeared in the small round window in the front door. For a second, his pupil regarded Alf with curious indifference: a specimen under glass.

"Hey, buddy," Pete said, as he opened the door.

Alf entered the dim, hot room with its reek of stale beer and gas: the compost of unhappiness. Staring at the TV, Pete let himself down into his plaid Easy Boy.

On the screen, football players broke from their huddle and trotted back to their positions. The screen was full of snow, and from time to time the picture swam upward, creating the odd impression that the room was sinking.

"American game," Pete said. His gaunt face—thin even for him—was dark with stubble. His gaze briefly brushed Alf's knees. It was the look a frightened man might give, checking out the sources of danger. "Get yourself a beer," Pete said. He had his own bottle—he had several—parked on the TV tray beside him. "You know where they are."

Alf heard a hint of accusation in this. *You know where they are.* As if Pete were calling to account their years of friendship, the years his house had been as open to Alf as his own. As if he were saying, *I trusted you.*

Alf fetched a beer and sat on the low couch, grateful for the distraction of the game. He needed time to think about what he would say. The announcer's voice, rich with masculine authority, rose and fell with the action. There were other voices too, higher and more nakedly excited, and the crowd roaring distantly.

Alf had the nightmarish sense he had lived all this before. Prince's motel room came back to him: the sailboats on the wall, Prince picking at his corns on the bed, and the football game: the same soporific blend of voices and crowd sounds, the sense of exciting things happening, but happening elsewhere. On the screen, a clutch of cheerleaders shook their pom-poms like the heads of vanquished enemies.

The picture swam upward again. Though the temperature in the room must have been over 80, Alf felt chilled and his throat was sore. Pete did not move.

"I'll fix that," Alf said.

"Just give it a rap."

The picture righted itself. He went back to the couch wondering how long Pete would have sat there if he'd been by himself.

When a commercial came on, he asked Pete how the job hunt was going.

"Had a few nibbles," Pete said, after a while. On the screen, in the land of happiness, an old man was pouring out cornflakes for a smiling boy.

"Oh, yeah? Who?"

Pete didn't answer.

"May dropped by our place," Alf said, steeling himself. He did not like to talk about emotional difficulties, his own or anyone else's. Better to be silent and let them solve themselves. But he had promised May. He said, "I guess she's pretty worried about you."

Pete took a swig of beer; he might have been deaf.

"Look, if you don't want to talk, just say so," Alf said, with an edge of irritation. He experienced a frisson; it was the first time since Pete's firing he'd dared to speak roughly to him.

"What's to talk about?"

"Your wife's over at my place, bawling her eyes out. She's worried sick."

"She tell you I hit her?" Pete said to the TV.

"Yeah, but she doesn't blame you. Anyway, that's not why I'm here. I'm worried about you."

Pete said nothing.

"Look, what's going on with you? Is it the job or what?"

He was daring Pete to accuse him. He had exposed himself like a target. But there was a hostility in his challenge, and more power than Pete could face. Pete flashed another sideways glance at Alf's knees, took a swig of beer, and continued to concentrate on the screen.

"I don't know," Pete said. He winced and shifted in his chair. "I get these funny ideas."

"What do you mean?"

"I don't know. I can get pretty black. Paranoid, like."

Alf waited.

"Just a mood, you know." Pete motioned with his bottle toward the screen, where a large black man with immense padded shoulders tore off his helmet and began to yell at another player. Pete said, "You have to wonder who your friends are."

"What do you mean?" Alf said, his throat tightening. If it's going to happen, he thought, let's get it over with.

"Just craziness," Pete said, moving his bottle in a dismissing wave. "Not important."

Alf said, "You think I had something to do with your losing your job."

Pete stayed with the screen for what seemed an eternity. Alf watched the thin face of his friend, laid back against the white antimacassar.

"Not you, buddy," Pete said finally. "Woody's the guy. Everybody knows that."

"I wouldn't give your name to God himself," Alf said, managing to produce a rasping chuckle. "Not that he'd ever ask for it."

Pete grinned.

Alf tried to turn his attention back to the game, but his heart was pounding. *Not you, buddy, Woody's the guy.* Did Pete really believe that or was he just trying to let Alf off the hook? I'll never let you down again, he promised silently. Yes, he'd get Pete through this bad patch and they'd go on together, better friends than ever. Talking, confessing, would do no good at all. It would only cause more pain, and their friendship didn't need more pain. Better to wrap what he knew in cement, sink it to the bottom of a deep hole, and let it stay down there forever. Let it disappear, as it surely would, with time. Unless Prince talked, of course. Or Woody. Discovering that he had stopped breathing, he sucked in air. On the screen, the cheerleaders were bouncing in another war dance.

The next program was a Roy Rogers rerun. Cowboys on horseback thundered merrily among the pale hills of California. Pete seemed mesmerized. Alf was moved by the images of dazzling sunshine and rollicking male freedom.

"You got to get out of the house," he said, with a sudden uprush of tenderness. "You're rotting in here."

"Where would I go?"

"Anywhere. We'll drive down to Port Dover. Pick us up a couple of

babes." They had actually done this years ago, before the war. On the pier
they had met two girls and driven with them to the sand hills: immense
crests of sand, and the green-blue of Lake Erie rippling far below them.

"This time," Pete said, "I get the pretty one."

THEY WENT THE next day, a Sunday afternoon of brilliant light
flooding the spread of brown land waiting for winter. Alf drove the Biscayne. Pete sat in his dark blue Stingers jacket, occasionally raising his
cigarette to his lips. He did not look to the right or the left and he did not
speak, unless prodded by Alf.

They were driving south, toward the great lake that had drawn them
all their lives. As a boy, Alf had gone down to Erie by train to attend Bannerman company picnics. Later, his father had taken him bass fishing at
Long Point, and in recent years Alf had occasionally rented a cottage for
a week at Port Ryerson. He never lost his excitement at seeing the lake
after a long absence, and now, crossing the endless flats of the hinterland,
studded with the green and red barns of the tobacco farms, he felt the
old anticipation rising, the old freshness of anticipation.

As they drew near Port Dover, little mounds of sand appeared beside
the highway, and the sky ahead seemed to change, to grow larger and
brighter. They swung onto the bridge and there it was, past the dull little
river and the derelict boats and the buildings and the pier: glittering,
turquoise Erie.

They ate lunch in a near-empty restaurant overlooking the public
beach, in the full heat of the sun streaming in the plate-glass windows.
Pete kept his coat on, zipped to the chin, and left half his whitefish
untouched. Out on the lake, a snub-nose fishing boat was plowing in
across the glitter, its shadowy silhouette trailed by a cloud of gulls.

On the way out, Alf stopped off at the washroom. Pete said he'd meet
him outside, but when Alf emerged, blinking in the glare, the scrap of
beach was empty. A cottage with boarded-up windows looked out
bleakly at the water. Alf went back to the street, walking past the Biscayne and along the line of restaurants and tourist shops, most of them

closed. He experienced a stab of panic. In some way it made perfect sense for Pete to disappear, to evaporate in broad daylight.

He hurried through the town, finally coming to the concrete pier with the stubby lighthouse at its far end. A boy on a bicycle clanked past him, with a fishing pole laid across the handlebars. The pier looked empty, though he could not tell if anyone was standing behind the lighthouse. He started to move swiftly, fighting down a rising sense of alarm.

He was almost at the lighthouse. Now he was past it. No one was there, on the guano-stained end of the pier. He looked into the clear water. An oil stain glittered on the swell; the body of a tiny fish floated upside down. The sandy bottom was just visible, ten or fifteen feet down—the rippled, empty, sandy bottom, wavering as though alive.

PETE WAS WAITING for him at the car. They'd just missed each other, apparently; Pete had gone into a store to look at some belts, he said. Driving home in the waning light, the long shadows of the tobacco barns reaching over the frozen earth, they talked more easily than they had on the way down. Pete told a story Alf had never heard before, one that began with Pete's ship putting into Marseilles, a couple of years after the war. He'd gone on shore leave and found his way to a small nightclub where a band was playing jazz. It wasn't like any jazz you'd ever heard, he said, it was faster, happier; one guy was playing a violin. Later in the evening he'd danced with a woman who had taken his fancy. "She was the prettiest thing," he said, keeping silent for a while. "Black eyes . . . God." He'd fallen for her, he said, to the point where he was ready to stay in Marseilles. But he had gone back to the ship. "I still think of her," he said. "Isn't that strange? I think of her like I met her only yesterday. I can still remember the way her back felt. So slim and—makes you wonder what could have been, you know? You do one thing different, and your whole life is different."

———

TWO DAYS LATER, a Tuesday afternoon, Alf was repairing a machine when Matt Honnegger told him he was wanted on the phone. Margaret, Matt said. Alf left his tools and walked toward the little office that overlooked the graveled roof of the dyehouse. On the sill, a pigeon regarded him warily before flapping off. On Matt's desk the receiver lay on its side, seeming blacker, heavier, than usual. In the eighteen years he'd worked for Bannerman's, Margaret had called him only twice: when Joe had been knocked off his bike by a car, ten years before, and last summer, when Jamie had been lost.

For a moment, her voice saying his name, crying his name, held in the balance the lives of his children. Who was hurt? Who had slipped away into the unthinkable? It's Pete, Margaret said, and he experienced a momentary relief before her voice carried him away from safety, away from the world that had existed only moments before. It was the car, Margaret said. She was sobbing. Pete had shut himself in the garage and turned on the ignition. May had found him.

22

THE MORNING AFTER Pete's funeral, under a faultless blue sky, each twig and branch bore a delicate slice of snow. There was a sense of hospital stillness, as if the snow or its sender, conscious of a need for convalescence, had swaddled everything in bandages. Joe dressed as quietly as he could—he needed to be at his job at the A&P by nine—and slipped into the hall. The closed door of his parents' bedroom, nearly as white as the snow outside, met him with a mysterious, oppressive blankness. He went swiftly downstairs, propelled by the expectation of escape. But his mother was at the stove, making breakfast.

She sat opposite him while he ate, from time to time taking long, noisy sips of coffee. He was irritated by this, by the way she put down her cup and sighed with a world-unsettling weariness. Her sighs seemed to go right through him, to touch his every secret dread and doubt. She had a way of filling his mind with the atmosphere of her own concerns; it was suffocating. He worked at his food and tried not to look at her sagging gown, where the white tops of her breasts appeared, ivory at the frail lip of her nightdress.

"I'm worried about your father," she said.

He hated it when she said *your father,* a phrase that seemed to block the light in his sky, as if a mountain suddenly loomed. Reaching for the ketchup bottle, he shook out the red sauce stubbornly. He did not want to talk, not now; he wanted only the isolation of his sleepiness.

"He hasn't been himself for weeks now."

"He's just sad about Pete," Joe said quickly, through a mouthful of egg. He felt he knew more, far more, than he was letting on. He remembered standing at the edge of Pete's grave, as one of the pallbearers. He'd seen a darkness in his father's face, shadowing his eyes; it had seemed to him that his father had a connection to the coffin that superseded all others, a yearning as if he wished he could go down into the earth with Pete.

Shocked, Joe had glanced away, down the side of the pit, and noticed a bit of root sticking out from the dirt. And this root—crooked and hairy and white at the tip, where the backhoe had sliced it—pierced him with a feeling so wild, lonely, and ungovernable that he had had to bite his lip to keep from crying out.

"It started long before Pete," she said.

"Well," he said, shrugging, wishing she'd stop. He sipped at the hot coffee. He found his mother's prodding wrong, even indecent. There were times when he talked willingly enough with her about his father, airing his complaints. But just now he felt a powerful identification with his father and his silences. For a moment he understood their deep usefulness, how pain and lesser but still bothersome things might disappear in them. He checked the clock.

"There's more going on than he's telling us," she said. "At least more than he's telling me."

At the window, a blue jay blundered into the glass with a soft thud.

"Of course," she said, "what *has* he ever told me?"

"Don't know," Joe said, lifting his cup.

"You know, he wasn't always like that," his mother said. Her eyes found him now, with a commanding brightness.

"Like what?" he said, frowning.

"So quiet. When I first met him, he was almost chatty."

"Dad?"

"He talked as much as I did, I'm sure. And charming? He could be the life of the party, your dad. I know it's hard to believe."

"What happened?" he asked, interested now in spite of himself.

"Well, the war," she said, with another long, dismayed sigh, and he felt the war enter the room in all its dark, mysterious glamour. He was insatiably curious about the war, all the more so because his father's reticence encompassed it so thoroughly. From an early age he had been instructed by his mother not to ask him about it: "We don't want to upset him," she'd say. So the war had become a presence in the house, something he was not allowed to mention, although it lived in his father's face, and sat down with them for meals, and hung among his father's tools, and hunkered in the spaces between his father's words. Joe imagined the worst, he couldn't help himself, for what but the worst could generate such a deep, long-held withdrawal? Perhaps his father had killed a man, or many men. He would look at his father's hands and see the backs of them, the strong nicked-up fingers with their dirty nails, roped with blood.

Now here was his mother saying that before he'd gone off to France his father had been a different man—a cheerful, outgoing person, who once came to a masquerade ball dressed as Rudolph Valentino, his blue eyes shining out of a black half mask, charming every woman there. After the war, he had come home moody and paranoid; he would throw himself face down in the street when a truck backfired, and he could not break the habit of crumbling up his cigarette butts, so that the enemy still lurking in every street could not find them. His mother hardly recognized him; he was not the man she had fallen in love with. She hinted to Joe that she had wrestled with the question of whether she still loved him, whether they should marry. Of course, she had gone ahead, had borne this particular cross of trying to lure (persuade, trick, love) a man who had left the mainstream of life back into it.

"What those boys went through over there," she said, to the haunted place beyond her coffee cup.

"But what happened to him?" Joe said, leaning forward abruptly. The gap in his knowledge seemed critical. His curiosity had not only to do with battles and guns and wounds but with how to become a man. The war was the central clue; it surely contained some secret of courage or survival or growing older that he needed himself.

"I'm sure I don't know," she said in a wondering way. "His brother was killed, of course—he wasn't there for that, they were in different regiments—but his mother never forgave him for it."

"Never forgave him because Joe died?"

"Joe was her favorite. She was always after your father to look out for him. By the time I met your father, he made a kind of joke of it. But when he came home from the war alone, I think she felt—well, I probably shouldn't say this, but if only one of them was going to come back, it should have been Joe."

THE NEXT MORNING, his mother asked him to come to church with the rest of the family. He hadn't gone for months, not since declaring his atheism, but he softened when she said, "I can't do this alone." She did not have to explain what *this* was. There was a sense of unhappiness dragging at the family, stemming from his father's desolation. It had fallen mainly to her—to the engine of her brisk English cheerfulness— to lift them back to normal.

They took their usual pew on the main aisle, about halfway to the altar. When the choir entered in their red robes, Joe looked automatically for his mother—he had done this since he was a boy—and watched as she sat, her posture self-consciously erect. Her air of weary concern had lessened a little, he thought. She had tilted her face upward and seemed to be hearkening to a kind of call that came from the old dark rafters, where the Union Jack and the banner of Saint George hung, and from the altar with its white embroidered cloth and tall candles and fretted golden cross. To Joe's surprise, he found himself moved—first by his mother's bearing and then by the church itself, warm and welcoming and all but full on this bright winter morning.

Penny and Jamie knelt beside him on the thin prayer board, worn into shallow hollows by the pressure of countless knees. Their father knelt at the end of the pew. Joe had often felt there was something out of place about his father here—his badly knotted tie, his stare of fathomless abstraction—but today this quality had deepened, as if his father, for all his trying, would never fit in. Joe felt pity, and remembering what his mother had said—that before the war, his father had been a different person—he kept glancing along the pew, as if he could find in the way his father held the prayer book, or absently turned a page, some trace of the happier, more talkative man he had once been. As the phrases of the general confession sounded around them, Penny sang out the responses almost rapturously. But Joe, aware of his father's silence, kept silent too.

Almighty and most merciful father, we have erred and strayed from thy ways like lost sheep. We have followed too much the devices and desires of our own hearts. We have offended against the holy laws. O Lord, have mercy upon us miserable offenders. Spare thou them, O God, which confess their faults.

Emerging from the church, they blinked in the snow glare, unused to the superior brightness of the outside world. Icicles dripped from the church eaves and the parking lot was flooded with exhaust fumes, billowing like cumulus in the warming air. Back home, Joe found himself thinking of Anna Macrimmon, though with some reluctance—it was like bringing her into a sad, squalid place that must make her think less of him. Yet he kept sensing her, up there on the hill, in her house with the white porch, a reminder that his life belonged, or might belong, to places other than this house with its chipped baseboards and stink of Brussels sprouts and deepening atmosphere of defeat. He wanted to be rid of his parents, whose troubles were not his. What did he have to do with his father's sadness or his mother's searching gaze, which seemed to beg of him a solution he could never deliver?

The next morning he put on his best slacks and cardigan, as well as the suede jacket with the knit sleeves, which after the Niagara trip had come back smelling faintly of Anna, and climbed the hill to school. It was another blazing white winter day, painful on the eyes, and in the dimness of the corridors he was momentarily unable to identify anything. The other students drifted like shadows amid the slamming of lockers. But his vision had adjusted by the time Anna came. Elated, he watched her feel her way down the stairs, in her cloak and tam.

"Joe, is that you? This light—" Smiling, she grasped his arm. "I wonder if this is what Hades is like," she said.

"I don't know," he said, his heart thudding. "I've never been."

She laughed briefly and let go of his arm and was about to pass on, when she added, in a quieter voice, "Joe, have you given any thought to the Christmas formal?" She spoke with a lilt he recognized as flirtatious. "Have you thought about taking anybody?"

He shook his head, but he was lying. He had thought of asking *her* but had abandoned the idea because of course she had forbidden any such thing, and anyway, he had to assume she was going with Brad. She touched his arm again, letting her fingers linger. "I was thinking it might be nice if you asked Liz. I shouldn't say this, but I know she's dying for you to ask her."

She was manipulating him, using her power over him to get something he himself might not want. He was a little taken aback, for he had held her morally above him, above all of them; she might know moments of weakness, but she was good—frank and kind and open—and everything she did, her slightest gesture, from smiling to reading an essay, was touched with rightness. He felt a flash of anger at her, for letting him down. Yet later in the day he talked to Liz. Her beautiful made-up eyes fixed his intently. "I'd love to go with you," she said, with a quiet directness that surprised him. He was more pleased than he expected: Liz McVey was attractive, and besides, by taking her, he would be close to Anna, whom he assumed was going with Brad. He would ask her to dance. His plan came to him with a leap of excitement—he would take her onto the floor, put his hand into the curve of her back. . . .

That afternoon Anna fell in beside him as they walked to Biology.

"Well, you've made one girl very happy."

"Who, you?" he said coldly. He had not quite forgiven her.

"Well, yes, me," she said. Her face reddened. "But you know who I mean. I hope you're not angry with me."

"It'll cost you," he said. "You have to promise me at least once dance." He dared to add, "A slow one."

She stopped abruptly, so that he had to turn back to her.

"I haven't told you, have I? I'm not going to the dance, Joe."

She was going with her parents on a Mediterranean cruise over the holidays. They would fly to New York and on to Lisbon. Then by ship past Gibraltar, Barcelona, Marseilles, Rome. He listened to her itinerary with a sinking heart. She had come from over there, and he had always feared that Europe might one day reclaim her. He was almost more jealous of Europe than of Brad Long.

He thought of breaking his date with Liz, but in the end he went ahead in a spirit of defiance. He would do it, but he would do it his way. He paid $2.50 for a corsage at Mills' and drove up the hill in the Biscayne, its front left fender bearing a fresh dent caused by his father's skid into a tree. He was not in the least embarrassed by the car; something in him was almost daring Liz, the whole world, to find fault with him. She wore a thin-strapped gown of black velvet and long matching gloves that she peeled off halfway through the evening and stuffed in the pocket of his rented tux. By ten o'clock she had wrapped both arms around his neck. They swayed in place, barely moving, while candles quivered at the perimeter tables and the Morganaires in their baby-blue jackets and frilly shirts stood up as one, their horns filling the dark with a swelling ballad.

Afterward, in the Biscayne, they necked in the school parking lot until their mouths were sore, and when he moved to touch her breasts it was Liz who suggested they go somewhere more comfortable.

She took charge so easily, he was sure she had done all this before—with Bobby the salesman, no doubt—but he had no jealousy of Bobby for he felt no particular claim on Liz other than the claim of pleasure. She guided them to Johnsonville, to a double-decker motel built around a pool filled with logs and snow. He found their room nice, tasteful, and far superior to anything he knew at home, with its twin beds, a painting of sailboats on the wall, a single lamp shedding a warm light over the flowered spread. "I'll be out in a minute," she told him, kissing him before she slipped off to the bathroom. Her theatrical look—eyes flashing meaningfully at him—made him feel he was taking part in a play. A moment later, turning to undo his tie and stiff collar, he was swept with doubt. What was he doing here? He wasn't sure he even liked Liz McVey. Just being with her, especially here, was a kind of lie. He went on undressing, though. From the bathroom came the sound of running water. When it stopped, he heard the familiar words of a Christmas carol seeping through the wall from a TV or radio in the next room. *Silent night. Holy night.* Sung in a high, clear, inviolate voice: a boy's.

23

"SEE, IT SAYS Crazy Horse. 'Crazy Horse grew up in a Sigh-Ox village,'" Jamie read, hesitating only a little on the hard words, "'on the Great Plains.' Can you read that?"

On the bench beside him, in the Children's Room of the library, Billy was grinning his grin that was not really a grin, showing his brown-edged teeth. They were alone.

"Try to read that."

"Crazy Horse," Billy said, giggling as if it were a great joke. Jamie was trying to teach him to read. One day they had met Billy's mother on the street, and seeing that Jamie had a book and Billy had none, she had said, "I wish you could get Billy here to read—get him out of that class with the dumbies." So he'd taken Billy to the library. Billy had just looked at the spines of the books on the shelves and then started walking on the benches, as if that was more interesting. So Jamie thought he'd find him a book he might like. *The Story of Crazy Horse* was one of Jamie's own favorites. But all Billy did was flip through, look at the pictures, and start balancing on the benches again. So Jamie read it to him in the hopes he'd get interested. "Read that!" he said, pointing. "Read the next sentence. It's really a good story." Billy stared where he was pointing, and his grin got more fixed. He pushed the book away.

"What's the matter?"

"I don't feel like it."

They went outside, into the slowly falling snow. At the corner, Billy said, "I got you a present."

"What?"

Billy wrestled inside his windbreaker and dragged out the Crazy Horse book in its clear plastic wrapper.

"You took this book?"

"It's for you," Billy said, in his flat voice. "I hooked it," he added, still grinning, and Jamie remembered the chocolate marshmallow cookies Billy had hooked the day before, from Kinnear's store. They'd eaten them at the rock in the Indian Trail.

"You don't have to hook things in the library. They're free. You can take anything you want. You just show them your card."

Billy grinned again. Okay, he knew that!

Jamie took the book from Billy, explaining he'd already read it, put it inside his coat, and returned it to the Children's Room. When he came out, Billy was throwing snowballs at a stop sign. They started across the road, and it was then, looking south toward Water, that Jamie saw his mother. She was crossing Water, marching briskly along in her gray coat, her arms filled with groceries. All she had to do was glance to her right and she'd see him with Billy. His father had seen him with Billy, one day on the main street, and had winked at him as if their being together was a kind of joke. It would be different with his mother. To her, wrong was on one side and right was on the other, and she never hesitated to tell him which was which. And he himself wasn't entirely sure he ought to be with Billy. He hadn't felt good about those cookies. But he had no other friends, and besides, Billy wouldn't leave him alone. He stuck to Jamie like glue.

He took a step back, to get out of her line of sight, then another. Billy grinned.

"What you doing?"

"Nothing. Walking backward."

Billy took a couple of steps backward himself.

They went along Bridge Street to the bridge and looked down at the streaming black water, at the weeds bending under its surface, and up the river past the dam to the rail trestle where a string of boxcars was rumbling against an empty sky. "We're Sigh-Ox Indians," Jamie said.

"Okay."

"You can be Crazy Horse, because you're the real Indian."

"You want to come to my house?" Billy said.

They walked to the Flats, along Willard and Pine to Billy's. The place made Jamie sad with its lonely-echo feeling and no pictures on the walls, just a couch with a rip down the back. Billy's bed was a mattress on the floor, his toys were scattered all over, and there was a smell of pee. After a while Jamie said he had to go; he and his dad were going to buy a Christmas tree. "Are you getting a tree?" he asked, and Billy said he was going to cut one right now. They could both go and cut one, okay? And because Jamie wasn't going with his father until later that night, and because cutting a tree would get them out of the house, he agreed.

Billy brought up a hatchet from the basement, and they walked up the road, under the rail trestle and up a short street to a forest of evergreens. In the forest, which was still and peaceful, the snow poured over the tops of Jamie's boots and chilled his feet; he was beginning to wish he hadn't come. But they waded on, talking about which tree would be good to cut, and finally they picked one and Billy started hacking at it with the hatchet. Pale gashes appeared, but though he was hitting the trunk fiercely, gritting his teeth, he couldn't get much deeper than the bark. Then Jamie took a try, and it was while he was whacking away that a voice sounded beside him. He was so scared he dropped the ax. He was ready to run, but Billy just stood there, looking at a man—an old man Jamie did not know. He was smiling at them with a mouth that had no teeth. "Trying to take my treesh, are you?" he said, in a rough but not unfriendly voice. "I know yis one," he said, nodding at Billy. "Who are you?"

Jamie gave his name. The old man was wearing an open coat and a plaid shirt underneath and a cap from which his ears stuck out like handles. He said they should come with him to the house, he'd get a proper saw. Jamie wasn't sure, but Billy fell in behind the old man, following in the soft trail his boots made.

The house sat up on a small hill above the forest. Behind it stretched the open space of a gravel pit, where Jamie could see cement towers and a snowed-over line of conveyor belts. Then he was in a big kitchen, not bright and neat like his mother's but warm, with bare-wood cupboards, a kitchen table painted bright red, and an oil stove with slits in its side that reminded him of catfish gills. The old man told them to take their boots off and sit down at the table. While the old man was rummaging in a cupboard, Billy leaned across the table and said to Jamie, "We'll get candy."

"Did I hear something about candy?" the old man said. He had taken off his cap, and his hair was as white as the snow.

He came back with a big glass jar full of different kinds of candy: jawbreakers and licorice and others wrapped in twists of foil. The old man set the jar on the table and said to Billy, "So. Shall we tell him our little game?"

"You take your pants down and he feels your dick and then you get the candy. Sometimes he sucks it. Then you get three candies."

Jamie wondered: Sucks the candy?

"I don't do anything you don't want," the old man said to Jamie. His smile had changed, he had teeth now, yellow teeth as straight as the boards in a fence. Jamie felt his face go hot and the old man giggled and said, "I think Billy here should go first, to show how it's done. Okay, Billy?"

Billy jumped out of his chair and went over to a couch near the oil stove. He lay down and the old man went over and sat beside him on the couch. "It's just a little game," he said to Jamie. "It feels nice. Why don't you come over here and look?"

Jamie didn't want to, but when the old man winked at him and gestured for him to come, he went. He stood beside the old man as he reached out his big lumpy hands and pulled down Billy's trousers. He thought of being in the doctor's office when Dr. Carr looked at his dink, carefully pulling back the skin, and he thought of when Carol Jenkins and her friend Chrissy Bell had pulled his pants down in Carol's outhouse and had hardly been able to stop laughing. All these other times seemed to be with him now, as he watched the old man move his crooked fingers very gently over Billy's thing, pulling and stroking it the same way he, Jamie, sometimes pulled and stroked Red's ear, feeling its smoothness. "There there there," the old man said (he had hair in his ears and even sticking out of his nose, Jamie saw) and he seemed almost to be singing, crooning like a mother to a crying baby, though Billy wasn't crying, he was grinning up at Jamie as if he considered the whole business rather silly. Then he stopped grinning and his eyes went far away, blank.

"See, that's all there is to it," the old man said suddenly, looking around at Jamie. "You want to try?"

"Aren't you gonna suck it?" Billy said.

"Not today, you rascal." The old man snapped the band of Billy's underwear. "You get yourself a candy or two. Just call me the Candy Man." He winked again at Jamie.

Billy pulled up his pants and got off the couch. The old man had turned to Jamie now with a friendly smile, showing his board-straight teeth. "Nothing to it," he said.

"He's chicken," Billy said, walking back to the table.

The old man patted the couch.

"Just hop on," he said.

Jamie lay down on the couch. He looked at the ceiling and at the old man's long chin with its spiky stubble and felt his pants being drawn down. When the old man said, "Just raise your hips a little," he did, and felt his nakedness in the air. Then the big fingers touched him, and it felt nice down there, nice and smooth, except the old man's hand was a little cold, just like Dr. Carr's, and the old man was crooning over him now, as he pulled his thing. "Oh, you've got a nice one," the old man said. "That one's gonna be a real beauty," and he bent over and kissed Jamie's dink. But his stubble scraped Jamie's thigh and made him twist away and the old man pulled him back, hard, jerking him back to where he wanted him, like you'd jerk a bag of sand. Suddenly, Jamie wanted to go home. He wanted to be at the kitchen table, drinking tea milk, and his mother there and all the lights on and the house snug against the cold. But he was here, and the old man was bending to kiss him again, and everything that had been so strange and nice—the old man, the candies, the touch of his hands and even his lips—suddenly was replaced by a loneliness so big he wanted to cry.

He heard his voice say, high and strange, that he had to go, but the old man kept his face down and his dink was in the old man's mouth and there was the wet drag of something else that must have been his tongue. The thing was, down there it felt good, but down there was only a part of him now, small and far away, and in the rest of him he did not feel good; he felt cold and lonely, and he had the idea that the old man was eating him bit by bit, starting with down there, and he could do nothing about it. He studied the ceiling and the old man's head, balding and covered with scabs. He turned and looked at the little table by the couch and saw the yellow teeth sitting in a jar, grinning underwater. "I have to go," he said again, and the old man lifted his face, which was red now, and said in a coy, pleading voice, "Arn you going to help ush cut the tree?" Putting his hands over his dink (he half expected it to be bloody though he didn't check), Jamie said he was going with his father to buy a Christmas tree. So the old man got up and put in his teeth and Jamie got up and pulled up his pants, not looking down there, not even wanting to know that down there existed. He did not want candies now, but he picked one out of the jar, fake-smiling when the old man made a joke, not wanting the old man to touch him again. Before he could go out the door, the old man bent down to him. He held Jamie's shoulder with one hand and said, "Who's your father?" For a moment Jamie, distracted by Billy, who was poking away in the candy jar, not upset at all by what had happened, could not think of his father's name.

"Alf Walker," he said finally, and the old man grunted. "I wouldn't tell anybody about this if I was you," he said. "This is secret, okay?"

Jamie said okay; he would promise anything if he could just get out. He gestured to Billy, thinking they could leave together. But Billy was chewing a candy and did not respond. "We can go," Jamie said, but Billy did not seem to hear him.

"Because if you tell," the old man said, his fingers tightening hard on Jamie's shoulder, "bad things might happen. Okay?"

"Okay," Jamie said.

"Look at me," the old man said, and he looked at the old man and saw the bad things in his eyes.

Outside, he trekked through the forest of Christmas trees. The sun was just going down, a fire behind the hill across the river, and the snow was blue, and their old tracks were blue. Though he was headed home, he felt he had no home, he was just here, with a lump in his throat and a wet, loose feeling in his pants, trudging in the blue snow that spilled over his boots and went on forever.

" 'COURSE," HIS FATHER said, and his voice filled Jamie so that he seemed, almost, to be listening to himself, "when I was a kid we'd cut our own tree."

Their headlights reached up the steep, winding road of Tapper's Hill, through a forest where trees leaned out into the light from banks of ghostly snow. They were on their way to Gowan's farm, and the heater was making a sound like a toboggan scraping over rough ice.

A car appeared up ahead, its headlights flicking down.

"How come we don't now?"

His father said nothing, and Jamie knew he hadn't heard. He's sad about Uncle Pete, Jamie's mother had said. They were friends when they were boys.

"Dad?"

"What?"

"How come we don't now?"

"Don't what?"

"Cut our own tree." He thought of Billy's hatchet, bouncing off the trunk without hardly cutting it and felt again the sadness of the forest of Christmas trees outside the old man's house, in the blue, lonely snow. He shouldn't have left Billy. He wondered if he was still in the house, on the brown couch, and he saw the look in Billy's eyes when the old man touched him, his eyes going far away, not scared, but distant, as if he were somewhere where no one could ever find him.

"Well," his father said, and still he did not answer. The tires crunched over a patch of ice, and up the road a long shape bounded through the edge of the light. "A deer!" Jamie turned but whatever it was had already vanished into the jail of shadowy trees that fell toward the river. His father slowed the car, and they looked off the road where a cable hung between posts. He couldn't see the ground there, it dropped away so sharply. The deer seemed to have flown into the darkness.

"A buck! Did you see that? Did you see the antlers on him?"

His father's jacket smelled of smoke, a good smell. Jamie peered past him out the open window where the cold air now flooded in. The trunks of the trees were lit dimly up one side.

"Did you see him?"

"Yup," Jamie said. But he wasn't sure what he'd seen.

"A big boy, eh?"

"Yup."

He didn't know if he was the big boy, or the deer was, but he was glad that his father was happy. The happiness of the deer had filled the car. He hoped it would last. His father put the car in gear and they went on, through the high-piled ghostly snow.

My love is in the blue snow, the voice said. Jamie sat alert, very still. He hadn't heard the voice for a long time, though he hadn't noticed its absence until now. *My love is in the blue snow.* The voice was deeper in him than anything, even his father's voice or his own voice, and at the same time it seemed to have come from the night, lit by the car's passing lights. He waited for it to speak again, but the only sound was the roar of the heater.

24

MARGARET WATCHED AS the Reverend John Ramsay, Jack to her, picked up his tea tray by the wooden handles and placed it carefully on his desk, the bone china rattling almost musically. There was also a plate of the biscuits his sister had sent from England: Fortnum and Mason's. Just watching him put out tea, the way tea should be put out, calmed her. She felt it was something people in this country didn't understand: the measure of peace that came with doing things right, ceremoniously. Taking the right amount of time. People here slurped their tea from any old sort of mug or cup, even paper ones, as if all they cared about was slaking their thirst. But tea was hardly about thirst, she felt. It was about conversation, and restraint, and good cheer: a bulwark against the failing day.

"What have you got this year, two angels?" Jack Ramsay said, taking a chair near her. He crossed his legs, in their priestly black serge: a tidily good-looking man, with a pleased, suggestive shine in his eyes, as though his occupation as the minister of St. Paul's Anglican were not only a pleasure but a bit of a lark. He had the English talent, so welcome to her, of making an instant party, a little conspiracy of merriment.

"Both shepherds. Penny had her heart set on being an angel but—"

"Well, she is an angel," he said.

"I'll tell her that," Margaret said, "if you don't mind. She's convinced she looks quite ugly in her bathrobe. Of course what she'd really like to be is the Virgin Mary. All the girls want the Virgin. I was the same, back home."

"I never wanted to be anything but a shepherd. The angels seemed sissy to me, and as for Joseph—unimaginably embarrassing."

"Why was that?" she asked eagerly. Any talk that led them back to her childhood was a joy to her.

In the main hall outside, children were making a racket. In another ten minutes they would begin the next-to-last rehearsal for the Christmas pageant. Besides singing in the choir, Margaret was assistant director this year, which mostly involved searching for lost halos and making sure the requisite number of bodies was trooping down the aisle at the right times.

"Well, if you were Joseph," he said, "it meant you were married to Mary. The other boys wouldn't let you alone about it. Reduced more than one Joseph to tears. Married to the mother of God at thirteen, not easy!"

He shot her a twinkling look, lingering a split second longer than necessary. She enjoyed his flirtatiousness. He was married to a Canadian woman much younger than she. But Grace was childless, and though she was pretty and good-hearted, Margaret found her a bit simple. She felt she offered the minister a taste of something a little more cultured, more in the spirit of his spirit.

"We've a lovely Mary this year," she said, suddenly uncomfortable. In the hall Stella Bridgeman, the pageant director, was shouting for order.

Jack Ramsay's voice dropped a tone. "You wanted to speak to me?"

"I suppose it can wait." She glanced at the open door.

He got up to attend to the tea.

They had never talked intimately, not really; intimacy had only been implied. Far from ever mentioning her problems, she considered it a point of pride to give the impression she had none. Others might come crawling to him for help, but she and he were equals, in their English cheer. She was no longer sure she wanted to confide in him.

He handed her a cup and saucer and went to close the door.

The cup steadied her: the milky tea, its soothing fragrance. She sipped and searched in herself, to find again the impulse that had brought her here. She was not quite convinced of the purity of her motive. Perhaps she had only wanted the distraction of his company.

But he was listening, waiting, only two feet away. The paneled room with its smell of old books and mildewed Sunday-school papers had filled with the pressure of expectation.

"It's Alf," she said, concentrating on his desk—and immediately felt as if she had betrayed her husband to a process she was not sure she believed in. Already, in her mind, she was backpedaling, portraying the situation as less serious than she knew it was. "I just feel, losing his friend and all, he's in a bad way. It's been nearly three weeks since—since the funeral, and he's—he's always been a very private person."

She sipped at her tea, avoiding his eyes. She had no way to convey, did not want to convey, what lay behind her husband's silence.

"What do you mean, a bad way?"

"It's nothing specific. He's just—well, it reminds me how he was after the war. Not really himself at all. The children feel it. I suppose it'll be all right."

She shifted in the hard chair. Her time of month was coming on, and for a moment her digestive tract seemed crammed with nails. She thought all this must show in a general unattractiveness. Yes, it was a mistake to have come.

"If he'd like to drop by for a talk," he said. His tone had hollowed, professionally sympathetic now. But *he* had actually withdrawn, it seemed—which made her feel even more the pariah. "Would you like me to speak to him?"

"No, no. He'd know I—he wouldn't thank me. He's very proud," she said, and a flash of love went through her, for her husband. It was something she was not often aware of but now rediscovered as true. In her husband's isolation, which she deplored, was something else, which she did not deplore at all. He was better than all the rest, better than Jack Ramsay with his friendly chatter. "No," she said, suddenly protective. "It's all right. Just let it be, for now." And thinking she must give Jack something for his time, she managed a smile and added, "It's been helpful, though, to talk to you about it."

"Not at all," he said. "Grief," he said, and the word sounded theatrical on his lips, "can take a long time to work itself out. You have to be patient with him, pray for him. I'll pray for him."

"Thank you," she said. She had been praying for Alf, but now this mention of prayer unsettled her. Prayer was such a private thing, the words leaping and stumbling from the heart. In talking openly about it, Ramsay had turned it into something vaguely shameful.

Yet prayer, really, was a joy to her, the leap of her silent words in the dark bedroom as she lay beside her husband: an electric current of joy as fine as singing, finer. Prayer was a kind of singing. What she wanted, almost more than anything, was for Alf to know the same joy. But he had never taken kindly to her suggestions that prayer might help. She suspected he did not pray. Watching him in church, from her place in the choir, he seemed set against the place and everyone in it, his mouth not moving during the responses or hymns, his eyes fixed straight ahead without any discernible emotion. In bed, in the dark, she had no sense of him praying beside her. It was disheartening, to think he did not know this joy. But then again, perhaps he did. He was so private. And prayer was the most private thing of all.

She left Jack Ramsay's office feeling uneasy, and followed the mob of children into the church. She separated the angels from the shepherds, the shepherds from the wise men and the animals. A few lights had been turned on against the leaden day outside. She noticed Penny, slumped by herself at the end of a pew. Her daughter looked forlorn. Since the onset of the diabetes, Penny seemed more prey to these moods; Margaret was perpetually wondering if her blood sugar was all right. She picked up a shepherd's crook and approached her daughter. "Is this yours, love?" In her abstraction, Penny appeared not to recognize her. Those eyes simply looked at Margaret, out of their alien blue.

———

LATER, AT HOME, she found Alf on the bed, lying on his back with his shoes sticking out from the bottom of the spread. The top was pulled up to his chin. He had been lying there in the cold bedroom, as the light grew dim, for God only knew how long.

Changing her dress, she snapped on the light over her dresser: an act of aggression, to make him stir. After a while, he threw back the spread and sat on the edge of the bed. He was wearing his trousers and an undershirt and his hair was splayed every which way. She was hopeful, but he stayed there, scratching at his thigh. It infuriated her, the way he had given in to sadness, if that's what it was. Even more than she wanted him to talk, she wanted him to bury his sorrow like she did. She wanted him to drive it out of the house, by force of will.

"Supper will be a bit late. I just put the meat loaf in." She went past him quickly. Turning at the top of the stairs, she glanced back along the hall and saw that he had not moved. He was facing her now, his shadowed eyes agleam. It was his postwar look, definitely, when he would watch her, fueled by such a fund of dark knowledge she felt she must scream or suffocate. There had been times when she wanted to leave him, go back to England. One day she actually packed her bags and carried them as far as the front door. But leaving was no longer a possibility. There were the children, and there was something else; she was married to him in a way she had never been married at twenty-three. Over the years, like two trees twining together, their trunks had fused. Perhaps they did not belong together, perhaps their natures were wrong for each other (she had considered all such possibilities), but there it was; their marriage was a fact that had somehow made its way to the core of her being and lodged there.

She met his gaze frankly. She would not be cowed by his mood as she had been, years ago. Even though she understood nothing about what he was feeling or thinking or remembering, she refused to be cowed.

"Come down soon," she said briskly. "I'll make you tea."

25

DEEP IN THE Lincoln the transmission shuddered gently and they were floating, Joe and Liz, past the parking meters and the strolling pedestrians and the show windows with their banners announcing post-Christmas sales. That night her parents were holding a New Year's Eve party, and he and Liz were off to Johnsonville to buy her a new dress.

He was in love with the car, the luxurious sweep of the seats sheathed in tan leather, the easy tug of power as he touched the gas. This was his first time behind the wheel and he was driving almost gingerly, wary of what the car might do. It floated so smoothly, almost without a sound, yet under the wide placid hood he sensed the reserves of power, something alive, even conscious, asking to be unleashed.

On the Bridge Street bridge, he laughed out loud.

"You like it?" Liz asked, with coy triumph.

She swung one leg over the other, with a whisking sound of material rubbing, a stretch of tweed skirt emerging from the soft, falling weight of her fur coat. She might have just presented him with wings.

Her legs, shapely and exposed nearly to the thigh in rose stockings, became part of Joe's excitement, as if her body and the luxury and power of the car were one. They passed onto the Flats. He was starting to accelerate, when suddenly Vern Melling's garbage truck was in front of them, stopped by the curb as Vern and his son loaded up an old couch. The opposite lane was blocked with oncoming cars, so Joe eased the Lincoln to a stop. On the sidewalks, Bannerman's employees were streaming home for lunch. As he waited for the lane to clear, Joe saw his father. He was walking by himself, wrapped in his thoughts, it seemed, his coat flapping open, his green work shirt partly untucked, and his hair, which was long overdue for a cut at Benny's, blowing wildly. Just then Alf looked up. His face registered recognition but Joe, hardly knowing why, glanced away. A moment later, he wheeled the Lincoln around the truck.

On Willard, he accelerated, scarcely aware of Liz talking beside him. She leaned forward to twist the radio dial, and the Beach Boys wrapped them in their frantic falsettos.

On the Johnsonville Highway, Joe opened it up a little. Effortlessly, the Lincoln took the long hill and swept down the winding road that people said had once been an Indian trail: past farmhouses and gray leaning barns and low modern bungalows and Kanter's Miniature Golf and Driving Range and the skeletal towers of hydro lines, stalking away over the snowbound fields like giants, arms outstretched under a lowering sky. Nudging the gas, Joe kept checking the salt-stained asphalt unrolling behind them in the rearview mirror. He was sorry they were only going to Johnsonville. He would liked to have kept heading south indefinitely, swept along by the Beach Boys, calling from a land where everyone was young and without regrets.

JOE SAT ON a low hassock while Liz tried on dresses. She would disappear for minutes at a time into the changing room, leaving Joe and the saleslady to share an awkward silence while tepid music played so faintly it might have come from a sunken ship. Then Liz would burst from cover, striding out decisively in a new outfit, her eyes meeting his with a blazing directness, as if to say *Well?* He liked this moment, the energy she brought back to the room, and the authority she placed in him, the freedom to scan her body. They had slept together only once, but now everything they did, he felt, was leading them again to sex. His anticipation lent an excitement to each new dress and kept his interest flowing as she stood in front of the triple mirror, turning studiously this way and that, cocking her head or twisting to glance at her reflected back, while the saleslady murmured comments or leaned in discreetly to flick at a hem.

Unable to decide, Liz took two dresses. The saleslady folded them into shallow boxes, whose lids bore the slashing stylized signature *Cardy*

Brothers, tied them smartly with string, and handed the boxes to Joe. "The man's job," she said, turning up the corners of her small mouth and all of them laughed, though the remark had not been funny. Liz thanked the woman effusively and turned away.

"Aren't you going to pay?" Joe said. He had remained beside the cash register.

"Daddy pays," Liz sang to him, over her shoulder.

Joe was mortified, hoping no one had heard; he despised her for these airs. At the same time she held him with something more compelling, even, than sex. She had a power that drew him after her, and when she stopped by the perfume counter he stopped too.

"I've just had an idea," she said, touching him on the arm, making an exaggerated show of inspiration. He had a distinct sense she had planned this moment. "Why don't we take a look in the men's department?"

"I don't think—"

"Please? For me? Just a look?" She dropped her gaze to his mouth.

The men's department was even emptier than the women's. A few solitary people—half of them clerks—wandered about in the maze of counters and racks. Liz guided him to a place where shirts were arranged in armless rows, under glass. She asked a clerk to measure him. The clerk was a slim little man of about thirty, with a bright, eager-to-please expression that oppressed Joe. The world would never appreciate the service this man seemed anxious to lay at its feet. But he managed the tape with expert gentleness, and it wasn't long before Joe felt a kind of collusion with him—they both had to endure the brisk, confident stream of Liz's instructions. She draped ties across folded shirts. She called for sweaters. She cajoled Joe into trying them on. The clerk and he exchanged looks, ironic and tolerant. Women.

Yet the clothes were so fine, he half enjoyed the process, the make-believe, which was what it had become. He was pleasing her by doing this, and pleasing himself by pretending that he could afford to shop here. Yet the whole time he was aware that he had only ten dollars in his wallet, and this knowledge began increasingly to bother him; he felt he was getting into a situation that would leave him uncomfortably exposed, in the end. When she'd sent the clerk off on another errand, he told her he'd had enough.

"Couldn't we look at some trousers? I'd like to see you *complete.*"

He frowned. "Look, I don't have any money."

"We don't need money," she said, drawing her finger over his chest.

When he understood what she meant, his face burned.

"No."

"It's Christmas," she said, her baby mouth pouting.

"It's after Christmas."

"You won't let me buy you a Christmas present?" She was still lingering at his chest.

"No. I mean, I don't have anything for you."

He had just thought of this defense.

"I don't care. I just want—"

The clerk had come back and was hovering discreetly.

"We'd like to see some trousers," Liz told him.

He couldn't find the escalator, which made his escape rather awkward. He blundered around Overcoats and finally had to ask another clerk. Outside, the cold, damp air sharp with exhaust fumes hit him like a blast of sanity.

It was nearly ten minutes before she appeared. Under one arm were the two dress boxes. Hanging from the opposite hand was a large bag, also bearing the store's logo. She marched grimly past and when she got to the car she stood for him to open the door for her, on the driver's side. She flung the packages onto the backseat, slid in behind the wheel, and pushed the key into the ignition. The Lincoln roared. He half expected it to take off without him.

But she waited. He got in and slammed the door. Neither of them spoke.

She drove too fast, with a fierce competence. He was the first to break the silence.

"Did you buy those things anyway?"

She was steering almost carelessly, the fingers of one hand at the bottom of the wheel, chin lifted.

He stretched over the back of the seat, for the bag. It was just out of reach.

"You did, didn't you?"

"I'll buy what I like," she said.

"Sure. But I won't wear them."

They were at a standoff. They sped past the School for the Blind, past the vast, rolling lawns covered with snow, the great maples and spruce. As a child, he had wondered how the blind children managed to avoid running into the trees. He had practiced being blind, by closing his eyes and feeling his way around the backyard.

They were in the outskirts of the city, with the open fields ahead. The speedometer touched 75.

"Slow down," he told her. She ignored him.

He settled into a stoic silence, hating her. Mercifully, the road was bare, though banks of frozen snow often obscured the view on both sides and the shoulders had all but disappeared. He glimpsed a sway-backed cow, standing in miserable immobility beside a steaming manure pile. He decided they were finished, he and Liz. He would tell her when they got home.

She was doing 80 now.

"C'mon, slow down," he told her. "It's not worth this."

She glanced at him with such cold, penetrating appraisal that he felt she had casually leaned across the seat and stuck a knife in his arm. At that moment the Lincoln, drifting to the right, scraped a snowbank and lurched back onto the road. "Liz!" he shouted. A hundred yards farther on she ran the car into the parking lot of a garage where a line of new cars sat blanketed in snow. They sat in silence.

He realized she was weeping, a thread of eyeliner darkened her cheek.

"Why did you do that?" he said. "I mean, for a few shirts?"

"I knew what I was doing." All her patina of sophistication had crumbled.

"You could have rolled us, back there."

"I didn't," she said. He had come up against her will, childish and stubborn and dark. A deep weariness seeped into his limbs. "What were you trying to prove?" he said, rousing himself.

She glanced at him: a little girl now, sulky.

"All right," he said gently. "Maybe I should drive."

He got out and circled to the driver's side, while she moved over. Before he could start the car she slid back to him and burrowed into his shoulder. She sought out his mouth with her own. At first he resisted but she caught his wrist and drew his hand between her legs. He worked aside her soaked panties while she moaned extravagantly and tore at his hair. In the end, she huddled against him with her ruined face, sniffling and saying she was sorry.

THAT NIGHT, HIS parents drove to a Couples' Club party at the church. Joe walked up the hill to Liz's house, where he was soon put to work behind the bar, near the floor-length windows that overlooked the snowbound patio. A decorated fir tree towered in the opposite corner, a fairy-tale mountain of white lights and golden globes topped by a golden angel with open wings of fretted gold, its mild face lifted as if toward a greater though invisible glory. The room was crowded, voices bubbling everywhere, and he was kept busy pouring wine and rye or scrambling to concoct fancier drinks, Manhattans and Brown Cows, one eye on the chart pinned behind the bar.

He was drinking steadily himself—beer—and soon felt buoyed by a pleasant tide of sociability. Familiar melodies from decades past rose from the hi-fi, carried on the harmonies of the Ray Conniff Singers. Through the doorway to the kitchen, he could see Liz, in her new dress of off-white silky stuff, talking to an older woman who kept touching her arm. Just by raising the fingers of his left hand to his nose, he could smell her: an earthy tang that soap had not erased.

"Oh, Joe!" Liz's mother, Mary, was approaching the bar, her brown eyes fixed on his with their habitual look of fractured but still game hope. In the bottom of her glass a lemon rind lay like a wasted flower.

Already that evening he had made her three gin and tonics; she'd been behaving noticeably less matronly with him, oddly younger. He thought of Doc McVey's girlfriend, Babs Wilcocks. In town people said that she and Mary McVey had found a way to live with each other, and he wondered if Babs Wilcocks would turn up at the party. Something in this thought, something about the mere *existence* of Babs Wilcocks, excited him. Anything seemed possible this evening. Below the steady hubbub of the party, a kind of subterranean energy was roiling.

Mary was towing an old woman with a shallow cap of thin bluish hair. A dot of cheese dip had lodged at the corner of her mouth.

"Marjorie, this is Joe, Liz's new beau." Mary seemed to love the word *beau,* with its hint of a life more gallant and risqué. All evening she'd been introducing him this way, as if the engagement ring were already on Liz's finger.

"So this is the young man."

"I've been thinking of running off with him myself," Mary said, looking straight at Joe. He dropped his gaze—there was some line she was crossing. Marjorie laughed with exaggerated glee, showing the gum ridge of her false teeth. "Maybe you'll have to compete with me," she said.

The women left. Joe wiped down the bar. He didn't feel he was Liz's beau (whatever that meant), but at least being presented that way made it impossible for him to be mistaken as the bartender, which pleased him. He hadn't come up the hill as a servant, but as practically a family member. He was enjoying himself, enjoying with an almost proprietorial ease the refined, spreading rooms of this house, owned by the town's richest man, enjoying the welcome of the town's best people—doctors and lawyers and businessmen and Bannerman's executives and of course their wives, done up to the nines in silky sheath dresses, their hair shaped in wavy bobs and high bouffants. He was enjoying being spoken to so familiarly by all of them, as if it were the most natural thing in the world to find him here. Even when someone said, "Oh, you're Alf Walker's son," the little tremor of misgiving he felt was answered by no hint of condescension or disapproval. His presence as Liz's boyfriend made him one of them.

Liz came down from the kitchen.

"Darling, I'm sorry about this."

Tonight, he didn't even mind her theatrical *darling*. The party was all drama, in a way.

"Sorry about what?"

"Having to meet all these people."

"I like it. I like your mother," he said, spying her across the room. Mary McVey had a large low-set bosom, nested under dark blue silk; he watched it as she put back her head to laugh.

"I think I'm jealous."

"You should be." And for a split second he intuited a place—exciting and ill-defined—where both her mother and she were his. He looked pointedly at the deep slit in the bodice of Liz's dress.

"Why don't we lie down behind the bar?" he said, deadpan.

He sensed that she, too, was inflamed.

Then her mother was there again. "I'm going to take him from you," Mary announced. She reached out and took Joe's hand into hers.

"Oh, Mother."

Mary squeezed Joe's hand and held it tight. Hers was surprisingly soft but cold, too, as if she'd been keeping it in a snowbank. "Don't listen to her," Mary told him. "Seriously now, Joe. Do you like older women? I think you do."

"Mother," Liz hissed, in a fierce undertone.

"Sure," Joe said. But this was too much. He managed to extract his hand.

Mary wandered off, strangely out of place at her own party. She bumped into a man in a garish orange sports jacket and veered away. Bing Crosby was skating effortlessly through "White Christmas."

Liz said, "I think you better cut back on her gin."

Liz was being awfully attentive to him following their drive back from Johnsonville. Perhaps she was beginning to fall in love with him. He felt remorseful, a bit of a fraud, and yet he felt so good, being there, flooded with goodwill. Leaning forward impulsively, he kissed her on the mouth and told her she was beautiful. And she was. As she looked up at him, testing his words, her beauty struck through to him, and he remembered how the small globes of her breasts had pressed against his chest in the motel. There was a hunger in Liz McVey's wiry body, as genuine and convincing as her social manner was false—a frank hunger that suggested danger and aroused him.

Her sister called her away just then, to see about the food, and he surveyed the crowded room with a fresh surge of excitement, thinking about the next time he and Liz might be alone together. A few minutes later Mary came back, drawing behind her a man with a bald, darkly tanned head and a look in his eyes of sharp, confident inquiry. Joe had noticed the man earlier, when Mary introduced him to her husband. His name, she told Joe, was Bob Prince. She had known him at school, in Toronto, and now by coincidence he was working in Attawan.

Joe took the man's hand and felt the shock of a hard, willful strength. As the pale blue eyes met his, Joe thought of his father.

"He's going to university next year," Mary said of Joe. "And when he graduates, we're going to run away together."

"Oh-ho!" Bob Prince said, in an effortless voice. He asked Joe what university he was headed for. Mary, who had been beaming at Joe as at a prize child, was called to the kitchen.

"Are you doing a general BA or—"

"I'll be majoring in history."

"Good. Good. Great preparation."

"Preparation?"

"For going on. Business. Law. What are you planning to do?" Bob Prince said genially.

"Just study history," Joe said, wiping at the bar. "Maybe teach, teach university. I don't really care for business."

This just came out, a flash of defiance. He sensed he was attacking the other man and that this showed him up as gauche. But he had taken an instant dislike to him; it was his polish, his smoothness, his irresistible voice, which under the velvet carried a suggestion of plate metal. He made Joe feel insecure.

Bob Prince darted a glance at Joe from his superior height—he must have stood about six-four—apparently amused. "And what's wrong with business?"

Joe shook his head. His contact with business was pretty limited; he wasn't quite sure how he'd come to think it was a second-rate activity, not really a profession at all. The men he thought of as businessmen— the manager of the A&P, Scott Dowd, or the various bosses he'd observed at Bannerman's, seemed perpetually consumed by trivialities, lost orders, and deadlines—tearing their hair out over matters that couldn't be worth it. Then there were the owners of stores on the main street and the men who came door to door, selling brushes; what struck him most about them was their false friendliness. Yes, business meant selling things, and that meant turning yourself, he thought, into a glad-handing phony.

"Just not attracted to it," Joe said, with another shrug. "Fumbling in the greasy till—"

"Those are interesting words."

"They're from a poem," Joe said. Anna Macrimmon had showed it to him one day in the library.

"I take it you're a socialist, then."

Joe shrugged, allowing that he was.

"Tax the rich and give to the poor, like Robin Hood."

"Something like that."

"The rich who've taken all the risks."

"You think poor people don't take risks?" Joe had heard his history teacher, Archie Mann, make this argument and had adopted it as his own. He went on. "A poor man puts his health, his body on the line, every time he goes to work. That's his capital, and he's risking it. If he loses it, he loses a lot more than some rich guy who drops ten thousand bucks he can afford to play around with."

Bob Prince laughed, a little too tolerantly, Joe thought. Joe's face was flushed. He was astonished at himself, his vehemence. He was not sure the other man was taking him seriously.

Bob Prince said, "But you're willing to enjoy the fruits of another's labors." He gestured in a general way with his scotch glass, indicating the room, with its deep white couches and chairs, the splendid tree, the fire licking happily behind glass. His gesture took in the whole house and, somewhere deep in the house, Liz McVey—or at least it seemed that way to Joe. He felt the contradiction at the core of his own argument and disliked Bob Prince for putting his finger on it with such casual accuracy.

He said, "I don't know. Is making money on the stock market labor?"

Bob Prince was shaking his head and grinning.

"I think we should all share, more fairly," Joe said stubbornly.

"You'd like to live like they live in Russia?"

"No," Joe said. "They're not free in Russia. But at least they've grasped a certain principle."

They sparred like this while Joe continued wiping at the counter with a rag, like a real bartender, though without the neutral equanimity. He was convinced that the other man was humoring him and this made him even angrier. After a while Doc McVey drifted over to refresh his scotch. Behind his glasses, his babyish face seemed always on the verge of laughter, as if the world were a source of perpetual amusement: only a fool would take it seriously.

"So, Bob, is our bartender giving you a hard time?"

"First communist bartender I ever met, Jack," Bob Prince said.

Doc McVey's loose mouth opened wider, happily.

"I'm not a communist," Joe said sullenly. He felt he was becoming an object of fun. The way they called each other Bob and Jack, with a pointed country-club familiarity, as if they had known each other for years, annoyed him.

"Communist, socialist," Bob Prince said, waving his glass. "Same thing."

Joe remained silent, refusing to be baited. He was convinced that Bob Prince, whatever his cleverness at making money, was essentially stupid. There was something blunt about him that made subtlety impossible.

"So when does the revolution start?" Doc McVey said.

"In ten minutes," Joe said. "You're all being taken to the basement and shot. Then your bodies will be dragged outside and burned."

Of course it was a joke, but there was a savagery in his remark that he instantly regretted. The difficult moment was quickly covered by the older men, who laughed indulgently and drifted away, but Joe, his face burning, felt he'd been hopelessly crude.

He stayed to the end, though, stayed through the uproar at midnight when everyone blew horns and kissed and on the TV Guy Lombardo and his Royal Canadians played "Auld Lang Syne," over the images of throngs packing Times Square. Just as the melee was subsiding, Mary found him and, pressing her body against his, kissed him hard. The quick darting of her tongue alarmed him and he gently extracted himself, but a minute later, remembering her soft mouth—the hint of experience beyond anything he had known—he became so excited he had to sit down.

Later, when the last guest had left, Liz asked him to come to the family room, where her mother and father were. She retrieved two packages from under the tree and held them out for him. "Your payment for tending bar so well. And because I like you."

"We all like you," Mary said, slurring a little. She was slumped beside the fireplace, in a wing chair, staring at his chest. Doc McVey stood at the window with his back to them. Out in the yard, a solitary black tree leaned into the floodlit space above the patio, releasing a few clots of windblown snow.

Joe took the packages, beautifully wrapped in gold paper. He could feel the flat softness of the sweater, the stiff horseshoes of shirt collars.

For a second he hesitated; something passed through him, leaving only a metallic taste, an emptiness.

Liz was beaming, a bit frantically, while Mary smiled sleepily to herself in her chair. Beyond Liz's shoulder, her father continued to watch the floodlit yard.

"For you, darling," Liz said.

In her chair, Mary clapped her hands rapidly, like a child.

26

IT WAS AFTER two when he got back to the Island. He found his father in the kitchen, standing with his back to the stove in his plaid dressing gown, which had sagged open to reveal the unbuttoned top of his pajamas, a scrawl of hair on his pale chest. He was drinking a bottle of beer. Something about him—his sunken eyes, with their aggressive glint, watching him sourly—put Joe's back up. He brushed past with his bag of presents.

"So how's life in the palace?" his father said.

"Better than here," Joe said. Why wouldn't the man just leave him alone?

"What did you say?"

Joe didn't bother responding. He had almost reached the door to the hall.

"Hey, you!"

He kept going.

"Stop!"

He stopped, let out an exaggerated sigh—this was nonsense—and turned to meet the man shuffling across the floor toward him. He knew he'd gone too far, knew it by an old yet familiar fear slipping through his chest like cold water.

He stared back, lifting his face.

"What did you say?" his father asked again.

"I think you heard me."

"So you think you're too good for us now, is that it?"

"Oh, God," Joe said, starting to turn away.

As his father gripped his arm, Joe tried to shove him away. They were at it in a second, slapping and pushing almost awkwardly, scuffling around the floor. Often, over the years, they had fought for the pleasure of it: wrestled or boxed on the living-room rug or in the backyard. But

they had never fought in anger, never set out to hurt each other. Even
now they were held back by old constraints, not quite sure what to do
with the energy surging into their arms. But the fury was real enough. It
had come up so fast it seemed to have been waiting in some deep well
where the resentments and rivalries and sheer hellbent love of chaos had
been put away over the years. Finally immobilizing each other in a tangle
of arms—in some part of their brains they knew it was less dangerous to
wrestle than to box—they crashed to the floor. The table went skidding.
The butter dish landed on a chair. They rolled together in a wave of tartan bathrobe, and Joe felt the soft flop of his father's genitals against his
leg. He shoved his father's head against the fridge. Outside, Red, waking
in his den under the back porch, put back his big head and howled into
the wraiths of snow drifting from Lookout Hill.

Then Joe's mother was there, shrieking for them to stop. "Is this who
we are?" she kept crying. She was almost singing, in a wild new voice,
tremulous and high. "Is this who we are?"

Beyond his father's head, Joe saw her shins, nicked by a razor.

"All right, fella," his father said hoarsely. They were lying locked on
their sides, in grim equilibrium, their faces inches apart. Joe could smell
the beer on his father's breath, the stink of his father's unhappiness.
"Let's get up," his father said.

Joe extracted himself, avoiding his father's eyes. As far as he was concerned, the other man no longer existed. This house no longer existed.
He was through.

A COUPLE OF days later, Joe found his mother vacuuming in his
room. "There's a letter for you," she told him, nodding at his desk,
where she'd propped up a small envelope with unfamiliar black-and-
orange stamps. Joe carried it down the hall to the bathroom, locked the
door, and sat on the lowered toilet seat to open it, in the steamy aftermath of someone's shower. It contained two sheets of blue airmail
paper, covered on both sides with Anna's scrawling hand.

Dear Joe,

I'm sitting on the deck of the S.S. *Independence*. We're sailing east, toward Italy. Yesterday we had a day in Cannes, the best so far. We had lunch in a little place called Pont-du-Loup, just outside town: red-tiled roofs and white facades and long green shutters, under bushy hills rising to cliffs. The country is rough but also beautiful. You wouldn't think people could live in it, I mean, as well as they do. The towns are wonderful, so many hills, so many views of the sea taking you by surprise. I'm looking at it now (the sea) where it hazes off toward Corsica (which I can't see) and Africa somewhere beyond that. I've always loved the idea of the Mediterranean, and now that I'm here again, it's wonderful.

Mom and Dad rented a car, and we went exploring in the hills. Father Campion came with us. He's American, a priest we met on the ship, and the best company—a great storyteller. He doesn't wear his collar on holiday, looks more like a retired businessman. He's plump, with a twinkle in eyes that, when you look closer, are as sharp as knives. He enjoys his food more than anybody I've ever met and loves to talk about it. When he picks up his wineglass he's likely to take ten minutes telling you where the wine comes from (he seems to have visited a million vineyards) right down to the exact hill. He says he's in love with me, and he's very gallant, but since he's sixty-something it's really just a game. I tease him and tell him he's not really a priest. Dad says he's probably having such a good time because we aren't Catholic.

While he and Mom and Dad were visiting a winery, I went for a walk. I climbed a hill and went through some fields. I met a shepherd. My first shepherd! He had a dog, and his sheep were milling around at the edge of a field where he sat eating his lunch on an old stone. (I guess all stones are old, but this one looked older.) Actually, the dog saw me first and came barking, till the shepherd called him off. We had quite a conversation, at least what I understood of it. The old kind of French they speak here is pretty strange. The sheep kept putting in their two cents. He might have been fifty or younger, but he had an unbelievably leathery face. He told me he'd been a shepherd all his life, ever since he was twelve, when his father took him out of school. I asked him if he'd wanted to leave school, and he went quiet. I felt no one had ever asked him this before, and he didn't know what to say. We were both embarrassed. But of course, being me, I couldn't let him off the hook—I mean, I didn't say anything to help him out. There's a part of me that would be cool in a train crash, I think, just watching to see what happens. I felt the sadness of his life, and something more than that: his fate, maybe. The shape his life had taken.

I wonder if people have fates anymore, or do they just have careers? Is everyone's life now so much like everyone else's, so bland and pre-dictable, that a real fate can't happen? Or do we just pretend we don't have fates—but they happen anyway, in a backdoor sort of way. No two fates are alike, and I think that's why we're afraid of our own. It means we have to embrace our aloneness, our uniqueness, and as much as we might say we want to do that, really, we're scared. Better to be like everybody else and not stick out too much. So life misses us.

In the end, he just shrugged. It was like he'd said, "This is how things are. No use regretting." He gave me some wine, in a thick little tumbler.

I saw three dolphins this morning.

Tomorrow, Italy: Livorno, Rome, Naples.

Thinking of you warmly,

Anna.

He read it three times. The thin paper seemed fabulous in its blue-ness, as if at any moment her dolphins might rise from its depths.

LIKE A SUDDEN influx of fresh air after weeks indoors, the letter intoxicated him, as if she were holding out the promise of a finer life; as if the landscape she had described—the blue Mediterranean glimmering at every turn—had sent its ranges and peninsulas into his own existence and he was already wandering with her, in a partnership he could not clearly fantasize, for he had known nothing like it before. He stared at the edge of the bathroom sink, where a single plastered hair appeared like a crack in the porcelain, and wondered if the letter didn't mark a sea change in her attitude to him (wasn't there some hint of it in that phrase *thinking of you warmly*)? At the same time, applying the lash of common sense, he told himself there was nothing there but friendship.

But just that she had thought of him, over there, that she had sat on the deck of a great ship and aimed these words at him! She had reached across the world to create this space inhabited by only the two of them. At the same time, her letter reminded him by contrast of his relationship with Liz, which every day seemed more false. In the past few days he had spent a lot of time at her house, he had driven around in her father's Lincoln, and yet he knew his link with her was temporary and even dishonest, because the truth was, as much as he enjoyed her physically—and really, he couldn't get enough of her in that regard—he had to admit to himself (and he saw this in the clarity Anna's letter had brought) he didn't *like* Liz McVey very much. The thought that Anna would come home and find him with her ignited an obscure shame.

The next Saturday he and Liz drove over to Johnsonville in the Lincoln to see a movie. All evening he kept meaning to tell her they were finished, and all evening he kept postponing the confrontation, though he managed to hold himself a little aloof. She must have sensed something was wrong, because she was even more attentive than usual, constantly touching his arm in the dark theater, keying her laughter to his. Later, in the car, she asked if he wanted to go to the motel. He'd been planning to deny himself that pleasure but found himself helpless when she started to kiss him. In bed, his excitement was extreme. But immediately afterward, he regretted the tawdry room, the vapid sailboats on the wall, her crouching nakedness as she washed herself in the long tub. They drove back to Attawan in silence.

27

ONE SUNDAY, SMILEY dropped by the house with his skates and stick. Joe was taken by surprise; he hadn't seen Smiley for some weeks, not since he'd dropped out of school and gone to work in Bannerman's dyehouse. But here he was, just like old times, planted on the kitchen doormat in his rolled-down rubber boots and bright blue-and-white hockey jacket, announcing that the Atta was frozen solid right up to the first rapids. Such perfect skating conditions hadn't been seen in years. There was no snow to shovel off, and the ice, Smiley said, making Jamie laugh with pleasure, was as smooth as a baby's bottom.

Joe leaped at the chance. He felt as if his old life—before the arrival of Anna Macrimmon and the complication of Liz McVey—had returned, offering him the chance of a forgotten, uncomplicated happiness. Penny and Jamie wanted to go too, so there was a general rush to dig out skates and toques and hockey sticks. They were nearly ready to leave when Joe's father appeared from the cellar, carrying his ancient stick and the battered skates with long, thin blades that Joe hadn't seen him wear for years. Penny and Jamie danced around him: Daddy was going skating! But Joe, standing by the door with Smiley, felt that the day had been stolen from him. In the days since their fight, his relations with his father had existed in a state of suspension. They were friendly enough, in a formal, superficial way, but Joe sensed that each of them was waiting for the other to make the next move—whether it would be toward reconciliation or fresh hostilities, he couldn't say. Just now, his father's gloomy face—smiling wanly at the young ones—seemed like the specter at the feast. There could be no joy around *him*. At that moment his father looked at him and—to Joe's complete surprise—winked. Instantly, something in him started, gladdened.

They set off in a noisy gang. Margaret, who had never learned to skate, watched them go out the door. "Don't fall in," she said dryly. Smiley promised her he'd keep an eye on everybody.

Behind Bannerman's old hosiery mill on West Street, they descended to the millpond formed by a dam across the Atta. Out on the wide ice, a dozen men and boys were playing shinny, gusting here and there like a flock of windblown starlings under the cloudless sky. They sat on logs to put on their skates. Joe and his father helped Jamie and Penny. Then the two of them sat side by side, lacing up with numb fingers.

"So you think you've forgotten how?" Joe teased.

His father did not respond. His fingers were attacking his laces fiercely, with what might have been anger. Joe felt the shadow of their antagonism.

Then Alf finished and picked up his stick. As he skated away, he tossed back a challenge—"No one catches the old man"—and the day was made whole again. Joe watched him skate toward the other players with slow, lazy strokes, accelerating suddenly for a step or two, his head down, then stroking easily again, rocking slightly as he sped along. He looked so natural, even more natural than he did walking down the street, as if all his life was an exile from the easy freedom of ice.

Joe followed a minute later. Smiley had dropped a puck, and he and Jamie and Joe's father were passing it back and forth. Joe streaked upriver. "Hey, Walker!" he shouted, and his father looked up and saw him. Joe took his pass close to his feet, lost it for a moment, then circled back with the puck, floating an easy pass to his brother. Jamie fanned and promptly landed on his back.

Joe was exhilarated by the expanse of ice. He felt he could do anything out here—wheel, fly, brake on a dime—under a sky that seemed to smile on every improvisation. He forgot about Liz McVey and Anna Macrimmon. What else mattered but to chase a puck across the wide dark river? After a while Smiley and the Walkers joined the game of shinny. There was only one rule: whoever got the puck hung on to it as long as he could. It was fox and hounds, with nearly everyone playing the fox at some point. Joe laughed when his father took the puck and started to dipsy-doodle through the crowd like a madman, with his hair sticking out from under his too-small toque. Joe managed to poke the puck away from him, but it went straight to the stick of Larry Langlois, easily the best player there. Larry was seventeen, tall and loose-jointed—it was said he'd been scouted by the Leafs—and he ragged the puck as if it were wired to his stick, covering the ice in effortless sweeps, his eyes laughing. He'd tempt you with the puck, throw in a body feint, and leave you crashing into air.

They started a proper game. Larry's team got only six players, to eight on the other side. The goalposts at one end were rocks and at the other, a hundred yards away, someone's cowboy boots. The boots looked forlorn and absurd standing six feet apart, their toes pointed toward the distant banks with their low clouds of winter trees. Smiley's father, who despite being bald was playing without a hat, got the first goal with an explosion of reckless windmilling speed that left the others whooping and laughing. As he coasted away from the goal, bent over his stick and gasping for breath, Smiley whacked him affectionately on the bottom.

After a while, Joe noticed that his father had left the game. Jamie hadn't been able to keep up with the older boys and men, so Alf had taken him off to the side and was laying soft passes on his stick. Jamie was working hard at it, digging along for the puck on ankles that barely seemed able to support him, falling down and bouncing up again with wild determination. Watching his brother, Joe felt a poignant stab of recognition. His father had once fed him passes in just the same way, and now, seeing Jamie, he was seeing himself, so eager to please his father, at once his god and his nemesis. But where was Penny? On the other side of the river, where some alders showed red against the gray of willows, he saw her, in her pink hat and mitts, pushing herself along with abrupt, erect strokes among her friends. Dipping, she opened her arms, extended a leg behind her, and became a gliding swan.

Later, tired of the game, Joe gave his spot to a new arrival and turned upstream. It seemed less cold under the high cliffs, out of the wind, and he skated steadily along, gripping his stick in one hand at his side as he passed tiny islands and the great leaning willow trunks, all floating by with a dreamlike smoothness, to the rhythmic swish of his blades. The river grew more shallow and he began to glimpse weeds and rocks, under the glass of the ice. He was soon out of sight and hearing of the players. At a bend where he had once caught a half-dozen bass, he met Penny and her friends, returning from upstream. They were laughing and gossiping—skating with the short quick strokes demanded by their burred blades. Penny, he noticed, was eating snow out of her mitten, though when she saw him she tossed it down. A few seconds later, as the girls fell away behind him, he heard them burst into giggles that finally died out around the bend.

He heard the rapids before he saw them: a soft, rushing sound that touched him with faint fear, a reminder that the river was still alive beneath him, that this afternoon of skating was a temporary gift, a kind of illusion.

Most of the rapids had frozen over. But the biggest wave was still visible, flowing like the smooth, darkly glinting body of a serpent amid jumbled crusts of ice. Water had spilled over the ice, where it had hardened in a yellowish mantle, like wax. He stood at the rapid's edge, wondering if he dared bypass it by climbing up one side. At that moment, he saw the fox.

It was watching him from above the rapid. He was sure the fox had not been there a few moments ago, and yet he had not seen it appear. It was standing almost broadside to him, head turned inquisitively, the fantastic orange plume of its tail tipped with white, stretching straight out, nearly as long as its body and, except for a stir of breeze in the thick fur, motionless. The fox lifted its muzzle, trying to scent him, and turned its head a little more. His heart pounding, Joe met the animal's unblinking stare.

Then the fox trotted off, without haste, followed by the great level plume. Something in the fox's movement seemed unusual. Joe saw that half of its right hind leg was missing, the thigh tapered into a dark stump. He just glimpsed the end of it, hanging uselessly below the fox's belly.

THAT NIGHT HE fell ill with a high fever. He lay shivering and sweating while a small cold moon moved over the house. When he glimpsed it between the curtains, the moon seemed to be seeking him out, like a flashlight whose glare hides whoever is holding it. Twice he threw up. The first time he didn't quite reach the toilet, and his vomit splashed on the hall floor. Then his mother appeared, and he felt about four years old again, helpless before her tender scolding. She put him back to bed with extra blankets and a hot-water bottle, which in his delirium seemed to be a part of himself he couldn't quite incorporate into his body. He dreamed he was in a bare white room that had no door. He had climbed up to a ledge and was balancing there, precariously, while the fox with three legs kept jumping up at him from below, showing its sharp teeth in a kind of smile.

The next day, Monday, he was still running a fever and vomiting, so there was no question of school. But he knew it was the day that Anna Macrimmon was scheduled to come back. What he feared—what he was powerless to do anything about—was the reception he knew she would get from Liz. He could imagine Liz telling her, with an air of subtle triumph, that she and Joe were steadies. Yes, she would somehow let Anna know that they were sleeping together, and this prospect seemed to expose him to the injustice of being misunderstood, though over what exactly he did not let himself think too clearly. Groaning, he turned violently in the bed and struck his fist into the wall.

By Thursday, his sickness had turned to a cold and he was able to go back up the hill to school. In Miss Todd's homeroom, Anna Macrimmon's desk, a sheen of birch veneer under a tall window, was empty. It remained empty, in its various incarnations in various rooms, all morning. Her absence gave him hope; perhaps she hadn't come back yet and so had not yet been informed by Liz. He still had time to tell Liz they were through, but there was one problem: Liz was absent as well. Sometimes the two empty desks were far apart, but in French they were side by side, a constant reminder of the strange partnership he had made with them both, and which in some obscure way they had made with each other. In the hall after French, he fell in beside Brad Long, drawing him into a conversation about the schoolwork he'd missed. He asked casually if Anna was back yet.

"Got back Monday."

Excitement and despair rose in him at once. She was here, but Liz had undoubtedly told her everything. Still, he had to be sure.

"Back here? At school?"

Brad looked amused. "Where else?"

"She sick or—"

"Some bug she caught over there. Some foreign bug."

Brad's eyes stayed trained on him, lit with mockery, and Joe had the feeling that his whole dilemma was common knowledge, as if Anna and Brad and God only knew who else had sat around a table discussing— having a good laugh over—the lovesick Walker.

As soon as school finished for the day, he hurried downtown to the florist and chose a small bouquet of dried heather, which he tucked inside his coat in its paper wrapper. Then up the hill again, walking so fast he was soon out of breath and had to stop to spit thick phlegm into the snow. Behind the houses on Banting, the sun sent low beams across the plowed street.

He mounted the front steps, under the little portico with its white pillars, in a straitjacket of self-consciousness, aware she might be watching. The house itself seemed alive. No light showed in the windows, yet each object he glimpsed inside—the top of an armchair, a lampshade withdrawing into dimness—seemed to take note of him.

He pressed the bell button. There was no sound. An Irish setter trotted alone down the street, its long matted fur carrying little balls of ice that clicked together. Joe fumbled open his coat and retrieved the small bouquet. The house went on considering him.

Then the door opened, and he saw a woman in a full-length white apron, her hair swept back from her face into an untidy bun. She was middle-aged and rather short, but there was something about her, a glint of humor, that was familiar.

"I'm Joe Walker. I'm a friend of Anna's."

"Oh, Joe, yes, she's spoken about you. I'm Estelle Macrimmon. Why don't you come in?" Her warmth gave him courage. Her accent made "in" sound like "een." He found himself in a small entrance hall, aware of a staircase in dark wood, the smell of cooking.

She shut the door and again stood before him, regarding him in an open, pleased way. There was pride in her carriage, creating an almost aristocratic effect, despite her plump figure. He explained that he'd just dropped by to wish Anna well and leave the bouquet; he held it up almost apologetically.

"Well, why don't you give it yourself? I'll go up and get her."

He waited in the hall. The house was much smaller than the McVeys', and more somber, with its heavy woodwork and faded Indian carpets. In the living room to his right, books were piled loosely on the floor. The walls were green with white trim (oddly, very like the walls in his own house) and hung with numerous framed photos and paintings. Propped on the mantel was a large oil painting of a seated woman with silver ha wearing a dress. Its pale green folds, beautifully evoked, filled much the old-fashioned frame. Her lips held a vague smile, but her eyes co veyed a certain wistfulness.

Anna's mother reappeared on the landing above.

"She wants to see you up here. Come up, Joe."

He shed his boots and climbed the stairs. Her mother gestur toward an open door.

"Just *entrez*."

Anna was sitting in bed with her knees up, under a quilted spread. In the window to the left, the molten orange globe of the sun was settling into woods. Books were stacked on the rug beside her bed. A crumpled Kleenex lay nearby, like the head of a ghostly chrysanthemum.

She unwrapped the bouquet. He noticed that her upper lip was chafed.

"Heather! How did you know?"

Her voice had thickened with her cold.

"Well, with a name like Macrimmon—"

"The hills go purple with it," she said, trying to smell the little dry flowers. "Have you ever seen it?"

He said nothing. He was standing beside the bed, feeling a bit like a servant who's delivered a message and will soon be asked to go. He could hardly believe he was here, in her room. Happy that he had pleased her, he stood secretly drinking her in, her pillow-flattened hair, the smocking of her flannel nightgown over her small breasts, her red nose. He could scarcely believe it. She had been over there, and now she was here. She had been sailing on the Mediterranean, the actual blue, wet Mediterranean. Yes, days ago she had been in Europe—fabulous, distant Europe, that he knew only from books. And now she was sitting in a bed in front of him, with a cold.

Her illness seemed part of her trip and its aftermath, as if going to another continent and back again, breaching the boundary between two different worlds, was a stressful thing, and the cold was the cost she paid for accomplishing the miracle of existing in two places.

She told him to bring the chair from the desk. Picking it up, he glimpsed something of her private life. On a sheet of paper, half covered by a book, he saw what might have been a poem—a ragged, narrow column of language in her familiar, jabbing hand. In the two seconds his attention lingered there, he saw the phrase *a mask of bees,* and in the same glance he scanned the framed photo standing by itself to one side. Anna, her hair bound under a kerchief, was seated in some kind of boat—he could see water in the background, the arch of a bridge—beside a handsome man with blond slicked-backed hair and intense, serious eyes; his arm circled her shoulders with a confident possessiveness. With a sense of excitement and grief, he felt as if he had at once embraced her life and lost it.

He sat beside the bed while they talked. It was all he could do to contain himself, to make his limbs behave and not go jumping around the room in some mad dance. He kept shifting positions in the hard-backed chair.

"Your letter was terrific," he said. This seemed lame, a cliché— sometimes he felt he offered her nothing but. "I mean, I could almost smell those hills."

"It's funny. I felt more like writing to you than to anyone else. I have this feeling that you hear me better than other people."

"I do," he said.

"I'm serious. You seem to make the thoughts come, to draw them out somehow. You're a good listener."

"Well, that's something."

"It's a lot," she said. The fading sunlight now left the room entirely. They sat in the dusk, not speaking. On her bureau, a clock ticked slowly. Everything he had ever wanted was here, so close at hand that all he had to do was—what? If he leaned over the bed and kissed her, he would spoil everything.

She blew her nose.

"Listen to me, a regular duck!" She sniffed and went on. "Liz tells me you've been seeing a lot of each other."

He had no doubt she knew everything and was being tactful. He felt fixed in his chair.

"We've gone out a few times."

"I'm glad you asked her to the dance."

"I did it for you."

"Are you still taking her out for me?"

There was laughter in her voice. She blew her nose again. He said nothing.

"Sorry, that wasn't fair."

"I don't know why I'm taking her out," he said. "I'm not sure I like her very much."

She was silent, but he could feel her attentiveness, holding him, holding the entire room with its books and ticking clock, in the mild gray light. His confession seemed to stand between them, not fading at all, something they had no choice but to consider. He felt a sad falling away, as if he had come to sobriety, a clarity. She was with Brad, and he was with Liz. Out the window, he could see the white fields of Wiley's farm, the thickets that bordered the Atta.

"Sunday I went skating on the river. Just down there," he said. "It was incredible. Everything was frozen solid. There wasn't any snow, so you could skate for miles. At the first rapids, I saw a fox."

He told her, as best as he could, about his strange sense of the animal as it looked back at him, the way their eyes had met, as if he were being given a privileged glimpse of life in its depths.

He told her how the fox had appeared in his dream. How it had seemed the same and not the same, with the stump of a leg and a menacing grin. "I was afraid, and yet I knew the fox wasn't going to bite me. It just wanted to come closer."

"And you wouldn't let it."

"No."

He felt a sense of failure. In her stillness, she seemed aware of it.

"You see," he said, "I couldn't tell Liz any of this—I wouldn't even think to tell her."

On the bed, Anna let her knees drop.

28

PENNY WORKED AT her bar of laundry soap, carving carefully with her paring knife, trying to bring out the fish's gills. The overheated classroom was filled with the clank of radiators and the smell of wool drying and the slow stomping of Miss Hobsbawn's oxfords as she strolled up and down the aisles with her hands behind her back.

Penny's fish was giving her trouble. Gouged from the hard yellow soap, its head, she thought, looked an awful lot like a sheep's. Putting it down, she tried to remember the fish her dad and Uncle Pete had caught on Lake Erie. Suddenly she saw Uncle Pete coming up the trail to the cottage with a bucket of bass. He had cleaned them on a board nailed between two cedar trees, a cigarette hanging from his lips, squinting through the smoke while he worked with his special knife. She saw the narrow blade run up the fishes' bellies and cut behind their heads, saw it traveling flat through their sides—feeling its way, Uncle Pete said, along the ribs, as if the knife had a mind of its own—and then Uncle Pete lifting off the white fillets and putting them carefully on waxed paper. No one could cut a fillet like Pete, her dad said; the man could have been a surgeon. She heard Uncle Pete talking, while the cigarette bobbled in his lips and seemed about to fall, talking about fish and what they could smell and what they liked to eat and where you could find them. He had picked up the waxed paper with the fillets and put it in her hands, letting her heft its weight while he grinned at her through the smoke of his cigarette, in the sunlight under the cedar trees: her uncle Pete.

"Penny, are you all right?"

Wiping one eye with her wrist, Penny looked up. Miss Hobsbawn wore a gray skirt and a white blouse with a frill down the front. The story was that the teacher had had one breast removed. Penny couldn't see her without wondering which bump was the fake.

"Do you need your snack?"

The teacher was peering through her little glasses.

"No, Miss Hobsbawn."

Out of the corner of her eye, she sensed Bobby Tuckett twisting in his desk to look at her. Sometimes he just stared at her, teasingly, and sometimes, running past, he'd whisper *Diabetic!* She wished Miss Hobsbawn hadn't mentioned her snack (the three Arrowroots tucked in her coat hanging in the cloakroom). She was supposed to eat them at recess, to keep from going into a reaction.

"Penny, that is wonderful! Absolutely wonderful!" Miss Hobsbawn boomed in her man's voice. "Class, look at this!"

She scooped up Penny's fish and turned with it for all to see. "See what care she's put into the details," Miss Hobsbawn said, holding the fish between thumb and forefinger. "The head—look at that, class! The head! Penny, I'm afraid they can't see. Why don't you take it around and show everyone?"

Penny went up and down the aisles, with the yellow fish in her open palm, trying to keep it balanced on its tummy. Some of the students hardly paid any attention, which was fine with her—she was embarrassed at having to show it—but a few studied it closely and murmured *Huh* or *Good* and Ginny Lamport smiled at her as if she was pleased not just with the fish but with Penny too. She tried to slip by Bobby Tuckett's desk, but he cried "Wait!" and plucked the fish right out of her hand and smirked under his long eyelashes.

At recess, she went off into a corner of the Girls' Yard to eat her Arrowroots. The whole yard, overlooking Shade Street and the river, was a trampled mess of slush. A black dog with a white streak down its nose was barking shrilly, while two girls picked their way between the puddles, trying to catch it.

"Still eating baby cookies, are we?"

Brenda Stubbs. Unlike her last name, Brenda was tall and skinny, with lank hair and red-rimmed eyes that were always getting infections. Ginny Lamport was with her, Penny saw, Ginny with her fair hair as smooth as silk, cut in a pageboy. How often Penny had stood in front of the bathroom mirror, wishing she had Ginny's hair, wishing she was Ginny.

Penny fumbled her last cookie into her pocket.

"Now be nice," Ginny told Brenda. "She has to eat them."

Penny heard the click of candy in their mouths.

She stood uncertainly, eager for them to like her. In her pocket, her hand abandoned the Arrowroot. She'd eat it later, in a washroom stall.

"I really liked your fish," Ginny said. Her eyes sparkled with amusement, as though Penny had done something cleverer than she knew. "We were doing soap carvings," she explained to Brenda. "Penny's was the best in the class."

Brenda held out a crumpled paper bag. "Want a blackball?"

"I can't," Penny said.

"Licorice?"

"I'm not allowed." Her eyes followed the bag as Brenda drew it back. For a few seconds, no one said anything and Penny felt she was letting them down.

"Shall we ask her?" Ginny said to Brenda.

"I don't care," Brenda said, screwing up her mouth as she looked away.

"We want you to come to our sleepover," Ginny said. "Next Saturday."

When Brenda turned toward the chain-link fence, Penny had the sense she was stifling a laugh. But Ginny was smiling at her, her mouth open, her lips and tongue black as tar.

29

IT SEEMED TO Alf that the only clean thing in sight was the beer. The yellow beer floating in cylinders on Sid Walters's tray, the spots of yellow rising and falling around the crowded MEN'S BEVERAGE ROOM of the Vimy House, the yellow pooling at the bottom of his own drained glass. Everything else was dim, squalid, dirtied by the light that fell from wall brackets and reflected dully off the dusty Venetian blinds. The room had a kind of womblike privacy—if you didn't count the ten or so other patrons, who for reasons best known to themselves favored the town's grimmest hotel. He signaled Sid for two more.

On the screen above the bar, players swarmed up the ice like insects: Leafs versus Red Wings. I never did get those tickets, he thought, lifting his glass an inch or two off the table and swirling the contents. He set the glass down. The memory had drifted to him out of nowhere, a fragment of normal life where fathers promised to take their sons to hockey games and sometimes forgot. But who was he fooling? He wasn't going to take Joe to Maple Leaf Gardens. Such things seemed as far from possibility now as the moon. Yet he kept on talking and acting as if nothing were wrong. *Do you want anything from the store? I'm just going out for a walk. Hand me that wrench, will you?* He watched himself go through the motions, but the motions had very little to do with what was actually happening to him—which lay beyond his powers of expression and even understanding, though it carried him like a cold current that swept him on, oddly fascinating.

At the small table opposite, Freddie Stone had been watching him since he'd come in: little Freddie Stone with his disheveled face and watery eyes above the flagrant red of his bunched scarf, smiling and nodding as if he and Alf shared some understanding that was a source of great pleasure to them both. He'd known Freddie all his life, retarded Freddie, who'd spent fifty years at least as an errand boy at Bannerman's. Now that he was retired he lived in a room at the Vimy House, supported by a couple of small pensions and a monthly stipend paid, people said, by Doc McVey.

Sid arrived with the beer, two tall tapered glasses of golden light through which strings of bubbles rose. Sid expertly corralled the empties with the fingers of one hand, taking them up with a clatter. When he was gone, Alf lifted a glass, and the cold, bitter beer slid under its own foam into his mouth. He wasn't drunk, not yet, but he had reached that state of clairvoyant wakefulness where he felt on the brink of insight, and this produced a sense of imminent danger, as if he were venturing out onto thin ice. On the far shore he glimpsed a deeper drunkenness, where the danger would be past because there he would feel nothing; it was what he was aiming for.

Across the way, Freddie smiled with his wet, shapeless mouth and nodded and seemed to be saying, *That's right, just keep it up and you'll get somewhere nice.*

Alf raised his glass to him and drank again. Behind Freddie, Ron Carson moaned an obscenity and let his bald, scabbed head nod forward. The television over the bar bayed its crowd sounds, and in the dim room a few men shouted. Alf had told Margaret he was going to the Legion. In the past he'd often dropped in there, of a Saturday night, for a bit of pool or to watch the hockey game. But he no longer had the heart for the Legion, with its noisy, forced camaraderie, as if the lot of them had only just got back from overseas.

He lit a cigarette and welcomed its mild fire on the back of his throat. At least Margaret had stopped asking him what was wrong. Is it Pete? she'd said once, prodding. And he'd said, Yes, it was Pete, of course it was Pete, what in the hell else could it be but Pete? and she'd responded by embracing him. He'd gone stiff and wanted to cry. In fact, he'd been on the verge of telling her everything, telling her that he'd betrayed his best friend and a lot of other people too, and now his best friend was dead because of it. But he'd stopped himself. Did his shame run so deep? Was he afraid she'd stop loving him? Each time he contemplated putting his crime into words, he felt he was approaching the edge of disintegration. He felt he could not survive confession. It had been the same twenty years ago, after the war. It was when he had tried to explain to Margaret what he had gone through that he had broken down. He had hardly told her anything. But the mere approach to telling her had unleashed terrors he'd somehow kept at bay for his two years in France. That's when the tremors had started, the nightmares, the fear of the streets. Better silence, he felt, than disintegration. Better grimly to endure than go to pieces and be of no use to anybody. It had been silence, finally, that had allowed him to bury the demons of the war. Perhaps he hadn't killed them. Perhaps they still lived in some red-line crisis zone from which they made brief raids into his dreams, his life. But he had largely banished them from the light. Couldn't he do the same now?

Freddie picked up his glass and shuffled across the narrow gap between their tables.

"Can I sit down, Alf?"

"Sure, Freddie. Make yourself comfortable."

Freddie sat with an odd formality, looking as pleased as if he'd just been invited into Buckingham Palace. His canny little eyes shone and his big lips hung open in a silent laugh.

"So how you keeping, Freddie?"

"Can't complain."

He had a rasping, fractured voice, as if each word was coated in phlegm.

Freddie said nothing more but continued to smile at Alf as if this were all the conversation he needed, as if the most pleasant thing two people could do was sit at a little table and look at each other.

"Doing any work these days?"

"Oh, yes."

"Over at Kelly's?"

"That's right."

Alf focused on his beer. It was hard to bear the trust of those watery eyes, that smile with its unguarded friendliness and innocence.

For some time they drank in silence. The Leafs got a goal and a few men roared. A snowplow rumbled in the street, steel on cement. Freddie said, "You found your brother."

He was grinning a crumpled grin, as if Alf would know exactly what he was talking about.

"My brother?" Alf said. Surely Freddie must mean Jamie, the night they'd found him up the river, with Lucille Boileau's boy. But how did Freddie know about that?

"You dove down and got him," Freddie said, beaming.

"I dove," Alf repeated. Then he remembered. One summer afternoon in the early thirties, he and Joe had gone swimming at Bannerman's Number One dam and his brother had disappeared below the apron. Alf hadn't been worried, not at first. There was a place where you could slip between the timbers and come up in a sort of leaky cave, behind the dam face; he had shown it to Joe himself. But after a few minutes, Joe hadn't reappeared so Alf dove to find him. His brother was there, in the dim cold cave streaked with the brown light of the Atta. He was sitting hugging his shins, crying in a muffled way, his mouth on his knee. Had he panicked? Alf didn't know. It had taken him a long time to calm Joe down. Finally, their heads had broken the surface together.

Freddie must have been there, standing on the apron or on the stepped cement wall to the west: a thirty-year-old man-boy in the old-fashioned striped bathing suit that covered most of his body, gaping at them as they swam to shore. Perhaps Freddie hadn't known about the cave behind the dam face. Perhaps he thought Alf had rescued Joe from the bottom.

Freddie had kept the memory fresh. Kept his admiration fresh. You found your brother. As if their slick heads had only just now burst from the icy spring-fed hole below the dam.

"You remember that?" Alf said.

"Oh, yes! You went far down."

"Not so far," Alf said. "He was all right, really." He did not have the energy to explain.

They drank for a while longer without speaking. Why had Joe been crying? Some hurt, some slight he would never understand. Alf felt he had spent most of his youth looking after his younger brother. *Make sure nothing happens to Joe:* his mother's battle cry. He had pulled Joe out of fights, fought fights for him, taken him everywhere, even upriver with his friends, when he didn't really want Joe tagging along with his manic gaze that broadcast the announcement that he was twice as ready as anybody for whatever adventure they had planned. At times, Alf had hated him, his mother's favorite. Once he had pushed him out of a tree, and once he had jammed a pea-shooter down his throat out of sheer spite. Mostly, though, he had done the job assigned him. He could never remember having an ordinary, relaxed time with his brother, because he was always looking out for him.

Yet he had loved Joe too, as he discovered that rainy night in the summer of 1944, near the Dutch border, when his sergeant had taken him aside to tell him his brother, who was serving in a different unit, had been killed. It had seemed impossible. Joe had had so many near misses over the years, in cars, on the river, in hockey games and barroom fights, that Alf had begun to think his brother was untouchable, a miracle kid. When Joe couldn't have been more than fifteen, he'd climbed across the Shade on the underside of the CN trestle, maneuvering along the black girders far above the water. Alf hadn't been there, but he'd heard. Why did you do it? he had asked. And Joe had said (Alf had never forgotten this), "When I think of something, I have to do it. Even if it's crazy. I can't rest unless I do it."

Alf's sergeant, his dirty face shining in the light of the hurricane lamp, told him that Joe had been napping in a ditch when a land mine had gone off beneath him. Apparently, he'd rolled over on it in his sleep. Alf left the barn where they were camped and stood in the rain. Sometime later, his sergeant found him and led him back to shelter.

"I wasn't always able to bring him back," Alf said.

"No," Freddie said.

"There are people you can't bring back. When you kill them, they stay dead."

Freddie shook his head; it was the sad truth.

Alf drank. He felt they understood each other perfectly.

Freddie finished his glass and stood up.

"Time for me to go upstairs, Alf."

He watched Freddie move off among the tables with his shuffling steps, nodding here and there in his courtly way. Across the room, a bottle broke with a pop and someone shouted *Attaboy, Coach!* When Alf looked again at the table where Freddie had sat before joining him, he saw that someone else had taken it. The man was wearing an old-fashioned tweed cap with a flat top and stubby visor. He had twisted in his chair to signal the waiter, so that Alf could not see his face, but Alf instantly experienced a terrified elation, as if he were about to fly off a cliff.

The man turned in his chair. Alf saw the scrawny-handsome features, the girlishly fine skin, the nose bent from a fight, the blue eyes fixed on his with a wild familiar merriment, as if the man were enjoying his little surprise. He was wearing the heavy tweed suit he had bought in Johnsonville for the victory banquet, after the Stingers had won the provincial championship in 1938. As Alf watched, transfixed, the man touched one hand to the knot of his maroon tie with a curious, suggestive delicacy.

Alf had stopped breathing. His brother had not aged a day in the twenty-one years since he'd last seen him. It seemed to Alf that since then he'd only been hiding. Joe had found some secret place where no one would ever think of looking, where even time, somehow, had been fooled into passing him by. His smooth skin was flushed with rose and there was mischief in his smile, as if he were more than pleased with himself. Happiness spread from him like the power and hope of youth itself, and this power flooded over Alf, engulfing him in a warm, calming tide. He started to rise from his chair—he wanted to go to Joe, to embrace him—and in that instant Joe was gone.

But the feeling remained, a sense of well-being that suffused his whole body. He wanted to call out, *Hey, it's my brother!* Everything in the dim room seemed to glow—men's faces, the flickering moon of the television, even the glasses in front of him, which contained a miraculous liquid, a distillation of yellow blossoms.

He had a craving for the dark and quiet of the night. At the door of the MEN'S BEVERAGE ROOM he looked back in wonder at the table where his brother had sat. Two other men occupied it now, two men in colorless jackets, talking to Sid Walters as he put down their beer. With a new shock, Alf remembered that it had been in this very room where the victory banquet had been held, in the days when the Vimy House still clung to a kind of propriety. He tried to recall the room as it had been that night: the long tables covered with white cloths, the draped flags and picture of the new king, the championship cup displayed proudly at the head table. He remembered roast beef and a tedious speech by the mayor, but he couldn't establish where Joe or he had been sitting.

Alf went on down the hall, conscious that his happiness was already fading. From the open door to LADIES AND ESCORTS came a wave of laughter. It seemed to wrap his body, to pull him toward the room. *You don't!* A woman cried. She was answered by another woman's scandalized bray. The hotel cat lay curled on the desk. Its green eyes noted his passage indifferently, his body of no more account than a movement in the air.

Realizing he needed to pee, he turned and went back down the hall. The stairs to the cellar washrooms were steep, and in his descent he experienced a moment of vertigo, as if the floor below him were exerting a magnetic pull. In the washroom he fell, landing on his back, on the tiny white-and-black tiles, in a puddle of what might have been urine. He scrambled to his feet immediately and for a moment stood gripping the edge of a sink. There was a mirror to his left, but he avoided looking at it.

He did his business in the ancient foul-smelling urinal, where the porcelain was webbed with tiny cracks, and stood for some time afterward, leaning his forehead on a cold, sweating pipe, aware of the soaked seat of his trousers, of the ruins of his life. *You're a fool,* he said, and with this pronouncement felt a little relief. *Just a bloody fool.* He wept a little, laughing at himself through his tears. In front of his face, the tan wall scribbled with graffiti somehow looked different from the way it had looked a moment before, the letters clearer. He supposed he'd always been a fool, only like most fools he hadn't noticed.

In the hall outside, he saw a pair of women's legs in jeans coming down the stairs. She wore low black boots with silver studs and a blouse of gray metallic-looking material. At her throat was a black choker with a cameo. Lucille Boileau. When she saw him, she broke into a grin. But it fell away as he went up to her and took her by the shoulders. When he bent to kiss her he half expected her to draw back or even strike him, but in the last second before he closed his eyes he saw her own narrow and darken, as she lifted her mouth to his.

30

SNOWFLAKES, ENDLESS SNOWFLAKES, fell glittering into the light Margaret had left on over the back porch, burning with a steady faithfulness that reproached him. He washed his face at the kitchen sink, scrubbed at it with a dish towel, then saw he'd put the stain of Lucille's pink lipstick on the towel. He took the damp cloth to the cellar and hid it under his workbench.

Climbing back up to the kitchen, he met Margaret in her dressing gown.

"Oh, it's you."

"Sorry. I didn't mean to wake you."

"I wasn't asleep. I'm worried about Joe. This snow."

"Where is he?"

"He told you," she said critically, studying him for a moment before she crossed to the window. Since he'd fought with Joe on New Year's Eve, she'd seemed more distant, just like Joe himself: the civilized side of the family, the Selwoods, closing ranks against the barbarian Walkers. "He and Liz McVey were driving to Toronto. Some kind of concert."

He watched her cup her hands on the window and peer out, then turn to him.

"Are you all right?"

"I was just taking a towel downstairs. I got some grease on me, I was sponging it off." He felt a need to explain everything, everything but.

There was an awkwardness between them, a mismatch of rhythms.

He was standing at the top of the cellar stairs and felt frozen there, as if he no longer had volition or reason to move. As if movement might betray him.

"Are the roads bad?"

"No, no. He'll be fine."

He bestirred himself, crossing to the sink and taking down a glass, glad of the distraction. Once again he had the feeling of being frozen in place, as if he had never been anywhere but here, watching the white rush of water from the tap splash and overflow his glass. The world seemed unreal, the glass in his hand both heavier and lighter than it really was. He felt he might drop it. As it touched his lips, he thought of Lucille Boileau, the dark mass of her hair spilling over his groin.

"He seems awfully serious about her," she was saying. "I don't know why he doesn't bring her by. I wonder if he isn't ashamed of us."

"Ashamed?" he said, turning. He had hardly been listening.

She left the room. For a long time he remained motionless. Behind him, the tap dripped; he'd been meaning to fix it for weeks. The wind shrieked briefly under the door. He went back to the cellar and took out the towel. It was dark with wetness, impossible to tell if the lipstick was gone. He hung it from a nail. Thoughts of Lucille Boileau kept coming back to him—the way she had knelt before him on her rickety bed. He bent to the space under his workbench and found the old metal tackle box that had belonged to his father. It opened easily, the tiered drawers revealing themselves like the terraces of a miniature garden. Each little compartment held lures: silver spoons with hooks and tiny beads attached; hand-carved wooden fish, their backs striped or spotted with yellow and brown paint, their clustered hooks tangled and rusting. One compartment was filled with various weights of sinkers, like little gray bombs, and different-sized hooks. There was a float, cleverly fashioned from a gull's quill, its tip painted red. When his father slipped off Bannerman's dam, the tackle box had remained on the cement ledge by the shore. Alf had left the contents just as they were.

In the bottom of the box were larger objects: pliers, a scaling knife, an old reel with black line, a gill chain, a book with a tattered jacket, all smelling a little musty. He took out the book, *The Thirty-Nine Steps,* by John Buchan. His father hadn't been much of a reader, and he'd been surprised to find the novel, though Alf hadn't actually opened it until several years after the drowning. The photographs were just where Alf had first found them, in an envelope tucked in the center of the book. He took them out and laid them on the bench.

The pictures had been taken on one of the fishing trips his father had taken with his old pal Shorty Bigwood. There was Shorty, with a beer bottle in one hand and a fishing pole in the other, mugging like a school-boy. And there was his father, standing near the stern of a beached row-boat, his slim face as brown as an Indian's, glowing with health and high spirits under his white hair. Alf guessed the photos had been taken sometime after the war, perhaps only a year or two before he'd drowned. He picked out two and set the rest aside. In the first, his father was standing beside an open railcar in whose shadowy interior a few people were sitting on benches. His father had a suitcase in one hand and was turned toward the car to help a woman negotiate the rather long step down to the platform. This woman was tall, with cropped hair and round dark glasses she might have worn to ward off the sun, though Alf couldn't shake the notion she was blind; it had something to do with the uncertainty of her smile, as if she were eager not to give offense by the burden she placed on others. In the second picture, his father was sitting up to his bare chest in water, directing a squint at the camera, while the woman in dark glasses sat on the steep, stony beach behind him, near the wild white roots of a fallen tree. She wore a bathing suit; her folded legs looked pale and shapely, and above the bodice of her bathing suit the tops of her breasts were just visible. Alf had no idea who this woman was. When he'd first discovered the photos he'd been intrigued, and a little shocked, but he had reserved judgment. He'd never had an inkling that his father had been involved with any woman save his mother. But now, studying the pictures, he felt sure that his father, in his early sixties, had had an affair with a woman at least a decade younger than himself, a woman who might have been blind. He found a magnifying glass and examined the woman's face. She had a strong chin and a small mouth.

She was handsome rather than pretty, and in her posture—it had something to do with her straight back and the lift of her head—was a bemused pride. Alf moved the glass over his father's face, which was slightly averted from the sunlight. There was a kind of smirk that suggested the two of them were united in a common knowledge. They were together. It was as clear as if they'd been holding hands.

You devil, Alf thought. What other secrets had his father kept? He returned to his father's face, at once so familiar and so distant. No son ever sees his father clearly. There is always a distorting glare that exaggerates or diminishes what is there, leaves areas hidden that might not be hidden to anyone else, and reveals secrets warped in the deep eddies of old emotions. His father had done what he, Alf, had done. This realization charged Alf with a roguish excitement. After a fashion, his father's sin justified his own, for it was simply what men did. "You old devil," he said out loud.

At the same time, as if he were a boy opening a door he would later wish he had never opened, he heard the long echo of betrayal.

31

PENNY, GINNY, AND Brenda were in Ginny's big bedroom, with its framed pictures of ballerinas in pink and lime tutus, and a pink frill—like a giant's tutu—around the dressing table. They were getting ready for bed when Ginny turned suddenly to Penny and said there was a game she and Brenda sometimes played. When they took off their clothes they'd look in the mirror, and sometimes they put jewelry on and sometimes they would dare each other to run around the house, bare naked. "We have to be quick, okay? 'Cause my mom will be back pretty soon. Okay?" Ginny smiled at Penny with a secretly amused smile, as if she found her a bit backward, but nice just the same. Over on the bed, Brenda was unbuckling her shoes.

Penny shrugged okay, though she could feel heat come up under her clothes, right into her face. She took baths by herself now, not with

Jamie, like she had when she was little. She didn't even like her mother to see her naked. Sometimes, when she got undressed in her room, she could hardly stand having no clothes on. The air on her—all over her— seemed to be gently touching her where she hardly dared touch herself. Watching herself in the mirror, Ginny unbuttoned her blouse. An excitement was in the air. Penny wasn't sure she liked it, this feeling that she was on the verge of things she didn't know about, wasn't supposed to do.

"C'mon, don't be shy."

Sitting on the edge of a chair, Penny bent to her shoes. She was breathing a bit harder now. The other girls were already down to their underwear. Under her white cotton undershirt, Ginny had bumps, where her breasts had started to grow. Penny couldn't keep her eyes off them.

"C'mon, you're getting behind," Ginny said. She slid her underpants down her long legs and stepped out of them with a little laugh.

Penny pulled off her undershirt. On the bed behind Ginny, Brenda was already bare naked. She was running strands of her hair through her fingers and staring absently at Penny. When she discovered Penny looking back, her face went blank.

"Take off your panties," Ginny said.

Penny did as she was told and sat with her shoulders scrunched up and her hands between her legs. A shivering was going up and down her body and through her shoulders, and she couldn't take her eyes off Ginny's bare chest.

"Come look at yourself in the mirror," Ginny said.

They were all at the mirror now. Ginny and Brenda were laughing and hardly able to stand straight, feeling each other's smoothness against their skins. Penny looked at herself in the glass, at her nonexistent breasts puckering in her thin chest, and at her straggly brown hair that was neither straight nor curly, and at her face with its wide blue eyes, looking back at her as if she—that bare-naked girl in the mirror—were looking at Penny and wondering what she was doing out there, not joining in the fun.

AFTER MRS. LAMPORT came home, they made popcorn—Penny had a special measured amount in her own bowl, no butter—and ate it up in Ginny's room while they leafed through old magazines. Later, in the dark, Penny lay on her side in the little bed that had been Ginny's when Ginny's sister Ella was at home, listening to the other girls talk in the big bed. They were chatting about boys, and it was all a bit alien to her since they seemed to have noticed and thought about so much that she hadn't—who liked whom, who was good-looking—though when Ginny said she was pretty sure Bobby Tuckett had a crush on Penny, Penny went hot under the sheets. "No!" she cried, really outraged. "I *hate* Bobby Tuckett!"

"Why?" Ginny said. "He's so cute!"

Penny fell silent, stunned by the idea Bobby Tuckett liked her. Stunned by the idea that he was cute.

After some time there was silence, the banging of a snowplow. Penny had started to drift off when she heard an eruption of giggling and scuffling from the other bed. Then Ginny said, in a loudish whisper, "Oh, darling!" which set the two of them, Ginny and Brenda, snickering into their pillows. Then there was silence again, and more scuffling, and Penny heard Brenda say, "I don't like tongues."

"Shhh," Ginny said.

And Brenda said, "She's asleep."

"Is she?"

"I don't think Bobby Tuckett likes her."

"Yes, he does," Ginny said.

"No he doesn't. Who's gonna like someone with diabetes?"

They said nothing for a while. Then Penny heard Ginny say, "My mother says diabetics can't have babies."

In the morning, the other girls pressed close as Penny gave herself her needle. She felt odd at having to do it in front of them—her mother usually left her alone with her syringe—but they had asked if they could watch. Mrs. Lamport watched too, hovering nearby and saying, "Girls, pay attention now, she has to do this *every* morning," the three of them peering as Penny stuck her needle into the little bottle of insulin—

plunged it right through the rubber top—and drew back the plunger of the syringe to the right amount, twenty-four units, and pulled the needle out and brought its tip to the outside of her upper arm.

"I can't watch," Brenda said.

They were all spellbound: Mrs. Lamport with her big front teeth; Ginny, her pretty face drained of color; and Brenda, her red-rimmed eyes moving from the hovering needle to Penny and back again.

Sometimes, at home, she hesitated for a long time before pushing the needle in. She was afraid of the pain—the thin, slicing pain that sang through her arm or leg. She tried to deny this pain. She told herself, her mother, her brother Jamie, "I like needles." But as often as she said this, she knew she did not like needles; she hated them.

Now, seeing their fearful, fascinated faces, she experienced a rush of triumph.

"I like needles," she said calmly, and pushed it in.

32

THE RAPID PIPING of the organ rose above the church, into the February sky. Bach, Margaret thought, pausing on the sidewalk; it was as if an old dear friend she had not seen for years had surprised her. The lower notes were muffled by the thick cobblestone walls, but the clear treble ran on and on, a joy that never exhausted or repeated itself.

She entered the church quietly, so as not to disturb Helen. Near a brass railing she paused again to listen. Now the bass was clearly audible, tossing themes back and forth with the treble. It seemed a wintry music, sunlight glancing off icicles, that also contained by some mysterious alchemy the depths of summer.

Helen botched a run, started over, botched it again. "Damn!"

Margaret laughed and moved to the steps.

"Oh, you're here."

"I've been listening. It was absolutely—"

"A mess."

"No, no. It was lovely," Margaret said with feeling. She slipped off her coat and laid it on a choir bench. "Are you playing it for the wedding?" Helen turned to her in the pool of light at the console.

"No, lucky for all concerned. Anyway, I don't suppose the Clarkes or the Williamses have ever heard of J. S. Bach." Helen screwed up her thin mouth as though suppressing a more sarcastic comment and held out some sheet music to Margaret. She was Margaret's age exactly, forty-two: a prematurely gray-haired woman with skimpy bangs and a slight stoop. Her husband was editor of the *Attawan Star*. Sometimes she and Margaret went off to Kitchener or Hamilton or Toronto in Helen's Buick, to operas and concerts. They had adopted a jolly, bantering, slightly superior tone, two women who shared a love of music and had little tolerance for humbug.

Margaret looked at the music Helen had given her: "Seven Wishes for You," by Anne-Marie Fletcher-Valois.

"Never heard of her. Are we going to do all seven?"

"If we want to get paid."

Helen picked out the melody with her right hand while Margaret read from her copy. Finally she stepped away from the organ. The empty pews seemed ready to listen. In a stained-glass window, a bearded apostle carried a book that shone like a ruby. Margaret lifted her face a little as she sang and her body swayed slightly. Her family often teased her about "wriggling around" and she tried not to. But it was her response to singing, the pleasure she felt as she became an instrument for the music, even the unexceptional music of Anne-Marie Fletcher-Valois.

"Seven Wishes for You" listed, as promised, seven things the newly married couple wished for each other. It was a sluggish, sentimental piece, although there was a string of notes in the refrain she liked immensely, that gave a haunting lilt to the word *you*. Each time she sang the word, shivers ran down her face and chest.

Unexpectedly, the sixth wish gave her trouble. "I'll listen to you, I'll hear your troubles," she sang, "even when you're far away." The words were innocuous enough, but on the first syllable of *away*, her voice broke and she stopped.

The organ died out behind her.

"Sorry," Margaret said. Unaccountably, her face was burning. She made a point of not looking at Helen. "Just give me a little lead-in."

It was worse the second time. As she broached the word *even,* a shudder went through her and she only stopped the note from turning into a wail by clamping her mouth shut. She sat down in the choir stall.

"Are you all right?"

"It's the oddest—I'm sorry." She leaned over, hardly able to talk. Helen came and sat beside her.

"I just felt faint," Margaret managed. "The oddest—"

"Would you like some water?"

As Helen hurried to the parish kitchen, Margaret pressed her forehead against the hard cool back of the next pew, struggling to fight down the impulse to weep. Tears wouldn't do, especially in front of Helen, any more than a confession would do. She considered Helen her closest friend, but theirs was not that kind of friendship. When Helen returned, they decided to stop for the morning. Walking home, Margaret paused at the rail of the Shade Street bridge. Below, the Atta steamed from a narrow fissure in the ice, making its peaty way toward its meeting with the Shade. For some reason, the water drew her thoughts to England—gave her a sharp intuition of the English spring, with its distinctive smell of earth and damp woods and petrol fumes. For a few minutes she was overcome by a deep nostalgia for her girlhood, for her mother and father, both dead now, for the green of a certain field, for the high chalk-veined downs with their glimpses of the distant channel, that gray, strangely heartening infinity. She wept, digging frantically through her purse for a handkerchief, thinking, *This won't do, this won't do.* All she could find was a paper napkin.

BY ELEVEN-THIRTY SHE was busy in her kitchen, getting the children's lunch. Penny's took a special effort—everything had to be weighed on the spring scale whose round numbered face dominated the counter—and dessert was always a problem, since Jamie still clamored for sweets. The dietician at the hospital had told her that the rest of the family should go on eating as usual, but when Margaret had set a lemon meringue pie on the table, Penny's face had fallen. Margaret had sworn never to torture her again.

Noon came with the plunging howl of Bannerman's whistle. A few minutes later Alf called to say he had to work through the lunch hour. She leaped at his voice, but though he was cheerful and warm enough, she felt he was impatient to hang up.

Then Penny came through the door, pigtails bouncing. She launched into a story about a schoolyard quarrel, and a moment later Joe and Jamie came in, pink-faced, having raced each other from the edge of the Island. Margaret watched herself go into gear—the cheerful mother setting out bowls of tomato soup and plates of bologna-and-cheese sandwiches, listening and commenting on the tales they had brought. She kept a special eye on Jamie, who had seemed distracted and oddly wary of late. Recently, when they were shopping in the A&P, he'd grabbed her hand as if he were suddenly four years old again. Startled, Margaret had glanced down the aisle to their left. But there was only an old man—it was Ron Carson from the Flats—standing behind his shopping cart as he talked to a woman in a red coat. He smiled and nodded at Margaret while Jamie, who had shifted his grip to the edge of their cart, kept trying to move them along. A few moments later in the seclusion of an empty aisle, a bit miffed at her son, she asked him what was wrong, but he only made a face and indicated he couldn't talk about it. "What is it?" she demanded. "I have to pee," he said, in a fierce undertone. Margaret thought immediately of diabetes. Before she'd been diagnosed, Penny had been going to the bathroom every fifteen minutes.

Soon her children were gone, in a gust, and she was alone. Life itself seemed emptied away. A dozen jobs called to her, but she sat at the kitchen table. The sadness that had threatened her almost violently all morning was now a still pool, a pool in which everything was submerged, even the white daylight at the window, the crumbs strewn around the oilcloth.

She had an urge to call Alf. "Don't be daft," she scolded herself, in her brisk English way, "Don't behave like some silly girl." She never phoned the mill, except in emergencies. Two minutes later, she picked up the phone.

Matt Honnegger, the knitting-room foreman, told her Alf had left an hour before. "Funny," Matt said, "I thought he'd gone home."

She didn't see him until he showed up at five-thirty. He was in a good mood, almost too good, and he'd brought her a bar of Cadbury's milk chocolate in its dark blue and silver wrapper, just like the old days. Margaret couldn't resist the tide of his good spirits. At the supper table, while Jamie was telling them about every turn and twist of some TV show, Alf looked at her and winked in happy complicity. Suddenly she felt insulted, patronized. It was the sort of wink you might give a child.

The next morning after the children had left for school, she walked over to the Flats. Passing the arena, its whitewashed walls blinding in the sun, she turned down the lane that led to the mills. No one was in sight, though she could hear the thrashing of machines from open windows. Furtive now, almost dizzy with tension, she pushed through a heavy door into the vestibule of the sweater mill. The wooden rack of time cards hung beside the clock. She searched the array of yellow cards until she found her husband's: *Walker A. #117*. Pulling it out, she swiftly put the card back again—someone was on the stairs above—but the footsteps faded. Again she retrieved the card and found the date she was looking for: yesterday. The unevenly inked numbers stamped by the clock showed that Alf had left the mill at one-forty and not returned until five after three. She replaced the card in its slot and went outside, blinking in the light reflected from the snowbanks.

MARGARET HAD A hundred questions seething inside her but dared not ask them until she was safely alone with him. Even then—it was ten o'clock that night and she was creaming her face at the dresser, while Alf read a paperback in bed behind her—she hesitated, sensing danger, as if one wrong word might plunge her into a situation she would regret.

She watched him in the mirror. He lay on his back with one knee up under the quilt, idly massaging the top of his head with one hand.

She heard her voice say, cheerfully disinterested, to the glass, "So, did you ever get lunch yesterday?"

He grunted, scarcely hearing.

"Alf." More sharply.

He looked up. For a moment, the blue of his eyes shocked her in the mirror. Such eyes that husband of yours has, Helen had said to her once. Faraway eyes, of a pale electric blue. She knew other women found him attractive, more so perhaps than she did herself. Now those eyes were suddenly fresh to her, a surprise and a rebuke.

"Yesterday, when you had to work through noon, did you ever get lunch?" She knew her question must sound queer, caring about so trivial a thing a day later.

He lowered the book. In his hesitation she sensed calculation. She turned on the bench to face him. A dog barked in the street.

"I went out to the Rendezvous," he said at last. "Had a yen for a burger." He cleared his throat. "Why?"

She faltered at his challenge. Of course she couldn't say, You were away for an hour and a half. Does it really take you that long to eat a burger? She would have to admit she'd read his timecard, and she didn't know enough to risk that. Maybe he'd gone for a drive. She could imagine him sitting in the car above the river somewhere, eating as he stared at the ice. But she couldn't ask him.

"Nothing, I just wondered how you got on. I worry you're not getting enough nourishment."

Immediately, *nourishment* seemed false on her tongue, a too-elaborate word, hiding her own duplicity. He gazed at her for a long moment, then raised the book. Instantly, she was piqued.

She said, "Are we all right?"

"Hmm," he said.

"Alf."

The book came down.

"Are we all right? Are things all right between us?"

She supposed she was making a scene, maybe unnecessarily. But there was something desperate in her, kneading with tiny fists in her chest and throat.

"Sometimes I think—we seem to be drifting away from each other."

"I'm not going anywhere," he said, warmly enough, and her spirit rose at that, eager to believe.

"You still like me then?" She lifted her face to him, defiantly, flirtatiously, feeling the remains of the cold cream like a mild burn.

"Hey, hey," he said, cajoling. He got off the bed and came toward her while she studied him with black, sober concentration, not sure whether he was approaching out of duty or desire. When he kissed her on the mouth, she strained to read him, his mind, through the pressure of his lips.

For the first time in weeks they made love. He was attentive and slow, just as she liked. She held him at the small of his back and focused with shut eyes on traveling to the place that was so elusive: the little patch of light that might, just might, expand suddenly into a meadow of pleasure. It seemed critical that she get there tonight, as if to seal a pact with him. Suddenly—she had never done this before—she thought of him being with another woman. For a moment she was that other woman, unknown to herself, holding on to Alf Walker's back, the back of a man who belonged elsewhere. And pleasure rolled through her in a smoothly swelling wave.

But just as she was about to slip into deeper pleasure, he pinched her nipple so hard she cried out in pain. Everything came apart for her then; the road to heaven filled with stones and briars. Alf was flustered and apologetic. Sorry, sorry, he told her; I forgot. In the end she was left feeling raw and used. She lay in the dark as he slept, wondering what it was he had forgotten.

THE NEXT MORNING, alone in the house, she searched his clothes. In the pockets of his dirty factory greens she found a screw, a broken latch needle, a note that read *#8 running slow,* written in an unfamiliar

hand, a half-used book of matches, bits of tobacco. Was he smoking
again? She'd smelled smoke on his shirts and now the golden shreds of
tobacco hinted at a life of illicit pleasures. She went into the cellar, to his
workbench. It had almost a shrinelike neatness: the tools hung in ranks,
the little jars of screws and nails graded according to size. She usually felt
a tenderness on seeing his bench. He had bought these tools for his carpentry business, back in 1949. They were all that was left of his plans,
the plans he'd once wooed her with, in England. But this morning she
rummaged irreverently through the drawers. She peered into cans and
boxes. In a deep drawer, under a bundle of electrical wire, she found an
envelope containing half a dozen old-fashioned tinted postcards. Two
were of French scenes: the Eiffel tower, the Place Pigalle. But the other
four were of naked women. They posed in boots and berets: young big-
bottomed women with short curly hair and heavily made-up eyes.

Their swaths of pubic hair shocked her. The young women looked
stagily surprised, holding up their hands, palms out. On the final card,
a blonde in a sailor cap was tweaking her own nipples. Her eyes with
their huge false lashes conveyed a look of amazed innocence, as if she'd
never thought of doing *this* before—tuning herself like a radio. Margaret remembered how Alf had hurt her in the night. Was this his
inspiration then? Was this her rival? Impossible, surely. Now she was
indignant, scarcely able to believe he kept these pictures. How could
there be any pleasure in such little-boy stuff? She flung the envelope
back in the drawer, not caring that the photos spilled out across the
bottom.

A dish towel hung from a nail, blue and white checked: she'd wondered where it had gotten to. In a moment, she found the stain; it was
lipstick, there could be no mistake, a pink halfway to cherry.

Margaret turned in the dim cellar and thought, Carrie Crean.

After lunch she changed into the rust-red corduroy dress she kept for
parties, pulled on her Sunday coat and boots, and marched across town
to Kelly's Irish Linens. Carrie Crean worked here as a clerk. At the New
Year's party in the parish hall, at midnight, Carrie Crean had wrapped
herself around Alf and planted a kiss on his lips that Margaret herself

would have been embarrassed to give him, at least in public. She had seen the same color lipstick then, on both their mouths.

Margaret entered the old store with its fresh linen and wool fragrance. Tablecloths, handkerchiefs, bed linens, and blankets were suspended under the pressed-tin ceiling; the place was a veritable forest of textiles, and Carrie Crean was in it somewhere. Margaret went up the aisle, alert. She felt that all she needed to do was look into Carrie's face, and she would know.

Evelyn Brockhurst was there, examining a display of fancy handkerchiefs. Her face was as wrinkled as a peach pit and her head shook continually with some kind of nervous disorder. She sang alongside Margaret in the Anglican choir, where her presence was a source of embarrassment. She whooped on the high notes, but no one had the courage to tell her she should quit.

"I hear you're singing for the Clarke wedding."

"Yes. Saturday."

Evelyn's head wagged back and forth, as if she were continually saying, Well, who would believe that?

Margaret smiled thinly. She was aware of life in other parts of the store, somewhere in that thicket of hanging cloths, that deep scent of wools and linens. Perhaps Carrie Crean was eavesdropping.

"What are you singing, dear?"

"I'm sorry?"

"For the wedding."

"Oh, just a little thing. It's called 'Seven Wishes for You.'"

"I've never heard of that. Is it nice?"

"Yes, lovely."

No, no, it's not, Evelyn's head said. Deep in the aisles, someone dropped a pair of scissors.

"And how's that boy of yours?"

"Joe?"

"Such a nice-looking lad. I'll bet he has to shoo off the girls. I think he takes after his father."

"Sorry?"

"So good-looking!" Evelyn cried.

It was a harmless conversation, except that Margaret felt that Carrie Crean might be listening and this made every word portentous, like a tolling bell. Finally she escaped. She moved on down the aisle and back up again, glancing into the bays, priming herself to meet Carrie Crean. But apparently she was not in the store.

IN A FEW days, Carrie Crean's presence had grown to fill the town, to the point where the rivers and the very shape of the hills suggested her: her blond curls, small twinkling eyes, her strange, wide, thin-lipped mouth—like a frog's, Margaret thought, with fascination and loathing. She couldn't visit the stores now without thinking she might run into Carrie Crean, without a sense of dread that quickened her pulse and left her as alert as a soldier.

She watched Alf, dissecting his every comment and gesture, while pretending that nothing was wrong. He seemed in a much better mood than he had been after Pete's funeral, and in fact was quite affectionate with her. She no longer trusted this affection, though, even when he suddenly hugged or kissed her with real exuberance; Margaret suspected she was not the real cause of his outburst but only catching the overflow. When he announced on a Saturday night that he was going to the Legion, she invented an excuse to phone him. And he was there, a familiar voice like an island in the babble of background noise. Her relief died within seconds of hanging up. What was to prevent Carrie Crean from being there too? She supposed the whole town knew about Alf and Carrie Crean. Yes, they were probably all laughing at her or pitying her, and from then on she saw the secret playing in the eyes of nearly everyone.

She told herself it was all nonsense, she hadn't a shred of proof. For a few minutes, an hour or two, she would keep busy enough to forget. But then she would remember, with a sickening plunge that seemed to prove by its very violence the truth of what she suspected. How could such strong feelings be prompted by nothing?

On Sunday she felt she would know. She would see Carrie Crean in the church choir. Margaret did not usually wear makeup, but before church she applied lipstick and rouge and a touch of eyeliner, then cleaned it all off in a fury of dissatisfaction. Carrie Crean was—what, fifteen years younger than she? There was nothing in Margaret's bottles to compete with that. In the end, she used lipstick and rouge only, and felt as if she were wearing a mask, grotesque and comical.

Even before Margaret saw Carrie, the church seemed alive with her anticipation. The old doors to the Parish Hall with their chevron pattern, the brazierlike lamps hanging from the high ceiling, the choir members in their dark red gowns, the familiar neat figure of Jack Ramsay, so brightly welcoming in his robes—all these were as vivid to Margaret as if she had never seen them before. She pressed into the passageway where the gowns hung. Beyond a half-open door, the piping, wintery notes of Helen's organ were filling the main body of the church. People were sliding into their pews. And there she was, Carrie Crean, standing right in front of her, talking to Brian Stokes, a gangly tenor who leaned over the young woman, grinning.

Margaret's gown hung just behind Brian. She advanced toward it, smiling through her makeup mask.

Carrie Crean's mouth moved. The thin froglike lips with their coating of pink lipstick shaped the words *Hi, Margaret!* and the tiny eyes brightened. Brian Stokes turned. Greetings fluttered in the close air.

"I've decided to get that organ," Brian told Margaret. His long face was at once boyish and sepulchral.

"Oh, yes?" Margaret drawled. His words made no sense to her.

"I was just saying to Carrie, we might as well have it now, while Mom's around to enjoy it."

"Enjoy it while you can," Carrie Crean sang, with a coy, knowing glance at Margaret. Blushing, Margaret managed to remember that for weeks Brian had been ruminating publicly about buying a Hammond organ. He'd been in quite a turmoil over it, but then, other than his sickly mother, with whom he lived in a tidy little house on John Street, he didn't have much else to be in a turmoil about.

His breath smelled as if he'd been drinking turpentine.

"I don't play that well," Brian said, "but Carrie was just suggesting that Helen might give me lessons."

"I daresay she would," Margaret said. Carrie Crean gave her another complicit smile, though exactly what it was trying to tell her, Margaret did not know. For a moment she felt faint; groping for her gown, she nearly dropped it on the floor in utter confusion. She'd been certain that seeing Carrie Crean would reveal in a twinkling whether she had been betrayed. But she couldn't tell, one way or the other. Either this woman standing an arm's-length away was destroying her life, or she was just blond, innocent, indifferently pretty Carrie, chattering in a rather mindless way to someone about organ lessons.

They went together into the Parish Hall. Walking behind Carrie Crean, Margaret was struck by how small and slight she was, almost built like a boy; petite was the word. Around her neck, the edge of her gown had gotten turned under.

"Here," Margaret said, suddenly commanding. "You're rumpled at the back. Let me fix you."

So Carrie Crean stood while Margaret smoothed her gown and passed her trembling hands over the young woman's shoulders for good measure. She was treating her kindly and controlling her too, dealing with her like a schoolgirl. If she was guilty, Margaret's kindness could only make her feel guiltier, perhaps guilty enough to stop whatever it was she was doing with Alf, if they were doing anything.

Touching her, Margaret felt an odd thrill of excitement, imagining how Carrie would feel to Alf. "There," she said, her voice tightening. "All done."

Turning, Carrie did an extraordinary thing, so extraordinary that the memory of it persisted for days afterward. The young woman puckered her wide pinkish mouth until there was just a little black hole at the center, shaped like a diamond, and blew Margaret a kiss.

The kiss was too much. Margaret was left in a state of outrage. It seemed that Carrie had flung her an insult, a taunt. All through the service, Margaret kept her eye on the other woman, who was seated just ahead and a little to the left, her cap of curls nodding now over her purse as she extracted a candy, unwrapped it with a rustle of cellophane, and popped it into her mouth. Margaret caught every twitch of her cheek. By moving her head, she could make out Alf, where he sat with the children, but at that distance she couldn't see whether his pale blue eyes were making contact with Carrie. She was certain, though, that there was something between them. The more she thought about that kiss, those lips pursing up at her, the more it seemed proof—terrible, mocking proof—of everything she suspected.

On the drive home, she was short with Alf and the children, and while making their Sunday dinner (she had put a roast in the oven before church) she managed to break a bowl and burn the scalloped potatoes. The curious thing was, she was no longer thinking of Alf and Carrie Crean. They had sunk into the blackness of a more general fury, for as she laid out her best plates—they were chipped and old-fashioned and not nearly good enough—her whole life felt like a mistake and an injustice.

That night, sitting as usual at her dresser, she nearly confronted him. She nearly asked (he was standing in his underwear while he hung up his trousers), Are you having an affair with Carrie Crean? But in the end she said nothing and went to bed feeling armed by her silence. There was something about knowing his secret that gave her an advantage. And, too, she was afraid of the truth, of the edge it might drop her over.

Then, lying on her back in the dark, all her cold, furious strength vanished in an instant. Tears slid down her cheeks and tickled her neck. Beside her, Alf seemed to be asleep. Moving very slowly, she touched the back of her wrist to his buttocks. She wanted to reassure herself of his reality. She remembered their first night together, in a small hotel in London, twenty-four years ago. He had been so excited by her nakedness: he had wanted her to stand in the light of the lamp while he marveled over her—worshiped her, really. She had been awkward and ashamed and embarrassed by *his* nakedness, though she made a half-hearted attempt to touch his erection. He had hurt her, and ever since she had felt sex was something she did more for his sake than for hers. She had pleasure, of course—you couldn't help but have pleasure if someone was touching you the way you liked, in certain places. But she'd never felt excited by him, not the way he seemed excited by her, with a fever of anticipation. In certain moods (she hadn't seen him in one for some time, mind you) he fairly pranced with eagerness, he couldn't keep his hands off her. It was all a bit of a mystery. She wondered if there wasn't something wrong with her—sex just didn't seem to matter very much. It all struck her as faintly silly.

Perhaps she hadn't done her job as a woman. Perhaps she hadn't worked hard enough at pleasing Alf or herself. She felt she had let her husband slip away through a net she might have mended. She pressed a little harder, with the back of her wrist. He smacked his lips and wiggled away.

The thought occurred to her that if she confronted him—if there was a blowup—he might move out. Where would that leave her? There was a woman, Edna Carnegie, who had lived in the North End, in a lovely old house with blue shutters, until her husband ran off with a hairdresser from Johnsonville. Now Edna Carnegie and her two children were stuck in a small house on Willard, beside the mills. Margaret saw her often, a tall handsome figure buoyed by desolate pride. Apparently she had taken a job in a factory in Johnsonville.

She had always thought of Edna Carnegie with a kind of indulgent pity, but here she was, only a whisker away, perhaps, from the same fate. What would she do if she was left on her own—give music lessons? That would scarcely bring in tuppence. She lay looking up at the ceiling, where a thin spoke of light was reflected from the street. Life was so precarious. You thought you were safe as houses; you had your family, your friends, your routines, surrounding you like the walls of a fortress. Yet the whole time you were hanging by a thread. "Oh, God," she whispered, "bless Alf and me. Help us—" Breaking off, she turned on her side. Her tears were coming freely now. "Bless Edna Carnegie," she murmured. Suddenly, she was aware of Carrie Crean's wide frog mouth. It seemed to be in the room with her, only inches away. Startled, she lifted her head, searching in the dark.

33

WALKING HOME FROM skating, Penny, Ginny, and Brenda stopped outside the Oasis, under the broken neon sign with its buzzing palm tree. The warm afternoon sun lit up the display of old-fashioned ice-cream-making equipment in the show window.

"So I guess you can't come in," Brenda said to Penny. She sounded stern, like somebody's mother.

"I can," Penny said, pushing past her.

Inside, she peered at the long glass counter with its jujubes and sea foam and licorice straps and candy pipes and candy cigarettes in little packages that said Camels and Lucky Strike. Putting her hand in her pocket, she touched her packet of cookies. She knew she should eat them, she could feel an insulin reaction coming on, but she was sick of Arrowroots. Besides, the cookies weren't in any shape to be eaten. Penny had left the packet in her boot while she was skating. When she'd come back, she'd forgotten it was there, and put her foot into her boot and mashed it.

Outside, they ran into Ginny's aunt Karen, who was pushing her baby, Jennifer, in a stroller. While Brenda and Ginny leaned over and made a fuss over Jennifer, trying to get her to respond, Penny hung back. The baby watched them solemnly, her huge grave eyes looking out from under her bonnet. She seemed uncertain about all the commotion. It must be so sad to be a baby, Penny thought, to be so helpless, while people came and stuck things in your face. When the baby looked at her, Penny smiled, and Jennifer, her toothless mouth opening, laughed a silent laugh.

They walked on down Water Street. Brenda and Ginny took bites out of their Choco-rolls, which looked like little round slices of chocolate cake, with a swirl of white icing through the centers. Penny fixed on the other girls' mouths; their voices started to sound far away, as if coming down a pipe. She was having trouble lifting her legs. On the bridge to the Island she stumbled.

"Clumsy boots," Ginny said. She held out her Choco-roll. "Want some?"

"She's not supposed to have candy," Brenda said.

"I'm having a reaction," Penny said. She meant she should have a bite of Choco-roll. She needed sugar, fast, so her insulin would have something to work on. But Ginny had gone on eating. Penny couldn't find the words to stop her.

They reached Brenda's house with its high porch and windows where the beige curtains were always shut tight. Ginny and Brenda started up the driveway. Penny kept on down the street. Getting home was the most important thing now. "Where are you going?" she heard Ginny calling after her.

Penny turned and saw her friends standing behind a snowbank. They appeared strange to her, with their white skates hanging over their chests like chunks of snow and their faces punctured with eye holes and mouth holes and nose holes.

"I know who your father's girlfriend is!" Brenda sang.

Penny heard the taunt as something small and bright and distant—nothing to do with her. She trudged down Water. There was something she was supposed to eat. She thought of a cookie: the sort of soft yellow cookie babies ate, with scalloped edges. This cookie existed somewhere, she was sure of it. The cookie was home, and home was in the sun that had turned the Island to a white blaze.

Girlfriend? Who your father's girlfriend is? Sometimes, her father called her his girlfriend. He said he'd take her out on a date, and Penny would say, No, you can't. Daddies can't do that. But she liked being teased by him.

Her legs were getting heavier with each step, like trying to run in Lake Erie when the water was up to her waist. She could see her house now, a shadow in the dazzling heaps of snow. Then she fell to her hands and knees. She had tripped on the curb. She stared at the white nicked toe of her skate on the sidewalk; where had that come from? She was so heavy and sleepy that she got right down on the sidewalk and curled up. But no, she couldn't sleep, she had to keep going. She rolled on her back and looked up at the blue, cloudless sky. It went on and on, as big as Lake

Erie, and there was nothing to do but sink into it. The sky came closer. At the same time, it drew into the distance, like Lake Erie when they drove away from it after a holiday, its light growing smaller out the back window of the car and a lump rising in her throat to think their holiday was over and it would be a year, a whole year of school and winter, until they could come here again, to the blue lake where the waves danced and sparkled—all the way, her dad had once said, from America.

A kick of panic—she remembered the cookie. She struggled to her feet and started up the sidewalk to her house.

She saw a squat, pimply nose with big nostrils. She saw a small eye and a red scarf. It took her a moment to realize that these details added up to Mrs. Horsfall, their neighbor. Mrs. Horsfall was blocking the narrow passage between their houses.

Mrs. Horsfall said something, in her deaf-and-dumb person's voice.

"Sorry, I have to go," Penny shouted. She stepped forward and fell into Mrs. Horsfall. She could smell her, a smothering wave of perfume exactly like the smell of the flowers at Uncle Pete's funeral. Her face pressed into Mrs Horsfall's bosom, but what she saw was Uncle Pete's sharp, waxy face in his coffin.

HALF AN HOUR later, Penny was sitting at the kitchen table, feeling almost normal. She had a headache, but she knew what was going on, clear as a bell. Her mother stood over her with her hands on her hips. Penny took another sip of orange juice. "You didn't touch your cookies," her mother said, pointing to the crushed packet on the table. "Penny— you let yourself go into a reaction. What were you doing? What happened to your Arrowroots?"

"I forgot," Penny said. This was half true. Below the table, she crossed her fingers.

"You could have—" Her mother broke off in frustration. But Penny knew what she meant to say: *You could have died.*

She felt ashamed for having a reaction, ashamed of frightening her mother, ashamed, even, of having diabetes; all of it was her fault. She moved her empty glass on the table, in a prickly misery of shame. With a lurch—she almost felt sick—Brenda's words came back to her.

"Does Daddy have a girlfriend?" she said.

At the stove, her mother stopped stirring a pot.

"What a ridiculous idea," her mother said. But her voice sounded high and hard. "Whoever told you that?" Penny put her head down. "Penny, who told you that?"

"Nobody."

"Somebody must have." Her mother turned from the stove. "Penny, who was it?"

"Brenda Stubbs," she said, barely audible. "I think she was only teasing."

"Just the sort of thing you'd expect from Brenda Stubbs," her mother said, suddenly rummaging in a cupboard. After a few seconds she slammed the cupboard door shut, walked to the cellar, and disappeared. Penny could hear the washing machine churning away down there, *glug-glug, glug-glug,* like a bored, unhappy person who hated her work.

She went up to her room, which she saw her mother had tidied. She'd told Penny to tidy it, and Penny had, but her tidying was never good enough. Her mother had put everything away on shelves; books, dolls, even the skipping rope, wound in a neat coil and tied up with string. The order in the room oppressed her. It was like nobody lived here, like Penny had moved away. She felt so unhappy she flung herself on the bed.

After a while, she rolled to her back and raised her foot in the air. There was a hole in her red tights where her big toe showed, and as she wiggled the toe, which seemed to have a life of its own—a funny little toe person waving around, saying hello—she remembered the soap. Jumping off the bed, she tugged open the drawer of her table and there it was: her bar of laundry soap.

One day at the stores, when she and her dad were shopping, they had run into Miss Hobsbawn, who had told him about Penny's fish. In her shouting man's voice she'd talked about how fine a carver Penny was and looked at her with eyes gleaming ferociously, pleased as punch. Afterward, Penny's dad had taken her to the A&P and bought this big bar of soap. "Don't carve it right away," he said. "Think about it a bit."

Penny put the bar on her table. She took out her small jackknife and pulled the blade open. She was excited now, like on Christmas when she was the first downstairs in the living room where the presents waited in the dimness under the tree. Everything else was gone. Brenda Stubbs and Ginny Lamport were gone, her diabetes was gone, her mother was gone. She was alone in her room, with her feet twined around the legs of her chair, staring in the stillness of happiness at a bar of yellow laundry soap.

34

THE WINDOWS IN Matt Honnegger's office gave onto the flat graveled roof of the dyehouse, where pigeons waddled in the late winter sun. Alf watched them absently.

"I'm afraid I'm stuck here again," he told Margaret, on the phone. A new bird, white as chalk, sailed with breathtaking grace to a landing. It approached the others skeptically, head bobbing like a boxer's. He had stood just here, watching these same birds, when Margaret had phoned with the news that Pete was dead.

She said, her voice young, plaintive, "Well, if you get free later, come home, will you?"

He closed his eyes. "Sure I will."

Each time he lied to her, he felt he was driving a small sharp blade into her flesh. The cut was so swift she did not feel it, and yet she was aware of something, he suspected. At these moments, oddly, he was certain he loved her.

He worked until nearly two, then punched out and drove off in the Biscayne, along Willard. The sun beat on the wilting snow, on abandoned porches; the Tuesday afternoon had filled with a Sunday languor, as if the purpose of life had failed. As always, he passed Lucille's street, Pine, finally turning up a stony lane that rose along the rail embankment toward the old pioneer cemetery. He turned into the dilapidated garage behind Lucille's house and sat for a while in the shadows, keeping company with the horned beast in the corner: the canvas-shrouded motorbike Lucille's brother Frank had ridden until a couple of years ago, when he'd died in a hunting accident up north. It was two minutes after two. Billy would be at school, while Lucille—who was now working part-time at the A&P—would be waiting for him. Advancing across her small backyard, past Fuzz's empty doghouse, he found the kitchen door locked: unusual. Light smeared the linoleum in the empty hall. For a moment she seemed not only away from home but gone in some more permanent way, dead or injured, and in his head a voice offered alibis to some faceless prosecutor. *I only arrived at two; they saw me in the mill at two. You can check my time card.*

Then Lucille came down the hall. Her tight gray T-shirt was molded to the abrupt mound of her breasts, showing the wrinkles in her bra. With the swiftness of light, the arrow of desire passed through his chest.

She twisted open the lock.

"Trying to keep me out?"

She cast him a hard glance and began to clear the kitchen table. Plates and glasses crashed into the sink. She turned on a tap.

"You okay?"

She did not answer. He found a towel and dried for her. He had no idea what he'd done, but his guilt was on a hair trigger these days. Penitent, cagey, he put away a glass.

"What is it?" he said, smiling.

She set a plate in the rack.

"I want to go out."

"Out?"

"You know, like people do. I'd like to get in that car of yours and go"— she waved her hand airily; soapy water flew onto his cheek—"out for a drive."

"We'd be seen," he said gently.

"Maybe we should be," she said, attacking a pan. "I think I'd like to be seen."

"But there's Margaret," he said. He spoke his wife's name warily, hating to invoke her. He never talked about Margaret with Lucille. It had seemed a way of protecting them both.

Lucille shrugged.

He did not love Lucille Boileau. At that moment, watching her shrug off Margaret, he half hated her. But he wanted her—with a fury of frustration that had dried his mouth.

"We can talk about it," he said.

"What's to say? I get my coat, we go out."

Her eyes burned now, furiously challenging, though at the same time there was something misfocused in them, that missed him by a hair.

"But if Margaret finds out—" He smiled again gently, placating. Why should he ruin his marriage for the sake of their pleasant afternoons? He was pained that she couldn't see this.

"Queen Margaret," she said, mocking. She studied him a moment. "You know, if all it is is sex, maybe you should pay me. You sneak over here, we go bang-bang, you pay me. A lot more honest, eh?"

"Lucille—" He felt she was tearing something valuable, in her anger.

"I've done it, you know. Out west there: Winnipeg, Edmonton. The good johns of Winnipeg!"

His face went hot.

"You're shocked," she said, with satisfaction.

"No," he said. "Yes."

She was darkly triumphant, as if she'd cut herself on purpose. "I started when I was thirteen. I can always start again."

"Don't," he said.

"Don't what?"

"Hurt yourself."

The look in her eyes reverted slowly from triumph back to mockery. She began to laugh, hoarsely and without joy. Then stopped.

"You kill me," she said. She tossed a sponge into the sink. "You don't want me to hurt myself. I wonder why that is. Do you love me?"

She knew he didn't love her; it was her trump card.

All her life, its desperation and defiant survival, seemed revealed in her face, daring him to answer. Beneath her lower lip was a small scar in the shape of the letter C. She had told him it was from a skating accident. Now he doubted it. He doubted everything he knew about her.

"I care for you," he said.

She snorted in disgust and stepped away from him, toward the bare beige wall mapped with cracks. On a calendar he saw a photo of a jet fighter, silver on blue, like a holy medal.

"You see, I've been here before. Except most of the others—I don't mean out west; I mean here in town—" She stopped. He felt he was being reconsidered, judged. She said, "I came back here to start over, you know. No more johns, just good honest boys. That's what I was going to have—good honest boys." Feeling neither good nor honest, he shivered at her words. "They at least thought they loved me," she said, a smile of pain twisting her face. "At least they said they did. And who knows? Maybe they did. I'm really not so bad, you know."

"No," he managed. She seemed not to hear him. An icicle fell outside, passing her head like a dagger.

"Then you know what happens?" she said. "You know what always happens? They leave me!" Grinning, she flung out her hand; it fell and struck her thigh. "They up and leave me, all of them. Do you know why that is?"

He shook his head and stood waiting. Everything he thought of saying seemed trivial. Besides, he knew that he too would leave her.

"If I can do anything," he said finally. This sounded so pathetic he dared not meet her eyes.

"I told you," she said. "You can take me for a ride."

He thought he would take her straight into the country, where they were less likely to be seen. But she insisted on a town route; she needed cigarettes from a particular store that "gave her a deal," she said. Glumly obedient, wondering what this deal was, he took the Biscayne across the Bridge Street bridge and up Shade, then over to Station. She raised her broad face to the windshield, in a show of defiance. She was going to have a good time, a pleasant, normal time, or at least act like she was.

An old man was shuffling up Station Hill. Folded at the waist, so that his face peered straight down at the sidewalk, he planted his cane in front of him and then caught up to it with shuffling baby steps. He traveled miles this way, like a snail: Ralph O'Grady.

"Give him a ride," Lucille demanded.

"He's all right."

"No, stop!"

He stopped. He'd always felt it was only a matter of time until his secret came out, though he never imagined it happening on an afternoon spin with Ralph O'Grady. But he was helpless to resist, already guilty about leaving her. Guilty, too, about getting her fired. He thought about her revelation that she'd once worked the streets. He owed her something, for the life she had had. Still, all these reasons were pathetic, weren't they? Weighed against even a featherweight of love, they were nothing.

And, too, he had not yet given up on his afternoon. In half an hour or an hour they might be back at her house, in her swaying bed. All he needed was fifteen minutes, even five. Just looking at her in her packed jeans, as she went over to talk to Ralph, made him want her. Maybe he did love her. In bed, she met him as no woman ever had, with an appetite equal to his, even greater. At certain moments they seemed to burn up the world, replace it with something entirely their own. He was grateful for that, grateful for the pleasure of knowing her naked: her strong, thick body and darkly budded breasts, as if life itself had taken her form and offered itself to him each Tuesday afternoon.

He watched as she brought Ralph to the car. The old man was so bent she had to turn him around and ease him, rear first, into the backseat. Ralph cracked his head on the top of the door but hardly seemed to notice. "Oopsies," Lucille said.

They continued up Station Hill. In the rearview, Alf saw the old man's twisted face and red eyes peering from under his cap. He wondered if Ralph knew where he was.

Lucille asked Ralph how he was doing.

"Oh, can't complain."

"At least the weather's warm, anyways."

"Is it?"

"We take you to your place then?" Alf asked.

"Who's this?" Ralph said. In the mirror, Alf saw the old man squinting at him.

"This is Alf Walker. You know him."

"Oh, sure, I know him."

The feeble mouth grinned.

The Biscayne passed the station and crossed the humpbacked bridge into the North End. Lucille had turned sideways, her arm crooked over the back of the seat as she chatted with Ralph. Alf was aware of her thighs snugged up together in her jeans, sloping toward him, her fingers toying idly at his shoulder. He was stalking her, he couldn't help it, even here where every window seemed to watch, where his reputation and perhaps even his marriage had already begun to unravel; all he could think about, really, was getting his hands on her. You pathetic bugger, he thought. He remembered sharks he'd seen once in a photo, swirling ecstatically in water reddened with their own blood.

After they'd dropped Ralph off in front of his little bungalow, they drove to the Junction, to Hank Hays' Lunch and Gas. Lucille strode briskly in front of the car, her head up like royalty, and disappeared in the door with its slanting ORANGE CRUSH sign. When John Henson's gray station wagon pulled up to the pumps, Alf averted his face, praying that Lucille would stay inside until Henson drove away. But in a few moments the stooped, grinning figure of the Anglican sexton leaned over to wave at him through the windshield. Alf had no choice but to roll down the window.

"Can you believe this weather?"

"Not really."

John Henson gave his fixed, wincing smile. He always looked as if something sharp were poking at him under his clothes.

The door with its Orange Crush handle opened and Lucille emerged.

"I'm just giving Lucille Boileau a ride," Alf explained, too soon. John went on grinning, clearly not understanding. Lucille passed in front of the hood. John glanced at her, but he didn't really take note until she climbed in beside Alf. Then the sexton's head came back down and he peered at the woman in the black leather motorcycle jacket.

"I don't believe we've met," Lucille said.

"Hah! Well!"

John was smiling at full wattage now, showing tortured gums. He was never at ease around women, except perhaps very old ones, where he got to play the gentleman with a gallant hint of all the risqué things he would do if they were younger.

"Alfie, introduce us."

Alf had no choice. Lucille and John's clasped hands shook in front of his face. He didn't doubt that John knew who she was, even if he'd never spoken to her. Every man in town knew who Lucille was.

"I'm just giving her a lift," Alf said, trying again.

"We're going for a little spin," Lucille said brightly, ruffling Alf's hair.

"Right," John said, his eyes bulging. He jerked up his thumb like an umpire calling *Out!* at home plate. "I'm just filling up."

They drove away. A slow freight was rolling through the level crossing, each boxcar floating with majestic, drumming grace behind the barrier. Far up the tracks, the invisible engine wailed. Alf asked for a cigarette and Lucille lit it for him before passing it over. He considered. There was no predicting what John Henson would make of seeing them together. It would be a test of his Christianity at the very least.

They followed Danson's Lane to the old one-room schoolhouse, now a residence, and swung north among thawing fields streaked with black earth, low ranges of dirty snow, rivers of glittering ice water. High behind them, the sun of early March poured down its brightness. Smoking, Alf began to relax. Light flickered through the woodlots, and in a muddy paddock a black horse broke suddenly into a trot, throwing its head as if tossing invisible reins.

He thought again of what she had told him earlier. He conjured up an Indian girl in a skimpy dress, or maybe stovepipe jeans, grinning from the curb while men like him looked her over. The vision prompted a cutting sense of loneliness, yet he was fascinated. In the seat next to him, Lucille had tilted her head back a little, her eyes gazing almost dreamily up the road as it unfurled beyond the smoke from her filtered Caporal.

By the time they reached the village of Cairn, her silence had turned gloomy. Nothing he said roused her. She smoked fiercely, ignoring him and his remarks. He drove through the backstreets to a place where a pond spread toward a cedar bush. The pond was still covered with ice and snow, perforated by a few dead trees. He stopped and rolled down the window. A woodpecker was tapping somewhere, with an irregular precision. The bird was in its own world, with work that wholly occupied it, a purpose. But they were in the smoke-filled car, trapped in a kind of vacuum.

"What's the matter?" he said. He reached along the back of the seat to touch her hair. A quarter to three; their afternoon might be salvaged yet. "You're so beautiful," he said. He meant it.

She scowled and a chill went through him. He felt instantly attacked. At the same time, she did not seem to really see him. He might have been any man sitting there.

They drove back to town by the Galt highway. The sense of oppression in the car had deepened. It was as if some terrible thing had happened between them, and now it was impossible to speak without calling up the terrible thing itself.

She smoked steadily, with an impatience that verged on fury. She had to get back to the house, she said; Billy would be home soon. He suggested there was still time for him to come in with her, but even he could see that the afternoon had slipped away. At the corner of Bridge and Willard she suddenly demanded that he let her out. But when he stopped the car, she went on sitting, staring straight, as if she were waiting for something: waiting with a stubborn defiance to receive something he could not imagine, which she seemed to believe she was owed.

3 5

WHEN LUCILLE SLAMMED the door of the Biscayne and walked away down Willard, Alf felt they were through. In a way, he was relieved; she'd taken the initiative, which saved him from playing the bastard, or at least of playing it to the hilt. Anyway, the stress of lying to Margaret, of always worrying they'd be caught, had often seemed too great. He had promised himself a hundred times he would give Lucille up. But then the anticipation of pleasure and, even more, the pleasure itself, obliterated everything, like a drug. By the end of the week he was having withdrawal symptoms. Even his hands seemed heavier, lonely for Lucille Boileau.

Friday night, in a windless silence, it began to snow. On Saturday morning large eyelid-catching flakes of indeterminate shape were still floating down from an invisible sky, settling pure whiteness over the yard. Alf and Margaret sat in the kitchen in their dressing gowns, eating a late breakfast. From another room came the squawk of the Saturday morning cartoons. The renewal of winter gave the house a feeling of snug isolation; it seemed to Alf he had managed to return to the simple pleasures of home and normality—a second cup of coffee, the scrape of a knife on toast, the Saturday paper—after a time of insanity that half perplexed him. When the phone rang, it startled them both.

"It's for you." Margaret held the receiver as if it were slightly repugnant.

"Alfie," the voice said. Lucille.

She might just as well have erupted inside him. Her familiar voice, raw with cigarette smoke, seemed in danger of spilling from the receiver.

"I've got a broken pipe," she said. "There's water everywhere."

"In the cellar?" he said, conscious of Margaret moving at the counter.

"It's an emergency," Lucille said.

"I'm not really a plumber," he said sternly. "I'm not sure I have the right tools."

"Oh you've got the right tools, Alfie."

He turned to the wall.

"Look, have you tried a plumber?"

"I don't have the money, Alf. There's a foot of water down there now. If you can't come—"

"I'll see what I can do," he said. "I've got to get dressed."

"Who was that?" Margaret said, when he'd hung up.

"Lucille Boileau. Her cellar's flooded. I told her—well, you heard me. I guess she doesn't have much money."

"I wonder why she'd call here?" Margaret said, in a muffled voice, to the coffeepot.

He shrugged, doing his best to look puzzled, innocent. But a wild, youthful happiness had invaded him; he felt like seizing his wife and dancing.

ALF HAD NEVER been in Lucille's cellar, with its rough stone walls and low ceiling. Against one wall, a broken pipe spewed a ragged plume of water that crashed noisily into the flood lapping at the bottom stair. Lucille watched as he sloshed around in his rubber boots, searching with a hoe for the main valve.

"Alf?"

Feeling under the icy water, he found the tap. In a few seconds, the stream had petered to a dribble.

"Don wants me to work at the store. One of the girls phoned in sick. Could you keep an eye on Billy?"

He looked at her on the stairs, stooping in the weak light, her breasts free (he guessed) under her loose plaid shirt. He was going to be here anyway, fixing the leak. Besides, he'd do anything to be back in her good books. It was a kind of madness. He was like the drowning man who observes with curious equanimity the diminishing spot of light above his sinking head.

"He hasn't been well," she said, with an uncharacteristically coy smile.

"All right."

She let him kiss her, briefly, on the mouth. "I'm sorry," he said, meaning he was sorry for their last time together—for whatever he'd done or hadn't done that ruined their afternoon. She tousled his head, like a boy's, and a few minutes later he heard the front door slam. As he was poking about with the hoe, trying to find the floor drain (wherever it was, it was plugged), Billy materialized on the stairs. He sat in mismatched socks, jeans, and a red T-shirt with ATTAWAN FALL FAIR printed on it. In his hand was a large toy soldier clad in army khakis and a GI helmet.

"You could float a boat down here," Alf said, trying to be friendly. He was in a good mood, feeling that he and Lucille were back on track.

Billy said nothing.

"I remember a flood when I was a boy. They had to come and take us out in boats. The whole Island was under water. That was before they raised the dikes." Again he saw the ghostly ice cakes creeping through the misted streets, the rowboats nudging up to isolated houses, the swift mysterious rippling of waters.

Billy maneuvered his toy soldier, making him jump—or fall—down a couple of stairs, making sure he landed on his head. He might as well have been deaf for all the attention he paid to Alf. Yet when Alf turned away, he felt the boy was watching. He was like a wild animal with his dark eyes, which darted away at even the suggestion of a look from someone else.

Alf found the drain. There was a rock in it, apparently, as smooth as the top of a skull, wedged solid. He tried to pry it out: with his fingers, with the edge of the hoe, with a screwdriver.

"Somebody's put a rock in here," he said. There was no response from the stairs. Glancing around, he saw the boy was gone.

He got the rock out, but there was still a lot of muck clogging the drain. As he dug around, he could hear Billy moving upstairs. After a while, he went up to check on him.

He found him in his narrow room, sitting on his bed—which was just a mattress on the floor—with a mess of comic books littering the disheveled blankets. There was a smell of stale urine; in the uncurtained window, a ferny garden of frost could not quite obscure the dingy clapboard wall of the house next door. Billy's gaze took in Alf's knees, fled back to his comic.

"Your mom tells me you've been sick."

"Yup." Billy's answer came from far back in his throat—a tiny man talking, a tough little gangster, almost comical.

"Feeling better now?"

"Yup."

"Good."

Billy was turning the pages of the comic book, too fast to be really seeing anything. Alf felt he wasn't just shy. The boy seemed frightened of him. Alf had an impulse to go away—to stop torturing him with his presence—but he was held by Billy's isolation. He wondered what his life had been, who his father was. Lucille had gone with a lot of men. It was as if Billy was the child of them all, abandoned and strange.

He said, "I'm Jamie's father, you know."

"Yup."

"I'm a friend of your mother's. We used to work at the same place."

"Yup."

"Are you hungry? Can I get you something to eat?"

"Nope."

Alf hesitated, at a loss. He had never met a boy like this. He remembered Billy's silence, that night he'd driven him home. He watched as Billy twisted his comic book into a roll and bit his upper lip. He seemed independent of the adult world somehow, of all worlds, locked in one of his own. He seemed to Alf to be guarding a secret and at the same time waiting for someone to come and guess what it was. *He* couldn't tell.

"My grandfather drowned in Lake Erie," Billy said, tightening the roll. The statement came out of nowhere.

"I knew your grandfather," Alf said, squatting down, hoping to find his way into Billy's gaze. "One winter—it was a long time ago—we cut ice together on the Atta."

The boy went on fooling with the tube of paper, but Alf felt he was listening.

"That was before people had refrigerators. They kept all their food in iceboxes. The iceman used to come around in the summer. He'd give us pieces of ice to suck. Sort of like Popsicles."

The boy's black eyes briefly met his. A stab of excitement—of life in the quick—pierced Alf's gut.

"Sure," Alf said, warming. "Actually, he didn't give them to us. We'd steal them, when he was away from his truck."

Billy's throat emitted a little laugh: *heh!* He understood *that.*

"We'd go down by the river and suck them. Or, if it was hot, we'd rub them all over our faces and chests."

The boy was grinning openly now, his round face with its brown-edged teeth shining up at him, happy and appeased. Yet still, Alf suspected the boy had eluded him. His smile was like a mask offered to a greater power—a smiling power who demanded a smile in return. Something else was going on behind it, though, in those evasive, unreadable eyes, that moved Alf and held him there, in the little room.

36

THE TELEVISION FLOODED the McVeys' den with fake flickering moonlight. Lying on the couch, his head in Liz's lap, Joe watched an old Fred Astaire and Ginger Rogers movie, that spry and dapper man moving like an elf down a broad staircase, taking his platinum-headed love in his arms.

Turning his head, Joe began to pick at the buttons of Liz's blouse, exposing her peach satin bra with its frilly edges. Without taking her eyes off the screen, she helped him slide the bra up. Absently, Liz smoothed his hair. They could not make love tonight because her father had taken the car, and her mother and sister were up on the second floor. Her father, he supposed, was with Babs Wilcocks. Joe had seen the two of them a few nights ago, walking into the Vimy House LADIES AND ESCORTS, the tall man with the stocky, plain, fur-coated Babs on his arm, both looking almost formal in an old-fashioned way, and—casting greetings right and left—clearly making no effort to hide their relationship. Joe had never understood it: Doc McVey, the richest man in town, drinking in the Vimy House. He was a regular there, and had once, the story ran, gotten into a shoving match with Bud Reed over some remarks Bud had sent his way.

Joe caressed Liz's breast while her blank face continued to watch the screen. Through the ceiling came a thump. He wondered if Liz's mother had fallen. Two weeks before, he'd witnessed her—she'd consumed one too many gin and tonics—lean slowly sideways, like the tower of Pisa, with a bemused here-we-go smile in her sad eyes. He'd just managed to catch her.

"YOU NEVER TELL me you love me," Liz said.

Joe looked up at the too-bright violet eyes. She had told him she loved *him* once, whispering it in a little-girl voice as he lay in her arms in the Executive.

"You know I care for you." Her face flickered in the lunar light, impassive.

"I don't want my mother's life," she said, tugging sharply at his hair.

"No. Well, why should you?"

"The way he treats her," she said, now touching his forehead, as though evidence of her father's sins lay there.

"Hey, now, I don't treat you like that."

Once—this was driving up to Galt in the Lincoln—she had talked with remarkable candor about her father's affair with Babs Wilcocks. "He thinks it should be nothing, we should take it as nothing. After all, he's still here, or he is most of the time, he still loves us. He can't see the unhappiness he causes. I mean, he thinks it's unreasonable for us to be upset. He can't see why we can't we all be in a good mood and just be nice to everybody, like he is. Why do we have to spoil things? Us, spoiling things! The crazy thing is, most of the time we play it his way. We pretend nothing's wrong. Then something snaps: Mom gets drunk or— Mom gets drunk." It was the most frank she'd ever been with him. He had liked her better for it, had felt closer to her, once she dropped her theatrical manner. But at the same time, she had set a level of openness he couldn't match. She was asking for that now, her stare full of demands he couldn't meet.

Abruptly, he sat up. Hand in hand, Fred and Ginger were strolling happily through a crowd of partygoers. Neither was out of breath.

"Do you love me a little?" Liz said, ghostly behind him. Joe went still. Everything in the room called out for his answer: the deep couch, the fine desk with its brass-handled drawers, the gilt-framed pictures, even Fred and Ginger, pausing now in an embrace to look at each other in suspended bliss, waiting for Joe's response to come winging to them and make everything exactly right.

The thought of Anna hit with such force he caught his breath. Earlier that day she had come into the A&P. She had seemed delighted to find him sweeping the floor in his apron and stood chatting for a good five minutes. Since the time they'd talked in her bedroom, something seemed to have eased between them. He felt held in suspense around her, as if a happiness he could not quite reach were hovering nearby.

"Joe?" Liz said. "Do you?"

"Sure I do," he said. He had scarcely heard her. But he managed to reach out and squeeze her knee in its patterned stocking.

IT WAS JUST after midnight when he got home to find his mother in the kitchen. She was worried about his father. Apparently, Alf had left to go for a walk at eight, saying he'd be back in an hour or two. She wanted Joe to drive over to the Legion and look for him.

"Why don't we just phone?" he said.

"Joe," she urged, speaking with a fierce, loaded concentration, "please do this for me."

The pressure of unspoken things was in the room, and rather than broach them he took the Biscayne and drove over to the Flats. It was snowing again, large flakes drifting out of the dark to settle, a delicate fleece, on windshields and tree branches. He parked by the curb and approached the old brick house with its drawn curtains. He had never been in the Legion before—you had to be twenty-one—and the building was a place of mystery to him. If the war was still alive anywhere in Attawan, it was alive here, and as he pushed through the heavy doors into the dimly lit entrance hall, he sensed the mood of the thirties and forties, preserved in these rooms like clothes in an old trunk. From around a corner came the roar of voices and music; "The White Cliffs of Dover" was flowing in a slow nostalgic wave from the jukebox and a few people were singing drunkenly along. He was about to go on when he noticed display cases on either side of the hall. They were full of flags and old photographs and newspaper clippings: GERMANY SURRENDERS! But what stopped him were the army rifles, going right back to the Boer War. The nicked, polished wood and oiled metal of the Lee-Enfields spoke to him of the battles he had read about: Passchaendale, Vimy, Dieppe, Juno Beach, the Scheldt Estuary. There was a Mauser, too, that seemed to contain the very essence of the legendary enemy. Beside it sat a German helmet, its mythic shape like a pageboy haircut forged in steel.

Inside, he asked the barman, Nick Maroni, if he'd seen his father. Nick hadn't, but he tapped his head—a signal for Joe to remove his hat—and said it was okay for him to have a look, so he went gingerly through the rooms, his toque crushed in his hand, past the large framed picture of the Queen in her blue sash, saying hello to people who greeted him. On his way back he stopped at a large photo of a brigade of soldiers sitting around a square of improvised board tables, eating Christmas dinner from their mess tins. He scanned the scene intently, moved by the merriment of the young men in khaki, envying them the adventure of their lives.

Outside in the snowy silence, standing by a small fruit tree, its branches loaded with white, he was again overcome with a familiar sense of having missed his father's life, having understood nothing about years that seemed laden with rich, unheralded meaning. For a moment, alone in the poorly lit street lined with snow-muffled cars, he felt bereft.

He drove around the Flats for a while, past the mills, as desolate as prisons, and then started toward home. On Bridge Street he saw his father tramping toward the center of town. Snow had collected on the shoulders of his gray overcoat. When Joe drew up, his father stopped, hesitating before coming to the car, almost as if he did not recognize the Biscayne. Then he moved quickly and got in, with a gust of cold air. There was a drop of moisture on his nose.

"Hey, fella, what are you doing out here?"

"Oh, Mom—you know how she is. Worried you got lost or something."

He was immensely glad to have found his father.

"I stayed longer than I meant," his father said.

"At the Legion?" Joe said. "You were at the Legion?"

His father glanced at Joe and looked away.

"I was just there," Joe said, a bit off balance.

Since they'd played hockey on the river during the Christmas holidays, they'd been getting along pretty well, as they usually did if they trod lightly. Now he sensed some uneasiness in his father, which made him uneasy too. He drove forward, the tires spinning a little on the ramp to the bridge.

"I must have missed you," Joe said, eager to save his father discomfort over the discrepancy: perhaps he'd been in the washroom when Joe went through. "It's a great place," he said. "That collection of rifles . . ."

His father said nothing. Joe might have taken that as a warning, but he couldn't stop. Leaving the Legion, he had remembered his mother telling him that before the war his father had been a different man. He wanted to make contact with that younger, happier man who could talk at his ease and enjoy himself.

"I saw this picture, Christmas dinner 1944? I wondered if you knew anyone there. It was obviously taken in Europe. They seemed to be in a ruined church. They were having a great time. You remember any Christmases there?"

His father did not respond; he had sunk into one those baffling silences that made Joe feel he'd done something wrong, been cast out into an isolation of his own. Waiting at Shade for the light to change, he saw another car draw up beside them: Doc McVey—his wide, bespectacled face emanating its usual arrogance. For a moment, checking for traffic, he lit on Joe and his father without apparent recognition and then sped the Lincoln away up Shade. "Coming home from his girlfriend's, I guess," Joe said, trying to bridge the gap with a joke.

"Just drive," his father said.

Feeling suddenly chilled, Joe put the Biscayne in gear and they went on, between the darkened stores.

37

STANDING WITH BILLY below Rat's Hill, Jamie was shivering, his mittens and the seat of his pants soaked from repeated trips down the hill on the piece of ruined cardboard that lay at his feet. He wanted to go home, but there was a problem. Billy wanted to come with him.

"We could play with your soldiers," Billy said, his mouth hardly moving. His eyes traveled cagily from the zipper in Jamie's coat to Jamie's nose to some spot in the air between them. Far above, at the top of the hill, Wayne Cox stood with one foot on his toboggan, eyeing the ice chute that gleamed like a long stream of saliva in the hillside. In a nearby house, lights had come on, signaling snugness and safety.

"It's time for supper," Jamie said. "My dad'll be home."

"We could go up to your room."

"I don't think so."

"I could wait in your room while you eat."

"I don't know. I don't think so."

Billy grinned, refusing defeat. He wasn't wearing mittens and his coat didn't cover his brown, skinny wrists: he too was shivering, and there was a drugged, sleepy cast to his face.

"I guess I better go," Jamie said.

As he walked away, Billy spat and fell in beside him, his rubber boots squelching in the wet snow.

"Anyways," Billy said, "your dad's going to come and live in my house."

Jamie stopped. Suddenly his body felt wrapped in hotness.

"That's stupid. He's not."

"Yah, he is."

"That's stupid."

"Want to fight about it?" This was said so quickly Jamie knew Billy'd been planning it all along. When Billy had a problem, he would fight. If something wasn't true, he would make it be true with his fists.

"No, it's stupid."

"I'm not stupid!"

"I know. But my dad's not going to live with you. That's—silly."

"He came to our house."

"No, he didn't."

"Yeh, he did. He kissed my mom. I saw him do it in the cellar. That means he's going to live with us."

"No he didn't," Jamie said. But his face burned at the mention of the kiss. It didn't sound like Billy had lied about *that*. The kiss made everything look different: the purple sky, the stain of the ice shoot in the hill—they all had the cruel, bright look of something true.

Billy's shove sent him staggering sideways.

"Hey!" Jamie said, but Billy had that fighting look he had seen so many times in the schoolyard, fixed now on Jamie's mouth, as if that alone had made Billy mad. He'd thought that being friends had made him safe from Billy. But now Billy no longer saw him, only a mouth, a chin, a chest: places to hit.

He was walking rapidly away when he heard the churn of Billy's boots. Billy was on him before he could turn. They both went down, punching and wrestling in the slush. At the crack of Billy's fist, numbness spread up Jamie's nose and into his forehead. A few seconds later, Billy had straddled him. Jamie bucked and twisted, struggling to free his wrists from Billy's grip, looking up into Billy's face, which was all fury now under the thatch of black hair, the bad teeth clenched in a sneer. He knew Billy had more fierceness in him than he did. He was going to lose.

He lay still.

"All right," Jamie said. "You win."

Billy twisted his wrists. "Say it's true," he said.

"What?"

"Say it's true your dad's coming to live at my house."

He studied the murk of the sky. He could not say that. It was not true, it could not be true, and—some strange intuition drifting through his body—he sensed that to admit it made it more likely. Words made things true, they made them be.

"Say it!" Billy twisted his wrists again.

Jamie heard a car pass, on the road by the hosiery mill, a sound that might mean rescue, growing weaker. Distantly, across the fields behind the mill, a chain saw stuttered and growled and he was filled with self-pity. He thought of his house on the Island: the lit kitchen where his mother would be starting to make supper. He realized that she did not know what was happening, which filled him with sadness. He saw the top of the kitchen table and the little glass dish that held the butter, the perfect square of yellow butter. "That was my mother's," his mother had told him.

"Say it."

He was filled with longing for his own life. At the same time, he felt this moment was something he had always known, though he usually managed not to think of it; he'd come down to the fact of the cold slushy ground and him lying on it, beaten. This was true, and it was there underneath all the other things he knew were true too—school, summer holidays, his father—this cold, wet place that made him want to cry.

"Say it or I'll punch your face in."

"All right."

"Say it."

"My dad's coming—"

But he couldn't speak the words. His throat swelled and he felt the first tear spill from the corner of his eye.

"Say it, crybaby."

He fought back, twisting and struggling. He got one hand free, but of course that meant Billy had his own hand free; it made a fist and the fist struck him in the eye like a stone.

"Say it!"

Again they lay still, locked. Another car went past. It seemed much darker suddenly, though the wet, dirty snow gleamed from the hillside. He strained to see if Wayne Cox was still on the hill. But the brow was empty, against the stark, high wall of a house.

His coat was soaked now; he was shivering harder than Billy.

"You can come to my house," he said. "We can play with my soldiers."

He knew his mother would never let Billy in.

Billy gave his wrists another twist and shifted back, letting them go. But he went on sitting on Jamie's stomach, deciding something.

"You can borrow my tank," Jamie said. His best Dinky Toy. "You can take it home."

Billy let him up and they walked in silence down West Street, their arms brushing as if they were friends. They approached Donnie Whittaker's dog. In its mouth was a bloody bone. The dog slunk into the road, watching them with sneaky eyes.

Then a car drew up, and it was Truck Cassidy's taxi, its sides feathered with slush, and Billy's mother was inside. She told Billy to jump in— time for supper, she said—and when he wouldn't, she got out and grabbed him by the ear and marched him into the backseat. "We'll see you later, honey," she said to Jamie with a big smile. He looked at her huge pink mouth.

The lights were on in Jamie's house, but the car was gone. He told himself Joe might have the car, but a moment later he saw Joe in the window, reading a newspaper. For a few minutes he stood shaking in his soaked pants, wanting to go in but wanting even more to know where his father was. If he was just driving around, that was all right, but if he had gone over to Billy's. . . . Jamie ran back to the corner but there was no sign of the car, not down Water Street, where the stores nested in the glow of the streetlights, or up West, where the road disappeared in thick dusk, or at the other end of Water Street, where the ramp climbed to the footbridge. When he saw a car, its headlights streaking among pines, he felt immediately it had to be his father, going to Uncle Pete and Aunt May's house maybe, or just going, as big people always were, on errands and trips that seemed to have no end. He ran down the street, up the ramp, and onto the bridge. The car was visible now, it tires rumbling on the snow-packed road as it hurtled through the dusk, but it was not his father's, he saw, not the brown Biscayne but a low black vehicle he did not recognize, speeding along the dead-end road as if it actually led somewhere.

At that moment he heard a sound like the report of a gun. He staggered sideways, then recovered, frozen in a state of hyperalertness. His heart seemed to be beating in his whole body. Peering through the chain-link mesh of the safety fence, he saw the river moving under him, a huge white snake, its rough back crawling slowly through the land. Now repeated gunshot sounds came, and a rumbling like a train on the Shade Street overpass. Climbing the mesh, he looked down and saw great blocks of ice shifting and clambering one over another. Below him, the bridge banged and hummed as the cakes of ice struck the abutments.

As he watched, one particularly large cake rose into the air. It reared straight up, taller than he was, taller than the bridge, and it was coming on slowly, toward the rail. Jamie gazed up at it, unable to run.

In the slab's underside, stones and bits of weed were embedded like eyes. Jamie thought of a creature he'd seen in the Christmas Parade, a giant leaning its huge grotesque head over the crowd.

"Mommy," he whispered. It was almost on top of him, and still he couldn't run.

It's all right, the voice said.

"All right?" he echoed, mesmerized. The creature sank. Just before it reached the rail, the slab bowed its great dripping head, sweeping so close to him he felt the chill of its icy body as it slipped beneath the bridge. Jamie climbed down from the mesh, hurried to the opposite side, and watched it reappear, a giant spearhead of white ice, moving away among its smaller brothers under the ghostly mass of Lookout Hill.

38

PENNY CAME DOWNSTAIRS with her soap carving. She felt elated yet nervous, the carving—which she had been working on for weeks and shown to no one—cupped carefully in her right hand. When she saw her father in his chair in the living room, solitary as if in another world, she caught her breath. But she had come down hoping to find him; he was her favorite audience for her artwork. Discovering her, his eyes blued, and he took the little soap dog in his fingertips.

Penny writhed with suspense at his knee. "It was supposed to be Red, but I think it's—it's just a dog," she said. The yellow soap dog was too thin for Red, the legs too short: the carving seemed a mess now, no good at all.

"It's terrific," her father said.

He turned in his chair and put her carving on a book lying on the windowsill. Beyond, boys were playing road hockey in the cul-de-sac. In the room the weak, silvery daylight was hollowed by shadow.

Penny climbed into her father's lap. "Aren't you getting too big for this?" he said.

"Nope," she said, and settled in with her head against his shoulder, while he swiveled the chair a little, back and forth. They both studied the dog. Penny had made its ears prick, like little tents, like the skunk cabbage sticking above the mud in Wiley's swamp.

"Reminds me of Queenie," her dad said: his dog when he was a boy. Immediately she felt hopeful. "Sure, that tail. That's Queenie to a T. He's almost the same color!"

They were quiet for a while longer, looking at the dog, at the boys running up and down.

"Am I your girlfriend?" she said.

Her father said nothing.

"Hey, you," she said, panicking a little. She poked him in the chest. She had felt funny saying 'Am I your girlfriend?' as if she'd dressed up in her mother's shoes and jewelry, which she did do sometimes but only in secret. She didn't want to say it again.

"What?"

"Am I your girlfriend?" She was blushing now, with a sense of touching forbidden matters.

"Darn right," he said, giving her knee a squeeze.

She was not appeased, not quite. She waited, hoping he would say more.

"Absolutely," he said, bouncing her a little.

"Am I your only one?" she said, her face hot now.

She felt him pause, in a little shock of surprise, and in that moment her own heart seemed to fail; she was on the edge of things she did not want to know. "Well, there's your mother," he said. "She's really girl-friend number one."

Penny let that sink in, and it seemed all right. Or almost. There was something, still, that did not quite fit, but it was so small, smaller than a speck of dust, that she was able to brush it aside.

"Tell me a story," she said. Her father appeared not to hear. She nudged him with her elbow. "Hey! Tell me a story!"

"Oh, I don't know—"

"Tell me about Johnny North."

"I think you've heard all my Johnny North stories."

"Tell me the old ones then." She wanted them all, a flood of stories to carry them both away.

For a long time her father was silent. When he began, she snuggled back down, looking idly at her yellow dog, with its pricked ears, as it watched the street. The dog was all right now; it had found a home. Her father's hand gently gripped her leg.

As a boy, her father had known Johnny North. He was a grown man but in some ways, her father said, he had stayed a boy. He lived in a shack on the banks of the Attawan River. He had worked for a few years as a mechanic in the mill, but one day, her father said, using the words he always used, "He just walked away from all that." Johnny made a paddle-wheel boat powered by a bicycle, and he would sit up on his bicycle seat, pedaling his passengers along, passengers who paid a nickel for a tour to the rapids. Sometimes he'd recite his poetry to these people. He wrote long poems about fires and train crashes and recited them dramatically, waving his arms as he guided the boat among the islands. In the newspaper he was known as JOHNNY NORTH, BARD OF THE ATTAWAN.

Johnny North was quite a character, her father said, chuckling a bit. "I don't think he ever took a bath, unless you count swimming in the river. The fellow stank—well, Pete used to say you could smell him coming around the corner."

"Around five corners," Penny corrected.

"As bad as that." Her father recalled how Johnny would dress up in funny costumes—women's dresses, or a Japanese kimono, with driving goggles to keep the dust out of his eyes—and go around town pulling a little wagon with a phonograph on it and a sign that said JOHNNY NORTH, ENTERTAINER. A few people hired him to perform at birthday parties, where he'd sing or do magic tricks. Not everybody wanted to hire him, though, because of the smell, and because you could never tell what he was going to do. "I remember once," her father said—and this was a story she'd never heard—"when Bob Drummond was killed in a fire, Johnny turned up at the front of the funeral procession. He was wearing a black dress and he did this strange, shuffly dance. Some people were pretty upset and wanted to get him out of there. But Lila Drummond— that was Bob's mother—she told them to leave him alone. She said, 'Johnny's just showing how he feels.'"

"That was good," Penny said.

"Yup, that was good."

Another time Johnny had saved a boy from drowning; this was one of Penny's favorite stories. Johnny'd seen the lad struggling, from his shack on the bank, and had rowed out to him. The town had given Johnny a medal and held a party, where he recited all fifty-seven verses of "The Wreck of Ninety-eight." The mayor's wife had fallen asleep in her chair.

In the winter, when people went skating above the dam, Johnny would keep a fire going onshore. He'd lace up the skates of the ladies and girls, always doffing his cap and calling each one Miss—"even if they were eighty-two," her father said. In the summer Johnny rented out rowboats he had built himself. "He only charged a penny, and if you didn't have that he'd let you have it for free. They leaked like the dickens, usually."

Penny loved the Johnny North stories; they were always happening, it seemed, in a sunny corner just out of sight. Hearing them transported her to a time when her father was young. She hadn't been born yet, but that didn't matter; she felt safe, not being born, knowing she was still to come.

When Johnny North got old, things were not so good, her father said. Penny went very quiet—she hadn't heard this one either. Johnny had arthritis, and in winter he stuffed his clothes with newspapers that made a rustling sound when he walked. He blacked his white hair with shoe polish. He still wrote poems, though. "I remember this bit—he must have written it for the town's New Year's party. They printed it in the *Star*.

> "Onward nineteen hundred and thirty-seven,
> I am out of my mammy's home:
> To wander in dark woodlands
> Alone, all, all alone."

"So sad!" Penny said, on the edge of tears. In the window, her yellow dog was walking with Johnny in his dark woodlands.

"Well," her father said, bouncing her a bit on his leg, "some rich people in town took up a collection. They paid for Johnny to go to an old-age home over in Johnsonville. He wasn't very happy there, though—didn't last more than a few months."

"You mean he died?" Penny said, sitting up. She had never thought of Johnny dying: that wasn't part of his story. It wasn't part of who Johnny *was*.

Her father seemed startled. He started to smile.

"Well, sure, eventually. We all—"

"No!" Penny cried fiercely. She threw herself back against him. In the street, the boys continued to yell at their game. She clung to her father's chest, while he rubbed her shoulder. She didn't want to hear about Johnny North or anybody else dying. She wanted Johnny at his fire in the snow, tying the skates of ladies. She wanted him pedaling his boat upstream, declaiming "The Wreck of Ninety-eight." She wanted her father to be with him, a boy still, and safe.

39

THE SNOW FINALLY left for good, swallowed by the slowly thawing earth. Only a few patches glowed among the bare trees on the northward-facing slope of Lookout Hill. But the season that arrived was no spring; it was an in-between time of black branches and soaked dead-looking lawns littered with paper and other rubbish. The months had run backward, as though November had begun again.

One day, lying beside Lucille in her unsteady bed, Alf felt it was over. "Maybe we should lay off for a while," he said, touching her on the cheek. His tenderness was real enough. He felt sorry for her, and guilty, for as she'd expected he was acting no differently from all the other lovers who had left her. Reaching for her clothes, she avoided his gaze. Her movements conveyed a stoic darkness—a despair that could not or would not rouse itself to anger or condemnation. Better that she had upbraided him. This way, he felt hopeless too.

He drove up to the cemetery. The Biscayne passed through the wrought-iron gates that were always propped open, past the red stone where his mother and father lay, following the narrow road into its final loop, where the gravestones petered out in a few acres of yellow lawn. Pete's grave was here, separated from the others under the tall gloom of a spruce, as if his death were somehow different from the rest. May had erected a small gray stone with a polished surface, where the word

MOON had been carved and, under it, slightly to the left, PETER WAT-
SON MOON, 1918–1965.

Alf stood under the spruce in whose branches the faintest wind could
be heard, like the distant hush of water over a low barrier. It was far from
the first time he had stood here, looking at the wicker basket filled with
plastic flowers May had set before the stone. But this time seemed more
vivid, as if it were the first. He felt he had come back to something. What
had his fling with Lucille Boileau been really but an attempt to escape
this place? To burn up his guilt in her bed? He plucked a pebble from
the half-frozen mud and cleaned it with his fingers. He never realized,
until his friend had gone, how much he had loved him. In fact, he
hadn't really known he'd loved him at all—*love* was not a term he ever
used in connection with his male friends. Now it was a torture to think
that, as he went to his death, Pete might have believed Alf had abandoned him.

"You dumb bugger," he whispered. Tears came to his eyes, in a rage
against his friend. "You should have fought it. You should have told *me*.
Hell, I should have told *you*." Yes, if only he'd confessed to Pete, begged
his forgiveness. The possibility of confession and forgiveness—with
Pete, with Margaret, with anyone—seemed as remote now as the dim
gray line of bush at the far edge of the field beyond the cemetery. Alf was
in a place no one could enter or even approach. Overhead, the tree had
filled with the cheerful rant of small birds.

EACH MORNING, HEARING the cry of Bannerman's whistle, he felt
that only moments had passed since it had released him from work the
previous day. He trudged numbly up the stairs of the mill with the silent
crowd, arriving in the room of tall machines that seemed to have been
waiting for him all his life. He no longer took even a minimal pleasure in
his work. He'd told Prince what he could do with the foreman's job; his
ambition had become an offering, an inadequate one, laid on the altar of
Pete's death. Yet several times he was appalled to discover himself staring
at the fading notice on the bulletin board, as though some small, craven

part of him still hoped to be made foreman. Matt Honnegger was staying on, temporarily. Alf was doing most of Matt's work for him. For now
the foreman's job—its burdens if not its title—had come to him by
default.

He did his work swiftly and automatically, with a curious sense that he
was alone. Sometimes, though, he was roused by a chance event that
broke through his isolation. He might drop a wrench and, bending to
retrieve it, be struck by the oddity of its existence, as if he'd never seen a
wrench before, or held its cool heft in his hand, or considered its square,
silently howling jaws. One damp, cloudy evening he had gone out for a
walk and was just passing along the rail platform by the station, on his
way to the old concrete steps that led to the Shade, when he heard a
sound, as if someone had spoken to him. Not seeing anyone, he stopped
and looked around. Above him a Manitoba maple made a rushing noise
as its dry seed pods—hundreds and thousands of pale brown tags hanging in clusters in the bare tree—stirred in a faint breeze. It was odd, but
he felt as if the tree had spoken, and peering through its branches he
glimpsed the moon in a blue tunnel of cloud—a little gibbous moon like
a battered stone—and a shiver of excitement, of life, ran through him,
though it was gone in a moment.

That night, he had dreamed he stood before a knitting machine taller
than any he had ever seen. On the machine's great head was a rack of
bobbins like a vast crown. It seemed somehow human to him—
fatherlike and commanding in its quiet power—and although it was not
knitting anything (the bobbins were still), he was sure the machine was
about to speak. It could not make a sound, though, and there was something painful and suspenseful in this failure.

ONE DAY, SOON after the midmorning break, all the knitters and fixers were told to shut down their machines and come to a meeting in
front of Matt Honnegger's office. The last to arrive, Alf peered over a
mass of heads and shoulders at three men who stood waiting with their
backs to the washing-up sink. Matt was part of this triumvirate, but the

foreman remained a little aloof, cradling his empty pipe against his plaid shirt while casting a bland smile at the floor, as if distancing himself from the proceedings. Beside him stood Wilf Thomas, the manager of the sweater mill: a solid-looking fellow whose Roman nose with its thick bridge lent him the gladiatorial air of an old football guard or hockey defenseman. Wilf was talking in low tones, his head down, to a man Alf had never seen before, a young man of thirty or so, with a taut, bony face and a brush cut so short his head seemed shaved. He wore jeans and a tight black T-shirt and stood with his well-muscled arms folded, revealing on his left biceps a fading, bluish tattoo in which the hooked head of a hawk or eagle was just visible. He was chewing gum—so rapidly that the lower half of his face might have been afflicted by a nervous disorder—his large eyes darting between the floor and the knees of the men and women who stood a few feet away, watching.

"All right," Wilf Thomas said at last, in his gruff voice, facing the crowd. Wilf gave off a sense of blunt integrity that inspired trust. Many of the workers had known him all their lives; the son of a spinner, he had grown up on the Flats. "I won't take too much of your time, folks. But as you know, we've been looking for a new foreman for this floor, and though we've had lots of good applications, we felt we needed a specialist."

Alf's heart pounded; in a flash he understood that he wasn't going to be made foreman. He had tried to convince himself he no longer wanted the job, but all the same, the tenacious weed of his hope had survived until now.

He heard Wilf out in a kind of dream; the manager seemed to be speaking about some other place that Alf knew little of, not the mill where they were now assembled, surrounded by the great crowd of motionless machines. "The reason we need a specialist," Wilf went on, "is that Intertex is going to be putting a number of new machines in here that none of us know how to run, so we thought we should have someone who does. I'm happy to say that in Kit Ford here we've got our man. Kit comes to us from one of the most advanced mills in North America, and I'm sure we're going to appreciate his expertise. He's already been telling me things I don't know." Here Wilf grinned, showing a gold tooth, but the people in front of him did not respond. "Kit's staying in a motel in Johnsonville, but he's going to be moving into town, and I know you'll make him welcome. Oh, yes. I should mention that Kit was once in the marines, so he'll waste no time getting us in fighting trim. Kit?"

"Yeah," Kit Ford said, with a slight drawl. He licked his lips and looked at them with a bright, earnest gaze and a thin smile. He spoke in rapid bursts, almost too fast to be understood, in an accent that seemed southern—from the Carolinas, maybe, or Georgia—and with a straining, plaintive quality, which gave the impression he was laying too much stress on his own sincerity. "Yeah, been knitting most of my life," he told them. "Fact, I see some machines here I haven't seen since I was a kid. The old Jacquards there—should be fun. Sure you've got a lot to show me. Look forward to that. Good to be in Attawan." Somehow he made the name of the town sound foreign, as if they'd never heard it before. "Used to come up to these parts as a kid, to fish, in Quebec there. Good to be back. Look forward to knowing you and working with you."

When the meeting was over, Wilf Thomas called to Alf, who turned back through the dissolving crowd. As he passed Dick Kenshole, the knitter leaned in close. "That job was yours," Dick seethed, demanding to know what Alf was going to do about it. Without responding, Alf went on to where the three men waited for him. He did not look at Kit Ford until Wilf introduced him and then calmly took the hard, damp hand and met the reaching, anxious sincerity of his gaze. In those wide-staring eyes he caught an insistent claim of innocence. I didn't do it, Kit Ford's expression said. Though there was no indication of what *it* was, Alf felt a tremor of misgiving.

"Alf's our best man here," Wilf was telling Kit. "Really knows the place like the back of his hand." He then addressed Alf, speaking in a slightly too-loud voice that betrayed nervousness. "Matt was going to take Kit on a tour, but if you don't mind I'd like you to go along with them."

Alf glared at Wilf—he couldn't help it—and was rewarded by a slight evasive ducking of the manager's head. He felt the least Bannerman's might have done was warn him this was coming. Hadn't he earned that much consideration in his years of virtually running the place? Behind Wilf, Matt was smiling nervously into his pipe.

Alf, Matt, and Kit Ford went down the aisles. Alf was in a state of turmoil. A taste of betrayal kept rising, bitter in his mouth. It made it hard to speak calmly about the machines and the routines of the knitting room.

Kit Ford didn't help. No matter what Alf told him he chewed his gum and nodded and said *Yep, yep, yep* so rapidly and continuously that he gave the impression he already knew everything Alf could possibly tell him; it was all old hat. Put off balance, Alf forgot names he normally knew and several times had to be helped out by Matt while Ford looked at them both in a sincere, slightly pained way, as if none of this incompetence surprised him in the least.

Finally, to give himself a break, Alf asked Ford about the new machines Intertex was buying.

"A lot faster than these old junkers," Kitt said, somehow managing to chew and talk at once. Alf resented hearing the machines of Number Six called *old junkers*. He had worked on all of them and kept them going for years beyond their expected life span, often by improvising spare parts. He took pride in them.

He listened to Ford talk about the new knitting machines. They looked a bit like a jet engine, Ford said, a curious description Alf could not quite picture. They were computerized. They would take fewer workers to run. "Fewer hands, fewer mistakes," Ford said.

"My, my," Matt Honnegger commented mildly, shaking his head.

Kit seemed startled to find his predecessor there, still smiling blandly over his empty pipe.

"Nothing against the old ways," he said. "Good in their time. But you don't keep up with the competition, you die." He looked meaningfully at Alf and Matt, which struck Alf as faintly comical—after all, they were talking about knitting, not cancer or war. At the same time, Alf caught a glimpse of a no-holds-barred tenacity, as well as a certain delight in the extreme vision he had just expressed. Kit Ford was telling them that in the game of survival they were playing, he knew the rules and was willing to abide by them, as a man should.

IN THE NEXT few days, Kit Ford moved up and down the aisles so quickly—his rubber-soled shoes squeaking on the hardwood—that the workers in Number Six knitting soon dubbed him the Road Runner. Despite his claim that he looked forward to knowing them, he went on confusing Alf with Art and Mary with Eileen, and he never stopped for even a few seconds to shoot the breeze, as Matt had done, or to join them on the fire escape for their breaks. Worst of all, he spread a spirit of resentment by letting them know that they were not working hard enough. He never accused them of sloth in so many words; it was the air of haste and disapproval he exuded, the cast of his pained eyes that seemed to be suffering their poor performance in outraged silence.

On the fire escape, they made jokes about him. "I don't think he ever goes to the bathroom," Dick Kenshole said, and quick as a whip Boomer Tomlinson came back in his droll bass. "I guess that's why he's so full of shit."

They laughed ruefully, weighed down by the knowledge that their jokes were ultimately futile and that an older, more friendly world was passing away. They did not know what was coming, but with the glum fatalism of those who must await change passively, many suspected they were not going to like the new order. The new machines Intertex was bringing in worried them because some workers would be made redundant. In their minds, Kit Ford and these new machines—fewer hands, fewer mistakes—were inextricably bound; the exhausting haste he had brought to the mill seemed just a foretaste of a still faster regime to come. Even before they arrived, the new machines promised a world in which workers were going to become creatures like Kit Ford, as fast and efficient as the equipment they served.

Alf also disliked Ford and his ways, though he tried to suppress his bitterness. After all, it wasn't Ford's fault he'd been overlooked for the job. He did his best to sympathize with the foreman, telling himself that, for all his experience, Ford was nervous in his new role and deserved a chance to settle in. When the complaints on the fire escape escalated, he decided to offer Ford some advice.

One evening after the mill had emptied, he dropped by Kit's office. The young man was sitting behind Matt's desk (Alf still thought of it that way), which he kept completely clear save for an order spike holding a mess of impaled papers, a clipboard, and a single orange pencil, sharpened to a clean point. There was something forlorn about all this. Alf was suddenly aware that Kit Ford was young, even younger in some ways than his actual age. Sitting with his large fingers hooked over the edge of his desk, motionless but for that perpetually working jaw, he seemed like a student awaiting some as yet undisclosed after-school punishment.

Alf started off gently. The workers were feeling a bit edgy, he explained, sitting forward in his chair and gesturing with open hands. They sensed there were big changes coming and were nervous. It might help if he, Kit, made an effort to warm up to them a bit. If he talked to them casually from time to time, even if only about the weather.

Kit Ford listened without comment, and it occurred to Alf that for this man chatting idly about the weather might be impossible. He was over-wound, as if he had never been taught—never had the freedom—to relax.

"So they sent you to tell me this."

"No, no," Alf said, smiling amicably, his face heating, "it's my own idea. I just think if you made a few goodwill gestures, you'd have a happier gang out there."

Kit Ford looked from Alf to the pencil on his desktop. He was chewing more slowly, and Alf sensed he'd confronted the foreman with a problem he did not know how to meet.

"So they're not happy—"

"Well, nothing too serious. I'm just suggesting—you know, make an effort to get their names right. It's a little thing, but—"

"So they sent you in here to agitate."

"I'm not agitating," Alf said, trying to make light of the idea. "No one sent me here. I'm just saying—"

"You were an agitator in 'forty-nine, isn't that right?"

Taken aback, Alf could only stare at the other man. All vestiges of the boy had vanished. Ford was the ex-marine now, hard, perfunctory.

"I wasn't an agitator," Alf said softly. A weariness was enveloping him, a sense he had started up a hill he could never crest. "I went out on strike."

"An illegal strike—"

"Well, that's debatable."

"Thank you very much for your advice," Ford said sharply. " 'Preciate it." The interview was clearly over. The foreman pulled the clipboard toward him and made a show of studying it. For a few seconds Alf did not move. He watched Ford—his angular face knotting and unknotting in a perpetual flow of tensions. In the window behind the foreman's close-cropped head, the evening sky had grown luminous, a kind of mirror in which Alf could not find his own face.

IN LATE APRIL there was a spell of unusually warm weather, and the workers on the sixth floor were able to take nearly every break outside. In the morning, before the sun reached the west wall of the mill, it was still cool enough for sweaters, and the hot thermoses of coffee and tea they poured into plastic cups were deeply enjoyed. But in the afternoon, when the sun beat down on the brick wall behind them and threw the striped shadows of the fire-escape railing over their knees, they opened their shirts and soaked in the warmth they had missed for so long. These ten minutes were precious, a time unclaimed by not just the tall machines, fallen silent in the room behind them, but also by the duties they owed their families. These little islands of rest contained as much undiluted freedom as most of the workers enjoyed in a day, and they used them well; they talked or ate or read or smoked or looked out through the railings into the deep cube of the millyard, where sharp geometries of light and shade shifted back and forth all day. When the buzzer finally sounded there was always a double sense that these minutes had passed more deeply and slowly than any others, but also that they had flown with the swiftness of a glance.

In the days when he had helped Matt, Alf was often so busy that he skipped break. But after just a week on the job, Kit Ford made it clear he wasn't needed, so he increasingly took up his old seat just outside the door, on an upturned wooden box topped with a scrap of foam rubber that had turned a rich golden color. He didn't join in the general conversation but listened with a secret pleasure, drawn by an instinctive need. Not so long ago, he'd felt he was a man with a purpose, a man with important things to do; he'd forgotten how good it was just to sit with these men and women, many of whom he'd known all his life. So he smoked and drank his coffee and gazed across the millyard to the gap between buildings, fixing almost unconsciously on the place where all their eyes tended, the little ribbon of river water visible between the dike and the cement wall of the opposite bank.

Often at these moments he thought of Lucille, with a longing that surprised him. She had started to appear in his dreams (he saw her, once, driving away in a red car, then looking back at him with a curious, watchful indifference). He worried that he had used her, though he never intended to. He felt badly, and the worst of it was a sense that he'd overlooked something when he was with her. At a distance, she—her beauty—appeared to promise an experience he could not name but was sure he had missed.

ON A WINDY Thursday under scudding clouds that seemed about to catch on the high soot-stained lip of Bannerman's stack, someone on the fire escape said, "I guess they found another cat." Alf, sitting on his box, looked up. He'd been aware that for several months someone in town had been killing cats. The plague of small corpses seemed to have petered out for a while, but now, apparently, the skinned body of a tom had been found hanging on a wire from the Shade Street rail overpass. Down the fire escape, Mary Carr cried out in dismay—she kept cats herself and didn't want to hear anything about it—but some of the others got into an animated discussion of the killer's possible motives. "He's just some poor sicko trying to prove he's a bigshot," Dick Kenshole said with angry revulsion, summing up the general attitude. Alf listened as the conversation drifted into humorous speculation about who the killer might be. A few tossed out the names of the town's most important citizens. The knitters howled expansively and then fell silent, sensing they had gone too far.

Suddenly Book Cummings, about halfway down the row, turned his big pimply face toward Alf and said, "I think Alf did it."

Alf was shocked, his body awakened from its torpor. It was not just the stab of accusation, which was obviously meant in fun, but the sudden exploding of his isolation. He had begun to feel invisible, sitting there quietly day after day on his foam pad. Now he saw that several faces had leaned out to catch a glimpse of him.

Struggling to keep his composure, he blew out smoke and, meeting Book's eyes, deadpanned. "That's right, Book." He let a beat go by before adding, "You're next, cool cat."

They roared, since the overweight, bookish Book was anything but cool; they were relieved Alf had taken the jibe so well. The only one who didn't laugh was Woody Marr; his pudgy face lifted sourly. He was habitually ignored by the other knitters, who believed he had ratted on the people laid off in the fall.

After the cat incident, Alf took a more active part in life on the fire escape, though he supposed he was never what anyone would call talkative. What surprised him was that when he did speak, everyone stopped to listen. He was sure he disappointed them, for he never felt that what he was saying was witty or important or interesting enough to warrant the expectant faces ranged along the balcony.

ALL THE TALK on the fire escape one morning was of the big news that was going around town: Bannerman's was closing its hosiery division. For almost a hundred years John Bannerman's original building on West Street (the tall mill with its handsome mansard roof and bell tower) had churned out hosiery renowned across the country: fancy dress socks, women's silk hose (the silk supplied by special trains racing with their bales from the West Coast), work socks, children's socks, sport socks. Now the whole enterprise would be shut down by August. Almost two hundred people would lose their jobs.

The earthquake might be shaking a mill on the other side of town, but the tremors reached right to their iron perch above the yard, reminding the Number Six workers of their vulnerability. They could do everything that was asked of them and do it well, but there would never be a guarantee that their jobs would not disappear from under them. Many had friends or family members working in the hosiery mill. Its closure was hardly a distant or abstract event; it cast a chilly shadow, and behind it they glimpsed the behemoth, Intertex. It was not lost on them that in almost a century Bannerman's had never closed a mill in town, yet within a year of acquiring Bannerman's, Intertex was shutting down a fixture that had seemed as permanent as the hills that faced it across the Atta.

"I heard the place was makin' money," Steve Johnson said, in a high complaining voice, as if beseeching the rest of them for an answer.

"How could it have been?" Mary Carr said tartly to the railing in front of her. She was from Newfoundland, a stringy, pointy-chinned woman with strong opinions. "They wouldn't close a mill if it was making a profit. That's what these guys are in it for."

"That's right," someone else said, and that seemed to settle the matter. For a few moments there was silence.

Looking at his own hands, which suddenly seemed alien, animal-like, Alf said, "Actually, they *were* making a profit."

He could sense the stir, the wakening attention his words evoked. To his left, he saw Steve Johnson anxiously staring back, leaning with his elbows on his knees. Other faces had turned his way too, blank and expectant. In the yard below, an iron-wheeled cart rumbled over the rough asphalt.

"How's that, Alf?" Mary said.

"Well, it seems there's profit, and then there's profit. They were making about two percent over there. I guess Intertex felt they could do better with their money elsewhere." Grant George, assistant manager of the hosiery mill, had told this to Alf a couple of days before the shutdown was made public, when Alf had run into his old boyhood acquaintance in the post office. Grant, looking harassed and sounding grim, had barely been able to contain his disgust at the whole business. "No flies on these boys," he'd said of Intertex. "They'd sell their grandmothers if they could get their price."

Silence greeted Alf's news. Below, the cart of bobbins rumbled out of hearing.

"They were making a profit?" Boomer Tomlinson said incredulously. "How could that be?"

"He told you," Mary said. "They're not making *enough* profit."

"But what about all those people who lose their jobs?"

"They're not in business to make jobs," Mary Carr said. "If they could run the whole thing off a control panel, like Harry Scott and his boilers there, they'd be rid of us in a flash."

"You got it there," someone said.

But Boomer, rubbing his hands and screwing up his face into a rumpled mask of disgruntlement, was not satisfied. "Alf," he said, peering down the row, "how much profit are they making here? In the sweater mill, like?"

All eyes were on him, intensely interested in his answer. Feeling his mouth go dry, Alf shook his head. "I don't know," he said. "Enough, I guess." They waited a few moments longer, sensing or hoping he had more to say, but he could only repeat his gesture of disavowal, unhappy at his failure to satisfy them, wary of the hunger he had glimpsed in their eyes.

THE WEATHER TURNED to rain and they spent their breaks inside, in the noisy third-floor lunchroom with its bare beige walls and unpainted wooden floor, where people from so many departments were mixed together that discussion of any sensitive subject was impossible in the general din. But when the sun came out, the workers from the sixth floor returned gladly to the fire escape. No more mention was made of the hosiery mill, as though Alf's answer, days earlier, and the intervening rain had swept their minds clean. Boomer Tomlinson and Eddie Ray began to talk about where they might take their summer holidays. Boomer told a story about a bear that had lumbered into a campground where he and his wife were staying, near Wawa, and created such havoc he doubted he would ever get his wife camping again. While he and Stella were huddled in terror in their little tent, the bear had pried out a window of their Plymouth. "He just slipped his claws in and peeled the whole thing out like the lid off your Tupperware," Boomer said. That set others off with their bear stories, the best of which was Mary Carr's tale of how, as a girl, she had been trapped in her grandmother's outhouse by a bear that sat down outside the door. "That door was so flimsy," Mary said, "a skunk could have pushed it over," and there was something so absurd in the notion of a skunk opening an outhouse door that they all laughed. "The bear looked like he was just waiting for his turn," Mary said. "I was so scared I was ready to jump in the hole."

The nasal bleat of the buzzer, when it came, sounded distant and irrelevant, like a parental command the children don't take seriously. Sterner warnings might come later, but for now there seemed no harm in sitting on in the sun. Someone began another yarn, and Alf, flicking the butt of his cigarette over the rail, thought of a bear story Pete had once told. There had been a campfire, and a bear lurking at the edge of the light. He couldn't remember the rest, but the image of Pete's face, eyebrows raised in innocent surprise, plunged a sickle of grief through him. He gave a little cry, like the small, muffled sobs people make in their sleep. His neighbor, Eddie Ray, started, just as a high scolding voice broke in above Alf's head.

"People, people, this isn't the way."

Along the balcony, all talk and laughter stopped. Alf glanced covertly to his right and saw Kit Ford's blue-jeaned leg and black running shoe swinging inches from his shoulder. The foreman was leaning from the open door, like a conductor from a train. Some of the knitters stared up at him with blank faces. Some turned away to look impassively into space. There was a sense in the air of obstinate denial. They were used to obeying the buzzer, obeying every order that came from above, but today, in the sun and intoxication of their laughter, they seemed to have taken a communal decision to ignore the foreman.

Kit Ford stepped down to stand on the board that served as a step. He clapped his hands. He might have been trying to raise a flock of geese. "Come on, people! Let's go!"

Still they sat on. Alf could feel the tension in the back of his neck, as if at any minute the man above him might strike his head. He could hear Kit Ford breathing, in a labor of controlled fury. Bending his head and shoulders forward, Alf slowly rose. As he climbed the steps, he avoided the murderous gaze of the foreman, who stood back with crossed arms. From behind Alf came the sounds of cups being screwed on thermoses, of lunch boxes being shut, of bodies shifting, taking their time, as the workers prepared to follow him in.

40

"SO WHAT WAS that?"

Alf stood before Kit Ford's desk. On its surface lay a scrap of paper, in which a twist of gum had been deposited like a pink grub. Ford's eyes, bright with rage, had locked on Alf's.

"What was what?"

"That!" Ford jabbed two fingers toward the fire escape. "Shut the door," he ordered.

Alf hesitated for a moment. Then he turned and slowly closed the door. The hum of the knitting machines subsided. He faced the foreman again.

"Sitting there five minutes after the buzzer went."

"I don't know," Alf said. "We weren't paying attention."

"The damn thing is *deafening!*"

They had heard the buzzer—at least Alf had—but it had seemed to sound distantly, from another life. He was a bit mystified by what had happened. But he would not be spoken to like this, as if he were fourteen. His defiance had taken the form of exaggerated calm.

He kept his hands in the pockets of his factory greens, looking steadily at the foreman, motionless.

"It's a beautiful day," he said, with a shrug. "We forgot."

"*Forgot?*" Ford's voice filled with outraged glee, as if he'd just caught Alf in a whopper. "Even after I told you to get in you still sat there."

"Yes, I guess we did."

"And why was that?"

Alf let a sigh escape him. He agreed with Ford that things had gone off track. To pursue it this way, though—there was something so wrong-headed about it.

"I'm asking you," Ford demanded.

"I don't know," Alf said. "You took us by surprise."

"You bet I did." The foreman's gaze roved in angry frustration, from the desk to Alf's belt, from the belt to his chest. His jaw worked, as if in need of gum.

"I've never seen it happen before," Alf offered. He doubted Ford would get the hint that it hadn't needed to happen before, but he had to try. "I doubt very much it'll happen again."

"I guess you can see to that, can't you?"

Alf was suddenly wary.

"You're the ringleader."

"There was no ringleader."

"What was it then, spontaneous rebellion of the working class? C'mon, man, I got eyes. They didn't move till you moved!"

"That's crazy," Alf managed. Still, he felt guilty, as if the foreman were speaking the truth. "It could have been anybody."

"Be that as it may," Ford said, fiddling with a clipboard, "I'm holding you responsible. They do it again, I know who to look for."

The foreman now made a show of studying the clipboard. Was the interview over? Alf went on standing, his calm in tatters. Slowly, he took his hands from his pockets. They felt weighted, as if all the blood in his body had poured into his fists.

AT TEN THE next morning, the workers paraded onto the fire escape as usual. Near the end of the break, when a cool breeze from across the yard was lifting a page of Book Cummings's paperback, Steve Johnson checked his watch and spoke the thought that was on every mind. "I wonder if the Road Runner'll be out today." Someone chortled darkly, and Alf felt the backs of his arms tingle. I should go in, he thought, before the bastard comes out, but he sat on, ignoring his better judgment. Kit Ford had taken up residence in his mind like a conqueror from a foreign country. He couldn't stop replaying their meeting, thinking of what he might have said, of the injustice of the whole damn business. He blew smoke and watched it pass, a shape-shifting genie, through the railings over the sunlit yard.

Just as the buzzer went, a motion to his right made him turn his head. Kit Ford had stepped swiftly from the mill and positioned himself at the end of the fire escape, facing his workers, his fingertips wedged in the pockets of his jeans.

No one moved. Then Boomer Tomlinson leaned forward as if to bang his head on the rails and let out a low groan.

"You have a problem, Mr. Tomlinson?" Kit Ford said.

"Just a headache," Boomer said, without looking at him.

One or two knitters rumbled their amusement—Ford was the obvious source of Boomer's headache—but they kept their seats, not so much out of defiance as because they were confused, made immobile by the foreman's presence.

Alf sighed, flicked away his butt, and prepared to get up. He was dreading the result, figuring the rest would follow suit, giving Ford more proof that he was the ringleader. But he was also doomed if he went on sitting, especially if the others also stayed in their places. He put his hands on his knees, but before he could rise, Mary Carr leaped up. "So let the fun begin," she cried out, with black irony. They stirred as one and shuffled into the mill after Mary. Alf was one of the first to brush by Ford; he pointedly ignored the foreman, who stood with his arms crossed, observing them with thin disapproval, as if they only barely passed muster.

By the time the afternoon break arrived, most of the workers were anxiously anticipating Ford's reappearance. They had talked enough about his behavior in the meantime to work up a good head of opposition; who knew what would happen if he tried his funny business again? But Ford was wiser than Alf dared hope. The foreman didn't come out at the end of the break, even though a few people waited half a minute extra. In fact, he didn't reappear again on any day, and the incident, with its two chapters, passed into the general fund of factory lore, a story to be told over beer and embellished with witty comebacks that hadn't actually been spoken, celebrations of courageous determination "not to let him get away with it" that had been tentative at best.

The atmosphere on the fire escape told a different tale. Alf noticed that now, as the end of a break approached, everyone grew restless. People furtively consulted their watches and put away their lunches and books a little earlier than before. Though they still sat on after the buzzer, the traditional period of defiance had grown shorter—to the point where it hardly existed.

SEVERAL WEEKS AFTER the fire-escape incident, Ford again called Alf into his office. On his desk lay a strip of patterned sweater cloth, loosely folded. Alf noted the deep blue fabric warily; he had made it himself.

"Alf," Ford began. The foreman was wearing his most sincere, concerned face. "I'm worried you're doing too much there—working the Richardsons and fixing too. It's a lot for any man."

Alf sensed where this was heading. Running his hand over his hair, he said, "Well, to tell the truth, since you've come I've had a lot less to do. As far as I can see, you're doing about three times as much as Matt ever did. I had to spend a lot of my time helping him out."

" 'Preciate that," Ford said, with the twitch of a gaunt cheek. "But 'fraid we got a problem here." He deftly flipped open the top fold of cloth. It was a rich subtle blending of dark blue yarns, with just a touch of red running through it. Alf had made it on one of the Richardsons, the only machines on the floor sophisticated enough to turn out such a pattern. "You see what I'm talking about?"

"Not sure I do." But his face was heating. The foreman's blunt fingers shoved the sample forward.

"You used the wrong red."

Alf picked up the soft length of cloth, the red surfacing in random streaks, glimpses of fire.

"It's supposed to be Persian Red. You used Barn Red. Too bright."

Carrying the fabric past Ford's desk to the tall unshaded window behind it, Alf held it up and saw that Ford was right.

Ford's high voice jabbed at his back. "There's fifty yards of it spoiled, Alf."

Alf saw the graveled roof of the dyehouse, the pulsing necks and breasts of the pigeons gathered there. An irony he did not fully grasp tugged deep in him, the shape of an obscure joke.

Alf returned to his place—how quickly and completely it had become his—in front of Ford's desk, tossing down the cloth with a gentleness that belied the tension in his face and chest. It seemed pointless to say sorry, to say anything. In nearly twenty years of knitting he had never made a mistake of this order, a mistake that would cost the company dearly. He could not understand it.

"What I've decided to do," Ford said, frowning with great seriousness at his desktop, "is take you off the Richardsons. If you're working on some of the easier machines, you'll be able to concentrate better, on knitting and fixing both."

The foreman looked at him. Behind his expression of concern, triumph glinted.

Alf felt oddly neutral, almost untouched by Ford's announcement.

"I want you to switch with Marr," Ford told him. "He knows how to run the Richardsons—ain't that right?"

Alf grinned bleakly.

"What's so funny?"

"Nothing," Alf said. Beyond the window, pigeons were ascending, a storm of gray wings.

HE LEFT THE office and walked by the motionless Richardsons, refusing to look at them but sensing their tall mass as if they were watching him pass their ranks like a disgraced soldier.

Woody Marr's stand was at the back of the room: four old underwear machines now used to make cloth for T-shirts. Alf reached them just as Woody emerged into the aisle, a bobbin of white cotton in one hand. The knitter barely acknowledged Alf as he went about his business. Since fall, they had done their best to avoid each other.

"Now?" he barked, incredulous, as Alf told him what Ford wanted.

"Seems so."

Woody shot him a look of pure malevolence. Alf felt jolted awake by the reminder of their mutual history. He turned away without expression, pretending to interest himself in the state of Woody's machines.

It is one thing to accept your fate; it is another to go on accepting it, as if there was no argument to be made for an alternative. Within half an hour Alf was scouring his brain to understand how he could have mistaken Barn Red for Persian Red. They were as unlike as a bottle of red wine and a Coca-Cola sign. Had he been operating in that much of a fog? After a few minutes he marched off to the yarn room, where he flipped a switch and sent a pale, shuddering fluorescence over the rows of deep wooden bins, scarred by generations of use. The containers of Barn Red and Persian Red stood side by side, heaped nearly to overflowing with the huge head-sized bobbins. He looked from one bin to the other, in a state of self-lacerating wonder. A child could tell the colors apart. He couldn't shake the sense that he'd been tricked—most likely by himself.

Still his sense of injustice—that something had been done to him—persisted. To his right, one of the long windows set in the thick brick wall framed the old house that held General Office. Bob Prince's dark blue Fleetwood was parked in its usual place under the willow, now showing a faint blush of green. At the sight of the wide polished car with its low fins, a current of anger surged through Alf, and for another few seconds he raged silently.

AFTER THE RICHARDSONS, running Woody's old machines was a breeze. Alf had more time on his hands than ever: time to be bored, time to hope for a breakdown somewhere, so he could fix it (though he hated meeting the condolences of the others, who felt his demotion was unfair), time to look bitterly up the aisle where Woody hurried around the Richardsons, time to chat with Coreen Appleton.

She ran the stand across the aisle, a young woman in her twenties with two young kids at home, pretty, with an open face and eager brown eyes that smiled at him with no hint of flirtatiousness or guile. She usually wore a plaid shirt tucked into jeans, which fit her in a way Alf found quite pleasant, emphasizing the fullness of her pear bottom, the sudden narrowness of her high waist, cinched with a white plastic belt on which was printed a red heart design. She sang sometimes as she worked, in a childish soprano, old Teresa Brewer songs from the fifties. She gave his days a lighter touch; though he enjoyed her fresh appearance, he wasn't drawn to her physically. She was so bright and cheery there seemed to be no mystery in her, nothing hidden—unlike Lucille—that called to his own hiddenness. He saw Lucille in vivid fragments. Bending to roll up some cloth, he'd flash on the caramel smoothness of her stomach or on her full mouth, drawing lazily to his.

He was tending his machines as usual when he heard Kit Ford's high-pitched voice across the aisle. The foreman and Coreen stood shoulder to shoulder with their backs to Alf, talking. Alf watched as the foreman's square hand reached out to rest for a second on her far shoulder. Then the hand dropped, brushing the hollow of her back and settling, palm open, fingers spread, on the fullness of her bottom, squeezing as Coreen tried to twist away. In three strides, Alf was by her side. He acted so quickly, so impulsively—powered by a rage against Ford that had never gone away—that his move seemed almost rehearsed, he accomplished it with such efficiency. Careful not to touch Coreen herself, he took the foreman's wrist and flung away his arm, flung it like something rotten he hated to touch.

"Hey!" Ford said, turning. Alf saw a stab of fear cross his face, a hint of the boy again, but it was gone in a second, buried under a smirk of patronizing satisfaction, as he recognized Alf.

"Keep your hands off her," Alf said, in a dry voice. The words seemed unreal, as if he'd taken up a role in a play.

"Back to work, fella."

"Please," Coreen said, to both of them. "Alf, there's no need—" Neither man was aware of her.

Alf had stationed himself in front of Coreen, a little taller than the other man. Ford pushed at his chest.

"Go back to your squaw," he said.

The foreman might just as well have held a red-hot brand to Alf's face. Alf pushed him and felt the plated muscle of Ford's chest, saw him briefly stagger. Then Ford advanced, and almost immediately Alf had absorbed two quick punches to the head. Instantly drunk, he was aware only of Coreen crying out, and of Ford stepping closer with his fists up on either side of his chest, like a boxer in an old photograph. Alf let his head drop. His own punch came almost lazily, as if out of a stupor, taking Ford unawares on the side of his mouth and sending him backward with a surprised grunt. His head roaring, Alf made a terrific effort to crawl up the slope of his own fatigue. They punched with staccato fierceness, bent on maximum damage, blundering between the tall machines, which went on churning out cloth with stately imperturbability, as if none of this could ever matter.

41

TURNING OFF THE engine, Alf examined his face in the rearview of the Biscayne: the slitted right eye, embedded in swollen flesh like a turtle's; the scraped, purpling cheek; the bloodstain, like a little brown goatee set crookedly under his cut lip.

His untouched eye looked back, expressionless.

As he let himself into the kitchen, he heard someone drop the lid of the piano bench in the dining room.

"Hello?" Margaret's voice.

They listened to each other's silence.

"Just me," he said, stooping stiffly to untie his shoes. As she entered the kitchen, he straightened, showing his face.

Her cry gratified him. In an odd way, he was proud of his damaged face. There was something honest about a fight; besides, if he hadn't won, he had not been beaten either.

She came over to him in her corduroy dress and stopped, her hands half raised, not daring to touch him. For a moment he felt as if he had done something extraordinary: crossed a desert or come back from the dead. He met her gaze frankly, with a sharp, threatening pride. He had not felt so alive in weeks.

"I was in a fight," he said. He was daring her to counter him, to breathe one word of criticism. This was what she had married. He would not hide it. He would not feel ashamed.

She took in his ruined shirt.

"Gave as good as I got," he said tersely. "Maybe better." He was fudging a little. After a couple of minutes, the knitters had separated him and Ford, and just in time: the younger man's strength was beginning to tell.

"Who did you—?"

"The foreman," he said.

"Matt?"

He grunted sardonically. "A new guy." She furrowed her brow. "I didn't get the job, Margaret. They gave it to somebody else."

She stared at him in confusion. He had told her nothing about Kit Ford, and now it irked him that he had to explain. It seemed as if she had brought it up to torture him.

"Somebody—"

"I didn't get the job! Is that so hard to understand?"

He glared at her, as if to punish her for her very existence. Her face reddened. He crossed to the sink, reaching into the cupboard for a glass. Water ran from the tap, splashing as he struggled to subdue his reawakening fury. He saw Ford's pale, grinning face, felt again the ridge of the foreman's cheekbone as it met his fist. His hand trembled with the effort not to crush the glass. Finally he drank, and the cold water traveling through his parched mouth and plunging down his throat gave him relief.

"I've been fired," he said quietly.

"Oh, Alf," she said. "What happened? Who fired—"

"Ford!" he cried. Did he have to explain everything? "The foreman. The guy I fought."

She said nothing more, staring into the space between them, as if seeing other realities entirely. Her reverie—how could she go away at this critical moment?—enraged him further.

"Well?" he demanded, almost shouting.

"Alf, I'm sorry!" There were tears in her eyes. But he did not want tears, or the threat of tears, and he turned away, leaning on the counter with both arms. She tentatively touched his upper arm. "Tell me what happened."

"The bastard's ruined the place," he said. "He's alienated everybody."

"The new foreman," she said.

"Yes, goddammit, the new foreman!" he yelled. Spittle swung from his mouth in a bloody thread. He had only begun to grasp his defeat and was wild at his own impotence.

———

AFTERWARD, HIS WOUNDS treated with iodine and bandages, he stood at the bedroom window and watched Penny coming along the road, on her way home for lunch. She was wearing her winter coat and was carrying pussy willows, like a sheaf of knobbed whips. Her skinny legs in their red tights skipped up the curb. Suddenly she paused and looked up at the house, wary.

He shrank back from the window.

Moments later he was hovering at the top of the stairs, listening as she entered the kitchen. First came her chiming voice, innocent and cheerful. Then Margaret's lower murmur. "Just tell them I've had an accident with a knitting machine," he'd instructed his wife. He was determined to stop the damage from spreading. He would keep everyone safe; yes, everyone would be all right if they just believed what he told them. "Say I look banged up, but I'm all right. Don't mention the job. We'll tell them later. It'll be okay."

As he came down the hall, Penny ran to meet him and, as if she were suddenly younger and smaller, launched herself with a cry into his arms. He carried her awkwardly to the kitchen, her head buried in his neck, though as they passed into the brighter room, she reared back to get a better view. "Oh, Daddy!"

Jamie burst in. "I ran all the way from the—" Stopping, he saw his father, and his sister crying. Turning from the sink with the pussy willows in a vase, Margaret tried to explain. But Jamie's face was ashen. "Are you going away?" he said to Alf, almost whispering. His eyes sprouted fat tears. "Is he going away!" he cried to Margaret as she bent to him.

"No, no," Margaret said, trying to inject a lighter note. "How many times do I have to tell you, silly goose? He isn't going anywhere."

Soon they were all eating in relative calm at the kitchen table, all but Joe, who had stayed at school to play floor hockey. When the phone rang, the sound jolted everyone, but especially Penny and Jamie, who started as if the knitting machine that had hurt their father were about to come lumbering into the room. It was Boomer Tomlinson. The whole of Number Six was in an uproar, he said. "They're on the verge of a sitdown."

"Sitdown?" Alf said sharply, not quite understanding. At the table Jamie froze. Wasn't he already sitting?

"We're gonna get you your job back, eh? I'm gonna speak to Wilf Thomas."

Alf returned to the table in a state of astonishment. In his mind, he and Kit Ford had been alone in their battle, and the battle was over. But now the entire floor seemed to be going to risk their necks for him.

The phone rang again: Coreen Appleton, weeping and scarcely comprehensible. He'd been so good, sticking up for her like that, and now—it was so unfair! She too said she was phoning Wilf Thomas, the sweater-mill manager.

Everyone stopped eating as he came back to the table.

"Just asking how I am," he said, picking up his spoon and contemplating his mound of ice cream. He wasn't sure if this was good news or bad. There was something almost disappointing about the idea of getting his job back. In a way, he liked the extreme position he'd gotten himself into. It was honest, and so was his fight with Ford: he felt he'd come down to ground after years of floating. And there was a sense of freedom. He didn't have to go to the mill tomorrow.

Again the phone rang.

"Aren't we popular," Margaret said, getting up. The children watched her make the trek to the shrilling phone. She spoke briefly and hung up. "Wrong number," she announced. In his chair, Jamie pulled a face and began to laugh—*hah-hah-hah*—with grating theatrical harshness.

"That's enough," Alf told him sharply. Jamie stuck out his jaw and glared at the butter dish.

LATER THAT AFTERNOON Alf was alone at the kitchen table, nursing a cup of cold tea and leafing without much heart through the help-wanted pages of the Johnsonville *Gleaner*, when the phone rang again. It was Wilf Thomas. He came straight to the point.

"Alf, I've heard what happened. Listen, if you can guarantee it won't happen again, I can offer you your job back."

Alf bridled at the implication that he was at fault.

"And Kit Ford? What does he have to guarantee?"

"Alf, he is the foreman here. I'm ignoring his wishes to make you this offer."

Without warning, on a tide of sudden defiance and clarity, Alf said, "I won't come back unless you get rid of Ford. He's destroying the place."

"Alf, be reasonable."

He wasn't reasonable. After he'd hung up, he returned to the kitchen table, stunned at what he'd just done. Yet he knew he'd spoken the truth. He couldn't—wouldn't—work for Ford again, any more than he could drink the man's spit. But he was shocked all the same, to realize he'd cast his life adrift.

HE BEGAN TO make the rounds familiar to the unemployed. He filled out forms and sat in company waiting rooms where stacks of ancient magazines spilled onto glass tabletops, where photos of company officers and sports teams beamed down from the walls with the confident serenity of those who know they have a place. Once on a loading dock he was interviewed by a foreman twenty years younger than himself, a stocky, harassed-looking fellow who scarcely glanced up from his clipboard and spoke in a coarse offhand way Alf found so insulting he refused to move when the man dismissed him. A moment later the foreman went inside and Alf heard him say, "If that asshole out there doesn't leave, call the cops."

He had become *that asshole out there*. It was how he sometimes felt. Maybe it was his face, still blotched with yellow and purple bruises, that put people off. Maybe (as he sometimes suspected) Kit Ford was reaching out to block his chances. Or maybe it was his lack of real interest.

Somehow his focus was still on Bannerman's, as if he were only waiting to come out for a second round and fight again under the tall machines. There were times when to be looking for work anywhere else seemed an abandonment of his principles. Of his rights.

Before long, he was sick of the whole business—sick, too, of knocking around at home on those days he wasn't out job hunting. Margaret was increasingly impatient, snapping at him for trivialities. He could hardly blame her. They were having to make do on his unemployment check, less than half of what he'd earned before. They were buying the cheapest grade of stewing beef, bread from the day-old bin. He tried to be helpful by tackling long-postponed jobs around the house, but increasingly he felt underfoot. One warm gray day in early May, he stuffed a peanut-butter sandwich and an orange into the pockets of his windbreaker and, taking Red, crossed the footbridge to the park, heading for the woods and river flats northwest of town. The big dog kept stopping to lift his leg against various trees and pieces of playground equipment. Alf chose the path along the top of the dike, aware as he walked of Pete's bungalow perched in the wooded hillside, of the closed garage door hiding the Saratoga, which May had insisted on keeping. He struggled not to glance at the house, but couldn't help it. Pete himself could almost have been hiding up there, watching him. Yes, Pete seemed very close; he was behind the next tree, or waiting for Alf on the wet track above the hurrying river. He was smiling, in revenge perhaps, now that Alf knew what losing his job felt like, or in simple merriment, preparing one of his stories. But it was all crap, wasn't it? Alf was alone, more alone than he'd ever been in his life. "You stupid bugger," he said to the house. "You should have fought harder."

He reached the end of the park and entered a grove of cedars, following the flinty main trail that kept closest to the Atta. Ahead, Bannerman's number one dam made its hushing sound as the river thinned across its wide apron. He was directly across from the hosiery mill. The tall building had a graceful presence above the dark river, and for a few moments he stopped to admire it. Several windows had been propped open, and he could see people working inside—they had jobs for now, though in a few months, when Intertex shut the mill, they too would be unemployed. Soon you'll be footloose and fancy-free, he thought bitterly, just like Pete and me.

Red reappeared and sat beside him. The dog's ears pricked as something moved across the river. Following his gaze, Alf saw a heron, standing motionless in the shallows. Very slowly, the tall gray bird lifted one leg and took a step forward. Then, as it darted suddenly downward, its entire body crashed in a belly flop among the stones. But it had caught a little fish, a wriggling streak of silver across its rapier beak. Alf watched, transfixed. He'd never seen a heron fall before, never imagined it might happen. Standing upright again, the bird tilted back its long throat, and with a couple of tosses the fish was gone.

Beside him, Red seemed to be laughing, his tongue hanging out.

He went on, a little more enlivened, past the dam and into the woods that bordered the millpond. The dog trotted ahead of him now, his curled tail bobbing above the trail. Occasionally he paused to look back at Alf. The trail had been hardened by generations of use, and nothing would grow on it, though in the woods to his left and right the first green flames were licking among the tree trunks. He caught the chirpings and wheedlings of invisible warblers and, from a distance, the tongueless cry of a crow forever saying what could not be understood. He knew exactly the grove of pines in which it was probably sheltering. Crows had sheltered there when he was a boy.

By two that afternoon, he and Red had walked to Devil's Cave by the high woods trail. Alf had always loved the place where the deepening Atta flooded the basin below the cave. As he stood by the river, Red disappeared. For a moment, Alf felt a stab of panic, as if he'd been abandoned by a loyal guide, though he knew the dog would eventually turn up at the house. He returned across the river flats, which were dotted with wild fruit trees just starting into blossom. In the woods beyond he found the shy white stars of trilliums, motionless among their leaves. The woods were still and warm. The sand-colored duff, soon to be smothered with new green, crackled under his feet as he left the trail.

He sat in the empty woods with his back to a large beech, listening to the birds. There was one song in particular—he had never known which bird made it, though he had heard it all his life—that had a curious spiraling quality, as though the notes came curling down a long pipe. The song was too strange to be called simply pretty; somehow it gave the woods an air of melancholy. Alf felt the threat of rain. His limbs seemed heavy. He never wanted to move again, but to remain under the tree as the woods sank into dusk.

He might have been sitting for an hour when he heard a new sound, far to his left. At first he thought it was an owl, hooting in its sleep, or a duck or a goose blundering inland from the river. It faded, then came again, growing stronger with each minute. He glimpsed a black coat through the tree trunks. A man was walking along the trail, weeping. He was openly and unself-consciously sobbing, as though it were the most natural thing in the world to be shuddering and howling as he plodded through the trees. Alf froze against the beech in a kind of horror. He didn't want to be seen, didn't want to interrupt or embarrass the man. Though the path lay not sixty feet in front of him, Alf guessed his best chance of remaining invisible was to stay where he was.

So the man passed, on the slightly elevated trail, appearing and disappearing among the beeches and maples. Alf did not recognize him, though he seemed familiar. He was in his sixties or seventies, wiry and stooped, with a deeply tanned face and a shock of white, unruly hair that for a moment put Alf in mind of his own father—except that this man's hair was patched with black, as if he had been painting a ceiling and spilled some. He was wearing a bright red tie that stood out sharply, like a long wound inside his coat. Just as he came close to Alf, he stopped. Afraid he'd be discovered, Alf lowered his eyes, and at that moment the man blew his nose with a terrific honk, followed by several minor honkings and snifflings. Then he continued on his way, still weeping.

Alf listened to the sound grow distant in the trees. All the birds had fallen quiet, as if listening too. A light rain pattered on the duff, among the great trunks. The shadows were becoming longer. Again came the sound of the man honking. Then the woods were still.

42

"I'M NOT SAYING it's bad," Mann said with a sigh. "It's just not up to your usual standard."

Joe was glad the lights were off in the deserted classroom. His face, his traitor face, was heating. He and the teacher were sitting side by side, at two student desks. Before Joe lay the twenty pages of his essay, "Hoboes and Handouts: A Study of Charity in the Great Depression." Mann had filled its margins with blocks of criticism, in his tiny saw-toothed script. He'd given Joe a *B,* the worst mark he'd ever had for a history project.

"Sorry," Joe managed, not looking at the teacher.

Mann waved his hand. "Don't apologize. It's nothing personal. It's just something, well—when you're writing papers in university, you'll have to use better sources than just your required reading. You didn't read any of the books I recommended. Couldn't you find them?"

"No," he lied, feeling his embarrassment increase.

"I asked Miss Keynes to put a number of books aside."

"I guess I didn't look hard enough."

Mann had twisted in his chair. In the hall outside the classroom, the janitor's broom hissed.

"What happened? Didn't you leave yourself enough time? It felt hurried."

"I guess it was."

Mann waited with unreadable calm. The teacher had said this wasn't personal, yet Joe knew he was disappointed. Now his silence, a silence Mann seemed perfectly comfortable with, had filled the room. In the corridor, a locker slammed. Joe felt he owed this silence something: another apology, maybe, or an explanation. He frowned and pushed his essay around a little. As Mann had guessed, he'd written the whole thing the night before. He hadn't thought it was so bad at the time. In fact, he'd congratulated himself on how smoothly and quickly it had gone. He'd made some clever points, he thought. But Mann said that "Hoboes and Handouts" (how proud he'd been of that title, and Mann hadn't even mentioned it) contained far too few useful facts and relied too much on speculative arguments that chased their own tails.

The thing was, he'd known this at the time. In his rush to finish the paper, and even in the midst of his self-congratulation, he'd had an uneasy perception that "Hoboes and Handouts" was a bit of a con job. He'd crashed on, though, ignoring the knowledge standing just outside his vision. He knew the truth was there, but he wouldn't turn and look at it: he had fallen into the habit of living dishonestly.

He was still with Liz McVey. In spite of having promised himself, scores of times, to break with her, he had drifted on as her steady. "Joe and Liz" had become one of the ongoing features of the school's social life, coupled in the same breath by their friends and even by their teachers. They were a common sight, coming down the halls together, Liz with her head up, and Joe at her elbow, playing a role, he felt, secretly critical of her so much of the time. He couldn't stand the way she called him darling in her fake accent, or fixed on the person in front of her as if he or she were more important than anything else in the world. She pretended an interest in history and in poetry, but her views always sounded cobbled together, as if she had lifted them from a bin of approved opinions. She only grew truly impassioned when talking about herself.

So why was he still with her? Was it sex? True, he couldn't get enough of her slim, round-shouldered body and her searching mouth. Sex with Liz always felt slightly off-color, somehow desperate and illicit. But it was never satisfying. It only promised to be satisfying, endlessly. Whenever they finished one of their trysts, the world seemed drained of meaning. He barely had the energy to put on his clothes, although at the same time he couldn't leave her fast enough. At these moments he most wanted to tell her they were through, yet he could never summon the nerve. It would have been unconscionably cruel, he thought, to make love and then announce he was going for good. So he would postpone the decision for another time—and when the time came, his desire to make love superseded his desire to leave. So he went in circles. He hated himself: for his weakness, for his inability to spare her from himself.

He continued being cheerful and helpful, to all appearances a contented young man. People remarked to Liz on his thoughtfulness. What other boyfriend touched his girl's hair so gently or reached up to pick a bit of lint from her sweater? He had the reputation, even among the staff (though he wasn't sure about Mann), of being a real gentleman.

He went on enjoying the privileges Liz's company brought: driving the Lincoln, lounging about her fine house, being one of the North End gang. There were some consolations, after all, for being with Liz McVey, and not the least of them was seeing a great deal of Anna. He and Liz went out frequently with Anna and Brad. They traveled in the Linc, or in Brad's Oldsmobile, to movies in Johnsonville or to concerts in Hamilton or Kitchener. Every hour of those outings was sacred because he was near Anna. He felt they had entered an understanding. They were closer, friends and perhaps more than friends, with a secret communication that ran deeper than their loyalty to their respective partners. When they were out with Brad and Liz, he felt his actual pairing was with Anna. Perhaps she shared this view. "Oh, Joe and I are leaving," she'd said once, in disgust at something Brad had said and Liz had seconded. And she'd put her arm through Joe's and drawn him off a few steps, laughing, while Joe's heart pounded. She might have been letting him know that she was waiving her old requirement that he keep a certain distance. Often he felt on the verge of asking her where he stood. But he was afraid of another rebuff.

His dishonesty with Liz had infected him. He could sense it, just below the surface of his life. He caught himself adopting some of the airs he disliked in her: referring in bored terms to "the Linc" or "J-ville," her family's name for Johnsonville. Increasingly he lacked patience and rushed almost angrily from one thing to another, without finishing anything. He had developed a mania for speed. On the nights when he should have been working on "Hoboes and Handouts" he was driving the Lincoln down the highway, pushing the needle of the speedometer into the 90s while Liz nuzzled beside him, saying languidly, "Be careful, Joe. You'll kill us both," and stroking his thigh as if she were half attracted to the idea.

Now he saw the reflection of his entrapment in Mann's gaze. Yes, he had caught Mann observing him and Liz intently—disapprovingly. He was ashamed before his mentor, as he was ashamed of his own weakness. Now Mann seemed to be waiting for him to confess all.

The teacher broke the tension. "The important thing now is to get ready for the finals," he said, frowning. "You're going to have to prepare a lot more material than what's covered in your history texts. They'll be looking for some kind of depth. I was thinking, if you wanted to brush up on the Depression, or any other topic—the two wars, maybe—I've got some books I could lend you."

"That'd be great."

"Why don't you come home with me now?" Mann said, bestirring himself. "I'll see what I can root up."

They went together down the hall, past the ranks of dull green lockers. Exiting at the rear of the school, they found several students unloading cartons from a van. "Hot off the press," said a boy with a high forehead and premature widow's peak: John Butler. He had ripped open a carton and was holding out a folded copy of *The Poet's Quill,* the school literary paper. While Mann examined the gift, John handed another copy to Joe. Anna had told him she had a poem in this issue. He tucked the paper among the books under his arm and strode off with Mann, momentarily lifted by the thought of her.

IN MANN'S UPSTAIRS study, under a slanted ceiling, several windows gave a view of the distant Shade. A long, scarred wooden table ran beneath the sills. There was a casual, slightly disheveled look about the place, created by the stacks of books on the floor, the old *New Yorkers* scattered around the jute rug. Joe loved the room: its light, its books, its feeling of important work being done. Mann, he knew, was writing a history of Attawan. Parts of it had appeared in the *Attawan Star*.

He felt privileged to be here, and almost forgiven for his poor performance. He wanted to be a historian himself, and to come to Mann's study was like being admitted to an inner sanctum, a starting point of the long process that would lead him forward. He was alert to everything, keen to make a good impression. He sat in a low chair—the pink cover seemed a bit incongruous, even shocking—sipping his tea and leafing through the books the teacher took from the shelves and rubbed with a cloth, before handing them to Joe.

"You won't want all of these," Mann said with a grin. Inexplicably, the teacher was blushing. "At least I'm getting my books dusted."

Mann handed him a large volume with a dark board cover and knelt with cracking knees beside the chair as Joe opened it. The book was full of black-and-white photographs from World War I: wagon wheels fattened with mud, ragged files of grinning soldiers, the lifeless common of no-man's land. Reaching over, the teacher leafed through the pages until he found a picture of several soldiers in a trench. They all had dirty faces and had paused in their various activities—eating out of mess tins, cleaning their rifles—to smile at the camera.

"That fellow there." Mann tapped on the page to indicate a figure sitting on a crate, his soup-plate helmet pushed straight back from his blackened forehead. "My brother Gordon."

Joe found the figure and caught a hint of Mann's own square face and dark eyes, circled with dirt or fatigue. "*Vimy Ridge,*" Joe read.

"Not long after they'd captured it."

"He was at Vimy?" Joe said with excitement. The great German strongpoint successfully stormed by the Canadians—after British and French forces had failed for years to take it—was a mythic name to him; as with all such names, it came as a surprise to discover that someone he knew, or at least a relative of someone he knew, an actual human being, had been there. It was like finding a ladder into a world that was bigger and brighter, infused, somehow, with immortality.

Again Mann tapped the page. "Look at those grins. They're always grinning in these pictures. It shows their youth, what good boys they were. They were living in hell, but they still couldn't help going on their best behavior when a camera appeared, which tells you a lot about how well disciplined they were—I don't just mean as soldiers but as social creatures. They were so eager to please. I always find it sad."

Joe studied the picture and was moved by a curious sense that he knew what it was like to sit there, in the cold mud in France, eighteen years old, with his friends.

"Maybe they're just happy to be alive," he said quietly.

Mann's brown eyes grew moist, searching—entirely too intense. Joe had to look away.

Mann went on kneeling beside Joe as they examined the photographs. The teacher's left hand rested on his shoulder. Joe shifted away, a little uncomfortable. He could sit in a crowded church pew beside his own father and hardly notice that their legs were touching. But with Mann he became increasingly self-conscious. He was aware of the chapped skin on the back of the teacher's free hand, which was trembling a little, and the white flecks in his nails, and always his unpleasant breath, like the smell of a machine. Mann, he remembered, was retiring at the end of the year; he was old.

When he left, Joe felt immediate relief at being outside, in the mild bright evening. From a lawn a robin sent out its shivering cry. He hurried to Shade Street and along to the corner of Banting, where he sat on a low wall of cut limestone and took out his copy of *The Poet's Quill*, hunting through its newsprint pages until he found her poem.

WHIRLPOOL

Eyes
in the green whirlpool
looking up at me,
blinking and darkening and letting go.
Eyes of water
emerging, submerging—
the eyes of some vast green beast
who knows it need only lazily
circle
until I fall—
devoured by my hunger for looking.

Then you
standing by the gray rock,
a land-man, not of the river
with your startled love-look
beyond mere looking.
I was more afraid of you than the river,
more afraid of you than death.
Your eyes offered something more complicated than water,
wilder than the turquoise river.

Let me go
back to the pleasures of looking.
Let me drown at the bottom with my words.

—Anna Macrimmon

He read it several times. Was he the "land-man"? Yes, surely he was.
He remembered the day he had driven to the whirlpool with Anna, Liz,
and Brad; he saw again the wild water surging past the rock where Anna
had stood.

What was she telling him? "Let me go back to the pleasures of looking." Was she telling him to leave her alone? He sat on, scarcely aware of the cars streaming past or of the Bannerman mansion across the road, its gray stone warming in the late sun. But she wouldn't tell him that, would she, unless he had power over her—more, maybe, than he had guessed?

43

A WEEK LATER, Joe and Brad pulled up in Anna's sloping drive. It was the evening of the Spring Frolic—clear, fragrant, unseasonably warm. With a slight stiffness, ever the wounded athlete fresh from hockey or basketball wars, Brad, resplendent in his tux, left the Olds and took a jogging step or two as he crossed the lawn to Anna's house. Joe got out and climbed into the backseat with the tiny carton that contained Liz's corsage. He couldn't stop thinking about the oversized black shoes he had borrowed from his father—clown shoes, surely, their toes stuffed with newspaper—shoes that reminded him of his father's current difficulties, of his unhappiness deepening through the house like an unpleasant odor. Joe had not wanted to wear them, but he owned only brown shoes himself. He was aware that his hands were shaking. Then the front door opened and he saw Anna in a coat he hadn't seen before, a beltless white coat that came to her knees but did not entirely cover the long pale skirt flexing below it as she picked her way across the lawn. "Joe," she said, smiling, as she got in the front. He had to remind himself that she didn't know he'd read her poem—the new issue of *The Poet's Quill* wouldn't be distributed until next week—and this helped him subdue his nervousness.

A few minutes later, the Olds swung into the McVeys' drive, stopping with a lurch behind the sky-blue Lincoln. As he plodded to the door, Joe could hear Brad's laughter in the car behind him. He felt barely composed, a just object of mockery, the evening already fraying beyond his control.

And yet, and yet: she was here. On the short drive to the school, the world seemed to cohere only by grace of the sleek head in front of him. Inside, gusts of music swept through the dimly lit corridors. Couples in fancy dresses and suits, in tuxedos and evening gowns, with hair creamed and combed, bouffanted and permed, paraded toward the gym with a sound of whisking cloth and tapping shoes. Joe glimpsed Sandy, whom he still went out of his way to avoid. She was wearing what looked like false eyelashes and a puffy Popsicle-green dress, and she was clinging to the arm of Sid Miller, a North End boy with a reputation. There was excitement in the warm air, almost anarchy, as though some long repressed power were nearing the point of release. Two teacher chaperones, watching from the shadows, seemed out of place.

They climbed the stairs to the classroom that was serving as a cloak-room. Fluorescent light fell harshly over the desks heaped with coats. Helping Liz off with her wrap, Joe stared past her coiled hair at Anna. She too had just shed her coat, and he was mesmerized by her: by the simple white form-fitting dress with a square neckline that mirrored the cut of her bangs, by her bare arms, her newness, and the beauty of her face, smiling across the desks as she discovered him. She wore no jewelry.

They went down to the gym and sat at the little table reserved for them. A candle fluttered in its bottle, signaling to the dozens of other flames winking around the perimeter of the vast room. The floor was crowded with dancers, their heads and shoulders touched by the racing moths of light reflected from the multifaceted globe turning overhead, above a ten-foot-high model of the Eiffel Tower, its girders wrapped in aluminum foil. On stage, the Morganaires had stood up in their pale-blue silver-trimmed blazers, leaning forward to release the deep voices of their horns. The outside doors were open and the mild night air stole in and mixed with the warmer, perfumed air inside, making the candles flicker.

Liz drew Joe onto the floor. She hooked her bare arm over his shoulders and drew in close, possessively. Her body seemed uncannily thin and hungry, pressing at him as if to stanch a wound in her midriff. They turned among the other couples in a slow, shuffling drift. Her hair smelled of some flowery scent he found too sweet. He pushed her away a little and tried to dance more energetically, aware that Anna might be watching: wanting her to know he was ready to break with Liz.

"Anna looks nice," Liz said, closing in again. He grunted something noncommittal and twirled her. She came back to him, her face with its gash of red lipstick expressionless in the blizzard of light.

Half an hour later all four of them were at the table, arguing in a slightly forced way about the Beatles. Only Brad seemed to be enjoying himself. With one elbow propped on the back of his chair, his open jacket revealing a frilled shirt and cherry cummerbund, he grinned in his amiable way and announced that the Beatles were for thirteen-year-olds. Joe glanced at Anna. She was twisting her paper napkin—they had been eating cake—and sticking out her jaw in an odd scowl.

"Would you like to dance?"

He was surprised by how collected he felt. He could sense Liz and Brad's sudden stillness, on either side of him. But Anna had not heard: her reverie had taken her elsewhere.

"Hey," Brad said to Anna. He seemed hugely amused. "You've got an admirer."

The Morganaires had started "Twilight Time."

He had never touched Anna Macrimmon, not really, though sometimes their hands had brushed as a book or paper passed between them. Now, out on the floor, she turned to him with a half smile, her face both revealed and hidden by the light that streamed over her head and shoulders. Her hand in his was cold and dry: was she merely tolerating him? He placed his right hand on her back, his fingers touching the firm groove there ever so gently, under the soft rucked material of the dress. As they moved off, she miscued a little and trod on his feet.

"Sorry."

"It's all right. My shoes—they're my dad's, actually—stick out too much."

He could not believe he had admitted this, but he scarcely felt in control of himself.

They danced a little awkwardly, unable to find each other's rhythm. His hands were sweating, and he lightened his touch on her back, not wanting to stain her dress.

Her face was close to his, a little below. He drank in the perfume she wore, which had almost a non-smell: a cleanness, like vanilla. A wisp of her hair brushed his cheek. Between them was the orchid Brad had pinned to her bodice, a senseless mouth gaping upward.

They grew a little more competent, and she settled in closer. The singer wailed his anticipation of the coming night.

Her breast touched his bottom rib. The entire front of his body felt as if it had opened, like a door. He closed his eyes.

Then it was over. They parted, standing at a loss among the chatting couples. He thought to move back to the table. But she was looking at him blankly, her head raised, a little to one side. He returned her look and held it for a breathless moment, until her eyes darted away. Terror was in him, and at the same time he was aware of a remarkable, remote calm. He had read somewhere that animals go calm, knowing they are about to be killed by a larger beast. He pretended to be interested in what the emcee was saying, up there in the spotlight, but he was only impersonating normality. He put his hand in his trouser pocket and felt the handkerchief folded there; it too was his father's.

"Hey, I read your poem," he said, turning back to her with a grin, as if his news was a little joke, nothing important.

He thought she flushed. In the whirling lights it was hard to tell.

" 'The Whirlpool,' " he said. "I got an early copy of *The Quill*."

"And what did you think?" Her voice was hard.

"I love it," he said. He could no longer be casual. His whole body had become a drum, pounding. "I memorized it. Actually"—he realized, too late, that "actually" was a word Liz used, ad nauseam—"I didn't set out to memorize it. I just read it so many times it stuck. It's a great poem. It's—"

He was smiling helplessly. Why wouldn't she help him? She was listening without expression, skeptical and distant. "I was wondering if it had anything to do with me. I know you often make things up, or people do, when they write a poem. But I couldn't help thinking—that day we went to the whirlpool. There was a moment—well."

"Thank you," she said finally, softly. He could not read her expression, but something had crossed her face.

The Morganaires started into another piece, mercifully: he was sure he was drowning in his own incompetence. His face must be the color of Brad's cummerbund. The loud music made conversation impossible. It was a fast tune this time: an orchestrally jazzed-up version of an old Presley song. All around, couples flung themselves into the music. Joe thought Anna looked reluctant—in fact, he wasn't very good at fast dancing, himself—and they left as if by agreement, walking back to the table. He was a failure. He had spoken his secret and nothing had changed. She was leading him away from the dance. The revelation he thought he had found in "The Whirlpool," that he was special to her, was not there.

Liz and Brad weren't at the table. For a while Joe and Anna made themselves busy trying to pick them out in the crowd. There they were, dancing in the swarm of little lights as if born to it. Brad moved elegantly, Joe thought enviously, with a certain casual grace, like a tall black man he'd once seen on television: Cab Calloway or Duke Ellington. Liz danced as if she were totally disinterested, but she too moved well, in her long dress, her body bending in a willowy way.

"They look good together," Joe said. His voice had caught in his throat.

Anna Macrimmon said nothing, although her silence had an oddly palpable quality, as if she had conjured up a large stone that now sat on the table between them. More than ever she seemed to belong to another world: a world with the blue gem of the Mediterranean in its center, so far from this one and so superior, that it must be torture for her to sit here at a dance called, of all things, *Springtime in Paris*. He felt as oafish as any farm boy, a hayseed wearing his father's shoes; perhaps someday she would laugh at the story of this night with friends he would never meet.

"There's Mr. Mann," Anna said.

In the balcony at the west end of the gym a number of people had come to watch the dancing. Craning around, Joe spied the shadowy groups sitting on the wooden benches. The teacher stood behind a railing, his white hair unmistakable. He was looking toward the orchestra, though Joe had an intuition that, only a moment ago, the teacher's gaze had been fixed on him.

44

THE FOUR OF them drove to Liz's to change into more casual clothes and then went on to Laura Becker's place, the first stop in a series of all-night parties. Laura lived on the river side of the Shade Survey, in a big ranch-style house of yellow brick, with a run of picture windows looking east across the backyard and the distant river, toward chains of lights that marked a gravel pit. Joe went into the yard where a group of boys were smoking and drinking by the fence. Petie Brennan, a broad-chested farm boy in thick glasses and an oversized white dress shirt open at the throat, held out a wine bottle. "Get loaded," he said thickly.

Joe took a deep swig from the flattish bottle—the wine was fizzy and sweet, almost like pop—and listened to the others talk. It was over, he felt, his long, solitary campaign to win Anna Macrimmon was over. Clumsily, he had made his move and nothing had come of it. He might as well get drunk.

After a while he turned, letting his weight sag on the wire fence. Above the yard, the expanse of candle-lit living-room windows suggested a dark aquarium, swimming with the flailing forms of dancers. He couldn't see Anna, though he momentarily glimpsed Brad's tall form sliding through the light from a doorway. Liz came to the window and peered out; then her pale face retreated. Below, in the rec room, a game of Ping-Pong was in progress. The wretched hopping of the ball seem to be taking place inside his own head.

He turned again to the valley. In the east, an orange fire raged: the moon, edging slowly from shadow. He drank again from the bottle and passed it back. *You can't say that*, a nearby voice said. *Nobody says that.*

"Anybody got a cigarette?"

At her voice—the familiar-unfamiliar light voice—he turned and saw Anna Macrimmon approach the crowd of boys. She did not look at him, though he sensed she knew he was there. Several of the boys began hunting for their packs, but Dick Christopoulos beat them all to the punch, and in a moment had his lighter going too, shielding its flame under her dipping face. She blew out a plume of smoke with an experienced, blasé air, like a woman in an old movie.

"So is this a special club," she said, "or are girls allowed?"

Strangers to irony, they all hastened to assure her that girls were allowed.

Petie Brennan and Bob Black signaled each other with wide eyes.

She stood with her back partially turned to Joe, in her tight, short sweater, talking to Dick Christopoulos and the others, but especially to Dick. Dick's usual type of girlfriend had teased hair, smoked as a matter of course, and had a reputation. His sharply handsome Greek face, under the droop of his forelock, leaned close to hers, his mouth twisted slightly in a wry smile.

Her smoking shocked Joe. She had revealed a coarseness that he'd never suspected, though he thought it might be an act. Just her being out here surprised him, behaving like some ordinary girl happy with the kind of chatter Dick Christopoulos specialized in. The other boys hung on every word that was said, occasionally putting in their two cents' worth. She talked to them all, laughing every so often. Only once did she glance over at him, with a look that seemed to brim with angry meaning. Had she been upset by his questions about her poem? Well, too bad.

After a few minutes she thanked Dick for the cigarette and ground it out under her shoe. "Think I'll have a look at the moon," she said. She went along the fence, away from them all, toward an old wooden gate held shut by a loop of wire. She unfastened the wire and let herself into the shadowy tangle of bushes and small trees. Joe watched her descend out of sight. A few seconds later, Dick Christopoulos, gently touching the fingers of one hand to his forelock, walked out the gate. He too went down the hillside, with his hunched, high-shouldered walk, his cagey air, disappearing into the mass of bushes.

Joe watched in despair. He could hear voices: Anna Macrimmon laughing, and Dick Christopoulos going on in a low monotone, making her laugh more. Then the sounds were lost in the throb of music from the house.

"Fuck me," a boy said in a low voice, near Joe. Andy Schull flicked his butt over the fence.

"Fuck her," someone said.

"Don't you wish," someone answered.

The boys were at the fence now, staring as one into the night. All of them, Joe suspected, were virgins. They were probably thinking that acts they could only dream of were about to take place, down there in the dark. He twisted the fence until it hurt his hands and turned around twice, in a spasm of indecision. He went back to the house. He looked in the window at the Ping-Pong players. He returned to the fence. The valley was dim, though as his eyes became accustomed, he was able to see more trees and bushes, picked out by the moon, as well as the tin roof of a shed. Farther away, the empty flats stretched toward the river. From the gravel pits across the water came a faint clanking sound; a truck grunted as it changed gears. Anna and Dick Christopoulos had been swallowed by the night. He felt he knew nothing about love or sex at all. She had chosen Dick Christopoulos: Dick the hard rock; Dick who was said to sleep in his car; Dick who spent half his life in the pool hall! She was down there with him now, doing God only knew what.

After a while the boys heard a rumor of food and went back to the house. A few minutes later, Brad came out. He was eating a slice of pizza; a second slice drooped from his other hand.

"You seen Anna? She wanted some pizza."

"She's down there," Joe said, pointing beyond the fence.

Beside him, Brad peered into the darkness, his mouth open in a silent, disbelieving laugh.

"She's with Dick Christopoulos. She might not want you disturbing them."

He felt wonderful, saying this, and terrible. The gloss of happiness disappeared from Brad's face. He went out the gate and down the hill into the darkness, with his pizza.

Joe went into the house. In the light from the rec room, he examined his stinging hand. Blood had trickled into his palm, from the cut the wire had made in his thumb. Upstairs, he stood by the huge fridge, pretending to nurse a glass of punch. The kitchen counters were loaded with food: several kinds of pizza and sandwiches with their crusts cut off and paper barrels of fried chicken and a chocolate cake dotted with jelly beans. Laura Becker's skinny red-haired mother, a woman whose voice seemed pitched at near-hysteria, was walking around with a paper hat and an empty glass, encouraging them to eat. Joe had no appetite. He considered going home. Liz came in and asked him to dance. "I don't know," he said with brutal evasiveness and continued to stand there, ignoring her. She hung on beside him, talking with an inclusive air to people who came by, as if Joe were actually present. She made enough social noises for both of them, pretending to be enthusiastic about things he knew she didn't give a damn about. Of course, he had sometimes done the same thing himself, but he didn't think of that now. Finally she went off with some other girls to dance. From time to time she danced near the light that fell from the kitchen, putting herself squarely in his sight, twisting her body in a way that was meant to attract him, while her face remained cold. She was his fate, the best he could do, and he loathed her. He looked up at the clock, its face like a pizza with numbers. One-thirty-two.

Sixteen minutes later Anna came in, followed by Brad, her eyes preternaturally bright. Her upper lip was stained with pizza sauce. He supposed they'd been kissing. But where was Dick Christopoulos? Had she been kissing him too? No, he no longer understood a thing. Maybe all you had to do, if you were a boy, was go over and kiss her. Maybe it was that simple. "Joe, you should see the moon!"

"He's seen the moon," Brad said sardonically. "We've all seen the moon."

Ignoring Brad, she took Joe by the hand—hers was as cold as ice—and began to draw him across the kitchen. "You have to see how it looks on the river."

He let himself be drawn to the stairs. Apparently, it was his turn. Maybe by the end of the evening she'd have them all down there, even Petie Brennan with his thick glasses. For a moment, he drew back. He'd be damned if he went one step farther with her. He followed her out of the house.

Beyond the fence, the paths in the scrub were worn deep, like troughs. "I think they're goat paths," she told him. "At least it smells like goats." She was proceeding down a slope ahead of him. The gray moonlight held sway, turning the trees and bushes to blotches of dull silver. He half expected to see Brad coming after them, but no one was behind him. He experienced a flash of triumph. Maybe she was only being nice to him, one boy among many, but he was with her, Brad wasn't. He stumbled along, following her down the hard-packed trails.

Under a grove of black willows that obscured the house, she stopped. "You were supposed to follow me the first time."

"What?"

"I look around, and there's Dick Christopoulos."

"You don't like Dick Christopoulos?"

She laughed bleakly, tapping his arm, and went on. Suddenly energized—the numbness and passivity of months seemed to be falling away, though he was still baffled by what was happening—he hurried after her.

They crossed the flats to the river, quickly enveloped by its cold atmosphere, with its smell of decaying weed and slime. On the black water, a swath of moonlight glittered like a school of minnows.

"Very nice," he said.

"Look at me."

He turned. His own face half-shadowed hers. The noise of the party drifted down the hill. She put her hands on his chest and shoved him backward, along the damp path.

"God, you make me mad," she said. And a moment later, a cry of dismay: "I can't believe I'm doing this!"

She strode away along the path that followed the river. He hurried after the white flicker of her running shoes.

"Anna. Anna, stop. Can't believe you're doing what?"

She stalked on, nearly falling at one point when she stepped into a small hole. He sensed she was crying—why crying? what had he done?—but was unable to see her face clearly.

Then she stopped.

"This is crazy," she said. "We should go back."

"Okay."

"No, wait!"

More used to the darkness now, he could make out her features but could not, quite, read her expression. Her cheeks were definitely wet. And her voice, when it came again, seemed to be struggling for breath.

"You want me, don't you? I mean, you want to be with me?"

"Yes."

He did not move.

"If we do this," she said, "we're going to hurt people."

"Yes."

He hardly dared let himself understand her; at the same time his understanding leaped forward, wildly.

"Anna," he said. They stood looking at each other, half seeing each other, in the dim moonlight. His months of holding back held him back now. Everything he wanted was here, but he couldn't move.

Suddenly, with a small cry, she lunged forward, took his head between her hands, and kissed him awkwardly on the mouth. For a moment she pulled away to look at him. Then she put her arms around him. Holding her now, moaning her name, he drank in the smell, almost a no-smell, that rose from her hair, scarcely believing he was feeling the pressure of her long body against his.

They went together up the river. They went silently, almost gravely, holding hands, conscious of a deed done. She kept sighing as if dismayed at herself. When he asked what was wrong, she shook her head and said nothing. The path ran above the sharply edged, shallow bank, descended to cross the mouths of streams, ran on again. Neither of them had ever been here. From time to time they stopped; he had to keep kissing her so he could remind himself that what was happening was true. Between kisses he forgot what her mouth tasted like, forgot what her body with its small breasts felt like as it pressed against him. Then he remembered; it was like this.

Now they could hardly go twenty steps without stopping. They embraced and separated, embraced and fell down. She was laughing with him in the hollow place behind a fallen tree trunk, laughing and weeping both, she was balancing above him on the trunk like a ten-year-old who cares about nothing else. The ground sloped up to what looked like a flat platform. Climbing up its side they saw a long pond, with a little dam gurgling at one end. Under the dark surface fish were rising, breaking the velvet membrane of the water with delicate kissing sounds. The moon was in the pond now, wobbling and broken. "There are many moons," she said, leading him around the path. She had grown somber, as if instructing him: a virginal priestess pointing out the mysteries of the place. "Every moon has a different name. They're sisters."

He had no idea if she was making this up or reciting some old mythology. It didn't matter: everything she said was miraculous. He threw himself into the game. "Every kiss is a fish, and every fish—is delicious."

She contradicted him violently. Fish were sacred to Aphrodite, she told him. "We don't eat them."

"Never?" he said.

"Not unless we want to lose her favor. Which I don't think we do."

She kissed him with slow deliberation, now, and before they could separate again took his hand and placed it on her breast. The moment had the formal aura of an offering, as if Aphrodite were not an old name from the past but a power hovering over them, infusing each touch with divine meaning. She watched him in the moonlight. "Sooner or later, everybody loses her favor," she said. "She's easily bored."

"I'll never be bored with you," he said. "I couldn't be."

But already he feared she might be bored with him. It might happen tomorrow, it might happen in the next five minutes. If he had suddenly found himself alone by this pond, shivering in the damp like the ailing knight in the Keats poem, he wouldn't have been entirely surprised. He wanted her to echo him: I'll never be bored with you either. But she laughed and touched his mouth as if to stop his words. A frog splashed from the bank.

There was a second pond, higher than the first, behind another gurgling dam of iron and cement. They were near a barn and could sense the slow presence of large animals—cows or horses—and smell the heavy sweetness of hay and manure. "You know, I can't smell horse manure without thinking of vanilla ice cream," he told her. "It's the ice-cream man—his wagon was pulled by a horse. You could hear his bell, all up and down the street." He was saying anything that came into his head, with no worry about its relevance, because tonight everything was connected. Moon, ice-cream man, horse manure, love, his soaking shoes: all part of the same thing, a thing that had no name but which contained them as the gray moonlight contained them in its silver bowl.

LAURA BECKER'S HOUSE was quiet; the great windows blazed from empty rooms. Everyone had gone on to the next party. Not quite everyone. Turning a corner into the front yard, they saw the black Olds waiting by the curb. Behind the wide windshield sat the twinned, accusing shadows of their guilt.

They slipped into the backseat. It was Anna who spoke first, telling Brad she wasn't feeling well—was it a lie, Joe wondered, or had the events by the river made her ill?—she wanted to go home. No one spoke as the Olds cruised the moonlit streets. Brad dropped off Joe and Liz first. "We can take the Linc," Liz said, as they climbed the steps to her house, as if they would simply continue to the next party.

She went up to the bathroom. He waited in the family room, feeling capable of anything—it was the promise of Anna's touch, given secretly across the backseat before he left the car. Behind him, Liz came into the kitchen. "Come here," he said softly, the executioner calling to his victim.

As he poured out his mixture of truth and lies, she watched him without expression, her heart-shaped face pale, her beautiful eyes fixed on his with their look of startled candor, at once ferocious and cold and completely vulnerable. Her silence unnerved him. She was doing nothing to defend herself, only waiting with the calm air of someone who has expected such treatment all along. He was fumbling now, fumbling out his apologies like a fool. "I'm sorry," he said, for the third or fourth time. "I know it isn't fair." Not knowing what else to do, he moved to embrace her. She was stiff in his arms. He let go, looking around uncertainly. "I guess I better go."

"Anna won't have you," she said, her voice small. "She was involved with someone else. She told me. She said she can't love anymore."

"Someone else," he said numbly.

"A man," Liz said. "Not a boy like you."

He moved away, but at the stairs to the kitchen he looked around again. She was gazing out at the starkly lit patio, at a glass-topped table where someone had left a pair of hedge clippers. He was chilled by her isolation, which gave her a strange authority, and for a moment he nearly went back to ask her what she meant. Finally he crossed the kitchen's glare and left the house.

45

THE NIGHT WAS full of sounds that drifted through the open windows above the table where Archie Mann sat working—music, voices, the clanking of conveyor belts across the river—all made small and enticing by distance.

Again he clinked the lip of the Glenfiddich bottle to the little earthenware cup. He was drunk, he realized, pleasantly and thoroughly drunk. I could sneak up on them, he thought with an amused grunt. He imagined his surprised students discovering him in the bushes, with his binoculars hanging from his neck. They could hardly fire me at this stage in the game.

He put down the cup, looked for a few moments at the small age-

browned snapshot lying on his desk blotter, and uncapped his fountain pen.

Dear Esther,

The photo you sent—well, to be frank, it was a shock. Only I
think it was taken in Regent's Park, that time you and Walter came
down for a play at the Old Vic, remember? I think you took it. The
four of us had a picnic beforehand on the lawn, just to the east of
the zoo. August 1935. Those are Nash's terraces in the distance.
Jeremy and I still enjoying our golden age, all five or six months of
it. But the photo's a revelation. I mean, every picture ever taken of
us shows something new, don't you think? If you look closely
enough? I think I look positively sheep-eyed, rather pathetically
devoted; no wonder he left me! Jeremy looks rather more intense
than usual, staring at the camera as if determined to impress it. He
had more vanity than I was ever willing to give him credit for.
Walter—that way he had of carrying himself—real noblesse in that
man of yours, though here he looks a little weary, as if secretly fed
up with the rest of us. Do you think he was ever fed up? Not with
you, my dear, but with Jeremy and me. We were rather déclassé
compared to him, I mean in every sense. But it's heartbreaking to
see us at the very summit of our youth and happiness, don't you
think? God, what life is!

Glenfiddich thoughts. I'm sitting at my long desk with the
windows open, pleasantly sloshed and listening to a group of my
students make merry at a house near here. I wish I were eighteen
again.

But Jeremy. I remember you said, one time after he'd left me,
that it was probably a good thing, for me if not for him: Jeremy too
self-absorbed, and likely, you said, "to pull me down with him."
But why couldn't I have pulled him up? People do pull other
people up, don't they? Or do they get pulled down a little too, no
matter what? Of course all this is irrelevant, really, because the fact
is, in the end, he didn't want me. I don't know if there was some-

one else. He was so damnably opaque, and I let him be, out of some misguided notion of kindness. I never pressed him. I wished I had, now. We talked so much, and in the end we talked about everything except why he was drawing away. That last summer in London, in the borrowed flat on St. Mark's Crescent, we were getting along so beautifully. Then one day (I don't believe I've told you this, forgive me if I have), I was pulling on my clothes, hurrying to get to work, and I saw Jeremy looking at me from the bed. His face had gone cold. I went cold. It was as if he'd really seen me, some fatal flaw of mine, for the first time. I'd always thought I was lucky beyond deserving to have him—he was better looking, smarter, the target of a thousand other boys, etc. etc. But I'd almost gotten used to him being there. And then this look: I believe I lost him right then. And I still don't know what it was about. But I can tell you this, there are moods—Glenfiddich moods—when I feel that look was the central event of my life.

Enough of this. Did I tell you I'm writing an essay about Abraham Shade? The man has gotten under my skin. I'm living in his house, of course, and maybe it's just old age, but I seem to feel him around here, more and more. From my yard I can see the hill, across the valley, where he sat on horseback one fine day in 1822 and looked down on the forks for the first time. He knew in a flash (this isn't fancy, I have his diaries) he had to make a town here. To my mind (a most unhistorical notion) he's still there, on the crest of the hill, holding the town in his gaze; and it's this, somehow, that allows the town to go on existing.

As I say, Glenfiddich moods. I feel sometimes as if thirty-five years have gone by in the time it takes me to put down one exam paper and take up another. But we make do, don't we? We rub on. I think your Walter was the best man I ever knew. He was older and wiser and funnier than the rest of us, and I loved him as I love you. Forgive your old friend his rambling. I will definitely come to Cambridge this summer.

Archie

He left the house. The party sounds had stopped. Distantly, across the river, the conveyor belts went on with their fretful clanking. The moon stood almost at the high midpoint of the sky. He drifted to the south side of the house and gazed down the valley toward Lookout Hill, where it commanded the deep center of town. On the hill's crest, not quite visible in the mass of trees and houses, he sensed the lone horseman waiting. What was time? Archie Mann was supposed to be a historian, but he felt he had no idea what time was, really. It certainly wasn't what got measured by watches and clocks. *That* time was a tidy illusion, made for businessmen. Real time was something else, wild and unknowable. Just now it seemed that time had only been born that instant. Everything was fresh with the impetus of new beginnings: the infant skull of the moon riding over his shoulder, the wild blue light in the valley, the dank-earth smell of the river, the lights twinkling downstream. He moved on a little, into a deeper darkness. Across the valley, the horseman watched, motionless above his dream.

46

THE LIME-GREEN EDSEL brought Alf to a halt. There was no mistaking those protruding rust-eaten headlights, the drift of papers on the dash.

"Alf!" That torn-cardboard voice. Doyle, dressed in a sport shirt flecked with tiny red dots, and shapeless gray trousers, was coming down the post office steps, one massive hand—a badger's paw—extended.

Alf, incongruously, felt he was being congratulated. He knows I've been fired, he thought.

"You got a few minutes?"

He had nothing to lose. It was one of the advantages of being unemployed. At first you sensed everybody's eyes on you. Then you realized you were invisible.

He followed the organizer into the Vimy House, past the empty desk where the same asbestos-colored cat slept, up three flights of stairs following a trail of filthy mismatched carpets to Doyle's room. Alf took the chair by the open window that looked down on the empty street. From nearby came the watery murmurs of pigeons. Wheezing from the climb, Doyle sat heavily on the edge of the bed and immediately began rolling a cigarette. His tongue swept the edge of the paper. "Trying to quit," he growled. "They say you smoke less if you have to make your own. Drink?" he said, nodding at a bottle of rye on the bedside table. The amber liquid contained a light of its own, faintly sinister. Alf looked at it for a moment. His social reactions had slowed.

"No thanks. I wouldn't mind a fag, though."

"I thought that was one fault you didn't have."

"I have them all now," Alf said.

Doyle chuckled darkly as he handed the cigarette across. He tossed Alf his lighter and silently rolled another cigarette for himself. Alf smoked and worried. He knew he hadn't been brought here to make small talk, and he feared the exposure of even a small part of what he had kept to himself.

After a while, Doyle said, "I hear you had some bad luck."

Alf shrugged. "Nothing worth talking about." He could feel Doyle waiting, on the low bed across the room. He could feel the powerful draw of Doyle's silence, tugging on his secrets. He resisted, settling himself, a man in a hole. Still, Doyle went on waiting, perfectly comfortable, it seemed.

Doyle said, "They treated you badly."

Again Alf shrugged, feigning nonchalance. But he saw Kit Ford sitting smugly behind his desk, on the day the foreman had taken him off the Richardsons.

"Tell me."

Alf studied the glowing tip of his cigarette, reluctant to offer a single syllable. Silence was the one province he still ruled. Now another man was asking in.

Doyle would not be put off. He sat on, like a statue, a man whose chief occupation and talent was waiting. He could wait ten years, calmly smoking, his small eyes glinting in his rough face, his big hand going slowly up and down with his cigarette.

"Kit Ford," Alf said, to the rug at his feet. "You might have heard of him."

"Oh, yes," Doyle said, with a tone that suggested he had both heard and disapproved. Alf experienced a slight opening inside himself: an access of hope, like a glimpse of distant water. He licked his lips and began, very slowly, to tell Doyle about Ford's arrival in the mill and the events that had followed. Occasionally he had to stop to catch his breath, which curiously kept failing him.

When Alf told the story of his fight with Ford, the organizer heaved with amusement. For the first time, Alf experienced a certain pleasure and even pride in what he'd done. Margaret had made him feel ashamed, but Doyle asked him questions about their scrap, clearly relishing it. As Alf told about being fired, the organizer shook his head and muttered *bastard;* it was as if he were pouring water into the mouth of a thirst-stricken man.

When Alf finished, they were again silent. In the street below, several schoolgirls were walking along with skipping ropes bunched in their hands. Their chiming voices seemed far away, a dream in the bright sunlight. In a few seconds all the relief he had felt in telling his story soured into remorse, a sense that he had given away some critical part of himself. He was exhausted. It had all meant nothing.

"So, you found anything else?"

Alf shook his head, reluctant to talk more. His failure over the weeks to find work was far worse than being fired. He had once thought any fool could find work, but he seemed to have come up against something impenetrable. Perhaps it was some flaw in himself he'd never sensed until now, or perhaps fate dealt in conspiracies. The effect was to make him feel foolish, unnerved, and, yes, inexplicably embarrassed. He had recently developed the habit of putting his hand over his mouth as he talked—as if he were casually scratching his upper lip. In fact, he was hiding the rotting, untrustworthy depths his words came from. He was hiding from his own suspicion that he was lying, without quite knowing whether or not he was.

"How you'd like to work for me?"

A brief laugh rasped in his throat. Doyle's offer seemed a bitter joke.

"I could give you sixty a week. Not much, but better than you're getting on unemployment insurance."

"And what would I do?"

"You'd help me organize this place."

Alf looked at him in disbelief.

Doyle nodded. "There's a lot of people on side already. It's the closing of the hosiery mill. They realize just how little they mean to these sons of bitches. There've been some changes with us, too. We've got more money. I've got some girls to help me. There'll be four of us. We'll visit people at home—wherever we can find them. In the evenings, mostly. Put on a real blitz."

The last time Doyle had played this game, several people had lost their jobs. Alf felt he was being asked to live his worst mistakes over again. Doyle's dim room brought back memories of another room, the sail-boats on the wall.

He went on smoking, staring at the labyrinth of pink roses in the filthy worn-out rug.

"You don't want me," he said at last.

"Why not?"

Again Alf shook his head. Given how he felt about himself these days, the answer seemed self-evident. But at the same time, he felt incapable of expressing it. That would mean confession, and he could no more confess than fly. His guilt had become a dark weight his body had accustomed itself to, like a tree growing around a buried ax head. He went on studying the dilapidated rug, his cigarette growing a drooping worm of ash.

"You're worth fifty votes to me," Doyle said, butting his cigarette. "Maybe a hundred."

Alf hardly trusted his ears. But the organizer was studying him gravely.

"People will follow you," Doyle said. "They know you were treated unfairly."

"That's no reason to follow anybody."

"No, but they trust you. You're a sort of leader to them."

"Oh, fucking hell," Alf said. "I wasn't born yesterday. You're out of date, if it was ever true. Which I doubt. I've fallen off the table."

Cigarette smoke drifted along the sloping walls and ceilings. In the street, a fire truck's engine rattled. "So what do you think?" Doyle demanded, after a while.

Alf remembered the old man he'd seen in the woods, the man who had come trudging along the trail that day, weeping. He saw again the black coat opened to reveal the red slit of the tie; heard again his sorrowful howling; saw him stop among the trees to blow his nose, then go on. It was as vivid to him as if it were all happening again, as if he were there in the gray mild air of the empty woods, with his back to the tree. Except that this time, grief welled up in *him*—who knew where it had come from? He felt tears and turned his face aside.

After a few seconds, he composed himself. The organizer had averted his eyes. In the smoke-layered dimness of the room, his pitted face gave the impression of great age, as though he had come through centuries of lifetimes. To Alf, Doyle seemed somehow connected to the old man in the woods, as if he were thinking of him too. Alf felt a stab of affection for the organizer; he hardly knew him, and yet here they were in this strange knot of intimacy—more intimate, in a way, than anything he had shared for weeks with his own wife.

LATE THE NEXT day, Alf stood across from Margaret as she sorted grimly through a heap of children's jeans. Through the vast barn of the Johnsonville discount store, tangled piles of clothes had been dumped out on long rows of trestle tables, under the arctic glare of fluorescent lights. There were suits and dresses as well, their hangers squeaking incessantly as people shoved them along the racks. He and Margaret had not come here in the days when he'd had a wage; he sensed it was a burden on her, to shop alongside the kind of people who frequented this wasteland of bargains. Not far away stood an Indian woman with long greasy hair. Under her pink slack-necked sweatshirt her vast breasts fell away to either side. She wore bedroom slippers, rimmed with fur, and brown pants with a stain like dried mucilage down one thigh. Yet there was something proud in her carriage, frowning and royally disdainful, as she flicked through the mass of clothes.

He pawed through the trousers and from time to time held up a pair, which Margaret dismissed with a sharp glance and shake of her head. He felt, almost, as if she were dismissing him as well, for the pretty pass he'd brought them to. For a couple of weeks now, she had been short with him. He had tried to blame it on her time of month, but it had gone on too long for that. He worried she'd found out about Lucille. It seemed possible; probably half the town knew about Lucille.

They paid for a pair of jeans and went out into the menthol brightness of the evening to the Biscayne. He asked Margaret if she'd like an ice cream. "We can't afford it, can we?" she said dryly, and this too was a jab. But this evening he would not take an insult. He drove to the Dairy Queen and bought two small vanilla cones. Heading home, he took a longer, more scenic route along unpaved back roads, past ditches where shoots of new green flamed among cans and papers. They were mostly silent, turning their ice creams under the steady lathing of their tongues, burrowing into the parallel solitudes that had become their habitual form of being together, comfortable after a fashion. On the horizon, the sun had begun to sink, filling the car with a bloodred light. Her face seemed younger. Suddenly he felt tremendous hope and in the same moment a sinking, afraid of how she would react to his news.

But it was too late. He had already spoken. "I've got a job."

As if in a trance, she did not respond. On her chin was a spot of ice cream, like a white mole.

"Margaret? I've got a—"

"I heard you."

He saw he had kindled nothing in her, nothing like his own wildfire of fear and hope. It was as if she had lost the meaning of the word *job,* its aura of safety. There was something helpless about her too, as if she had been cut adrift. He saw she was as alone as he was. Something in him reached out to her.

"Do you remember last summer, that Irish fellow who came around to organize a union?"

"No."

"Doyle. Malachi Doyle."

"When all the people were fired," she said.

He bit his lip. "He's actually not a bad fellow."

"You're working with a union," she said, her voice flat with disapproval. "After all the unions have done for you." She had been irrational on the subject of unions since '49. Even more than he did, she blamed his involvement with the union for the failure, later on, of his house-building business.

"It's a job," he said. "I'll be making sixty a week."

She blew out derisively.

"What's the matter with a union?" he said. "They're not perfect, but they've done a lot of good for people."

"Yes, like Pete."

"Goddamn you, woman!" he roared, to the road. Ice cream was running over his hands, over the steering wheel. He managed to get the window down and fling out his cone. "Goddamn you," he said again. This was more than a job to him. The last couple of days, knowing he would work with Doyle, he'd begun to feel like himself again. But this feeling was weak, and here she was killing it.

They were silent for a while. The sun had disappeared. In the darkening blue, intersecting jet contrails made a cross of St. Andrew's.

"I can help those people," he said, struggling for calm. "The people who were fired. If we can get the union in, we can negotiate their jobs back." Doyle had promised him this: it was one of the main reasons he'd taken up the organizer's offer. It would be a way of making up, at least a little, for what he'd done. But she seemed unmoved. She went on staring out the windshield. "Anyway, it's not forever," he said, "If the union goes in, I'll get *my* job back."

"According to Doyle," she said, with infinite sarcasm.

"Margaret you've got to trust me!"

"I've trusted you well enough," she said. She was sitting with the remains of her cone, like a miniature version of itself forgotten in her fingers. "I trusted you with Carrie Crean."

"What?"

"I think you heard me. Or are you going to pretend you don't know her name?"

Her black eyes were glazed with tears.

"I know about her, Alf. I know what you've been doing."

He steered blindly, hardly seeing the road. That she had come so near to the truth, without actually striking it, made him feel a bullet had singed his hair. It was more shocking, in a way, than being hit. Somehow she had struck on the essential fact of his betrayal. He had not seen Lucille for months, but his sense of guilt was still raw, and she had put her finger right on it.

"Bastard," she said, "bastard."

He had never heard her use that word. The runt cone was melting over her fingers. A small muscle in her face twitched. He felt as if a craziness had broken out in the car and infected him. He was a hairbreadth from driving them into the ditch.

"Stop the car," she told him. "I want out."

He kept driving, in a kind of panic.

"I'm going to be sick," she said.

Even before he had completely stopped, she opened the door and climbed out, stumbling a little in her flats on the gravel. They were beside a kind of paddock. There was a metal gate, which she climbed awkwardly, her skirt riding up to expose the white straps of her garters. Beyond was a green area spotted with cow dung and the ruined foundations of a barn. She walked toward its caved-in doorway as if she lived there.

As he clambered over the gate, she went around the corner of the ruins, out of sight. When he finally caught up to her she was standing stock-still, looking at a mass of cattle in the corner of the compound, under the skeleton of a dead elm. They were returning her look from their furred dirty-white faces, lowering their heads and backing against each other nervously.

"Come on," he said. He took her arm but she shook him off and kept staring at the cattle, her head down, almost like them, as if the key, the secret of her life, lay there, among their broad hooves squishing in the mud, their wild pink-rimmed eyes.

"Margaret, there was never anything between me and Carrie Crean."

"You're lying," she said numbly to the cattle.

"I'm not lying."

In the corner, a few of the cattle were drifting from the herd, lowing and moving toward them. The second time he took her arm she allowed him to lead her off, in her mud-clogged shoes.

They climbed the gate. But when he opened the car door for her she turned to him, her huge eyes searching his. He told her he loved her. He did his best to look back at her candidly, but he was sure she could read his guilt in his face and much, much more. Her own loss was there, it seemed, her own confusion, as if she were no longer sure what his eyes meant, or his mouth. She no longer knew him.

47

LATE THE NEXT afternoon he returned to Doyle's hotel room. Doyle had been joined by his fellow workers, Shirley and Deirdre, who were to help with the organizing. Mary Carr, Alf's old mate from the sweater mill, was there too, as a volunteer. The little Newfoundlander walked up and down the soiled carpet, exultant at being the center of attention, jabbing at the air with her cigarette while she gave Doyle the names of possible supporters. The organizer sat on the edge of his bed, writing her suggestions down while he squinted through the smoke from his own cigarette, stuck like a white peg in the corner of his mouth. The air was full of smoke, blue ranges and uplands of smoke, drifting and slowly dissolving.

Alf had his old chair by the window. With each name Mary came up with he grew more uncomfortable, taking hard drags on his own cigarette. Down on the sidewalk, two women had stopped to talk. The world outside seemed a haven of sunshine and normality. But here, in this room, they seemed to be up to something else: an activity of shadows, conspiratorial, illicit.

Mary stopped. For this special occasion she had rimmed her small eyes with liner and painted her lips bright red. But there could be no disguising the oddness of her scooped-out face with its pointed chin.

"Can you think of anybody else, Alf?"

He frowned thoughtfully.

"What about Matilda Barnes?" she said, wondering.

The name jolted him. Matilda had been a friend of his mother's, a woman in her sixties now, who worked in the cutting department of the sweater mill. As a boy, he had often visited her house. Her husband had kept pigeons. Alf had loved to feed them, while the soft birds balanced on his shoulders and even his head, their little claws needling his scalp.

His whole instinct was to protect Matilda. He suspected that if he asked, she would sign a union card. Still, he didn't want to lead her into a situation where she might be fired.

"I wouldn't think she'd go for it," he said. "Too close to retirement. Not really the union type."

Across the room, Deirdre and Shirley were watching him. Deirdre Hoar was a stocky woman of perhaps thirty, with short black hair and beautiful fine eyebrows, a hooked nose, and a look of pent-up outrage, like a baby owl or hawk. Shirley Dearing was about the same age, tall, with hunched shoulders and an long attractive face within a thin fall of hair. Alf was aware of a certain shrewdness; her presence intimidated him more than Deirdre's, because she made him want to perform well.

"I don't know," Mary said, demurring. "Matilda's a pretty independent type. Ain't her husband in a union, over in Johnsonville?"

"Well, I could be wrong," Alf said.

"Anyways, you know her, don't you?"

"Years ago," Alf said evasively. He could feel his face heating and was glad of the dimness of the room.

Silence descended. Alf felt caught on the slippery slope of his own lie. He could almost hear the others thinking incredulously, *If you know her, why don't you approach her?* His subterfuge had shaken him. He had come to this room full of enthusiasm, wanting to help. Something about surrendering names had awakened an old reluctance, though. In a way, he had come full circle. Again, there was a man with a notebook, waiting for names.

"I'd give her a try," Mary said, to Doyle.

Doyle raised his thick eyebrows in Alf's direction; it was his call.

"I wouldn't," Alf said, as nonchalantly as he could.

"All right," Doyle said. He looked at the tip of his ballpoint. Alf licked his lips. Across the room, Deirdre was motionless in her chair. But her black eyes were fierce.

"Well?" Doyle said.

Alf realized that several seconds had passed. He had lapsed away.

"I'm sorry, I—"

"Mali just wondered if you knew any other names?" This from Shirley, with a note of gentleness, of provisional support.

"Right." The door's pale scarred rectangle stood only a few feet away, just beyond the gauntlet of legs and feet and shoes. Alf could stand up and say, I'm sorry. I've made a mistake. Or he could simply walk away. But he sat on, not knowing what he was going to do, only knowing he would have to do something. He was, almost, a fascinated spectator of himself, waiting in a clarity without foreknowledge or understanding. Was he simply afraid to leave? No, something else was keeping him here, the pull of something he did not understand.

He said, "I don't want to put these people at risk."

Deirdre swore.

Doyle frowned. "Alf, I think I told you we're not having any more meetings like the one at Pete's. At least not until there's so many of us they can't fire us."

"You said no meetings at all."

"What's going on, Mali?" Deirdre said. There was something comical in her anger, it was so immediate and extreme. Doyle ignored her.

"If we can collect enough cards, there won't have to be any meetings— not before ratification. After we're ratified, it's a whole new ball game."

"Have you ever done this before?" Deirdre asked Alf, critically.

"Not for many years," Alf said.

"Because this is pretty basic—"

"All right," Doyle said, placating.

"So give us some names!" Deirdre cried, slapping her thigh.

"Not if you ask like that," Alf said, fixing her with hatred. There was a certain joy in looking at her like this: all his strong emotion finally finding a focus. For a few seconds they simply faced off through the smoke.

"All right, brother," Deirdre said finally. She sat back in her chair with her sinewy forearms crossed, scowling.

There was silence. Everyone waited for him now: the two women in their chairs; Doyle on the squeaky bedsprings, his carved, ancient face hovering in smoke like a tribal god; and Mary Carr, with her back to the door, her bleak white face with its circles of eyeliner turned to him without expression, the hardness of her life having purged her of any airs, any bother with false, encouraging smiles. All the people in the room were hard, he saw. There was something desperate and pinched about them; they had the air of underdogs. But at the same time they were true, as a chunk of rock or a good hammer is true. They had given their hardness as an instrument, to a cause.

He said, "Ellen Kelly."

"Good!" Mary said, stabbing her finger at him. Doyle printed the name while the others watched, like people who don't write themselves and have an immense, almost superstitious respect for the scribe in their midst. Alf was momentarily lost in the associations conjured by Ellen Kelly: the narrow house on the Flats, a bed of prize dahlias, Ellen's fleshy arms. Yes, a name was more than a name. It was a life. What business did people have even uttering other people's names—flinging them about like stones? There was no telling what might happen. He remembered reading about an Indian tribe where everyone had two names, one for public use, the other a secret, unknown to anyone else. How well he understood this. How he wished Ellen Kelly had another name, to make her safe.

"Any others?" Doyle said pointedly.

Alf looked up wondering, his brow sweating. He saw faces but could remember no names. He saw eyes, and gardens, and front porches; he saw a rowboat, tethered under willows, and a green Plymouth with furry dice hanging from its rearview. But he could think of no names.

The only name that came to him was his own. It stuck in his head like some fragment of a song he couldn't shake: *Alfred William Walker, Alfred William Walker*. As if he were five years old, chanting it like a bit of magic.

Then another name occurred to him.

"Sidney Clarke," he said.

SIDNEY LIVED ON West Street, about a hundred yards north of the Island. Alf and Doyle found him in his backyard, bent over his hoe on a strip of black earth. Below the sharp cut of the bank behind him, the Atta churned up pom-poms of foam. Smoke poured from a pile of branches and leaves. Walking ahead of the organizer, Alf saw the stoop of Sidney's laboring shoulders and was filled with second thoughts. What business did he have walking in here, asking Sidney to risk his peace and quiet? He felt the warmth of pity, only a step removed from self-pity.

As always, Sidney was glad to see Alf. He kept his eyes fixed brightly on Alf's, as Alf explained what he and Doyle were up to. When Sidney glanced at the organizer, his smile revealed a hint of something hard and suspicious. Then when he turned back to Alf, his rapt expression returned. Alf was reminded of Pete. Had he pulled Sidney's name out of the air because Sidney was so much like Pete? If so, this was the last place he should have brought Doyle. What in the hell was he trying to do?

To make matters worse, Sidney agreed almost at once to join; said *Yep, yep, I'm in,* even as Alf, shifting his feet in the dirt, silently urged him to refuse. He felt Sidney was joining on his account only: the man didn't know what he was doing. As Pete he felt had not known.

"The deal is," Doyle told him, "you sign a card, pay us a dollar, and when we get fifty-five percent, the union's in." He had taken a card from inside his jacket. The grin froze on Sidney's face as he eyed it with blank apprehension: a good patient watching the doctor load his hypodermic.

There was no flat surface to write on. So Alf bent over and Sidney signed the card on his back.

Sidney had left his wallet in the house. As he trekked away to fetch a dollar, Alf and Doyle strolled toward the river. It was beautiful just now, a hurrying ribbon of bronze lit with the elusive earth tints of the spring evening. But Alf felt unconnected to the scene in front of him; he had stepped over a frontier, onto the questionable side of good. He turned, at a cry from the house, a woman's high-pitched voice leaping in anger. Alf was appalled. A surging unhappiness invaded his limbs; he had to do something. He found a flat stone and whipped it sidearm over the river.

"Her father went out in 'forty-nine," he told Doyle, accusingly. "Lost his job, in the end."

"Well maybe this time," Doyle said, "she'll learn who to blame."

"We're all part of it," Alf said, striking back at him. For a moment, before Alf bent to find another stone, their eyes met and their easy companionship was exposed as an illusion.

Sidney came back down the yard, pale and trembling but with a smile still struggling for prominence on his thin face. Protruding from his hand, the way a child might carry it, was a stiff new dollar bill. As he handed it over, no one spoke of what had just occurred, but Alf could see Jeanie Clarke's small face peering out a window, a vision of concentrated fury.

FIFTEEN MINUTES LATER, they were sitting in Ellen Kelly's front room, surrounded by wallpaper in a suffocating floral print like a dying jungle. Ellen worked in sewing: a heavy gray-haired woman with doughy arms that wobbled underneath as she handed around a dish of peppermints. The scooped top of her flowered dress showed a sun-roughened chest, like so much pink crepe. Sitting back in her armchair she rolled a peppermint around her mouth with a clicking sound and occasionally glanced at her husband, Jared, who had dragged a chair into the doorway to the dining room and sat bent over with his elbows on his thighs, staring at the floor as though his back and his patience had given out together. The house stank of Brussels sprouts.

"So you can't get enough trouble," Ellen said to Alf, in a loud, demanding voice.

"Guess not," he said.

"It's all right for you boys," she said. "If this blows up, you still got your jobs. Not like us. They catch us signing one of your cards and we're gone."

"That's right," Jared said absently, to the floor. The bald patch at the back of his thinning brush cut gave off a yellow shine in the lamplight. He had been a mechanic in the air force and now worked in a garage in Johnsonville. There was a weariness about him, as though he had long ago lost interest in life and was only waiting, a little disgustedly, for it to end.

"I'm three years from retirement, I got my pension to think of," Ellen said, glancing angrily at her husband as if this were his fault. "Maybe if I was twenty—"

Her big jaw worked on her candy and her eyes demanded *Well?* Her refusal was enough for Alf; he stirred on the couch to signal he was ready to go. But Doyle went on sitting with a faint smile as if he were settling in for the night, oblivious to the uncomfortable silences that fell. He said, "Think of it maybe as a legacy. Something for the younger ones who've got a lot more than three years to go."

"I got eleven grandchildren," Ellen barked at him. "That's legacy enough for me."

"Eleven!" Doyle said. "That beats me. I've only got nine."

Ellen went on rolling a peppermint around on her tongue, apparently unimpressed. She was dead set against them, Alf saw. Why was Doyle wasting everyone's time? Feeling embarrassed on behalf of them both, Alf cleared his throat and pretended interest in the pots of African violets and baby's tears in the window. He was beginning to believe that Doyle was more than insensitive; there was a kind of brutality in him, unsoftened by pity or remorse, like a salesman who means to exhaust his victim into submission.

Doyle said, "My daughter's husband, he's in this plant in Toronto, makes shock absorbers for trains. Good union—he's a steward—sits on the board alongside the bigwigs. They actually have a say in how the place is run."

Jared said, "Fat chance of that here."

"That's what they said there, apparently," Doyle said coolly. Jared snorted. Ellen glared at her husband. Alf felt he had stumbled into a secret life—a life of submission and unsatisfied rage—contained in this orderly little house where everything was spotless and exactly in place.

Doyle went on for a time about unions he was familiar with, talking about how normal things got once they were established. Even the big-wigs ended up being happy with the situation, he said; a long contract let them predict their costs accurately, without surprises. Hell, he even knew one boss who bragged about what a good union he had—and this guy was one tough cookie. He'd fought the union like a Mafioso when it first went in. But he'd come around. He seemed almost proud of it, as if he knew he was finally on the side of the angels.

As Doyle talked he took a union card out of his shirt pocket and toyed with it in his big hands. He bent it between thumb and forefinger, stropped it on his index finger like a blade, touched it to his red pitted nose. Ellen scowled at the little white card.

Suddenly Doyle stopped. He looked at the card and seemed almost surprised to find it in his hand. He looked at Ellen, as if to say, What am I going to do with this? He raised his thick black eyebrows.

"All right," Ellen said, "give me the damned thing." She shot another poisonous look at her husband, who had lifted his face, apparently in shock.

Doyle gave her the card, and she signed it on the small table beside her chair. She sent Jared out of the room to find a dollar, which he brought to her with evident distaste, holding out the bill and averting his head as she took it. She extended one arm, and as Doyle took the dollar and the card from her, she looked over at Alf and, without changing her dour expression, slipped him a wink.

AFTER, IN THE car, Alf said, "I was ready to walk out of there."

"Sometimes it's the right move," Doyle said. "You develop a feeling. That one was a believer. I knew it when I came in."

"A believer," Alf said, gently mocking. He was beginning to think

Doyle was a bit of a hot-air artist. They were driving down Shade, between the closed stores.

"She's mad," Doyle said. "You could see it in her face. She knows there's injustice in the way things work, knows it in her gut. The whole time she's saying *No, no,* and doing the sensible thing, inside there's a tough old gal standing with clenched fists saying, *Just give me a shot at the buggers.*"

"You seem so sure," Alf said critically.

"You must have sensed something yourself there," Doyle said.

"Not me," Alf said.

"Then why'd you give me her name?" Doyle asked. Alf was startled. Why *had* he given Ellen's name to Doyle? He looked out at a passing tree, its new leaves orange in the tide of light rolling in from the west.

THEY GOT FIVE signatures that night, with four refusals. The last refusal came at a house in Erie, a village a few miles outside of town, where the door was slammed in their faces with a report that filled the silent, shadowy street. They drove slowly back toward Attawan. Through the open windows came the thick, drowning sweetness of lilacs, wafting from roadside groves as big as transport trucks.

"A good night's work," Doyle said. He was slouching back with one arm falling over the seat behind him, the other straight to the wheel, his big head on an angle: the posture of a fulfilled man. Alf envied him his lazy pleasure in his achievement. Doyle seemed someone who believed, who had brought home the harvest of that belief. There was nothing sweeter in life, perhaps, but Alf could not share his sense of a job well done.

"I feel like you did it all."

"We wouldn't have got half those cards without you."

"So what am I, a pretty face?"

"That's right," Doyle said. Alf chortled. He had felt moments of satisfaction in getting the cards; there was something about being with

Doyle that normalized the whole enterprise and made it seem more possible than he'd imagined. He'd even experienced a sweet surge of vengefulness—against Bannerman's, against Prince, against Kit Ford. But revenge wasn't enough. To do this work properly, he sensed, you had to be a believer. He wanted to believe, with the same kind of certainty Doyle had, or even with the inchoate angry faith of Ellen Kelly, but he kept coming up against a barrier in himself.

"How do you justify it to yourself?" he said. "Risking these people's jobs on the chance you'll get a union in?" It was the question that troubled him most, just now. He hadn't worried about it when he'd worked for the union in 1949; he'd been so excited by the tactical, almost warlike side of the campaign, so caught up in the hope of making a better world, and, yes, so mesmerized by the head organizer, Cary Winner, that he hadn't really taken in the risk to anyone else. Now, though, he was older, and what had happened to Pete and the others had made him wary.

"Hey, what we're doing is legal," Doyle said, with gentle sarcasm. "And what they do, I mean firing people for organizing, that's illegal, brother." After a while, sounding a good deal more weary, the organizer added, "I worry about it, of course I do. I guess I believe in the big picture. To be frank, I don't believe in it the way I used to, when I was a tyro. But I believe, I guess, that we can push this bloody society to a place where the values are a little different. Where an ordinary person's job, just a decent bloody wage for God's sake, is more important than the ability of some obscenely rich bastard to add a new wing to his house in Palm Springs."

"But if he's earned it?" Alf said. It was the old independent businessman in him speaking, the guy who had once wanted to build houses, to someday build a fine house for himself.

"*Has* he earned it?" Doyle said, a new ferocity in his voice. "Or has the unfairness Ellen Kelly knows about just allowed him a god's leverage on things, a leverage no human being should have? I mean, I don't deny the punter his reward, but too much is too much. I know men who'd rather let a hundred or a thousand other men go to the dogs than give up a straw of their privileges. They haven't earned it any more than I've earned the air I breathe. They've just taken it away from the rest of us."

Alf knew Doyle had a point. A world where a few men had a hundred pairs of shoes and millions had none was not a just world. But hell, wasn't there room somewhere between those two extremes? What, after all, was the matter with wanting to have a nicer house, a better car? Yes, for all he'd been through, he was still hopeful he might rise one day. And a union wasn't about rising, it wasn't about life lived on the vertical. It was about the horizontal life, it seemed to him, where you couldn't rise unless everyone else rose with you equally. The thought of a purely horizontal life depressed him.

They were crossing a bridge; the murky waters of the Attawan drifted in mist. Alf was caught, he realized. He was not a committed union man. He felt he was working with Doyle to help those who had lost their jobs and to make up something to Pete. And, yes, because he needed the money. At the same time, he was afraid that history might be repeating itself. If their campaign was discovered, there might be even more job losses than last time. There seemed to be no way out. He struck a match and lit two cigarettes. For the rest of the way home, he and Doyle smoked silently, turning their faces occasionally to the windows, to exhale into the rush of night air.

THEY PAID THEIR visits mostly in the evenings and on weekends. That left the days free: long, tedious stretches of time in which Alf worked around the house. Sometimes Doyle came over, and they sat outside, drinking juice or beer on the picnic table under the apple tree. They were becoming friends. Whatever the difference in their politics, a deeper current was at work—a kind of sympathetic vibration. They liked each other, they shared a similar sense of humor, they had both fought in the war, Doyle as a member of a British regiment, an experience that had grated rather hard on the young man's Northern Irish, Catholic, nationalist sentiments. "I was just like Hitler," he liked to joke. "Fighting a war on two fronts."

For Alf, Doyle's presence was a kind of gift. After Pete, he hadn't expected to have a close friend again. In a way, he was already closer to Doyle than he had ever been to Pete. With Pete, he had always felt a bit superior, a big brother looking out for a younger. But he and Doyle were more like equals, mutually respecting. He had a sense he'd never had with Pete, a sense that Doyle understood him.

One afternoon, he and Doyle climbed with their beer over the dike and sat on a log near the deep bend of the Atta where it swung below Lookout Hill. They were talking about the war, and Doyle told a story about falling asleep one night on sentry duty. That night, the Germans had attacked the camp he was helping guard, killing three men, one a friend of his. No one had known he'd dozed off, and in any case there had been several other sentries, so no one had blamed him, but he obviously blamed himself. "If I have one regret—" he said, and broke off his sentence. In the silence that followed, Alf watched a gull that had settled on the river, like a small white boat adrift under the shadowy bank. His mind was full of Pete. Hadn't it been the same with Pete and him—his one slipup leading to a result he'd never intended, to a regret that would never go away? He had thought it impossible he would ever tell anybody about what he'd done to Pete. But now, his heart surging, he felt he was about to.

He shied away at the last moment, not at all certain his friendship with the organizer could bear it. Not sure *he* could bear it. Instead, he told Doyle about the German boy he'd shot in the wine cellar. Except for the death of his brother, it had been the worst moment of the war for him—when the cellar door was flung back and he saw the boy at his feet, the broken wine bottle in his hand. "I suppose he meant to kill me with it, but he couldn't have. I'd got him in the heart."

"Jesus," Doyle said.

Alf dug at the sand with the heel of his shoe. He hadn't told the story well, hadn't conveyed his shock at what he'd seen: the freshness and youth of that lifeless face.

And Pete was still alive in him, a pressure.

48

ONE SUNDAY EVENING when Doyle was out of town, Alf got a call from Mary Carr. She'd been fired. "Somebody must have squealed on me to the Road Runner," she told him. "Can't figure who it is."

Joe had the car—he was off with some girl, a new one, Margaret said—so Alf walked over to Mary's house on the Flats. It was a tiny stuccoed place, one end of a long, oddly curved building that had once been a rail station, in the days when a line fed into the valley. His father had left from this spot to go to France in 1915. Red roses bloomed against the brown stucco.

Mary lived here with her twin daughters. Her husband Carter had decamped years ago for the west, a runty little guy with an aggressive manner who, as Alf remembered, had been in trouble as a boy for stealing a shotgun. When Alf knocked on the door, one of Mary's twins (was it Susie or Sharon?) looked out with wide-set eleven-year-old eyes.

"Who's that?" he heard Mary bellow. From deeper in the house came a sound of childish sobbing. The girl withdrew her head. The door swung open a little.

"Alf, come in! I'm on the phone with Deirdre."

He waited in the cramped living room. There was a couch, which probably folded out into a bed, two armchairs, a couple of small tables, and an old-fashioned radio topped with a statue of Our Lady, her robe painted a bright blue, her arms out in succor. One of the hands had broken off. Mary stood with the receiver in the kitchen doorway, saying "Yeah, yeah, yeah" and gazing blindly in Alf's direction. The twin who answered the door had disappeared. The sobbing had stopped, replaced by sounds of a TV pumping out the opening theme of the *Ed Sullivan* show.

Mary hung up the phone and threw herself into a chair opposite Alf. Her shorts revealed slim, very pale legs.

"The fucker," she said angrily. "He had the nerve to take a cup of tea off me. He comes to fire me, and he sits right there where you're sitting and takes tea!"

"Who?"

"The Road Runner! The son of a bitch smiled as he told me. We know you're with the union, he says. Well, I didn't deny it. I should've denied it, I guess. I mean, what proof did he have? But I couldn't. There was something in his face—I just wanted to hit him with the truth. He's lucky I didn't hit him with a brick. I did it to myself, no less!"

She held Alf's eyes in disbelief, as if he might tell her why she'd acted against herself, why she'd admitted to the Road Runner that she was with the union, when all she had to do was deny, deny. Of course, as she said, he might have fired her anyway, but then at least she could have said she'd done everything possible to defend herself and her girls.

"The bastard wanted me to spy for them," she said, throwing one long leg over the other.

"Spy," he said. He woke as if from a dream state, in the deep chair.

"You know. If I find out who's signed cards, I can keep my job. The swine."

"And you refused," he said.

"I guess I did!" she said. She shook once, a brief silent laugh. Then tears glistened. "What am I going to do with my girls? I can't keep this place on unemployment!"

"I'll talk to Doyle." He struggled to find his voice. "He'll put you on salary," he said, promising wildly. "At the least, when the union goes in, we'll get your job back."

"That's what Deirdre says."

"Well, there you go. We'll fix you up."

IT WAS NEARLY dark when he left her house. He walked down Willard to the corner of Bridge and stopped for a moment by the raceway, the mills in their Sunday stillness. He had spent nearly twenty years in those buildings; his mother and father had spent most of their lives there. But now the mills seemed opaque, a mystery, with their countless windows reflected dully in the water below. In his chest, a little anger flickered and was gone.

He went on up Bridge past the mound of the arena, came to the bridge, and leaned on the rail. A hundred yards away, Bannerman's dam made a thick, white, churning line, a deep *shush* of falling water.

He felt tired, too tired to move. He thought of smoking a cigarette, but even this was too much effort, so he went on staring at the river, his forearms braced on the rail in a kind of hopelessness. He spat and watched the fleck fall in a long curve, under the bridge.

The car arrived soundlessly behind him. He heard only the hush—like an emissary of the dam itself—of a window sliding down. The Fleetwood seemed darker than black could be, in the feeble streetlight.

He stooped to the open window. Prince was leaning toward him across the seat, smiling affably, as if whatever had passed between them had left only a residue of casual goodwill. The executive's handsome face, over the open collar of his shirt, shone a little in the glow from the instrument panel.

"I was wondering if we could talk?"

Alf experienced a moment of triumph, realizing he was beyond the man's power. *I was wondering if.*

"The union," Prince said. "I may have a deal."

Doyle had warned him this might happen, he recalled. If the company felt they were going to lose, they might offer to let the union in unopposed, for considerations.

"I'm not the boss," Alf said, not bothering to hide a note of hostility. "I don't have the authority."

"For this you do."

"What is *this*?"

"Why don't you get in? Probably not too good for either of us if we're seen together."

Checking up and down the street, Alf got in. He knew he shouldn't, but he was curious to see what Prince had up his sleeve, and at the same time he hardly cared. Before him, the wide windshield framed the main intersection, where a red light glowed. Just beyond, a man in a baseball cap, oddly familiar, ducked into the porch of the Vimy House. Prince swung to the right, and they began to rise into the North End. "Got some kind of ping under the hood," Prince said, apropos of nothing. "The garage can't seem to find it." They swept past the gray bulk of the Bannerman mansion, a grim fairy-tale castle set back on its sloping lawns, and down the maple-shaded avenue.

Beyond the high school and the hospital, Prince turned down Golf Links Road. He drove with his head up, with that sense of easy nobility that emanated from him so naturally, two fingers lightly touching the bottom of the wheel. He talked about sports—he had been to see a softball game behind the arena, and the quality of play had impressed him. "I played shortstop myself. Loved not having a base to cover, you know? That sense of freedom."

Alf said nothing. The air-conditioning made him feel enclosed in a bubble, removed from the night. Even the road itself felt far away, its imperfections smoothed by the magnificent carriage of the Fleetwood. They floated past the high hills of the golf course, past a mink farm crowded with long pens, past old trees that for a moment grew huge in the sweeping scrutiny of the Fleetwood's headlights. Off to the right, a darkness watched by silent groups of cedars, the Shade ran toward town.

"So what's the deal?" Alf said, bestirring himself. Already he regretted coming.

"Well, Alf, I hope I'm not out of place here, but I want to make you an offer."

Alf let a beat go by. "I'm not too fond of your offers."

Objects materialized in the dream world outside. In a weedy field, a white horse bolted, its neck flattening. "We made a mess of that," Prince said at last. He sounded genuinely aggrieved, sorry. "You know, I really did want you for that foreman's job. But I was under pressure to bring new people in."

"I'm not interested."

"I can't blame you for being teed off, Alf. Having to see someone walk in and take the job that belonged to you. I'd like to make amends if I can." Prince paused and seemed to be considering his next step. In the headlights the asphalt gave way to washboard, a distant rumble. "How would you like to be assistant manager of the sweater mill?"

To Alf, Prince's words seemed as unreal as the countryside startled by their lights.

"As you've probably heard, Gordie Henderson's left. You could start right away."

"You must think I'm one eager whore." Alf was taut with anger. Yet there was a place in him, beyond defiance, beyond conscience, where he was still hungry for a different life, where Prince's words had raised a ripple of excitement. Disgusted by his own weakness, he added, "Or some kind of idiot. You're just worried we're getting close. You're trying to buy me off."

"Of course there's some truth in what you're saying," Prince said, after a while, "but the offer's real. I think you'd do a good job in that office."

"If you mean it, you'll offer it to me after the union goes in."

Prince was silent. Alf chuckled bleakly to himself, thinking he'd scotched him.

"Take me back to town," Alf said. "This is pointless."

They were nearing the top of a long rise. The Fleetwood slowed as Prince guided it sharply to the left, the headlights revealing an unfenced earthen track, and a spot fringed with tall grasses where the car came to a halt. Prince turned out the headlights. They were looking over the edge of the Reid Hills, with woods at their back. Three or four miles distant, the glow of the town dusted the horizon.

The engine remained idling, a nearly imperceptible vibration. The air conditioner put out its steady exhalation. Alf shifted impatiently.

"If I can have a few minutes," Prince said, "I'd like you to hear my side of things."

Alf shrugged. He had little choice. Besides, he was curious. It felt safe to give his curiosity play; he was impregnable in his refusal, protected by his hatred of this man. Like the sailor in the old story who had himself tied to the mast, he could resist the sirens' call.

He listened to Prince's voice as it went on: reasonable, humorous, intelligent, self-deprecating. Under the surface, though, was a hardness of will not quite disguised by these other qualities. In some sense, Prince was acting. While he seemed relaxed sitting behind the wheel of the Fleetwood, turning over ideas at random, he was in fact pushing, pushing, with a directness of purpose that irritated Alf and kept him on his guard.

"You don't like me," Prince said. "I can hardly blame you, not after the way things turned out. But let's just say, for the sake of argument, that the circumstances were beyond the control of either of us. That might be hard to believe, but I don't own this company, I'm only a vice-president—one among many." He chuckled before continuing. "What I want to say is this: I have great respect for you. I respected you when I first met you, that day you showed us around the floor. Later, I asked for your help in putting down the union. You balked at that because it would have meant betraying your friends. I respect that too. Of course, I was on the other side, I had to play for keeps, but I admired you for your decision. Really, Alf, I did—I still do."

Above the vivid white of his shirt, Prince's head seemed as much shadow as flesh. He was smiling at Alf with a strange, boyish eagerness.

"The thing is, the story of what you did—or didn't do—is out there now. I'm afraid it's being given a dishonest slant."

"What are you talking about?" Alf said, suddenly alert.

"I was talking with Kit Ford, trying to demonstrate the kind of fellow you were, to show what we were up against. So I told him the story of what happened between you and me in the motel room. To me, it showed your integrity. But Ford, I'm afraid—well, he pounced on the fact that you gave away one name. He's spreading the story that you were a company plant—a stooge, as you might say. He's telling people you helped us break the union in the fall. He's suggesting, ah,"— Prince paused and then went on, reluctantly, it seemed—"he's suggesting you're helping us break it this time too. He's just doing his job, of course, trying to undermine your side. But I'm afraid it may leave you caught in the middle."

Alf sat in shock. Yet he was not entirely surprised. This moment seemed to have been coming at him for months. He'd hoped to elude it, but that was clearly foolish. Too many people—Woody, Prince, now others—knew what he had done. Beyond the dashboard, he caught the twinkle of the distant town.

Prince went on. "So what I'm saying is, you may find—not to put too fine a point on it—that the union doesn't want you anymore. I could be wrong, of course. Maybe this will all blow over. Speaking on a personal level, I hope it does, for your sake. But if it doesn't—well, you could find yourself out on the street. If that happens, the assistant manager's job is there for you. You might be glad of a place to jump to."

Alf was silent. He could not tell if Prince was being sincere—he sounded sincere, painfully so—but in a sense it didn't matter. What had trapped him seemed more like fate than the machinations of an enemy.

Prince continued. "You're a management man at heart. You have the ability, the authority. It's something that can't be taught. You've got it, Alf. You're meant for better things than knocking on doors with Mr. Doyle."

Outside, the night seemed far away, a few isolated lights in darkness. A reddish star throbbed faintly.

"You want me to hold that job open for you, until after the union goes in? Or until the union kicks you out? I'll do my best. The thing is, right now I know we can bring you in. Later, who can say? Once you're in, you can prove yourself. A promotion that came to you under, shall we say, special circumstances, will seem perfectly natural. It's certainly deserved."

The steady hum of the air-conditioning filled the car. Doyle, the union, felt distant, insubstantial. The real world was here, in the comfortable bubble of the car. Here in the quarter light behind the complicated, glowing instrument panel of the Fleetwood was all the world, all the future a man needed. Alf thought of Margaret, and a wild sensation of regret pierced him. He went on sitting in the wash of coolness from the dash. He licked his lips and was about to speak, when suddenly—a rising panic in his chest—he felt he was suffocating. He needed a cigarette. He grappled for the handle and pushed open the door. Immediately he was met by a rush of scents, warm, earthy, sharp. A cricket was picking an out-of-tune banjo.

Behind him, Prince said, "People respect you, Alf. Whatever you decide."

Alf shut the door and stepped a few feet from the car, sucking in the night air. He lit a cigarette and stood smoking as he looked off at the burnished horizon where the town lay. For a few moments, all he was aware of was what reached him: the ground underfoot, the smell of the night, the faint howling of a dog down on the plain, the burn of smoke in his lungs. He was this and only this—this tenuous finite thing, the glow of a cigarette in the dark.

He started walking. He passed the Fleetwood and reentered the road, between its high bushy banks, striding down the hill toward town. Behind him, the Fleetwood's headlights struck out over the shadowy fields. Then the car crept up behind him, its tires crunching on gravel. A window hummed down. Prince spoke with humorous irony.

"Hey, buddy. Give you a lift?"

Alf gave no sign he was aware of Prince's existence but went on walking, walking and smoking, along the shadowy road.

49

WHEN MARGARET HEARD Jamie's cry her heart slammed against her ribs, as if she too were struggling from nightmare. She raced to his room and gathered up the wiry, trembling body in its soaked pajamas, rocking him against her. "Was it the same dream?" she asked, and the damp tousled head nodded fiercely. His father was driving away in the Biscayne, and Jamie, stuck in the cellar, could not run after him, because an old man with no teeth and fire in his eyes was hiding in a box by the cellar stairs, threatening to eat him. For several weeks he had been so frightened of this dream he had resisted going to bed. Margaret got him into fresh pajamas and changed the sheets. Finally easing him to sleep—he lay as he had when he was much younger, with his knees up and his thumb in his mouth—she carried his damp things to the cellar and put them in the laundry tub to soak. Reaching for the box of Tide, she knocked over a jar of soapy water the children had used for blowing bubbles; it tumbled off the shelf, breaking with a loud pop on the cement floor. Margaret cried out, furious, and kicked at the shards among the spreading pool. By the time she'd cleaned it up she was weeping quietly to herself. Her period wouldn't come and she felt as if she'd gained twenty pounds; she was irritated with everything and everybody—especially with Alf, who had said he'd be back in time to help put the children to bed. She was set against him perpetually these days. Their fight by the roadside had solved nothing. What had or had not happened (or might be happening still) with Carrie Crean had lodged in her stomach like a cold stone.

Returning to the kitchen, she had started to make tea for herself when she heard a knocking she at first thought was Penny, padding down the hall to the bathroom. Then she realized. Someone was at the front door.

A tall, strongly built bald man in a white shirt, open at the collar, was waiting with bowed head. Seeing her through the screen, he raised one hand, palm open, as though wanting to communicate that he was harmless.

"You're Margaret Walker," he said, as she opened the door. He had beautiful teeth and a low voice and seemed so marvelously at ease she thought of a movie actor. For a moment, understanding nothing, she experienced a stab of fear. "Bob Prince," he said. "I'm an executive with Bannerman's."

"Is something wrong?"

"No, no, not at all. Sorry, I didn't mean to frighten you."

"Alf's not in right now."

"We had a talk a little while ago. I just wanted to add some things to what I was saying."

Behind him she saw the expensive-looking car gleaming in the weak streetlight. Despite his reassurances and friendly manner, a sense of something ominous was in the air. She was wary.

"He should be back any minute."

"Ah," he said, and when he did not move, she added, "Would you like to wait?"

She had made the offer out of politeness, and was a bit disappointed when he took her up. He perched on the edge of her couch, in his faultless khakis and loafers, which showed a couple of inches of beige sock, pulled up tight. His legs were oddly short and spindly looking, she thought, for such a big man. But what really struck her were his eyes. They were the same blue as her husband's.

He did not want coffee or tea. She made a few attempts at small talk, but Bob Prince seemed almost oblivious, sitting with his big shoulders hunched forward, frowning at his own thoughts while he drummed his fingers on his knee. She felt a bit put out, having him see the shabbiness of her house, and disloyal somehow, to Alf, though she could not quite say why. Of course, with Alf in the union now, this man was on the opposite side of the fence. Bob Prince. The name came back to her. Wasn't it Prince who had praised Alf last summer, when Alf had taken him on a tour of the mill? It was Prince—wasn't it?—whom Alf had gone to see, that night he'd phoned during supper?

"I offered your husband a job tonight," he said abruptly. He had been staring at her rug—her old green rug with its streaks of burlap backing showing—but now he concentrated on her. "He turned me down, as I feared he would. Or at least I think he turned me down. I just feel I didn't make all the arguments I could have."

"What kind of job?" she said, not quite trusting him. What kind of job could it be if arguments had to be made for it?

He seemed not to hear her. He sighed as if the weight of the world were on his shoulders. Suddenly he seemed to see her—a flash of those eyes, as if surprised to discover her there. "Assistant manager of the sweater mill."

She snapped awake, with a clarity of disbelief. "Not foreman? You want him to help run the sweater mill?"

"That's right." He smiled his dazzling smile. "You seem surprised."

"Well, you did fire him." Her cheeks burned, at the sharpness of her tone.

"*I* didn't; that was some fool down the line. He's one of the best men we've got. Or had. We let him slip through our fingers, I'm afraid."

She had given up hope that Alf would ever rise. It was a dream of their youth, like wanting to be rich or famous or simply extraordinarily good at something. That fate only befell a very few, and she was resigned that it would never be theirs. She was just intent on surviving, getting them all through this bad patch.

Her visitor's news was incredible, yet there was some spark in her, never completely extinguished, that leaped to it. She watched the pale blue eyes that struck her as so familiar, scanning her poor rug, lighting on a sagging armchair. She felt a surge of affection for Alf. He *was* a good man and finally others were realizing it too.

"I guess he's committed to what he's doing with the union," Bob Prince said. "I must say, though I disagree with him, I have to respect him for it. Your husband's a man of great integrity, Mrs. Walker."

He was a big, strong, bluff man with an important job. But there was a touch of helplessness about him, she thought. He seemed overworked, judging by the shadows under his eyes.

"You know," he said, holding her with his gaze, "he left the door open a little. He did say that after the union went in he'd be happy to take a look at our offer."

She watched him closely, alerted by something in his tone.

"The trouble is—and I've explained this to him—I don't know if we'll be able to make the offer then. I mean, if it was up to me alone, he could have that job any time he wanted. But some of my superiors—" Bob Prince hesitated. He ran his hand over his bald head.

The slightly parted drapes gave a view of his car, glinting under the streetlight. A cat jumped to its hood just then, padding gingerly on the warm metal. It's me he came to talk to, she thought, not Alf at all. She turned back to her visitor. "Perhaps the best thing is for you to go," she said. "I'll tell my husband you were here."

AFTER THE FLEETWOOD drove off, she spent a restless half hour waiting for Alf. She swept the kitchen floor, washed a few dishes, put on coffee. Thinking she heard Jamie cry out, she went up to check, but the boy was asleep on his back, his mouth open, one arm flung out across the pillow. Downstairs, the screen door ajar, she found Alf in the kitchen.

Her husband was sitting at the edge of a chair, stripping off a sock. She cried out at the raw, round spot on his heel and brought him iodine and a bandage.

"How did you get that?"

"Walking," he said grimly.

"You must have walked some distance."

He went on tending his wound, intently, like a boy, his foot up on the chair. From outside came the faint, stuttering cry of a nighthawk.

Shutting the screen door and the inner door, she sat down at the table.

"Alf, we had a visitor tonight."

He grunted, more interested in his doctoring. He tore off the flap of rucked skin.

"Alf—"

He looked up at her, his eyes hard.

"Oh, Alf," she crooned, forcing her affection a little.

When he considered her—not quite sure, apparently, what she intended—she flushed, then plunged into the heart of the matter. "Bob Prince was here tonight."

He stopped short, a bandage in his hand.

"He came to see you. He told me about the assistant manager's job. He said there were some things he neglected to tell you—"

"He came here?" he said. "When the hell was this?"

"Tonight."

"When tonight?"

"Please don't raise your voice," she said, struggling to smile. "He came about ten o'clock. He left half an hour ago. Alf, we have to talk—"

He smashed his fist onto the table, making the glass top of the butter dish jump. She was startled and put out by his outburst.

"You can't just throw this away so easily—for what? For the union?"

Again he struck the table, in real fury.

"Oh, good," she said. She spoke sarcastically, powered by anger she could no longer repress. "You get the offer of a lifetime and you can't even talk about it."

She watched him stand up and go to the sink. There was something animal-like, bullish, in his shoulders, she thought, as he filled a glass with water and drank. This is what she had been struggling with in him, all these years: this roughness. It enraged her; she had borne so much because of it.

"You've worked years to get ahead," she said, trying to remain calm. "For heaven's sake, at least hear what he has to say."

He went very still, stooped over the sink. Was he just going to slip away into another of his silences? She was at full throttle now, remembering all the silences she had endured. This was part of his roughness too, wasn't it? Her husband hardly spoke to her, not when it came to important things, not even when it came to the simple matter of keeping her company. He might as well have been deaf and dumb, like Bob Horsfall.

"You had a business of your own once," she said. "Now you're knocking on doors for signatures."

A bit of spit had bubbled at his lower lip. "It's honest work," he said.

"Digging ditches is honest work! Why can't you see where your advantage lies?"

"Be quiet," he said, glowering at her.

"Tell me," she said, getting out of her chair and going to him. "Just tell me—since I apparently don't understand it—why knocking on doors with Malachi Doyle is better than assistant manager. Assistant manager, Alf!"

He turned to her, eyes flashing. Good, she thought, good; this is long overdue.

"The people who sign, they depend on me," he said, in a surprisingly rusty voice. His gaze seemed almost unfocused, lost in space, as if he was reciting some idea by rote.

"And what about me?" she cried. "What about your children? Aren't we depending on you? Your son's up there—did you know he has night-mares every night about your leaving? It's no wonder, is it? You're away every night. We hardly know you anymore!"

"This is what I'm doing," he said, after a moment.

He was so thick, she thought. How could she make him understand?

"You're ruining yourself. You're ruining this family."

"I have a job," he said flatly.

Her fury mounted, at the dead end of her life.

"I think you're a coward," she said. "You're afraid of the responsibility, that's what I think. You like being mediocre. It suits you. It doesn't mat-ter what happens to us, so long as you can go on digging your miserable little ditches with—"

The back of his hand caught her in the center of her face. He had never struck her before or even threatened to. There was the surprise—the sheer force of it—and then numbness, almost unreality, as she sensed the kitchen retreating. The pain had not started yet, though she wondered if her nose was broken. Her laugh came in an odd cry, hyster-ical. She leaned over the table, nursing her face with one hand, half expecting another blow. When it didn't come, she looked around. He was standing with his back to her, at the window. His shoulders were heaving—she thought he was weeping—while his reflected face hovered in the darkness beyond the glass, seeming to peer into the room at her like a ghost.

50

ALF SPENT THE night tossing on the couch, pacing and smoking in the backyard. He had done it now, he felt. He had crossed the line beyond which there was no forgiveness, no return, he had done the unthinkable thing he had despised other men for doing, and now he was no better than the worst of them. In a sense, he did not understand what had happened. He had struck his wife, yes, but at the same time it was as if a wave had come up out of nowhere, a vast, powerful wave that had rolled them both about, and in the confusion and fury his arm had gone out and caught her, willy-nilly, on her nose. The next morning, Margaret, setting out the breakfast things, ignored his attempts at apology. Her lower lip was swollen—one section pale and inflated like the thick part of an earthworm; a bruise shadowed her cheek and nose. He hovered in remorse, trying to be helpful; then froze as Jamie and Penny tumbled in for breakfast. It didn't take them long to discover Margaret's face. "What happened?" Penny said in a hushed voice, her eyes moving from her mother to her father and back again. Alf couldn't speak and was gratified when Margaret told them almost cheerfully that she'd run into a cupboard door; she was all right, she said, and would they please eat their shredded wheat, they were late for school.

AT ELEVEN, DOYLE came by. Alf met him outside and took him to their usual place by the river. He seemed to be moving in a dream now; he felt he knew nothing, but he clung to certain thoughts he had to express. Doyle sat on the driftwood log, smoking as the Atta drifted by. Alf stood woodenly before him, speaking in a rasping voice of the things he'd kept hidden: Prince's offer the previous fall, his betrayal of Woody Marr. He did not mention Pete. But he told Doyle about his latest conversation with Prince, the news that Ford was spreading the story, the offer of the assistant managership. He spoke mechanically, without much emotion, knowing only that he owed Doyle this. The shame that had attended his secret scarcely affected him. Nor did he feel any relief.

When Alf had finished, Doyle said nothing, the smoke twisting above the forgotten stub of his cigarette. To Alf, his silence seemed to open a gulf between them that deepened with each second; he was sure their friendship had ended.

"I wish you'd told me about this before," Doyle said finally. He squinted up at Alf, whose back was to the sun. "What do you want to do?"

Up in Joe's bedroom window, Alf could make out the small pale moon of Margaret's face, the bruise barely visible at this distance, watching him. She still had not spoken to him, and yet there was some quality of expectation in her look.

"I'll quit if you want," he said, his voice a dry, foreign thing. His shadow stretched over the sand before him. "But what I want—is to go on with the union. If the union will still have me."

Doyle got up heavily, paced. Snapped away his butt. Swung his thick scabbed arm at a scrub willow.

"All right, mate," he said. "I think we'll be all right. Everybody knows you were fired unfairly. They won't believe Ford's stories—or very few of them will. We'll just keep on, steady as she goes."

Alf nodded. The sun beat on the sand, on the stunted bushes, on the back of his neck, on Malachi Doyle's red face. He stood with his eyes half closed, aware of nothing but its heat.

51

PENNY RODE HER bicycle up West. Near the bridge, several girls were skipping Double Dutch, the two long ropes turning against each other like the beaters in her mother's Mixmaster, slapping the road under Ginny Lamport, who in Penny's opinion was the best skipper on the Island, her ponytail bouncing, her white socks jogging up and down, faster and faster, as the ropes snicked under her. The other girls, the turners and the watchers, sang out in saucy voices:

> One two three a-Laura
> Four five six a-Laura
> Seven eight nine a-Laura
> Ten a-Laura Secord!

Ginny ran out through the speeding ropes and another girl ran in. Seeing Penny go by, Ginny, her face flushed, called out for her to join them.

"Can't," Penny said, and kept riding. Pedaling off the Island and up West—it was pretty much on the level all the way to Bannerman's hosiery mill—she could hear the girls' voices crying out behind her:

> First comes love, then comes marriage,
> Then comes Linda with a baby carriage!

At the hill, she stood up to pump—the heavy old bike with the balloon tires and wicker basket had once belonged to her baby-sitter, Joyce French—and managed to ride halfway up before she had to get off and push. Far below, to her left, the river glittered through the trees that crowded up the steep bank to the road. She was not quite sure where the path was—at least a year had passed since her father had showed it to her—and when she turned off the road, hid her bike below the guardrail, and started down the narrow slot in the weeds, she still wasn't sure she had the right place. But she soon came to the clearing. It was shielded from the road above by trees and reached through a gap below. Yes, there was the weedy hump, the sticking-out bits of old boards and a crooked window frame with slivers of glass hanging in it—the remains of Johnny North's shack. She was here because of a dream. She had been lying somewhere, unable to get up for the heaviness of her body, lying in misery, as if she had been abandoned by everyone, and cold, for she had no clothes on. But a man had rescued her—Johnny North. He was wearing a black coat and he was young. His hair was really black, not stained with shoe polish. He had smiled down at her with his broken teeth—she had not been frightened—and then scooped her up, putting her right on his shoulders. Suddenly, Johnny North had turned into a giant. And she was so high she had been able to see the whole world as he walked over it: the countries, the mountains, the islands dotting the silver oceans like stepping-stones.

She looked around a bit nervously; then she began to remove her clothes, putting them on a flat rock: her sleeveless T-shirt, her red leather sandals, her shorts with her package of Arrowroots in the pocket, her underpants with their blue Bannerman's label. When a car passed on the road above, she searched around wildly for a hiding place. She knew she had to do this; the idea had been with her ever since she'd woken up. She had to do it, though she couldn't have said why. She stood straight and closed her eyes and felt the air on her body. When a fly landed on her arm, she brushed it off. "I'm here," she whispered. She wasn't sure whom she was talking to, the trees or Johnny North or the river rushing over its dam or the sloping fields of Wiley's farm or someone who was all of those things and more. She breathed in the presences. She could feel them close by, touching her with their fingers of air, drawing faint perfumes by her nose—

But there, that darned fly was back. She opened one eye and glared at it.

52

THEY LAY ON her bed, kissing and talking. Anna was watching him a little distantly: her green eyes, their irrepressible spark of humor. On her cheek was the birthmark. Up close, it revealed its subtlety, like a burn of many colors: the white, the tinges of pink, blending into tan. He had stroked it and examined it and kissed it, this badge of her uniqueness.

"I don't have much feeling there," Anna told him, as his hand closed on her breast. He lifted her blouse, licked, and sucked. The little buttons of pink flesh remained flush with their aureoles.

She pushed at his head.

"I really don't enjoy that."

"I'm sorry, I just thought—"

"That you, my Prince Charming, would succeed where all others have failed." She touched his hair affectionately, but he was chagrined. He didn't like to be reminded that there had been others. What had she done with these others? That was the question. He'd assumed they would sleep together, as he and Liz had slept together: had assumed that Anna Macrimmon was at least that experienced, but for two weeks now they had necked and petted only. He wondered if Brad had gotten any farther—Brad, who these days was acting as if he, Joe, didn't exist (except, that is, for a floor-hockey game when Brad had thrown a vicious elbow Joe had barely managed to slip). He wondered about the handsome man with the swept-back blond hair, so clearly older than she, whose arm cradled her possessively in the boat, in the gold-framed photo facing them even now on the back of her desk. "A friend," she had told him, with a casualness that gave away nothing.

She was fussing, almost maternally, at his hair. She had not told him she loved him. Twice now he'd told her he loved her—and he did, with a feverish certainty unlike anything he'd experienced—but it seemed wrong to press her for the same avowal. There was something in her he was a little afraid of. More than anyone he'd known, she seemed provisional in her presence. *I will stay here if,* she seemed to say, but there was no telling what came after that *if.*

"Are you a virgin?" he said. The light went out in her eyes, and he feared he had just committed the act that would make her disappear. The atmosphere around her was charged with invisible sanctions.

"No," she said, looking at him frankly.

"Then why can't we—"

He burned red, not at the sexual innuendo but that he was exposing his own eagerness, which seemed clumsy, a failure to appreciate some subtlety.

"What, *do it?*"

"Yah, why don't we do it?" he said, catching her tone of mock coarseness. "Don't you want to do it? I mean, what did those other guys have that I—"

She rolled swiftly from the bed, went to her dresser, picked up a brush, and stood dragging it fiercely through her hair at the window. The late-afternoon sun made the flying wisps shine.

"Anna?"

It was the first time she had reacted so sharply toward him.

"Don't ever refer to *other guys,*" she said. "I'm not a highway!"

"I didn't mean that."

"Then don't imply it!"

"Anna, I love you!"

"That's no excuse," she said, really angry now. He sat up in a kind of shock. "You can't just say *I love you* every time you get into trouble, like some kind of abracadabra to fly you out of there. I won't have it!"

"No," he said bleakly. He was still not sure what he'd done wrong.

"Love is the biggest alibi in the world," she said, and sighed, letting the hand with the brush fall to her side. Her blouse hung out over her skirt.

"I don't understand you," he said.

"You weren't meant to."

She came to the bed and sat facing him.

"I just want to go slowly. Is that all right?"

"Sure it is. I'm sorry." He was thinking of what Liz had told him: Anna can't love; it was a man, not a boy like you.

A man, not a boy like you.

"You told me once you'd had a bad time," he said. Her look darkened. "Does that have anything to do with wanting to go slowly?"

"I suppose."

"Maybe one day you'll be able to tell me," he said.

He was touching the back of her hand, with its two silver rings. Suddenly she leaned forward and kissed him, more openly, softly, than she had before. He resisted the desire to pull her down with him. He was willing to be a patient suitor. Unlike Sandy or Liz, Anna Macrimmon inspired him with a hunger to be better than he was.

HE ATE SUPPER with her family in the backyard, at a small table her mother had covered with a white cloth. They sat under a large maple tree, where the bare earth was littered with chains of greeny-yellow seeds that fell from the branches, almost caterpillar-like, sometimes into their plates of stew, even into the glasses of red wine Andrew Macrimmon kept refilling with a slightly wicked insistence, as if determined to get them all drunk. Anna's father was a slim, fair-haired man with wire-rimmed glasses through which small, intelligent eyes the same color as hers—though not the same feline shape—peered a little sadly. He was nearsighted and a bit stooped (his posture seemed to Joe to go with his position as senior accountant at Bannerman's; he imagined him slaving over a tall old-fashioned desk like Bob Cratchit in *A Christmas Carol*), but he also had a robust laugh that subsided to a silent up-and-down shaking of his body. Joe felt that Andrew Macrimmon had to know about his father's firing, and his work with the union, and almost certainly disapproved. But if he did, he tactfully kept his opinions to himself.

Anna's mother, Estelle, sat very erect in her chair, her plump face held a little up in pride, as if conscious of some higher standard of behavior, some Old World noblesse that was under constant siege. Joe was reminded of his mother, who carried her Englishness like a badge of honor. But there was something frantic about Estelle; he saw it in the way her hair strayed from her untidy bun and in the restlessness of her square hands, which kept touching things on the table as if to reassure herself of their proper placement, or perhaps of their very reality. She spoke English with the same enthusiastic articulation as French, so that her conversation was rich and dramatic, if sometimes incomprehensible.

Joe liked her and felt a gallant urge to support her; he imagined she must feel out of place in Canada. He tried out his poor French on her, which set her smiling with pleasure even as she winced at his pronunciation. He wanted desperately to be a success with her and her husband, not just for Anna's sake but to be accepted by her family, which seemed so much more desirable than his own. His father's attack on his mother had brought a cold wind into the house on the Island. He wanted to escape it, the tawdriness that always seeps in after violence. Now, every imperfection of his home life—the worn kitchen linoleum, his father's guilty, disheveled presence—seemed part of a morass that threatened to swallow him. Here, at the table under the tree, was another world.

But escape was difficult. As he was telling a story, in French, he watched Estelle's face grow hard. Thinking he'd made some terrible gaffe, he rushed his ending and fell silent. A train was passing—the main line connecting Toronto and Windsor ran across the hillside, just below the back fences of the houses along the south side of Banting—and for a few minutes, conversation became nearly impossible as the cars throbbed and clattered by, out of sight below the edge of the yard. A stink of oil and heat crept under the maple tree. Estelle picked solemnly at her food. A deep unease had spread around the table. Joe felt he was catching a glimpse of some ongoing family crisis. There was tension, as if Anna and her father were half expecting an outburst. Estelle's ears, below her untidy nest of hair, had grown bright pink.

When the clattering and rumbling finally grew distant, under the retreating wail of the diesel, Anna began to chat volubly about some restaurant in France, but Estelle remained under her cloud. She scowled and pushed her food around and generally gave the impression, for all her dignity, of a sulking child.

Suddenly interrupting her daughter, she turned to Joe.

"This is your last year at the school?"

"*Oui.*"

"*Et l'année prochaine? L'université?*"

"*Oui, l'université de Toronto. Je vais étudier l'histoire.*"

"*Ah, bon!*" Estelle spoke rapidly in French to Anna, seemingly irritated. Joe hardly understood a thing. He did, however, catch the word *Sorbonne*. It was where Anna planned to go, in the fall. He had glimpsed a letter on her desk, bearing the rich purple of a French stamp with The Sorbonne, Paris, as its return address. He'd tried to persuade her to go to Toronto with him, but without actually contradicting him, she had seemed amused, at best, by the very idea. She was planning to leave in August. Already—and it was only May—he was dreading the end of the summer.

Anna was quiet under her mother's scolding. She shook her head and smiled with closed lips in a way that suggested she was making a familiar refusal, in a state of bland tolerance. But she was upset, he could see; her hands were moving out of sight below the edge of the table. He supposed she was tearing at her hangnails.

Andrew was murmuring to his wife in French, placatingly.

Estelle looked haughtily around at their empty plates and asked Joe, with great formality, ignoring the others, if he would like dessert.

After supper they escaped for a walk. Down Banting, the rich, low light of the spring evening saturated the bark of ancient maples, making them glow like golden cork. She had shown him a special way of holding hands, two fingers interlocked, and they fell into this manner now. To him it was a secret language, a pledge that established a claim on the future.

Her hand was fine-boned and light. She seemed a creature of lightness. She walked with her mother's erect bearing, her head held up and a little back.

"Mama's not very happy. I guess you saw that."

"I thought she was ticked off at something I said."

"No. Every time a train passes, she's reminded of where she is. She has no friends here. She doesn't understand the way of life. She thinks people here are crude. It's all about hurry and money, she says, and—a lack of pleasure in things. She'd go back to France tomorrow, if she could."

"Is that what she was saying to you?" He felt included in her mother's criticism.

Another train was rumbling behind the houses, sounding its blatant horn. Her hand slipped out of his.

"She likes you," she said. "She was telling me I should go to Toronto with you."

"A wise woman!"

"An angry woman," she said. "She talks against herself. It's like there's a splinter in her, and she has to push it deeper. I'm just glad it wasn't worse."

"You mean she doesn't really want you to go to Toronto?"

"I don't think she knows. But she likes you, she really does. It's wonderful the way you spoke French to her. . . . Let's go down here," she said suddenly, pulling him to the right.

The sidewalk on Peter Street gave way to packed earth thick with spruce needles. They passed an old mansion, gloomy behind its wall of dark green, and came to the black iron railroad bridge. It rose a little in the middle, and from this summit they looked to the west. The tracks gleamed in their great arc, rounding toward the junction where an old water tower, like a block on legs, stood silhouetted against the sunset. To the left, from the depth of the valley, thrust the mansard roof of Bannerman's hosiery mill, with its dormer windows. "Like a château," she said. That it reminded her of France both pleased and saddened him. Sometimes she seemed to be traveling away from him and coming closer, both at once.

Beyond lay the sloping fields of Wiley's farm, fringed with darkening woods that hid the bend of the Attawan as it made its way into town. A huge molten sun had settled on the horizon.

"Sometimes I wish I were a painter," she said, leaning forward at the rail. "I'd paint this. Though I'd never get it. No artist ever gets anything, really. It makes you ill—the failure to get anything."

"It's beautiful," he said.

" 'The edge of terror we're just able to bear.' "

"What?"

"It's from a poem."

"One of yours?"

She shook her head, apparently amused.

"What's so funny? You're laughing at me because I don't know the quote."

"No I'm not."

"You are. You think I'm a bit of a clodhopper."

She looked at him with great seriousness, alarmed.

"I don't," she said. "I don't at all."

He was only half appeased, and embarrassed at exposing his own insecurity. The sun was a low hillock now, quivering as it sank. "Anyway, I'll bet this is just as beautiful as anything in France."

The light in her eyes was wounded and fond. He kissed her gently, holding the back of her head with his hand. When he opened his eyes, to peek, she was still looking at him. He wondered if his kiss had touched her at all.

"You didn't close your eyes," he said.

"I wanted to see you."

Overhead, a jet was outracing its own vacant, drifting thunder. Down the sky, a few solitary clouds had turned sumac red. He drew his fingers across the small of her back, stroked her hair. Though he wanted to reach out and seize her, seize it all, he knew that only a delicate touch would do. There was a sadness in him, a faint, sad desperation. Life could not be taken by force: life was elusive, this light brighter than noon was elusive, a thing to be briefly touched, not held.

———

THEY DESCENDED INTO the shadowy lower town. On Station Hill, near the house where the Catholic sisters lived, Anna stopped to watch a cat hurry across a lawn. It was long and black, with a look of slinking determination: a cat on its way to kill.

"Take me to your house," she said impulsively. "I want to meet your family."

"Now?" He had taken pains never to mention his family. He wanted to be born out of thin air to her, with no past.

"You've seen my family. I want to meet yours."

He told her she could meet them another time—perhaps she could come to dinner some Sunday—but she insisted with such tenacity he finally gave in.

Flush with her victory, she went along swinging his hand, excited by the idea of a neighborhood called the Island. He knew she was bound to be disappointed—as he told her, it wasn't exactly Hawaii. At the bridge over the race, she stopped and peered at the dark water littered with old boards and rubbish while he watched in a misery of apprehension. "You see what I mean?" he said, "It's not much of an island."

"Shut up," she told him. "It's an island to me." She looked down the little street crowded with houses. "Actually, I think I was here once, on one of my walks. I just didn't notice it was surrounded by water." Nearby loomed the metal sheds of the town yard, with its dimming piles of sand streaked with salt, a scarred yellow road grader—signs, to him, of the decline in the neighborhoods since they'd come off the Hill. But she spied an old snowplow, its curved, rusted blades rising like wings. "An iron angel," she declared, running her palm over the scabbing paint.

When they reached his house, she stopped, while he fidgeted beside her. "We're planning to move," he said, clutching at the family myth, which normally he despised. Before them, the whitewashed facade with its dark green shutters (one had begun to sag badly) exuded a starkness that appalled him.

"It's like another century," she declared. This was apparently a compliment, though with her he could never be sure, irony shadowed so many of her enthusiasms. A sprinkler was throwing twists of silver around the tiny front lawn.

His mother was in the back, working in her garden. She had seemed weary and remote of late, her eyes shadowed with a darkness he found painful to contemplate. But it was the yellow-purple bruise staining much of her nose and cheek that he was acutely aware of now. She had told him the whole sordid tale—his father refusing to take the job of assistant manager and striking her—in a tone of cheerless exhaustion he had never heard her use before, all the while watching him steadily, as if demanding to know what he was going to do about it. Not long afterward, he had confronted his father in the backyard. Alf had borne his embarrassingly tearful recriminations—hadn't he taught Joe never to strike a woman?—in a silence that unsettled Joe because it made him wonder, later, if he had the whole story. In any case, his mother's revelation had gone on working inside him like a chemical reaction, producing anger and revulsion. He was set against his father, but really he was sick of both of them, of their standoff that filled the house with deepening tension.

To his relief, his mother roused to her bright English self. In the dusk, the bruise on her face hardly showed. He was hoping they could have a few words in the garden and leave, but she insisted they have tea. Joe followed miserably into the kitchen, where Anna walked around the table, complimenting his mother on her decorating—that blue with that yellow—so cozy and bright! "It reminds me of farmhouses in France," she said.

"That's what I was thinking of," Joe's mother said. "I used to go on holiday there when I was a girl." They talked cheerfully of Normandy while Margaret boiled water and put out a plate of Peak Freans at the kitchen table. "We don't keep much in the way of biscuits anymore," she apologized. "Not since Joe's sister got diabetes." Joe sat beside Anna, smiling thinly, conscious of the bruise on his mother's face. It seemed to him that the good cheer that filled the kitchen was a sham inspired by Anna's presence. He was aware—surely Anna was too—of the nicks on the chairs, the cracks and worn spots in the linoleum, the sad weak light from the overhead fixture.

A noise in the hall startled Joe, who feared his father was about to appear, but it was only his sister and brother. Joe watched Penny sneaking glances at Anna's birthmark. Jamie, dressed for bed in yellow and brown polo pajamas, was more straightforward. "What's that on your face?"

"Jamie," Joe's mother scolded.

"Did you hit it on a cupboard?"

Joe's mother turned away, clearly mortified.

"No," Anna said, laughing. She explained to Jamie about birthmarks, while he stared like someone at a zoo. "You can touch it if you like," Anna said. As the boy tentatively put out his fingers, she slipped a smile to Joe.

A few minutes later, they were all sitting at the table when Joe's father came in, his face weary, his hair in its usual tousle. Joe was instantly on guard: he felt he no longer had anything in common with him. Yet he didn't want Anna to think ill of him, so he managed a warmer note than usual as he introduced his father.

"You're even more handsome than your son," Anna told Alf.

"Well, I've tried to teach him as best I can," his father said. His pale blue eyes, suddenly decades younger than his face, blazed happily at Joe, who looked away.

"She's got a birthmark!" Jamie cried.

"Yes, I can see that," Joe's father said. "I'd call it more of a beauty mark."

Anna laughed, charmed. To Joe's dismay, his father made himself comfortable at the table. Across the kitchen, his mother had retired into silence. Whatever was between his parents was in the room: a dark pool spreading beneath the merriment. "We've been talking about France," Anna told him.

"Ah, yes, France," Joe's father said, running his hand over his head in a contemplative way. "I once spent a good many months in France."

"On holiday?" Anna said.

"No, no," Joe's father said, blushing a little, with a glance at his wife. "The war—"

"I forgot," she said. "You were in the war!" A new tone had come into her voice, at once excited and reverential, almost breathless. Joe waited in suspense; mention of the war seemed bound to drive his father into an awkward withdrawal. Around the table, Joe's brother and sister lowered their eyes to their half-finished glasses of milk. Like Joe, they'd been brought up not to ask about the war.

To Joe's astonishment, however, his father seemed not the least bothered by Anna's questions. Sitting back in his chair, he told a story Joe had never heard, about borrowing two bicycles with a soldier pal of his and heading off into the hills. They had stayed with a French family. He recalled their warmth, and the fine bread the woman had made in an outdoor oven. "It was the only time I actually felt like I was in France," he said. "The rest of the time, you were just too wrought up. You'd see some spot—some village or a grove of trees—and you'd know it was beautiful, you'd know you wanted to spend time there, but even if you did, you weren't really there, you know? You couldn't really get comfortable. France was—I don't know—sort of a dream. I kept thinking, Later—when the war's over—I'll come back; I'll really have a look at the place."

"And did you?" Anna said. Joe's father shook his head. Joe could hardly believe his father was telling her, a stranger, details he had never told *him;* he almost resented it.

"Nope, never made it back," Alf said, coloring. He seemed embarrassed by his failure to return.

"Oh, you have to go!" Anna cried. "It would be a pity if you didn't go. Mrs. Walker—you both love France, you have to go back!"

Joe shifted uneasily. Anna seemed unaware of the tension in the room, just as she seemed unaware that not everyone could just go off to France. His father looked over at his mother, his eyes bright. "Maybe we will one day," he said softly. Joe saw that his mother was staring at the floor and missed his father's glance.

"Did you drive a tank?" Jamie said. Everyone turned to him. His voice had chimed into the silence like a small bell.

"I should have been so lucky!" Alf laughed, tousling Jamie's head, "No, I'm afraid I walked the whole way."

Outside, in the dark, Anna took Joe's hand.

"I love your family," she said, as they went along. "I think that's how a family should be—noisy and happy. Not gloomy like mine. We don't live in our house, we haunt it."

Joe said nothing. He wasn't about to tell her what she had missed, if she had really missed it. There was no point dwelling on their unhappiness. It was like admitting failure—yes, unhappiness was failure. Whenever he looked into her face, her beautiful face, he knew this.

53

———

ONE EVENING LATER that month they climbed the steep stairway between two short fluted pillars, pushed open a heavy door, and climbed still farther, into the high-ceilinged main hall of the library, with its deep rose walls and white trim, its polished, creaking hardwood that made every step significant. Anna stood before the unused fireplace, held by the twin portraits of Abraham Shade and his wife, Rebecca. Both were seated, both wore somber clothes, their strong bloodless hands gripping the arms of their chairs, their pale faces stern, stark as ax blazes against the paintings' shiny black backgrounds. "A pretty grim couple," Joe said, beside her. His arm tingled where it brushed against hers. "But look at his eyes," she said. "There's real life in them."

He saw the dots of brightness in the Founder's pupils. No matter what he showed her, she pointed out some detail he had not seen. He wanted to resist this constant revision of a world he thought he knew.

"He wrote poetry, you know."

He told her about the sonnets and other verses Archibald Mann had found in one of Shade's diaries. Most of them were nature poems, Mann had said, Shade's stolid attempts to evoke the beauties of the valley. As he spoke, Anna's green eyes roved over his hair and his mouth, as if she was not only listening but taking in all of him. Her gaze thrilled him like a stroking touch. Still, he couldn't help worrying that she already knew what he was telling her, or that he was making some mistake—he was talking about poetry, after all.

"Have you read them?" Anna asked.

"No. But maybe Mann'd show them to us."

"Why don't we visit him? How about Saturday?"

She was squeezing his arm as she urged him. There was a force in her that was always saying *yes, yes!* pulling him on to the next novelty. Her glad, hectic approach broke some barrier of caution in him, but at the same time he was suspicious of her recklessness, as if she might be leaving out some piece of vital knowledge. She did not seem to remember that the rose had thorns; perhaps she simply did not fear them.

At the counter, the librarian cleared her throat in discreet warning.

"I have to work Saturday," he whispered, a bit put out that she never remembered this.

"Sunday, then."

They studied at a table behind tall shelves crammed with nineteenth- and early twentieth-century novels—three copies of *Lorna Doone,* complete sets of Dickens, Thackeray, Eliot, James. The worn covers smelled pleasantly of decay. They turned pages and made notes, her feet planted between his on the floor, held between his insteps with a snug rightness that kept distracting him. When he checked, she was nearly always deep in concentration, pushing unconsciously at the birthmark with the rubber end of her pencil or picking at her cuticles as she stared at a page. He returned to his book. He was studying a chapter in his Latin compostion text entitled "Constructions with Verbs of Fearing, Preventing, and Doubting." Looking up, he saw she had pushed her text aside and was busy devouring *Daniel Deronda,* fished down from a nearby shelf.

He scowled, watching her for a while before he spoke. She was slouched back in her chair now, her mouth a little open as she read.

"You should be studying."

"I don't think I would have liked George Eliot," she announced.

He sighed and tried again. "Study your Latin, girl! These are important exams!" Their finals, in fact: for all purposes their entrance exams to university. He tapped with exaggerated sternness on her Latin book, sheathing his command in a smile. She looked at the book and then at him, with a sharp, penetrating candor, almost hostile. Her anger always seemed close at hand.

"Okay, don't study your Latin," he said with a shrug. She went back to her reading. He acted indifferent, but her look had chilled him. Anna's independence was something, for all his desire to honor her freedom, that could gall him. She might have at least entered into the spirit of his reprimand, which rose out of concern for her. But she had regarded him so coolly she had made him feel like a stranger, a person of no account.

For the rest of the time in the library, he brooded. He was so on edge around her. Security lay with her; if he could only draw close enough, he could have it too. But the way was fraught with traps and a terrible provisionality. He could not forget for more than an hour that she was going away in August; everything they did lay in the shadow of that fact, and there was nothing he could do about it. This was bad enough, but what really unnerved him was that she apparently was not the least bit upset about leaving.

When the library closed, he walked her up the hill. *Daniel Deronda* rode with the other books, pressed to her chest by her folded arms.

They reached the edge of King's Park, stepping through its border of old trees. Up ahead was the little bandstand. The grass had been cut, leaving drifts of dead clippings here and there, a smell of hay.

"*Fieri non potest quin te amem,*" he said.

He had memorized the sentence from his Latin text—*It is impossible for me not to love you*—and now waited with pounding heart for her response. His textbook had translated the sentence; he'd gotten the message that she didn't like to hear him say *I love you,* at least not as often as he had been. But he couldn't help himself. He was fishing desperately for an answering avowal.

"Is that you talking," she said after a moment, "or page 167?"

"I find I agree with it exactly," he said.

She stepped along over the grass. A slight rain had fallen earlier; a scent of blossoms drifted from somewhere, sickly sweet.

"How about you?" he said nervously. "Would you say the same holds true for you?"

"I'm suspicious of the word *love,*" she said, a bit impatiently. "I mean, I always feel a bit queasy about putting it in a poem. I think that tells me something."

"What does it tell you?" he said, taking up her line of thought reluctantly. She was avoiding his challenge.

"I'm not sure," she said. "It's as if it means too much, so it ends up meaning nothing."

"Too vague?"

"Something like that. And maybe sentimental. And maybe a bit . . . easy, somehow. If you feel that way about someone, better to show it in your actions."

"So better that I jump off the railway bridge?"

"No," she said. "Definitely not that."

He walked along in silence, then said, "But it is a definite feeling; everybody knows what it is. Even you know, I'm sure. But if we can't say it, then—I don't know, the whole world's going to be pretty frustrated."

"I'm just talking about me, not the whole world."

"But if you think it wrong for you—and for me—don't you think it's wrong for everybody?"

"I guess I do," she allowed.

"You'd like to do away with the word *love* altogether?"

"A ten-year moratorium," she said. "Then we'd see."

"So even parents shouldn't say to their children, *I love you?*"

"Even that."

"That's monstrous," he said, stopping. She turned to face him, perfectly calm. "Without love," he said, gesturing with his free arm, "there'd be—I don't know, no glue holding things together. It would be awful."

"I'm just talking about the word," she said. He felt her smile was false, placating, a bit patronizing. "I know there's something the word refers to. I just think we should think about it a bit before we throw it around."

"So what I just did was throw it around, even in Latin."

He was breathing hard, really upset. He felt his heart had been laid bare and, in some way he could not quite put his finger on, mocked. He kicked at a little pile of dry grass. "Now I feel you're trying to put me in a straitjacket, telling me what I can and can't say."

She came up behind him and leaned her head into his back. They stood like this for some time. He was sulking, really hurt. He could not understand why it wounded him so much, this refusal of hers to let him tell her he loved her. To her, it was just an intellectual matter; to him, it was as if she had rejected his deepest self.

He turned. In the weak light of the streetlight her face seemed misshapen, as if bent by the atmosphere. But there was concern for him there, real concern, though he saw that spark of amusement in her eyes that nothing could quite quench.

"You say what you like," she said quietly.

"I will," he said. "You can just take your chances."

She reached up suddenly and kissed him on the mouth. He seized her by the shoulders, intending to plant a firmer kiss. His tongue sought hers. But she pushed him firmly back with her free arm. They went along through the park. The sense of disjunction between them seemed stronger than ever to him. It seemed to come out of the ground, out of the damp hay and blossom scents, out of the branches of new leaves. Like a trapeze artist, he had abandoned his swing to throw himself into the air toward her and he had to be sure her hands were there to catch him. Perhaps, he wondered with a kind of terror, she was warning him off love in an attempt to get him back on his perch. But it was already too late. He was tumbling through the air, his arms outstretched, his hands open.

54

ARCHIE MANN PULLED the plastic wrap from one of Shade's diaries, exposing the leather-bound volume to the air of his study. He opened the book carefully, turning its parched, crackling pages. At his elbow, Joe and Anna saw the brown loops of the Founder's hand.

"I like this one best," Mann said, giving the book to Anna. "Be careful. The pages are halfway to dust."

Anna held the book at chest level, bowing her head to decipher the block of writing. As Mann stepped out of the way, Joe moved in beside her.

> The flowing streams of this enchanted place—
> Enchanted and enchanting both, a boon
> To whomsoever haps upon its tune
> Of waters—trees, hills, Arcadian grace
> Bidding at every turn—

"Rather Wordsworthian," Mann said.

"Rather hackneyed," Anna said, with a laugh. Joe felt the stab of her comment. He wanted her and Mann to get along; he wanted her to find pleasure in Shade's poems. Her brutal judgment put a chill in the room. He struggled with the dense tract of handwriting but gave up before the end.

"I like it," he said. "It sounds as if he meant it, anyway." He did not actually know if he liked the poem or not; he was trying to smooth relations between Anna and his teacher.

"I think he did," Mann said, a bit testily. He had picked up a magazine. Now he tossed it down again. Anna turned a page.

"Are there others?" she said.

"Two pages over," Mann said.

Again Joe read at her side. She had recently torn a hangnail from her thumb: a livid red stripe beside the tan page.

"'The robin tenders his note from the vale,'" Anna said, quoting. "That's a nice phrase."

Mann said, "I think it's rather wonderful that a man as busy as he—he was a very successful businessman—would write such a thing. I mean, it's graceful, even if the phrases, as you say, have been used before. I wonder how many businessmen would attempt such a thing today?"

"Not too many, I hope," Anna laughed again.

Joe flushed at her lack of tact. He saw Mann's face knotting, the dark, hooded eyes frowning. Joe wanted to please the teacher, and to see him so obviously displeased unsettled him. It was a bit shocking. Anna wasn't speaking to Mann as one would to a teacher, with a note of deference, but candidly, as if he were just another person. To Joe, she was verging on disrespect.

She said, "But there—he fumbles the next stanza entirely."

"Well, I'm not making literary claims for him," Mann said, sounding really piqued. His brown eyes flashed. "You see, to me the poems are evidence of a very interesting man. An unusual man. I mean, he had practical reasons for founding a town here. But he was much more than practical, in the narrow sense. He fell in love with the place, really. He never got over it. I think it would be a very good thing if *our* businessmen wrote poetry or painted—or were at least interested in poetry and painting. They might come at things in a broader way. We'd all be better off."

"But if their poetry is bad . . ." she said, lowering the book.

"It doesn't matter. The point is, by coming into contact with the complexities of poetry—by paying some sort of homage to it—they're going to enrich themselves." Mann smiled at his choice of verb. "In more than the usual way, I mean. Shade was an enormously complex man. Just read his diaries. . . ."

The teacher gave them dessert in the old belvedere. Sitting on its narrow unpainted benches, facing each other a little awkwardly, they scooped at the little dishes of homemade chocolate mousse. "You wouldn't find better in France," Anna enthused, mollifying Mann a little. Far below, the Shade glinted under the rail trestle, as it spread toward the deep center of town. The spring evening, a Sunday, was unusually warm. A bumblebee drifted through the belvedere, rising toward the green sky over the treetops. Mann took up his old theme again, talking about Shade. He seemed determined to make Anna understand his fascination. "He was a more complete kind of man than is generally found now," he insisted, gesturing absently with his tiny spoon. "He was a woodsman, an entrepreneur, and an alderman and mayor for many years, a much-loved figure, really. Many's the needy family he helped out. He was a farmer—"

"A farmer poet," Anna offered graciously. "Like Virgil."

Mann bowed his head in acknowledgment and went on. "And all this was part of the same ambition, somehow."

"To serve God?" she suggested.

"Something like that. But here's the interesting thing. He wasn't formally religious, which was very unusual in a man of his position. He didn't go to church. Still—this is where the poetry comes in—he had this passion for place, if I can call it that. He loved what was here, it was in his care, somehow. In his later years, he could get tremendously exercised if—well, if someone was going to change a view by chopping down a grove. And this was a man who'd chopped down thousands of trees in his time."

Mann paused. Mostly he spoke to Anna. Joe was still guarding the bulwarks of propriety (long after they'd been breached), while these two went hammering each other as equals. It was thrilling and a bit disturbing.

"I think he was in love with beauty," Mann said. "He was in love with poetry, with—you know, the beauty of life that passes us by with hardly a glance. You're a poet, Anna—that was a wonderful poem you had in *The Quill*—so you know what I mean. It's the thing that should make us happy, and does, but also makes us melancholy, because we can't keep up with it; it's too quick for us, too eternally—young."

When the visit was over, they trooped down the hill. Joe was carrying a knapsack and a rolled blanket he'd taken from the Biscayne; when it got dark enough, they planned to do some stargazing. Mann had suggested they visit the old pioneer cemetery on the east side of town, where Shade and his family were buried. Joe had never been there and was as keen as Anna, so they crossed the Bridge Street bridge to the Flats and found the stony, deeply rutted lane that climbed behind several houses to a locked iron gate. They clambered over, into the isolated scattering of small pale tombstones, with the rail line and the gravel pits guarding its back and, to the west, the roofs of the town gleaming in the dusk. Joe had never seen the town from just this angle and stood picking out familiar buildings. The dark pyramid of the Presbyterian church roof dominated all, but there were other spires to the south and a rolling sense of buried life, under the dark canopy of trees.

The Shade monument was the largest in the graveyard: a tall plinth of white marble with a wider base on which the names of the Founder and his family were carved. They prowled around it, reading the inscriptions out loud, deciphering the Shade family tree, their scrutiny touched with a bittersweet sense of familiarity. They drifted among the other stones. Anna found notice of an eight-year-old boy, Julius Broad, who had drowned in the Attawan in 1896. The inscription read, *The river took him. Now God has him.* "It must have been wonderful to be able to believe that," she said. "If they really did believe it." She sniffed, and he looked at her, realizing tears were running down her cheeks. "What Mann said was wonderful," she said. "The truth is we're just shades ourselves. We're only here for about two seconds. Then—well."

"Yes," he said, slipping his arm around her. Her bare shoulder was cool under his hand. He was not feeling what she was feeling, but he was grateful for the chance to comfort her. After a few seconds, she dug her little notebook out of the canvas knapsack and went off by herself. He continued his tour of the cemetery, reading the fading inscriptions on the leaning white stones. From time to time he caught her bare legs, or her shoulder, sticking out from behind the Shade monument, where she sat on the ground, writing in her book.

One time, he saw that the notebook now lay several feet away from her, open on the rough lawn. He crossed to her. She was hugging her knees, staring blindly.

"Are you cold? Do you want your sweater?"

She shook her head, almost imperceptibly. He went and picked up her notebook, glancing at a page before he closed it. There was a scrawl of words and darker, crossed-out bits.

He held out the notebook. She glanced at it and looked away.

"I'm no good," she said and, a moment later, "That's not true. I'm very good. But very good for a poet—oh! It's no better than no good at all. The world doesn't need any more very good poems." She spoke angrily, with tearing sarcasm. "Very good poems. They're about as useful as a—a three-legged horse. If you're not a genius, you shouldn't even try."

"Maybe you *are* a genius," he offered, with complete sincerity.

She snorted. "You don't know anything. Emily Dickinson was a genius. Sappho was a genius. I'm just a pretender."

She took the notebook from him and abruptly got up.

"So what do we do now?" she said.

"Well, the stars are almost out," he said hopefully. "We could put down the blanket."

But she was too restless to settle. She walked around the cemetery while he spread the red tartan blanket. They had brought a bottle of wine and a corkscrew she'd taken from a cupboard at home. Joe drew the cork and placed the bottle on a fallen stone. "Wine's ready!" he called out. When she made no response he looked around and saw her stooping in the tall grasses at the back of the plot. Finally she came to him with a bouquet of wild grasses, which she presented rather formally, with a clumsy curtsy, apologizing for her outburst. "You must be getting heartily sick of me," she said.

"I'm a tolerant guy," he said.

"I know you are," she said, "and I thank you for it." He sniffed the bouquet she had brought him: the stiff, whiskered grasses, trembling in his fist.

They lay on their backs, watching the stars. They picked out the Big Dipper, Ursa Major, aslant across the sky, and the North Star, beaming feebly. Orion tilted in the south, with his sword belt. She pointed out constellations he did not know, pressing close so he could sight along her arm. The Milky Way was a vast twinkling road; it passed, she said, not only across the dark fields of space but through their bodies as well, entering just at the bottom of the breastbone and exiting out their backs. Could he feel it? He thought he could.

After a while they changed positions, sitting up with their backs to the Shade monument, trading the bottle back and forth. When she laughed at some joke he made—laughed with an almost shocking abandon—he realized she was getting drunk. He felt tipsy himself, released to a giddy freedom beyond his usual restraint and deference. They drank toasts to the stars and to individual constellations. He told her his old childhood fantasy, that the night sky was really the roof of a great tent, and the stars were pinholes where the light came through from beyond. She was intrigued by the idea of a light from beyond: a light so bright it could not be borne by human eyes, she said, like the radiance people attributed to the naked presence of God. That set her off wondering about the power of God; if there was a God, was he wholly benign, as people generally supposed, or a dangerous and even destructive force that might on a whim destroy people's happiness—hadn't he done that to Job, for the sake of a mere bet?—or burn the earth to cinders. Her imagination was apocalyptic. She began to talk about nuclear war and how it was impossible to think about—all those Russian and American missiles pointed at each other. The end of the world, at any given minute, was only a few minutes away. She was appalled by this, and yet she thrilled to the idea of such power, as if the devastation sleeping in those warheads were simply another facet of nature, great and mysterious like the stars.

They lay down and kissed for a while. Suddenly she rolled away on her back. He made to roll on top of her, but she pushed him off, instructing him to lie beside her.

"On your back," she said. "Lie perfectly still, your arms at your sides."

He remained quiet, looking up at the stars. One was blinking: a high jetliner, picking its way through the constellations. Its roar sounded soft and far away.

"We're lying like they're lying," she said. "Only a few feet above them."

"I don't like pretending I'm dead," he said, after a while.

"We are dead," she said, very quietly. He felt his breathing stop. The winking jetliner crossed the sky, in the remoteness of another life.

AFTER A TIME they heard the blare of a train's horn, in the countryside to the east. Soon they saw its headlight, striking through the night past the little cemetery toward the trestle that crossed the Shade. They could make out a few passengers in the sad isolation of the nearly empty cars, reading newspapers, looking out into the dark.

The engine rumbled onto the trestle. There was a deeper thunder, as hundreds of iron beams and wooden ties shook and thousands of fittings rattled like crude tambourines above the valley. Then the train was gone. They could hear its mournful bleat as it tore toward the Junction, straining for the fields beyond town.

Anna got up. "I hadn't realized we were so close to the bridge." She began to walk rapidly through the cemetery, clambering a bit drunkenly over the grassy mound at its border, over the ditch, and up the embankment to the tracks. Joe stumbled after her. Ahead, the surface of the trestle stretched away, with darkness on either side. The two sets of rails glinted in the weak starlight, across the infinite articulation of the ties. There were no guardrails.

She was walking with some difficulty between the rails, where the gravel was not quite level with the ties.

"What are you doing?" he said, as he strode behind her.

"I"m going out on the bridge."

"You can't," he told her. "People get killed out there."

"You don't have to come," she said with disdain. Immediately, she stumbled on a tie. He seized her arm, but she pulled away. Again he grabbed her.

"Don't!" she cried.

"I'm telling you, it's dangerous."

He went swiftly ahead of her, to the trestle, and saw the Shade in its calm lake behind Bannerman's dam, a hundred feet below. The lip of the dam glistened and put out a soft roar of falling water. He had crossed the bridge himself, once, with Smiley. But they'd checked the passenger schedules first and put their ears to the tracks to listen for approaching freights. And they hadn't been drunk.

He turned to face her on the tracks.

"I won't let you," he said. "We're too drunk. We'll do it another time."

She tried to get by, but he met her every dodge. She stamped her foot and made demon faces at him. He had become simply an object in her way. She flailed when he clutched at her and once scratched his face. In despair—he was convinced he was throwing away his chances with her—he was tempted to give in. Still, he clung to his sense he had to protect her.

Finally she gave up and stalked back to the cemetery. He followed, disconsolate. Off in the distance, a diesel horn sounded. He realized that another train was approaching, this time from the west. In a few seconds the freight thundered onto the trestle. Anna seemed oblivious to it but went about folding the blanket and putting the bottle away with a cold briskness that dismissed him utterly. He stood in amazement, watching the boxcars rumble and bang past. "You see?" he said. "If we'd gone out there, we would have had to dodge *that*." She wasn't listening, and he felt like some old fuddy-duddy, a parent who can only say no, who must fence life around with common sense and fear. Even if he had saved her life—and who knew, perhaps he had—his role was negative, secondary.

They left the cemetery and went down the hill to the Flats. Under the branches of maples, their foliage bright green in the streetlights, a few cars gleamed by the curb.

He had to hurry to keep up with her; perhaps she wanted him to vanish. He stuck to her stubbornly, wild with a sense of unraveling love, angry that she couldn't see what he'd done. At the corner of Willard she stopped. She closed her eyes and put back her head, taking long breaths. He waited in trepidation, thinking she was preparing some final speech. But she turned to him suddenly, pressing her forehead into the side of his neck. She said she was sorry: she'd been childish, an idiot. She said she didn't deserve his love. He had saved them, and she had been terrible. He circled her with his arms and felt her slim, trembling body under her cotton dress.

SHE DIDN'T WANT to go home, so for a while they wandered on the Flats. They walked slowly, with their arms around each other, up dim lanes past garages and gardens and silent porches. A black and white cat followed them for a while. They came back along Willard, under the vast east wall of the mills that rose sheer from the race.

They looked at the cloudy, inverted reflection of the mills. A duck quacked sleepily and glided off, leaving its trembling wake to glitter in the streetlight. Above, the white-framed windows, many tiers high, gazed out from the dim brick. They came to the narrow metal foot-bridge, with its pipe railing, that crossed the race to the mill. At the other end, a windowless door had been left ajar. The door looked small and secretive, a single opening in the vast wall.

"Can we go in?" she said.

"I don't know." He knew the night watchman must be about. Perhaps he was just inside. He couldn't imagine the door had been left open by accident. But he let her draw him forward.

"Come on," she said, cajoling. "We can't be killed here, can we?"

He didn't want to be always saying no, so he followed her across the bridge and in the little door. He shut it behind them but did not draw the bolt. A single bulb lit a corridor. He picked his way warily, hushing her at every turn and listening in the great stillness of the mills. To her, he sensed, this was an adventure, a glorious lark, as if these huge buildings, even the specter of the watchman, had been put here for her amusement. But he took trespassing more seriously. He was the son and grandson of mill workers; he had worked here himself; to take the place casually was impossible.

They stole through corridors and up stairways, into vast rooms where long trestle tables shone dully, in the pleasant odor of new cloth. She put her face to a stack of finished garments and breathed in deeply. She touched her fingertips to the cool, oddly shaped metal of machines. "It's so strange," she whispered to him. "I never thought of cloth coming from anywhere. Cloth, our clothes, just *are*. But then there's all this—it's like looking underground and seeing the elves and dwarfs working away." At one point they spotted the watchman crossing far below them, his light darting here and there through the millyard. He disappeared into the power plant, near the vast round base of the stack. Joe was anxious to leave, but for her sake he went on with their tour, listening all the while.

He showed her where his father had worked. The tall knitting machines stood silently in their rows, uncannily still under their wide crowns of bobbins. She had to know everything: how the yarn flew up through the loops of wire above and down into the churning drum of needles. She stooped to look at a knitted tube, hanging between a machine's legs. She could not get over how it seemed to appear out of nowhere. From just a few strands of yarn appeared this pale blue cloth, as soft and fragrant, she said, as a baby's skin.

A sudden clattering startled them. Outside, pigeons—wakened perhaps by a collective nightmare—swarmed from a roof, their wings whirring past the windows.

They moved on, walking through a covered bridge, several stories above the millyard, to another building. In one hall bales of raw wool were piled to the ceiling. The wool was rough to the touch and exuded a sharp smell of dried dung. They passed through farther rooms, past great shining vats and tubs, and came to a large bin. Inside was a mass of clean, whitish wool, smelling richly of lanolin. To his surprise, she climbed over the side of the bin and threw herself back in the wool, like a child playing on a mattress.

"Come here," she said, holding out her arms.

"I don't think—the watchman—"

"Come here."

The wool was too scratchy on their naked skin, so they spread the red tartan blanket. Even so, the wool curled over its edges, around them. As he moved on her, it tickled his sides, his forearms, and formed white balls, like snow, around her face.

55

ONE WARM JUNE night, several weeks after his fight with Margaret, Alf sat in the Biscayne, too tired to get out. Cooling metal popped. In the dim yard, the apple tree rustled and the humped, ungainly shape of a raccoon hurried into the garden foliage. The back of his shirt had stuck to the seat. For all the visiting he had done that night—he and Doyle had taken to working alone, to double their effectiveness—he'd picked up only one card, while the women hadn't done much better. The union was just fifteen or so cards from the total needed, but something in the atmosphere had changed. Many people didn't want even to open their doors. They spoke through screens, shadowy prisoners of their fear, or simply gestured through windows for the organizers to go away. Mary Carr, whom Doyle had hired several weeks before, blamed the change on Kit Ford, who was playing the heavy for the company. "I'm telling you, everywhere we go, seems like the Road Runner's just leaving. Lila Soames didn't even want to open her door to us. I don't know what the Road Runner's been saying, but it's working."

It wasn't just the Road Runner. Ford, Alf had heard, had taken to driving around with a bodyguard, a big fellow from Johnsonville whom Doyle usually referred to as "that goon." This development had occurred after several union supporters had threatened Ford in a restaurant. The goon accompanied Ford when he was visiting workers after hours. Ford hadn't unleashed his henchman yet, but he hovered in the background, a hint most people weren't slow to pick up. The atmosphere in town was getting more tense by the day, and Alf, who remembered the violence of 1949 all too well, was afraid they were slipping toward a repeat of that mayhem.

He got out of the car and trudged to the back door. Margaret had left the light on in the kitchen; it seemed a good sign. He was foraging in the fridge for something to eat when she came in, crossing in her dressing gown to the sink. "Your tomatoes are coming along well," he said. "That was a good idea, getting the greenhouse starts." She said nothing, just filled a glass at the tap and turned to leave.

"Margaret, we can't keep this up!"

She sighed. He heard Jamie call out, upstairs.

"Tell me what I can do, Margaret, and I'll do it."

"Jamie wants a drink," she said, and moved toward the door. When he put out his hand to touch her shoulder, she twisted away. A bit of water slopped to the floor.

She was soon gone, her slippers scuffing quickly down the hall. Then Joe was there, pushing in from the night. Greeting Alf tersely, he went to the cupboard.

Alf watched him take down a glass. Everything he had wanted to say to Margaret was still burning in him. "Joe," he said, his voice parched, "what happened with your mother? Joe, I need to talk to you—"

Joe turned, his face impassive. Alf sensed the common front between mother and son. They had their reasons for punishing him, good ones maybe, but in some obscure way he felt the entire story had not been told. That night in this room, just before he'd struck Margaret, she had touched something in him that should never be touched—she had reached inside him and cut his very soul. He felt she had meant to do this. He had reacted with the fury of someone who, in an instant, senses his life threatened. This seemed absurd to him, though. How had his life been threatened?

Standing before his son, he struggled to explain something of this. "I know there's no excuse for a man striking a woman. But you see, I love your mother, and so when she says—"

His throat had constricted, and he stopped. They were both embarrassed.

"Okay," Joe said softly. His fingers brushed Alf's arm as he went out, leaving his empty glass on the counter.

THE NEXT EVENING, Alf left after supper to visit Carl Schmidt, a spinner who lived a couple of miles outside town. The man had already turned him down once. Alf drove down the back roads in a fatalistic mood, not hoping for much.

As he headed along the dead-end lane that led past Carl's place, he glanced in the rearview and saw a red Chevelle turn in behind him. If it was Ford—and the sudden leap in his gut told him it had to be—then the foreman was clearly following him.

Impossible to visit Carl now; it could get him fired. The Chevelle was keeping well back, hardly visible in the dust drifting behind the Biscayne. "Come on, it could be anybody," he told himself, "Get hold of yourself." But the blood was pounding in his face. He passed through a grove of old maples, out into the sun in front of Carl's place. A movement of his eyes showed him Carl's dilapidated front porch, flickering behind the gray decaying survivors of an orchard. Carl was nowhere in sight, though his Ford pickup was parked on the grass outside the kitchen door. Alf drove on.

A turn in the lane cut off the view behind. Dust hung, shining, under a pine. Alf eased the Biscayne over a rib of white bedrock, down through a pasture spotted with wild fruit trees.

The river was there, swimming under the willows on the far bank. The road ended at a rotting wood barrier that blocked the ramp to a ruined bridge and forced him to the left, along the sand flats, where he finally stopped by a clump of scrub willow.

Feeling vulnerable in the car, he got out and walked to the river. A length of driftwood was lying at the water's edge. He picked it up, aware of the other car in the pasture now, its engine growing louder as it descended toward the flats. Making a show of indifference, he found a stone, tossed it up, and whacked it with his heavy stick, sending it knifing across the river.

As the Chevelle crossed the flats behind him, he turned. In the passenger seat was a mop-haired, dark-skinned fellow in sunglasses. His massive forearm hung outside the door with a queer indolence, as if it were broken. Behind the wheel, erect as a soldier, was Ford.

Alf went back to his game. Rattled now, he swung at another stone, and another, missing both. Hearing footsteps on sand, he turned.

"Kit," he said. He let the stick droop at his side.

The foreman stood a few feet off. His eyes, shadowed with fatigue, took in Alf's weapon.

Ford's goon had stopped a couple of steps away from his boss. He was well over six feet, too heavy for his height, with a look in his face of lazy contempt. Held loosely in his left hand was a tire iron.

"You guys got a flat tire?" Alf said.

He was ready to fight, but at the same time he almost didn't care what happened. There was something absurd about them all standing there like schoolboys preparing for a brawl. He wondered if this was Ford's idea of revenge. He'd considered his fight with the foreman to be pretty much a draw, but maybe Ford didn't see it that way. Alf waited, with the river at his back, feeling no need to talk, holding Ford's gaze.

Ford's shrunken pupils evaded him somehow, finding their focus just in front of his face. Alf was put out by this. For God's sake, he thought, at least look at me.

He sensed the goon shift his weight.

"Alfie," Ford said, his voice more strangulated than usual, "I want you to stay away from our people, anybody who works for Bannerman's. I don't want you near them. You got that? Or do we have to teach it to you?"

Alf chortled. Ford was sounding an awful lot like some movie cowboy.

"What's so funny, asshole? Stay away from our people."

"Is this how you want to spend your life?" Alf said quietly.

Ford's head jerked, almost imperceptibly, as if he'd been struck, and for a moment he looked directly at Alf. Not for the first time, Alf saw the boy in Ford, the lost, plaintive boy at the center of all that hardness. Alf, too, was affected by the unexpected contact. A kind of shock went through him.

Tossing down his weapon, he kept looking steadily at Ford.

"You just watch it," Ford said. But his voice was hoarse now, without authority; in his eyes was a watery sheen.

He walked quickly away, toward the Chevelle.

"Watchit," the goon told Alf, pointing at him with the iron. Scowling, he turned to follow Ford across the sand.

Alf watched the red car bump its way up the pasture road. Returning to the water, he found himself swept by unexpected emotion. It was as if some old grief had been exposed in him, a heaviness that verged on sorrow. It saturated everything around him: the warm air smelling of sand and willows; the implacably moving water, carrying along bits of grass and weed, funneling under the ruined bridge. He had no idea what had just happened between him and Ford, but the world had changed, he could feel it; the world had grown sadder and heavier and somehow more present. The very light seemed to lie on the land with a slow, viscous, golden weight. He watched two swallows skim the river, twisting and dodging with breathtaking alacrity, rising on wings so quick they seemed aflame.

56

THAT NIGHT, HE made four visits and picked up as many cards, including one from Carl Schmidt. "I guess I'm just sick of being afraid," the spinner told him, as he signed at his kitchen table.

When Alf got back to the Vimy House, he discovered that the other organizers had been successful too. In fact, they had put the union over the top in fine style. They'd signed up 57 percent of the workforce, two percent higher than was needed to achieve automatic certification. People who had held back for weeks had suddenly found reason or courage or weariness or anger enough to sign a card. Something had tipped the mysterious mechanism that releases a decision. Doyle couldn't explain it, though he said he'd seen the phenomenon once or twice before. "An earthquake in China?" he said, shrugging. "Who the hell knows?" As the organizers celebrated, Alf felt oddly distant, though he had a pleasant shock when Shirley, her head snaking forward almost apologetically, planted a long dry kiss on his mouth.

THE FOLLOWING WEEK two union negotiators arrived from Toronto to hammer out a first contract. They asked Alf for the names of people who had been laid off or fired over the past year as punishment for supporting the union. The idea was to lever these people back into Bannerman's as part of the collective agreement. Alf put his own name on the list. He told the negotiators he didn't want to go back to knitting, he couldn't stomach the idea of working again under Ford, but anything else would be fine. A few days later, he was offered—and accepted—a job on Bannerman's maintenance crew.

He was soon spending his days patching and painting, often working alone and often out-of-doors, which suited him well enough, though it all seemed a bit tame after the drama of organizing. One of his first tasks was on the roof of Number Six, his old mill, repairing some leaks around a ventilation shaft. He progressed at his own pace—it was a relief not to be hurried by machines—and from time to time, with a melancholy sense of freedom, paused to gaze across the roofs of the town toward the humped hills of Wiley's Farm, cutting the fresh sky of early summer.

In late July, the workers approved their first contract, and the union held a victory party in Lion's Park. All afternoon, tall clouds drifted from the west, casting sun and shadow over the thousand or so people who spread their blankets on the parched grass, in the shade of maples and willows. Taking a chance, Alf asked Margaret to go. She was speaking to him again, but she said she had a choir rehearsal at the church. Jamie and Penny went gladly, though, excited by the promise of hot dogs and prizes.

Doyle had returned to town for the celebrations. Dressed in Bermuda shorts even redder than his face, he insisted on making the rounds with Alf. "It wouldn't have happened without this guy," the organizer told people in his gruff way, while planting his large moist hand between Alf's shoulder blades. Alf was chagrined by the attention—Doyle's praise seemed exaggerated—but also secretly pleased. Everywhere, he met approving faces: that look of admiration and hopefulness he'd first encountered on the fire escape. It had unsettled him then, and it unsettled him a little now, this discovery of something in himself people seemed drawn to. When the time came for speeches from the band shell, Doyle barked into the microphone that Alf should stand. He got up warily, from the picnic blanket he was sharing with Jamie and Penny, to the largest ovation anyone got all afternoon. Then, sitting down, he found himself gazing at Pete's house, on its hillside above the park. The garage door was open. Pete's Sarasota was there, facing outward, its windshield dark.

Later, he stood talking to Doyle by the river. Below them, the shallow current collared rocks with foam. Alf felt a certain poignancy. Something was coming to an end. After this picnic, Doyle would get in his dusty car and he might never see him again, though they had promised to get together.

"So I can't persuade you to change your mind, you bastard?" Doyle said. Despite Alf's lack of interest, the organizer had kept pestering him to join him as a staff organizer for the UKW.

Alf grinned at his friend's persistence. "I don't think organizing's for me," he said. "I never got over the feeling I was just bothering people."

"Pah! People need to be bothered. Someone has to wake them up."

Linda Connaught, the new secretary of the local, called Doyle away. He was to be starter and general announcer for the races. Jamie ran up to Alf with Billy Boileau. Billy's dark eyes fixed fiercely on Alf's chest.

"There's a fathers-and-sons three-legged race!" Jamie said.

"You think we can win, eh?"

"Sure!"

Alf turned to Billy. "Shall we get you a partner then?"

Billy glared into the air, at nothing.

"C'mon, I bet we could get Dick Harmer to run with you."

"Nope," Billy said, in that trapped hard voice of his. With his fists jammed and working in his pockets, he seemed to be expecting something that had not been offered, demanding it.

Over at the course, Alf tied Jamie's leg to his. There wasn't much time to practice. The mothers-and-daughters race was already being run. Penny had found a partner in Alf's old school chum Annie Stone; they stumbled their way along in the middle of the pack, and soon the fathers and sons were ready to start. Bellowing "Go, brothers!" Malachi Doyle dropped his big arm and the horde of men and boys hopped over the grass toward the strand of red yarn held taut by Mary Carr's twin daughters. Alf and Jamie finished fourth or fifth, Alf laughing so hard he nearly fell over, while Jamie kept yelling at him, put out at his lack of seriousness. For prizes, all the children received mechanical crickets that soon filled the park with their clicking.

Afterward, Jamie went off to the swings with a group of other boys. Alf noticed Billy sitting up on a picnic table by himself, intently watching the others, and took him a cricket.

The boy merely looked at the toy in Alf's outstretched hand. Alf set the cricket on the table and climbed up beside him.

"There's going to be regular races. You don't need a partner for them."

Billy made his trapped-in-the-throat sound: "Heh."

"I'll bet you're pretty fast."

It was like talking to a post. Again Alf found himself drawn, almost painfully, to this skinny little boy with the luxuriant hair, sitting hunched beside him with his hands on his knees and a faraway slit-eyed look in which Alf glimpsed just the trace of a smile. Alf began to talk about the different kinds of runners, the sprinters and the long-distance runners, the ones who could keep going all day, like Tom Longboat—an Indian, Alf dared to say, and caught for his reward a slight turn of Billy's head. So he told him about the great Tom Longboat, how he was from a reserve not far from here and how he'd beaten all the top marathoners, including the Englishman Alf Shrubb, flying along in the tradition of the great runners who in the old days used to carry messages long distances between villages without stopping to eat and only drinking what they could scoop from streams as they splashed through them.

Once, twice, suspicious interest flickered in Billy's narrowed eyes. But a deeper gleam was there too, perhaps delight. Alf reached out and touched him affectionately on the back. It was like making contact with a little dynamo. The tension there was palpable, in the hard flesh.

"So maybe you could give it a try," Alf said. "I think they're almost ready."

Doyle, holding up his clipboard, was calling out in his raw voice for runners. First, girls, eight to eleven; then boys. Jamie and his friends were trooping back from the swings. Alf noticed his son eyeing him and Billy warily. Just then, Billy jumped off the table and walked rapidly toward the trees at the south end of the park. He was like a wild animal, bolting at God only knew what tremor of danger. In a few seconds he had disappeared into the woods of Lookout Hill.

Jamie, who had turned nine that month, came in second, despite being matched with older boys. The lad was obviously a sprinter, Alf thought, as his Uncle Joe had been. For a moment, Alf saw his brother bursting through the tape at the high school track meet, his head tossed back, his mouth open in a crazy, tortured smile of triumph. Afterward, he'd stuffed his ribbon in a drawer as if it was nothing.

Jamie came over to the table, his face shining with pride.

"Ah, you'll do better next time," Alf told him, as if he'd failed by coming second, and felt his own heart sink as he saw the shadow cross his son's face. Why had he said that, when in fact he was proud of him? He tried to make it up, praising the boy, ruffling his hair. But the damage had been done. Alf watched him go off toward the crowd with his prize, a red balloon, bobbing behind him.

He sat disconsolately. Why did he hurt people, his own family most of all? It was as if there were a blade in his hands that had a life of its own. He looked off toward the woods, flowing up the side of Lookout Hill. He'd been kinder to Billy Boileau than to his own son. What in hell was he trying to do? He thought of Billy—he imagined him walking hard up the narrow trails or sulking on a rock. The image pierced him, but he suppressed it, feeling disloyal to Jamie.

Well, he would make it up to the boy. He looked around. The last race had just finished. The crowd was dissolving and Doyle was in deep conversation with two other men, his voice growling under theirs. A cloud was just passing over the sun, the park had slipped into shadow. He was unable to pick out Jamie among all the people. He felt he'd made the boy vanish by his cruelty.

He saw Lucille. He had not spoken to her for months, though in truth he'd never stopped thinking about her. Here she was, as if emerging from one of his own daydreams, striding toward him. He half expected a rebuke. Unusually for her, she was wearing a dress, short and scoop-necked, her brown knees flashing as she walked.

He knew she was working again at Bannerman's, in her old job as a seam stitcher. Alf himself had put her on the list. Her smile surprised him. He wondered if she'd found out he'd helped her.

"Do you know where Billy's gotten to?"

He supposed she had noticed him with the boy. But he felt it was him, really, she had come to see.

"He went off to the woods."

"That kid—he's a regular escape artist."

Her black eyes, suddenly empty of expression, searched his. He had left her without an explanation, simply walked away. He felt he deserved hostility from her, but there was something else here instead, girlish, wondering. Shame heated his face, but he was glad, very glad, to see her.

It was threatening rain. The air was soft, close; the park felt wrapped in sadness. He was aware of her bosom, rising below her smooth, exposed chest, and of a faint twist in the left side of her mouth.

"So I guess you're a hero now," she said.

Was she speaking ironically? He could not meet her eyes.

"I wouldn't say so," he said.

"Why did you leave me?" she said.

"I'm sorry Lucille, I—"

"Well, you're a busy man." She turned away and stared at the crowd for a moment. He wanted her and was appalled at himself, that this should crop up again. "I really hated you for going," she said. "I sort of thought—well, stupid me, eh?"

"There's nothing stupid about you," he said.

"I just thought we might have, you know, talked about it."

"I was a bastard," he said.

The space between them filled with an awkward silence.

"Well," she said, "I guess I better find Billy."

"I'll help you," he said.

As they walked off, he realized people must be watching. Before, he had taken great pains to hide his connection to her. Now he told himself they were only going into the woods to hunt for her boy: they were innocent entirely. Careful not to touch each other even accidentally, they crossed the dry grass together, her sandals slapping at her heels. They did not speak. He wondered if she were only tolerating him. Men stuck to her, clung to her like burrs; it was something she was used to. He didn't care. That was the main thing, he didn't care. At the woods they had to separate, to enter the mouth of the trail. He followed her down the dim path that smelled of mud in hidden springs, aware of the white tag of her dress where it had stood up against her neck, white on brown.

57

JAMIE SAW THEM go into the woods. His balloon tickled its string lightly through his hand and slipped away, unnoticed. By the time he reached the trees, it had sailed, a red dot, high over the river and the Island.

He climbed through the dim mass of trees. After a while he stopped, below a tall clump of cedars. Water slimed and rutted the trail. The fragile, tentative tap of a woodpecker came from space grown ominous.

Billy had said, *He's going to be my father now,* and it had happened. He'd watched Billy go into the woods. Now his father and Billy's mother had gone after him. The three of them were together.

He heard a laugh from just up ahead—his father's laugh! For a second he felt everything was going to be all right—that's what his father's laugh meant to him—and he remembered a time when they had gone swimming at Devil's Cave. His father had stayed a long time underwater and then burst up, the water pouring off his head, laughing. A flicker in the leaves told him his father was close by. Stopping, he turned a little and saw his father and Billy's mother. They were standing right in front of him, facing each other, and his father's hand was on her face, touching her cheek.

"Dad," someone said.

For a minute he thought it was Billy who had spoken: that hard little voice. But it was himself, Jamie, his voice like a stone.

His father's hand dropped to his side.

"Jamie, hey! We're just looking for Billy."

Looking for Billy in Billy's mother's face. His father came forward with a grin. "Hey, guy, you seen Billy?"

His father mussed his hair.

They went back down to the park together, the three of them. Billy could find his own way home, his mother said.

In the park, she went off. His father took him across the bridge and off the Island to the stores. He wondered, Were they still looking for Billy? His father took him into the Oasis and bought him a double-scoop of chocolate—for running so well against the older boys, he said. They walked back toward the Island. On the bridge, his father stopped, lit a cigarette, and tossed the flaming match toward the water. Jamie stood licking his cone and observing his father's face. Ice cream melted cold on his fingers. Somewhere down the shadowy millrace a mourning dove was cooing.

"What you saw there," his father said, "that was just Billy's mother being sad about something. It's okay, really. We don't have to mention it to your mother. Okay?"

Jamie licked at his cone. "Are you still my dad?" he said, in his strange new voice. The mourning dove had stopped.

He was falling, falling through the mild air. His father laughed. A large hand caressed the back of his head. "What a crazy idea!"

58

THESE DAYS—THE long summer holidays of sun and burnt lawns and the whining lathes of the cicadas in their high, secret workshops—Joe wanted to spend every hour he had with Anna, who was leaving in a month. But he had to work. He had to prowl the dim aisles of Bannerman's shipping department, invoices in his sweaty hand, taking down sweaters and T-shirts from their shelves and fitting them into cardboard boxes stamped with the logo of the Boy Scout with the banner. The place was miserably hot under its flat roof and, despite the pine scent of dust-bane sprinkled liberally everywhere, it stank of human waste. The toilet faced directly into the workplace, its saloon-style doors revealing the naked shins of whoever was sitting inside. The shins always looked vulnerable, pathetic, the source of endless jokes—*Show us your knees, Maggie*—which quickly grew stale.

One low, filthy window opened onto the straw-pale playing fields behind the arena. By putting his face close to the left-hand side of the glass Joe could peer over the arena roof and just make out the cloud of trees obscuring the North End. They seemed alive with Anna's presence, like the blank sky above and the steep roofs of the Bannerman mansion. He was impatient to get up the hill again, to renew the spell at its source. He kept glancing above the shipping room door, where the hands of a large clock jerked arthritically through the day, and was startled by a paradox. He was wishing the hours away, but every one of them, when it was past, was another sixty minutes deducted from her time in town. She and her mother, who was going back to visit family, had already bought their tickets.

When the five o'clock whistle went, he was always first down the stairs, first across the playing fields. At home: a shower, fresh clothes, then a quick bite, and out again. His mother kept asking if he didn't want to invite Anna home for supper. "Such a lovely girl" she said warmly, more than once. "Clever, too." But Joe resisted. *Love you,* he'd tell her, as he brushed past with a quick kiss. He did love her, it was easy these days; love seemed to spill from him without effort. He even loved the cozy, familiar kitchen with its banged-up furniture; he loved his brother's bicycle, abandoned on its side on the dry grass.

Something had shifted between him and Anna. It was their lovemaking in the mills that had done it, he felt—pitching them into a new level of intimacy. He had never forgotten Liz's words: *Anna can't love; it was a man, not a boy like you.* Well, he had proven her wrong, hadn't he? Now surely something could be worked out about France. He told Anna he could visit her in Paris; maybe he could become a student there himself in a year or two, if he could find the money. Yet his enthusiasm never generated anything definite from her side. They made love a few times more, in her bedroom when her parents were out, and once, at his insistence, in the lowlands beside the Shade where they'd first gotten together on the night of the graduation party. But even so, he began to fear that, for her, nothing truly essential had changed. She actually seemed to be looking forward to going away. He wondered if she felt any pangs at all. Couldn't she see, couldn't she guess, what he was going through? His desperation grew cagey, his desperation and, yes, his jealousy. He wondered if her old boyfriend was still in the cards, the man friend Liz had mentioned. He wondered if it was the man in the picture on her desk.

One Sunday afternoon they were reading in her bedroom. Sitting at her desk, he could hear Anna flipping pages on the bed behind him. Unable to concentrate, he kept studying the photograph in its gold frame—the picture he'd first seen that winter afternoon he'd brought her heather. He worried over the handsome face, the heavy eyebrows, the unreadable expression of the deep-set eyes, the sense of casual ownership implied by the loose draping of his hand over Anna's shoulder. In her head scarf she had the air of a convalescent, bundled against the chill.

The man was movie-star handsome, Joe thought, although there was something vacant in his face, as though it had been hollowed out from within. It was a mask of handsomeness, from which unhappy eyes stared. He had constructed a theory. This was the man Liz had referred to. Anna had fallen in love with him, and he had abandoned her. She had had a terrible time. Here, in the photograph, her unhappiness was already upon her, because the man, with his cold, careless face, was in the process of leaving her. She had been a long time recovering, and now she was wary of love, of love's abandon, because she could not allow herself to go through it again. Even if she loved Joe (and he was almost convinced she did), she could not let herself feel it. He needed to go slowly. She needed patient, tender care, and of course he was willing to give it to her, only there wasn't much time left to be patient in.

Twice he nearly spoke, to the rustling on the bed behind him. Each time he hesitated. Any attempt to enter her intimate space always seemed to embroil him in difficulties. She was a nest of trip wires. You never knew what anger or rebuke you might set off.

Offhandedly, he sang out, "Say, who's this handsome friend of yours?"

When she didn't answer, he turned in his chair. She was lying on her stomach, propped on her elbows over her book. She was wearing Bermudas and a sleeveless blouse. Those green eyes looked at him, across the carved mahogany of her bed.

"In the photo," he said.

"Enrico," she said, in a matter-of-fact way. "He was my best friend in Europe."

He conducted a rapid analysis of her words. She had spoken so casually of this Enrico that he wondered if he really had been only a friend.

"Very good-looking," he said, struggling to maintain a disinterested note. "Were you in love with him?"

"In a way," she mused, still watching him.

He could no longer stop himself.

"Will you be seeing him—when you go back?"

"Yes," she said, in a muffled tone, looking down at her book. Staring over the back of his chair, with the false smile dying on his face, he felt suddenly emptied. In two seconds, the happiness and confidence of the entire summer had evaporated.

"So this is my rival," he said. His voice came out as a croak.

She turned a page. Her bare feet were twining with each other, which seemed to him the twining of naked bodies, of which his was not one.

"Anna," he said.

"I feel like you're picking me apart," she said, to her book.

"It's a natural enough question," he said. "I'm naturally curious, in a jealous sort of way, about my rivals."

"He's not your rival," she said, in a flat voice.

"He's here on your desk. You don't have a picture of me on your desk. What happened to that little picture I gave you?"

She looked up at him again, without expression: she was displeased. But he brazened it out, making no attempt to hide the misery on his face.

"He's homosexual," she said finally. She sighed and pressed two fingers into her closed right eye, as if to force back some incipient pain.

"Homo—"

"He sleeps with *men*," she said.

"I know what it means," he said, flushing. He stared at her. He might know the word, but he didn't know any homosexuals himself, though occasionally some boy at school would be denigrated with taunts of *homo!* or *faggot!* There was something otherworldly in the term, since no one really knew what a faggot was, in any experiential sense; the boy might as well have been called a centaur.

On the bed, Anna rolled to her back, holding her book with one hand above her face. After a moment she flung it aside, as if in impatience or disgust, while he watched intently from across the room.

———

THE DAY BEFORE she was to leave, they walked up the Atta to Devil's
Cave. In front of the cave was a sandy depression littered with the
remains of old fires: charred logs, nuggets of wadded tinfoil, cruel shards
of brown glass. Clearing a place for their blanket with his feet, he
watched as she stooped to peer into the deep recess between two enormous slabs of limestone. She was wearing white sneakers, jeans, and a
white T-shirt that barely reached her belt. It had slid up, revealing the
softly notched serpent of her spine. They had not made love for a week,
not since his questions about the photograph.

She came away from the cave without comment and stood near him,
looking at the river where it slid into the pool—the deepest place he
knew of on the Attawan, formed by the river as it rounded a sharp bend
and met the sudden resistance of limestone. The water here, opaque
with its burden of soil, was in a constant state of agitation, its surface
alive with little whirlpools that popped up mysteriously and just as mysteriously disappeared. Upstream, the bank ascended gradually to a cliff
of gray clay, sharp-edged against the almost painful brightness of the sky.
With one hand shading her face, she was staring now at the cliff—
oppressive, rudely prehistoric—as if it had endured from the era before
life, the slick, leaden clay falling almost sheer to the water.

"There's an odd feeling about this place," she said, coming back. "It's
like there's somebody else here. I keep feeling I'm being watched."

"We could go somewhere else."

She trailed along the edge of the bank without answering. He went on
putting out their picnic things. Every object he touched—the pink Tupperware container of sandwiches, the thermos of coffee, the tinned cheese
from France he'd bought in the A&P—seemed oddly insubstantial, cardboard fill-ins for the real thing.

They sat side by side, picking at the ham-and-cheese sandwiches his
mother had made, absorbed by the coursing water. He had come here
all his life, first with his father, then with friends. It was a favorite
swimming hole, though at least two drownings had occurred here,
when weak swimmers had been trapped under the bank. He told her
about these deaths now, with a secretly hostile eagerness, unable to stop

himself. "One fellow, Graham Lessing—he used to be in my class—
when they pulled him out and worked on him, he came to. He sat up
and asked for a glass of water and then he lay back down and died."

"He asked for a glass of water?"

"I know. It's like he didn't appreciate them pumping his lungs out."

"How did he ask? I mean, was he conscious?" she said.

Joe admitted he hadn't been there; he'd only heard the story later.

"Aha," she said.

He was deflated; he'd failed to communicate the strangeness of the
drowning. Upstream, near the cliff, the river swished at a broken willow
branch. He had always loved this spot, but today it had a heartless quality, as though it cared nothing for human beings. "I have to ask you
something," he said.

She glanced at him, a bit guardedly.

"What happened to you, before you came to Attawan? You said you
had a bad time."

She worked the remains of her sandwich between her fingers. Earlier, he would not have dared to ask, wary of the limits she had imposed
on him. But now he wanted facts, no matter how treacherous.

"Yes, well, it wasn't all bad," she said. There was something new in her
tone, a calm, simple sincerity. "I had an affair," she went on, tossing the
little ball of bread toward the water. "This was in France, in Paris, and—
well, I sort of got in over my head."

She paused, digging with her heel at the sand. He scarcely breathed.
The word *affair* sounded mature and somehow dangerous.

"He was a painter," she said. "The previous fall, he'd taught a few
classes at our school. All the girls were crazy for him. When he asked if
I'd model for him, at his studio, I jumped at it."

She told him about Guillaume, who had traveled the world and kept
in his studio a drum from Borneo he said was made from human skin;
chunks of temple carving from Thailand; a six-foot papier-mâché
dragon from Mexico, its fierce jaws clamped on the body of a hapless
victim. He wore paint-stained jeans and T-shirts. He painted richly colored oils of the human figure—nearly always a naked female extended

diagonally across the canvas like a rough, tilting landscape. He was thirty-three. She had just turned seventeen.

She didn't describe how she came to sleep with Guillaume, sparing Joe that, though he gathered that she had been happy with him in the beginning. "My parents didn't know," she said. "At least at first." She broke off and stared bleakly in front of her, as if whatever came next somehow deprived her of speech.

"Things started to go wrong," Joe said, prompting. He wanted—needed—that part of the story.

Bitterness entered her voice. "If you think someone doesn't like your body, there's really no place to hide. He'd tell me I was too heavy. Too slow. I was *stupide*. I was reading the wrong books. He didn't have much money, so I'd steal francs from my mother and give them to him. I even stole paint. I'd go into a store and come out with my pockets full of tubes. He used to call me his *petite voleuse*."

She shook her head. She seemed baffled and dismayed by her own behavior and at the same time fascinated by it.

"I wasn't eating," she said. "I wasn't doing my homework. In school, all I could think about was getting out so I could go to his studio. Then he started making these little speeches—I needed to get out more in the world, I needed to have a boyfriend my own age. One afternoon he told me he had to go away for a few days. Stupid me. I started standing in the park across the street, watching his building. When I finally went in, the concierge told me he'd moved."

She raked at the ground with her fingers, once, twice, three times, gouging a small trench. She flung away a handful of sand.

"I saw him again, one day in the street," she said, "and it all started up again—for a couple of hours. Afterward, he went completely cold. He was like that. He said he didn't want to see me again. He meant it this time."

Joe tried to hug her, but she pushed him away. When she began to speak again, her voice had flattened, gone almost dead.

"Everything seemed raw, too bright. I began to get headaches all the time. I wouldn't leave the apartment. I refused to go to school." She glanced up at Joe, and he saw she was ashamed to have gone to pieces over this, ashamed, now, for him to see what had happened. "It was weeks. My parents didn't know what to do." Finally, they sent her to a psychiatrist, but after three sessions she had quit. "He was an iceberg," she said. "I hated him." Her real doctor, she maintained, was Enrico, the man in the photograph on her desk. He was the son of her parents' friends. She had known him since she was a little girl. He spent hours visiting her; he coaxed her outside, on walks.

Then her father, who worked in Intertex's Paris office, was offered a chance to set up new accounting procedures at a mill in Canada, a job that would take one or two years. "Canada seemed safe somehow. I hadn't lived here since I was ten—my dad was from Montreal—but I had good memories. I had the idea I could start over again—you know, live a kind of normal life, a schoolgirl's life, nothing so . . . extreme."

She fell silent. Her story had come to an end, and yet he still didn't know the most important part. She was dragging her fingers through the hole she'd made in the ground, with an awkwardness that to Joe's eyes made her seem much younger. His impulse was to comfort her, but he wasn't sure she wanted him to. She seemed far away, isolated in her unhappiness.

"And it worked," he said, "coming here?"

"We didn't come right away. We went to visit my mother's family in Brittany. That's where I started to get better."

"Ah," he said.

"It's been fine here," she said. "It's just that—well, I don't think I'm really a small-town person. I can't pretend I'm someone I'm not. It was foolish to think I could." She spoke haughtily, almost angrily, as if lashing out at him, as if he were somehow to blame for her failure to belong in Attawan.

"Liz says you can't love, because of what happened." He had thrown the accusation at her sharply. He suspected now she had never loved him.

"What does Liz know?" she said. She got suddenly to her feet and walked toward the river.

"I love you," he breathed. The words—the tremendous emotion—

had come swimming up from his desolation like a new discovery, one he was fated to make over and over.

THEY STRIPPED OFF their clothes and walked upstream, following a narrow path that ran along the base of the cliff to the fallen willow that lay aslant the current. He studied her intently as she moved ahead of him: her wide shoulders, her long legs, and her skin, so smooth it seemed unnatural. In the shadow of the cliff, she hugged herself and complained of the cold. He showed her how to climb out on the trunk of the willow and drop into the current. She plunged in with a cry, and the river carried her off. He caught up to her downstream, in the pool by the cave, where they kissed briefly, her legs wrapping him in the coursing, tickling water.

Immediately she had to get out and do it again. He stayed in the pool, watching her hurry up the narrow path below the cliff. At the willow, she turned and waved to him. Her nakedness hurt him, yet he could not tear his eyes from her.

When she dropped into the water, he did a surface dive and swam for the bottom. It was dark almost immediately, the yellow-brown of the top layer turning to impenetrable purple. On the bottom was an old water-logged pine trunk, the stumps of its branches stippling it like the cruel knobs of a medieval club. He managed to grasp one of these, using it to keep himself down. Crouching on the cool ooze, he peered up into the haze above, hoping to get a glimpse of her. He stayed down as long as he could—he and Smiley used to play this game; their record for staying under was about a minute and a half—and finally, with burning lungs, he kicked toward the surface.

Broaching with a gasp, he could see no one. She was not in the river. She was not anywhere on shore. He called her name, turning and turning in the pool with rising concern. His feet scraped bottom: the current had carried him toward the exit. Swimming back to its center, he dove again, clawing his way down to where the current was weaker, making his way along the bottom while groping blindly with his hands in the dark. Finally he touched a limb. But it was only the end of the pine tree, slippery with algae. Again he rose to the surface. Again, there was no one there. Panic took him now, ice in the gut. Upstream, the sun blazed above the dank cliff. Then she was there: popping up not five feet from him, her head slick as an otter's. She had not seen him.

She was crying his name, sending it out with thrilling desperation to the empty shore. When he spoke, she screamed and turned to him, her eyes filled with fear. "What happened to you? What happened to you, why did you do that?"

"I just dove," he said. "I must have missed you when I came up." He was feigning innocence, secretly gratified by her alarm. He had meant to worry her with his first dive; he had meant to make her afraid.

She swam to him. He realized she was weeping, her face rubbery like a little girl's, weeping and hanging on him. Inwardly, he triumphed. On shore, he wrapped her in the red tartan blanket. Shivering, she huddled against him.

"You see," he said, hugging her protectively, "you do love me a little."

THAT EVENING, HE ate with her family in the backyard, under the maple tree, on the old deal table with the game leg, which swayed a little under its white cloth. Her parents were mostly silent—there seemed to be some tension between them—but afterward Joe and Anna were able to escape in her father's Bel Air. They drove north out of town, following the winding highway across a plain sectioned into farms. At Anna's prompting he turned down a gravel side road that ran straight east. They came to a small pioneer church, sheltered in a grove of maples. The arched doors were locked, but they walked in the churchyard, past the cobblestone walls with their even rows of smooth, egglike stones. The foliage lashed above them with a dry, wild sound like surf, in a wind that seemed to carry the orange light. To the north, the wooded Reid Hills crept out, blue skirmishers at the edge of the plain.

Anna had more energy for exploring than he, so he trailed around after her, faintly pleased when something pleased her—an old gravestone, the absorption of a wire fence by the bark of a tree—but also resentful that on their last night she could bother with anything but him. He could not forget her story. It was obvious that compared to her painter he had hardly touched her.

He watched as she stopped to scratch a bare leg, watched as the wind plastered her dress against her thighs, revealing their shape. He might have been seeing her for the first time, everything about her seemed that novel, that fresh—though it occurred to him that this might be the last time, too. The last and the first—the two times had become one, painful in its vividness. Then in the field behind the church he saw with a start someone walking there, a tousle-haired child of three or four, walking by himself through the wind-whipped grain. His heart leaped in recognition, though of what he couldn't have said. A moment later, he saw the child was only the upright iron seat of an old mower, abandoned at the edge of the field. The vision had moved him. He turned to Anna, thinking to tell her about it. But words seemed pointless now; words could do nothing.

IT WAS AFTER eleven when they embraced at her kitchen door. He was planning to come back in the morning to see her off, but still he didn't want to let her go. They clung to each other in a kind of inert exhaustion, like marathon dancers he'd seen in old newsreels. He was trying to convince himself she was holding on as tightly as he. Finally, she broke away.

That night he woke at three. Unable to get back to sleep, he dressed and walked up West Street, past the old hosiery mill, its windows boarded now, and up the rail embankment to the Macrimmons'. The wind had subsided, under an obscure sky. The yard was still, ghostly: the table where they had eaten so many suppers, stripped of its cover; the dim mountain of the maple; their four chairs scattered forlornly on the packed dirt. He sat with his back against the maple, in view of her window. Sometime later, the chaotic caroling of birds woke him, and he shook off his stiffness in the yard before resuming his vigil in a chair. He must have fallen asleep again, because the next thing he saw was Anna's face. She was kneeling before him in her dressing gown. For a blissful moment, he forgot she was leaving and simply smiled at her.

She scolded him delightedly as she led him into the kitchen. "You should be in a novel, waiting out there like that." He sat at the kitchen table while she made eggs, standing at the stove in a dark green dressing gown he had never seen before. The overly long sleeves she kept pushing back, her slender wrists—there was so much about her he didn't know; it seemed unfair that her novelty should go on unfolding so effortlessly before him, even on their last morning.

"What about Guillaume?" he said, and immediately felt sickened by his need to ask, in the face of what she'd been through. From upstairs came the sound of voices. Her parents would soon be down. "Do you think you might run into him again?"

At the stove, she went motionless. Spatula in hand, she looked at him in what seemed incomprehension. She shook her head a little. Did it mean no, he wondered, or did she mean she could hardly believe he'd asked?

"Anna?" he said.

"If I do," she said, almost cheerfully, "I'm sure I can handle it."

"Good," he said. "That's good."

EVERYONE ATE BREAKFAST on the fly, while trying to do a dozen other things. Her father, who was driving Anna and her mother to the airport, acknowledged Joe gruffly and went off to call his office. Her mother hurried here and there as she kept changing her mind about the clothes she would wear on the plane. He tried to make himself useful by cleaning up the kitchen. He helped Andrew Macrimmon carry the heavier luggage downstairs. The day was remarkably, nightmarishly, ordinary. He saw a squirrel leap to a lawn chair and sit up on its haunches to eat something. It struck him as curiously human—those dark little handlike paws—and when it scampered away behind the house, he followed its disappearance in astonishment, as if it contained a key to what was happening.

A few minutes later, he sat on Anna's bed, watching her make some last-minute changes to the contents of her carry-on. Her mother called up the stairwell, *"Vite, vite, allons-y! Ton père nous attend!"*

He helped Anna close the little case. They kissed, almost gravely, and with a quick movement she escaped his arms and went out the door. He followed with her bag. Outside, he put the carry-on in the trunk and closed it, in the sickening gust of the exhaust, while Anna slid into the backseat. Her mother extended a hand from the front window. "You're a good boy," she said. The remark stung. He did not want to be a boy, did not want to be good. The man Anna loved had not been good.

Anna had rolled her window down. He was taken aback by her tears, which made the mark on her cheek glisten. His throat tight, he leaned down to her. Their lips brushed—that smell of her, that scent of vanilla that was almost a no-smell, the scent of space itself—and the car began to back up. He walked down to the front sidewalk and stood watching as the Bel Air backed into Banting and then, with the slight jolt of the gear change, began to slide smoothly forward.

59

LATE AUGUST OUTSIDE the sweater mill, and the scream of Alf's saw, bees floating in the goldenrod towering beside his half-finished steps. Through an open window he saw a carousel turning inside with a load of white bobbins. Swiftly, swiftly, the pale planets fled the deeper darkness of the hall behind them. Other machines were invisibly at work with a steady brushing clash, like a waterfall, as thousands of needles and small metal parts raced through their tasks, above the deep organic hum of the drive belts. Regret lodged a small stone in his chest. He had once been at the heart of that work himself, and though he had never cared as much for knitting as for carpentry, he was alone now, outside the ark of easy purposefulness men and women made when they worked together.

Kneeling, he fit the board into the deck and nailed it home. Already, the fresh pine of the other boards was dirty with the confused prints of his work boots. Descending the stairs, he picked up a plank and was about to place it on the table saw when he noticed that the carousel had stopped. Minutes later it still had not moved. Above the stilled bobbins, threads moved slightly in the breeze. The knitter in him was instantly alert, critical; no machine should stand idle for long. As he stared up at the high window, he realized he could no longer hear the thrum of work. Suddenly—it was like the uncanny feeling he got when his heart skipped a beat—the mill seemed wrapped in the silence of desertion.

He looked around, the miraculous sole survivor of an event he could not grasp. Nearby, the bees, audible now, flew from frond to frond. A few moments later, he heard a cry. It might have come from a man or a woman, he could not tell, but it sounded from the depths of the sweater mill like some outburst of pain or alarm by the building itself. A little later he heard other voices, shouting and arguing; phones ringing; the sound of breaking glass. The din was coming mainly from the sweater mill, from all six floors, though as he listened it seemed to spread, a contagion of anger or panic that soon echoed from other buildings as well. Standing on the unrailed deck, he stiffened in amazement. Then he heard it: a drumming on the stairs that grew louder and continued to grow as workers streamed into the yard. His first thought was fire.

He saw Lil Hepworth stalk out purposefully, thick legs working under her shapeless skirt. Immediately behind came Jim Corcoran, a spinner, and his cousin Sid Corcoran, gripping the hair on the crown of his head as if he meant to tear it out. Everyone seemed dazed. They stood in the yard, facing the doorways from which yet more workers were streaming. They were coming from all the buildings now: not in a solid mass, as they did when the sirens released them (he looked at his watch to make sure it wasn't noon yet), but more raggedly, in twos and threes, from the dyehouse, the knitting mill, the spinning mill. Some were grim-faced, silent. Others were arguing volubly. A couple were laughing and smiling as if they'd been released on holiday. Behind him now, people came clattering down the plywood ramp he'd rigged at the loading dock. Seeing Joe emerge, Alf called to him. Joe didn't hear; he was listening to Eddie Baker, who was holding forth with clenched fists. But a woman who was closer to Alf—it was Linda Koch—raised her freckled face and shouted, "They're shutting the mills!"

Stunned, Alf watched her plump back retreat toward the gathering in the yard. A man and a woman—Lottie Connor and Art Freud—were arguing so violently, red faces inches apart, it seemed they must soon fight in earnest. Some were trying to calm them. The growing crowd seethed.

Alf left his perch and stood at the edge of the melee. Beside him, Davy

Clark, a tall man of sixty with a haggard, sour look, blew through his lips in little explosive bursts like the release of steam through a safety valve. Alf realized he was laughing.

When he asked what was going on—he could scarcely believe what Linda Koch had told him—Davy regarded him with bright, dismissive scorn.

"Closing her down," he said finally, as if he had seen the event coming for weeks, and Alf, like the others, was some kind of ass not to have seen it too.

"What do you mean?"

He still had not grasped, would not let himself grasp, the full truth. There had to be some other explanation: a fire, a burst pipe, short-term layoffs.

"It's over. Finished. They just announced it. They're moving the whole damn thing to Quebec."

"Quebec?"

"They say anyone who wants to work down there can apply. They'll get priority. How about it, Alf, you like Quebec?"

He felt Davy's viciousness, the personal hostility that added an extra current of confusion to the news that Bannerman's was moving. Disbelief was pounding in his chest, his face. He felt curiously exposed, as though the closing was somehow the result of his own missteps, his own naive miscalculations. He had the image he'd had so often as a child—he could see blame making a wide turn in the far distance, like a winged predator that had seen him on its first pass and now, despite his hope that he had been overlooked, was returning for the kill.

"When?" he said.

"November," Davy said. "Soon as we're finished the fall lines."

Bruce Mason, the new president of the local, had climbed onto the loading dock of the sweater mill, where he was conferring with two other union officials. Some people in the crowd were watching them expectantly. Others were jeering. By now, Alf understood what had probably happened. The foremen had called the workers together to announce the closing—or perhaps the news had come over the PA system—and the employees had stormed out spontaneously. He'd seen the same thing before, in 1949. But it was one thing to stage a walkout; the question was always what to do next. The workers seemed at a loss. They were jostling about, looking for leadership, but when Bruce finally came forward with his hands raised to instill calm, he seemed helpless before the milling crowd.

"Brothers and sisters," he began.

"Fuck your brothers and sisters!" someone cried out. New arguments exploded around the perpetrator of this remark. Beside Alf, Davy Clark continued to snort his silent, bitter laughter. None of this surprised old Davy; it was what the fools deserved.

Bruce said something about "fighting this with everything we've got." He would talk to management. He'd go to Montreal and talk to the president of Intertex himself, if that's what it took. He drew a flutter of weak applause from many, but the sniping of boos and epithets continued. In the windows overhead, a few people leaned at the sills, looking down like casual spectators of an arcane blood sport. On the sixth floor, Kit Ford observed the proceedings intently, as though memorizing every detail. Across the yard, a fight broke out. Alf heard angry, surprised shouts, the desperate scuffling of feet on gravel. There was the sense of a society unraveling at the seams. No one knew what to do or what to expect.

Just then, Alf noticed Lucille, standing with a group of her fellow workers from the sewing department. Instantly, he experienced a surge of the old hunger; she seemed a point of solace—of escape, really—in the dismal confusion of the yard. Since the union picnic, he'd been hoping they might get together again, at least to talk. He watched her tuck in her blouse, watched her hand plunge into her wide belt, watched the deep equine curve of her lower back.

A man was approaching her group: Bud Reed from the dye department. He was a well-built fellow of about thirty, with a cockiness in his gait. A tight T-shirt showed his biceps. He leaned over to say something to the women, then remained beside them, standing so close to Lucille that their arms touched. Alf came awake, as he watched their fingers entwine.

—

ARRIVING HOME AT noon, he said nothing to Margaret but washed his hands and sat at the table, staring over the array of pink Melmac, the ribbed juice glasses she put down with crisp efficiency.

When the phone rang, Margaret answered. "It's for you."

The voice on the line was male, and toxic with rage. Alf could not quite tell who it was—half a dozen possibilities flashed through his mind, until there seemed to be not one but several persons there, speaking with a single voice. He heard profanities, a barrage of accusations. The closing of the mills was the union's fault, the voice said. The union had priced the mills out of the market. Because of the union they had lost their jobs. "I hope you're happy now, Walker."

"Who is this?" he demanded, and was answered with the clatter of a fumbled hang-up.

"Who was that?" Margaret said, from the sink.

He barely heard her.

"Alf?"

"They're closing the mills," he said, distracted, the voice on the phone still seething inside him.

"Closing—"

He looked at her sharply.

"Alf, what's going on?"

"The mills," he said. "Intertex. They're shutting them down."

"Who says they are?"

"I say!" he cried, furious. He saw Joe standing by the door. His son had simply materialized and now stood apart, remote. It had been his mood for weeks, ever since his girlfriend left. Alf had tried to console him—*Plenty more fish in the sea*—but the boy scarcely seemed aware of his existence. Two or three times when blue aerograms had arrived from France, Joe had hurried them to his room like a prisoner expecting a reprieve.

Margaret turned to Joe.

"Your father says they've closed the mills!"

"For God's sake, Margaret!" Alf said. Did she trust nothing he told her anymore? He stalked down the hall, pausing at the door to the living room, where Jamie and Penny were watching TV. Bud Reed, he thought suddenly. Bud Reed. Wasn't the guy a bit of a jerk? In a trance, he stared at the screen. The Three Stooges were up to their usual tricks: whooping like cranes, poking fingers in one another's eyes, driving one another's heads into trees and parked cars and telephone poles.

60

THAT AFTERNOON, BACK at work, the idea came to him that he should talk to Prince. He'd demand an explanation, cook up some deal that would keep Bannerman's in town. He had the notion he might somehow reach into the mechanism of power, as if it were an idling car engine, and make some fine adjustment that would stop Intertex in its course. He knew it was a long shot, knew he was a fool to think he could change the course of events, but his relationship with Prince gave him hope. He couldn't rest till he'd tried.

After supper, he set out in the Biscayne. At G.O. the Fleetwood was not in its usual place under the willow. He drove to Johnsonville, where the clerk at the Executive told him Prince had given up his room a week ago. He went back to his car and sat behind the wheel, distracted by the wobbling glow of the pool. Children cannonballed, sending up geysers with their cries. Prince's disappearance seemed the final blow. He and his company had swept in out of the blue, done what they wanted, and flown off with their spoils, to places where you couldn't get at them. The thing was, they'd always had the power to do this, whenever they wanted. All the contortions Alf had put himself through—they'd all put themselves through—hadn't made a whit of difference. They might just as well have done nothing.

Driving back into town, he kept looking for the Fleetwood; he couldn't help himself. The hood of a large black car waited at the corner of Shade and Bridge, its body concealed by a store. As it drew away, he saw it was Rick McArthur's Cadillac hearse, the same vehicle in which Pete had made his last ride, its long bonneted cabin decorated with a stylized chrome **S**.

He hardly slept that night; the next day, punch-drunk, he dragged himself through his eight hours at Bannerman's. Later, feeling a little better, he walked over to the Flats for a special union meeting about the closings. Arriving at the prefab barn near the mills—it had been built by the Lions as a clubhouse—he stood at the back in a press of heat-dampened bodies. Set up in front of the seated, noisily gabbing crowd was a long table where Bruce Mason, the union president, tapped experimentally at a mike. Bert Hatch, an old Bannerman's executive who had grown up in Attawan, sat beside him, his face with its dark jowls looking exaggeratedly mournful. Beside him, Linda Connaught, the secretary of the local, was bent over a three-ring notebook, writing, with her wide face close to the paper, like a schoolgirl.

Just then Bob Prince slipped in from a door at the rear of the stage and took the chair beside Bert Hatch. He was wearing a light tan summer suit but no tie. Instantly alert, Alf observed him closely: the slight superior tilt of his head as he leaned to murmur something to Bert Hatch; the casual rubbing with one finger of a place under his right ear as he coolly took in the rows of faces.

"Can everybody hear me?" Bruce Mason said, his disembodied voice suddenly booming from the speakers.

"Unfortunately!" someone barked behind Alf. In the middle of the hall, a heavy woman in a T-shirt—it was Gail Phipps from Number Six sewing—rose to her feet and raised one arm in a kind of salute. She looked around defiantly, shaking her fist as if she were holding aloft a trophy, or perhaps a weapon, as others shouted for her to sit. It took awhile for Bruce to get things under way.

Alf had trouble concentrating. He kept looking at Prince, while his mind drifted in and out of the proceedings, always returning to some blank, burning space of its own. But when Bert Hatch said he thought that what Intertex was doing was shameful, he joined vigorously in the applause. The workers were not used to hearing terms like *shameful* from their business leaders. They listened intently, clearly hoping for more from Bert, some further echoing of their moral claim—maybe even the announcement of action that might save the situation—but as Bert droned on it became clear his disgust was not leading anywhere and they grew restless again.

When Bruce invited questions from the floor, Jimmy Quinn demanded to know if Bannerman's was leaving because the union had come in.

The people at the head table glanced at one another, as cries erupted around the floor.

"Answer him!" several people shouted.

"Maybe Mr. Prince should handle that one," Bruce Mason said, looking down the table.

Prince waved aside the mike Bruce pushed toward him. He leaned forward, arms folded on the table (he had taken off his suit jacket and rolled his sleeves artfully halfway up his tanned forearms).

"I'll be as frank as I can," he said, and his rich voice immediately established a calm that had not been in the room before. One or two workers heckled him, but they were quickly silenced. "I fought the union coming in. I had orders to fight it, and I lost. Intertex didn't like the result, a lot of people here—probably some of them in this room—didn't like it, but there it was, we had a union." Prince bowed his head a little and frowned, as if girding himself for even more painful acts of candor. He looked exhausted, his face pale, bluish shadows under his eyes. At least this costs the bugger something, Alf thought, if only a few nights' sleep. "Sure," Prince said. "Having to pay more in wages, at a time when we were making some expensive changes, didn't help. It was a consideration. But it wasn't the only consideration. I mean, we're not leaving because we're sore losers or to get back at anybody. This is purely a business decision." Though Prince did not look at Bert Hatch, Alf sensed he was reprimanding the manager for that *shameful*.

This was not the simple answer Jimmy Quinn was hoping for; it seemed to cut both ways. The shipper tried again.

"Let me put it this way. Would you stay if we got rid of the union?"

Immediately, a dozen people tried to shout Jimmy down. Others shouted at the shouters. It was another minute before Prince could continue, during which time Jimmy waited patiently, his wizened face lifted with a kind of moral loftiness. In a life of filling boxes with sweaters, Jimmy, it occurred to Alf, had never before enjoyed such public importance and probably never would again.

"No," the executive said finally. "We've discussed this at Intertex and, no, it wouldn't be enough."

The silence that answered his announcement had a bruised, stunned quality. The crowd had given Prince authority. Now his authority had rebuked them: delivered a sentence from which there could be no reprieve.

Jimmy said, "What would be enough?"

Again Prince frowned before he spoke. "Look, Jimmy, this wasn't easy for any of us. We didn't take this decision lightly. But hell, the only reason Bannerman's is here is because John Bannerman needed the power from the rivers. Well, we don't use that kind of power anymore, we need to be closer to our markets, we need to shed departments that are losing money, we need newer buildings, ones that don't cost so much to keep up. There's no room for sentimentality—we'd soon be dead if we were sentimental—we just have to do it."

Jimmy tried to speak again, but Prince continued.

"We all make business decisions. That's what you people did when you decided to ask more for your labor, just like suppliers sometimes ask more for their wool or their dyes. Sometimes these decisions are good ones, and sometimes they aren't."

Jimmy sagged reluctantly to his chair. People were shouting at him, telling him what he should have said, what he might still say. He held out his hands palms up and shrugged, as if to say, What? what? Others sat in silence or talked among themselves. When Alf put his hand up, Bruce Mason pointed.

"Another question for Bob Prince," Alf said. His words seemed to travel out in the hall in a parody of his voice, nothing to do with him.

He watched Prince find him, the executive's face resolving into clarity at the distant table, the blue eyes flashing in recognition. "When Intertex came in here last year, all the talk was of turning the company around. You said we had the people here to put Bannerman's on track—people second to none, you said. Well, now you're turning your back on us. I'd like to know what made us so second rate all of a sudden."

"The union did!" someone yelled. "You did, Walker!"

Other voices exploded around the room. Alf went on standing; Prince fiddled with his papers as order was restored. Finally, wearily, the executive spoke. "As I said, Alf, it's a business decision—"

"Don't patronize us," Alf snapped. "As if business decisions are better than other kinds of decisions. As if we wouldn't understand them, these business decisions. As if we have to take it on faith that there's no other way. You're leaving us in the lurch here. You're running away. We've had this company for a hundred years. A lot of our grandmothers and grandfathers worked for Bannerman's, we feel like it's ours—hell, I think it *is* ours—and you're taking the whole thing out from under us. Why didn't you ever ask us what we think should be done here?"

The hall filled with applause. Even many of the anti-union people applauded, though others sat scowling. Alf, the blood pounding in his head, waited it out by staring at Prince, who stared at his papers.

Finally Prince said, "Look, the decision is made—"

Several people booed.

"I really don't think this gets us anywhere," Prince said, scowling. Each time he tried to speak, the noise erupted.

Bruce Mason, sheltering behind a weak smile, raised his hands and leaned into the mike. "Brothers, sisters," he said, to further boos. "I think we need to move along." But anarchy had been freed in the crowd. Standing up to point accusingly, or sitting in their chairs, people argued across the room while those at the table looked unhappily around, guests at a family quarrel.

Alf turned away. He no longer believed that Prince had anything for them, no longer believed the man was worth his attention. He pushed through the crowd into the parking lot, walking past the rows of cars until he reached the relative dark of the baseball infield behind the arena. Stopping, he fumbled for his smokes.

"Alf!"

He heard his own name with despair. The young man who slipped to his side was Lloyd Tindal. Alf remembered his father, a drunk with one eye, a breeder of German shepherds, now living somewhere else. He knew everyone in town, it seemed, and everyone in town knew him: he wished to God it was otherwise.

Lloyd Tindal's intense eyes met his with the excruciating frankness of youth. "That was great, what you said in there."

Alf went on smoking.

"Alf, look, some friends and me, we've got a plan. We want to know what you think about it. Maybe you'd help us."

Then he noticed the others, three or four of them, hanging around at the end of the bleachers like shadows waiting to be asked into the game.

IN THE VIMY House, their little table was soon crowded with glasses topped with pure high foam. The television was shouting from its perch above the bar: a woman weeping, her marine husband dead in a jungle across the world. To Alf, her suffering was just one more irritation. He concentrated on his beer and tried to ignore the circle of expectant faces.

They explained—it was mostly Lloyd explaining, calf eyes fixed on Alf's as if his, Lloyd's, life hung on convincing him—that they wanted to take some action. Take over G.O. Or sabotage something. "We want to burn the place down," Andy Morris said, his flat, smirking face suddenly red. The others looked from him to Alf. "Let them take that to Quebec," Andy said.

Alf stubbed out another cigarette. "All you'll do is ruin your lives," he said. "Look at you. You're all young; you can do a hundred other things. You know you'll get caught. It's certain you'll get caught." As he spoke his warnings, their gazes met his with sudden courage, then dove shyly for the beer. On the TV, Dinah Shore was seeing the USA in her Chevrolet.

He worried after they'd left. Maybe he should have said more. He lit another cigarette and wished he was with them, back at the beginning of his life. *Yai, yai, yai,* the TV cried harshly, and he looked up at black-eyed dancers whirling: see Spain!

LATER, STANDING IN the street, he was uncertain as to what to do next. Distantly, cars were gunning into life: he supposed the meeting was just breaking up. Shouts floated across the river from the Flats.

Walking home, he turned the corner onto Water and saw Jamie— Jamie, in his striped pajama tops and jeans, slowly riding his bike along the sidewalk, like something from a dream, scarcely credible. Trotting along ahead of him was Red.

"Jamie!"

Startled, his son stopped abruptly by a streetlight, hopping on one foot to keep his balance.

"For God's sake, what are you doing out here?"

His head down, the boy said something Alf couldn't make out, in that queer, flat voice he'd had for a while now. Alf supposed he'd snuck out past Margaret, who must have gone to bed early.

"Speak up. I can't hear you."

"Were you at Billy's house?"

Taken aback, Alf caught his breath. When the boy glanced up, what Alf saw in his face pierced him. "No," he said. "No. It's all right. Come on, let's get you home."

They went through the still summer night with Red trotting beside them in the road, his tail high, past the house where Alf had grown up, under the dim cloud of the maple his father had planted, past other, darkened houses, into the cul-de-sac.

In the kitchen, Alf made chocolate milk for Jamie, tea for himself. "You can stay up just for a bit," Alf told him. In truth, he felt an urgent need to keep the boy near him. They carried their drinks into the living room, where Alf turned on the TV, flipping the dial and stopping when he recognized an old movie from the fifties, *Moby Dick.* They sat together on the couch while Alf explained the plot. The great whale swam toward the tiny distant ship (so obviously a model) like a cruising low mound of snow. Then Ahab's peg leg stamped down the decks while his men crouched below, listening in hatred and fear.

"How big is a whale?" Jamie said.

"Oh, the biggest ones might be over a hundred feet. From here all the way to Olmsteads' over there." His son checked the porch light across the road, where it flickered among leaves. Something in the boy's expression, the curiosity and trust, moved Alf, and he reached out to squeeze Jamie's knee, feeling with gratitude the little bony knob under the denim. He wanted to be here: that was the realization he kept glimpsing. He wanted to be here, in this house, but he didn't feel he was, not entirely; a faint panic was unsettling him. He looked at the stairs in the hall, the white rails leading up into darkness.

Standing up, he went back to the kitchen and cut some bread for toast. Billy's house, he thought suddenly. My God, how much did the boy know? From behind came a quiet tap at the door and, turning, he saw a large moth fluttering outside the screen. He watched in a kind of stupor as the insect, so frail and yet so tenacious, banged repeatedly at the mesh, banged out its life, it seemed, with no idea it was harming itself.

When he heard the shattering of glass, he thought immediately it was the television tube. Then came the peel of tires, Red's howling lament from the yard. Racing down the hall, Alf turned the corner and saw Jamie just where he had left him, sitting on the couch in his jeans and pajama top. The television was still working—in a long shot, Moby Dick was pounding and lifting the little ship with its toothpick masts— but pieces of the shattered window littered the rug like the leavings of an ice storm.

Jamie's face was pale, his eyes glassy, filled with the faraway look of someone listening to the meander of his own thoughts. At the side of his forehead, just starting to bleed, was a rising lump. On the couch beside him, as if he had been playing with it, was a dark smooth chunk of rock about the size of a lopsided baseball. Bound to it with masking tape was a piece of paper.

It was not until the next morning, returning from the hospital with the police, that Alf read the crudely lettered note. HOPE YOUR HAPPY NOW WALKER THIS IS YOUR DOING FUCK YOU DIE.

61

AT THE HOSPITAL, they had covered Jamie's eyes with gauze, to keep them from drying out, and held the pads in place by strips of tape that masked much of his upper face, giving him the appearance of a bug with bulging eyes—an insect boy, resting against the huge pillow. Three days after the rock had come through the window, he was still unconscious.

Alf sat in a leatherette chair by the bed. It was nearly eleven o'clock. He had been in the room since seven. He watched in a kind of trance, adrift on his own thoughts, at the same time sensitive to every sign—or at least to the possibility of a sign—from the bed. Jamie's mouth was open a little. Alf couldn't hear him breathe in, but the exhalations came in huffs, too brief to be sighs yet suggesting to Alf a dangerous weariness, as if the boy were close to giving up. Alf had the impression that Jamie was at work—some vast labor—alone in the dark. He wanted to help, would have given his right arm to go down into that darkness and put his shoulder to the immense weight Jamie was lifting by himself, whatever it was, but all he could do was watch helplessly from the sidelines, not even sure what was going on. He thought of a time in the arena, years ago, when Joe had been knocked out during a hockey game. Joe's coach had vaulted over the boards and run slipping across the ice, while the other players had milled around the motionless little body in its purple jersey. Watching from the stands, Alf had not joined them. He didn't want to appear hysterical, didn't want to embarrass his son, didn't want to break the unspoken masculine code that forbade overreacting to physical danger. And after a minute Joe had gotten up, slowly, and skated to the bench, grinning at the applause from the other parents, while Alf watched in relief and pride. The boy had proved he could take it. Alf tried to wrap himself in the same spirit of resilience now—his boys could take it—but Jamie had been unconscious for so long. True, the doctors had reassured them that though it might take time, the chances were good that Jamie would recover. Yet Alf was experiencing a dread unlike anything in his life. He was alert to every movement in the bed. If Jamie's breathing paused, he was up in a flash, worrying. If the flow of IV seemed to stop, he was in the hall, looking for a nurse. Everything in his body craved action, the leap over the boards, the slipping run across the ice, but this time he had no choice. All he could do was watch.

Alf smoothed the blanket and touched his son's forehead, which was warm. The bump itself, mostly hidden by the eye patches, had begun to subside, a purplish swelling no larger than many Jamie had sustained before and yet worse, the doctor said, because the rock had caught him on the temple. The word had turned odd, traitorous, in Alf's mind. A temple was a place where people prayed (he thought of fluted pillars, like the ones outside the post office in Johnsonville), and at the same time it was part of the forehead, a fragile, small, mysterious spot. One inch either way, and Jamie might have been spared.

Above the bandages, Jamie's hair flamed in wild tufts. Alf smoothed them down and bent to him, whispering for perhaps the hundredth time. "It's Daddy, Jamie. I'm right here." For a moment the breathing paused. It seemed to him that Jamie might be listening. Perhaps he was considering the word *daddy,* down there in the dark. Alf imagined him wandering in a labyrinth, trying to feel his way out. Hearing the word, he might turn in the direction it had come from, and so start up the long passage that slanted toward the light. The breathing resumed. Perhaps he was on the right path now, and perhaps he was heading the other way, confused, into a deeper darkness.

Alf threw himself back in the leatherette chair. Bastards, he thought. Who had done this thing? Someone who blamed him for bringing the union in—for driving Intertex out. Someone with a grudge going back years, who knew? The police, so far, had come up with nothing.

He lurched forward again, thinking he caught a movement from the bed. But the bandaged face lay as still as before. A bubble rose brightly through the throat of the intravenous bottle.

Then Margaret was there, entering the room with swift steps.

Alf sat upright in his chair. Her attention was fixed on the bed. In her arm was a paper bag, which he knew contained things she would need for the night. The hospital was willing to supply an orderly to sit overnight with Jamie, but Margaret insisted on doing it herself. Alf had offered to spell her, but she'd refused.

He watched her drop her bag on the cot the nurses had set up for her and bend over Jamie. She touched the boy's hair, murmuring something Alf could not catch, touched the back of his hand.

"Dr. Samuels checked in," Alf said. Samuels, the specialist from Johnsonville, was consulting on the case. "He still thinks the chances are pretty good."

Margaret looked at Alf, her eyes hard, bright, as if she were testing the truth of his words. He flushed.

After a moment, he stood up. "I guess I'll leave you to it."

Margaret didn't answer but went back to ministering to Jamie, feeling his cheek with the back of her hand.

"Well," he said. All he wanted was a word from her, some acknowledgment, but she kept her back to him as she shook out a blanket.

Then she turned. "You're tired," she said. "Go and get some rest." She told Alf this in a crisp, factual way, her eyes meeting his only briefly. The weary flatness in her voice unsettled him more than anger, for it suggested she wasn't surprised by what had happened. It was the sort of thing she'd come to expect now, in the place Alf had brought them to.

HE GOT HOME to find Joe and Penny in bed. Far from sleep, he sat at the kitchen table in the dark. From the distant gravel pits, the faint clank of conveyor belts floated intermittently through the screen door. He stared out into the night, across Margaret's garden toward the shadowy bulk of the dike and the more distant grayness of Lookout Hill, where a streetlamp dropped a cone of light over the road running past the park. He hardly saw these things.

At one point he became aware that his thoughts were twined with a rushing sound that came from the river, from a place where a lone rock, known to him since boyhood, plowed stolidly upstream. He let out a long breath and shifted in his chair and, when a siren went off, lifted his head a little. The blasts kept coming, at short intervals. In the street, a car suddenly accelerated, as if it had been waiting for just this signal.

Sometime after the siren stopped, the phone rang behind him. For a few moments he sat without moving. But then, remembering Joe and Penny asleep upstairs, he rose to silence it.

"Alf, the mills are on fire!" It was Jack Cornish, his foreman on the maintenance crew, his voice narrow and distant, as if calling down a pipe.

Alf flicked on the light and blinked at the calendar. In the square for August 30, Margaret had printed PENNY'S TWELFTH BIRTHDAY! Another life: where people stroked exclamation points in acts of hectic enthusiasm, as if happiness might be commanded.

"Alf, are you there?"

Those buggers, Alf thought, those stupid goddamn buggers.

"Alf?"

"I'm here."

"The fire department's just come. Johnsonville's sending two trucks. We need more men."

Alf felt his heart punching its way through his ribs.

THROUGH THE WINDSHIELD of the Biscayne he saw at first only roiling smoke, reddening as it billowed over the mills. The lane off Bridge was blocked with vehicles. Hoses ran everywhere, veining wet asphalt. Several dozen people, many in bathrobes, had gathered under the wall of the arena. Passing the mouth of the lane, he glimpsed the livid mill windows: story upon story of fire, as if a party were going on, a party of fiery creatures, their laws and language unknown to men, filling the rooms with their dances, their roaring conversations.

There was no place left to park, so he drove around the corner, finally drawing into the parking lot of General Office. No flames were visible from here, though getting out of the car he could hear the hollow, cascading roar of the fire, the small shouts of men calling for hoses. The glowing smoke from the far side of the mill complex rose over the flat rooftops, shedding an eerie light. Everything he looked at—the walls of the mills, even the asphalt roadway—seemed on the verge of exploding into flame. He crossed the deserted street, reaching the fence that bordered the millrace. A stink of mud—the race had recently been emptied for repairs—mingled with the smell of smoke. Down the street, by a lone fire truck, several men with hoses were shooting water into a building. He began to walk toward them, glancing up from time to time at the windows of the mills. Here and there smoke seeped from under a sash. He was breathing hard.

A voice caught him. It had come from above, but squinting at the upper windows he could make out nothing.

The voice came again. It seemed, almost, to be sounding inside his own head.

"You there! Help me!"

Putting his hands on the fence bordering the race, Alf strained to see.

"Get a ladder here!"

Shouting harshly, trying not to scream: keeping to the last edge before the fall into hysteria.

The voice seemed somehow familiar. But when Alf found the right window, the figure was half hidden in a streaming veil of smoke. He could not make it out.

"Alf! Bring a ladder!"

He went on staring, spellbound. The man seemed so small and faraway, absurd in the vast, empty buildings. What was he doing there? Perhaps he had something to do with the fire itself, was fire's creature; or he was the beleaguered, desperate spirit of the mills themselves, shouting out a last request for life. *And he knew who Alf was.*

Smoke was pouring around the figure now, he was entirely invisible.

Alf turned at the rail, looking for help. To the south, the hoses were

sending thin, ineffectual arcs into the mill. There seemed to be no lad-
ders there. He would have to go around to the back of the mills by
Bridge Street. It would take too long. To his right, he saw the narrow
footbridge that crossed the millrace to the base of the building. At the
other end of the bridge, a few wisps of smoke coiled gently into the
night; the metal door was ajar.

At the truck, Phil Jones gave his place at the nozzle to another man.
His hands were stiff, his shirt soaked by a leak spraying from the hose.
He'd been in bed with the flu when the siren sounded. Now, feeling
both feverish and chilled and more than a bit sorry for himself, he
glanced to the north and saw, in the light of flames, a figure shrouded in
a blanket, crossing the footbridge. Phil watched it break into a run—it
seemed, under the cowl of the blanket, to be headless—and vanish into
the smoking side of the mill.

62

BY MID-SEPTEMBER, THE poplars along the Atta had turned yellow. Their leaves trembled with the faintest movement of the air; their inverted reflections, just visible in shadowy water, suggested the presence of another world.

For Joe, there was no question of university. He had failed to win a scholarship, and his mother's new job as a clerk at Millie's Dress Nook didn't bring in enough to support the family, so he had gone to work in the liquor store. He spent his days filling the shelves in the back room with cartons of Seagram's and Baby Duck—a task he preferred to serving at the front counter, where he sensed people were observing him. He felt ashamed, as if the events that had befallen his family were in some way deserved, the punishment for moral failure, perhaps, for having had the father he'd had.

The back room of the store overlooked the iron water of the Shade. On the far shore, past the dike and the playing fields, the blackened shell of the mills was being knocked down. All day he could hear faint explosions as the wrecking balls assaulted the thick walls and bricks fell in showers. Above the ruins, dark flocks of pigeons, like gusts of ash, beat away and frantically returned. One morning he was startled to see that the mills were gone.

They had found his father on an upper story, his head wrapped in the red tartan blanket. "Smoke was too much for him," Patch Cooper, the fire chief, told Joe a few days after the fire. He said that one of his men had seen his father enter the mill, but by the time the crew had found masks and gone in after him, it was too late. "We don't really know why he went in there. Myself, I think he was trying to help someone."

"Maybe that was it," Joe said thickly.

Patch Cooper paused before continuing. "Yes. Well, two or three foremen went into Number Six a little earlier. They were trying to close doors, save records, like. Maybe one of them got into trouble and he tried to help. It could be—'course, the investigation isn't over yet—it could be he did a brave thing there."

The fire chief avoided his eyes as he said this, and Joe had to wonder what his real opinions were. He knew Patch Cooper had to be aware, as he himself was, of rumors that his father had himself started the fire. He had tried to refute this possibility, but the only man who could answer his doubts was no longer there. Joe often still felt set against his father, as if his dying were one more affront. He'd be walking down the street, and a voice in him would carry on an argument—*Why did you do it you should never have gone in there why didn't you think of the rest of us why?*—that met only a silence deepening like a kind of winter.

A few days after his meeting with Patch Cooper, two provincial police detectives came to the house. They sat on the couch with their notebooks on their knees, interviewing Joe and Margaret. They were trying to piece together Alf's whereabouts on the night of the fire. Apparently, someone claimed to have sighted the Biscayne near the mills an hour or so before the alarm had been turned in.

"What exactly are you implying?" Margaret said, indignant. Joe, seated nearby, watched her draw herself up. She had aged, he thought, her face gone sharp, her eyes too bright in their sunken sockets.

One of the detectives, the softer-spoken one, said they weren't trying to say anything; they just had to tidy up all the loose ends.

"I think I've had enough," she said, standing up abruptly.

"I know it's been hard for you, Mrs. Walker."

"You don't know anything," she said.

When the policemen went on sitting, she left the room.

"I got one more question," the other detective said to Joe. "The night of the fire—after your dad came back from the hospital—were you aware of him leaving the house at any time?"

Frowning, Joe glanced down at the rug. He'd heard the Biscayne leaving but had no idea what time that was.

"No," he said. The detective held his gaze for a couple of seconds while Joe, his mouth dry, brazened it out.

Later, he found his mother in her garden, mucking furiously around her tomato plants with a hoe. As Joe approached she cried in a full voice, "They don't know anything. Your father—" She broke off and for a moment some new thought rose brimming into her eyes, into features that now looked soft and oddly unformed. He tried to hold her, awkwardly embracing her and the upright hoe together. After a minute she stiffened and pulled back. "All right," she told him. "Let's go in."

TEN DAYS AFTER the fire, Jamie woke up, and in another few days he was well enough to come home. The side of his head still bore the shrinking, yellowish traces of his wound, and he seemed slow and abstracted. When Margaret told him what had happened to his father, he went very still. A minute later he asked if he could watch television.

He had no desire to go outside to play. Hoping to rouse his interest, Joe gave his brother his old fiberglass bow and three new arrows, beautifully feathered. One afternoon, from his bedroom window, he saw Jamie standing on the shore of the river, aiming his bow toward the far bank. He wasn't strong enough to pull it back to its full extent, but the arrow he released drifted over the Atta, .a flash of orange, and disappeared into the foliage of Lookout Hill. Joe nearly shouted out the window—those arrows were expensive—but something in the rapt way his brother lowered the bow and stared at the hill restrained him, and he kept silent as Jamie sped the remaining arrows across the water.

Penny took it hard. At the cemetery, she had broken from her mother's side and run to the coffin as Joe and the other pallbearers carried it toward the grave. Lately, she seemed possessed by an extreme urge to do something. She was often busy in her room, her table a mess of paper and paints and soap shavings. She made a papier-mâché figure, three feet high, with a black coat and a rather grotesque face which she told Joe was Johnny North. Sometimes, for a few seconds, his father seemed to be looking out at him from her eyes, making some demand— for recognition, for help? Joe did not know what.

Gradually, by day, a kind of normality settled on the house. But at night came the sudden cries, the drumming of his brother's or his sister's feet down the hall to their mother's room. Jamie wouldn't go to sleep unless someone sat by him, a job Joe often took on. One night, while Jamie tossed and kept opening his eyes to check if his brother was still there, Joe sat on the bedroom floor with his back to the wall, rereading Anna's letters by flashlight. In August, she had written to say she was sharing rooms with two English girls, reveling in the fact that each morning they awoke to the smell of fresh bread from the shop below. As for Joe's standing with her, it seemed ambiguous at best. She wrote that she missed him, but her pleasure in her new life made him wonder.

He had written to her about the fire, omitting anything too specific. Of his father he said only that he had died while attempting to save another man. In one way, he was glad to have miseries to report. He felt he had earned the right to her affections. At the same time, these events filled him with shame.

Two days after he sent his letter, he found another of her blue aerograms waiting at the post office. Her father, she said, had told her what had happened. *Oh, Joe, my dear Joe, this is terrible!* Immediately, the warmth of her sympathy flooded him. She had written him a poem, which, like all her poems, he soon memorized. It was about their last evening together: the churchyard where they'd walked in the wind. She'd been more aware of the poignancy of that moment than he'd realized.

He went to the post office every day. In early October, another letter arrived. He took it to the little park, at the end of the main street, by the war memorial. Sitting on the step behind the monument, his back to the cool stone, he read her news. She was studying German, she told him, and she'd just made a weekend visit to Chartres. After several paragraphs about the cathedral, she mentioned Doug, an American friend.

He's a philosophy major, very interested in Sartre. You know, you can actually see Sartre almost any day here, walking to his favorite café. He looks like a garden gnome. He has a wall-eye. It seems to be looking at things no one else has seen, that have scared one part of him witless. Doug's trying to get up his nerve to speak to him.

I should tell you, Joe, it doesn't look like I'll be able to get to Attawan for Christmas. We can't afford it, and of course with the mills gone, my father is making arrangements to come back to France. They've promised him his old job again. But I want you to know how much our time together meant to me . . .

He put the pages aside. On the scarred wall of the old Capitol Theater, fading advertisements for long-ago films were just visible, including the image of an immense tiger with a red tongue. He had no idea who Sartre was.

THAT EVENING AFTER supper he took a walk along the Atta. Moving slowly, he reached the dam and for a while sat on the bank looking out at the thin skim of water racing down its long, sloping face. Above, the edge of the millpond approached the lip with a glassy stillness before it slipped over. He had been thinking of Anna. But when a late dragonfly skimmed across the pond, he had an awareness of his father so powerful he stopped breathing. This was a spot his father had known—he had swum and skated here as a boy; his father had been saturated with this place, as Joe himself was. He knew what his father had seen and felt here, because he was able to see and feel it too.

Then, with a cold breeze rising from the Atta, everything changed. What did he know about his father, really? What could he ever know, now, about what lay behind his father's eyes, behind his silences? Joe looked downstream, where the current surged over a rusted, weed-clogged bicycle, and knew the chill of unrecoverable loss.

Over the next few days, a weakness infected his body. He only wanted to lie in bed, not reading, not listening to the radio, but drifting in and out of shallow sleep. The yellow trees of Lookout Hill filled most of his window. His gaze kept drifting to a spot of delicate orange-pink—a young oak perhaps—about halfway up the hill. He would fix on this tree first thing in the morning, upset if mist obscured his view. In the evening, he watched with feverish interest as it dissolved in darkness. He had no idea why the tree compelled him so; but one morning when he discovered that a big wind had stripped most of its leaves, he was distraught.

His mother usually came in after work to give him the news of the day. And Penny liked to bring him his meals, what little he was able to eat. She'd begun to adopt Margaret's manner of brisk cheerfulness and would sit on the edge of his bed chatting about school. One afternoon she brought him a small figure, carved in yellow soap. It was of a young man with a hockey stick in his hand, about three inches high. As Joe turned it over in his hands, Penny waited, tense. "It's you," she cried finally, piqued that he hadn't guessed. "You remember, when we all went skating above the dam." And he remembered the hockey game, that day of blue-sky freedom. She had carved him skating alone upstream, his head bowed, his stick held idly upside down. She had caught the stoop of his shoulders, and his old jacket with the torn sleeve, and something else, some indefinable thing that was him. He was astonished—she had only just turned twelve—and he remembered Penny and her friends, their chiming voices, as he skated up to the rapids. Again he saw the fox, its long floating tail.

After a week or so, he began to make small forays around the house. One Sunday morning, when the others were at church, he ventured outside. Everything was new and bright, almost painful to look at—the green of the yard, reviving after a summer of drought, the sun glinting off the Lion's Park bridge. He still felt frail, unsure of his legs, and also frail in another way, as if what little courage he had for this walk might disappear in a moment. Soon his mind was racing with a nameless panic, as if the future had ceased to exist. When he put out his foot, he half expected it to fall on nothing. He had to be alert, he had to concentrate, to keep from being swept away.

That first day he got as far as the band shell in the park, where he sat relaxing, or at least pretending to, before he retreated to the house. Some days later, feeling much stronger, he dared a longer walk. He passed the dam, following the edge of the woods that curved around the fields of Wiley's farm. Though a bit light-headed, he began to move more quickly, lengthening his stride, swinging his arms. But then, pausing for breath under a grove of pines, he broke into a sweat. All his fear had come back, full force. The sky was too huge, every distance too vast.

He looked up the long hill, to where the fields crested against the sky. That was the shortest way home, he realized, straight across the fields and over the hill—much quicker than retracing his steps by the woods. The fields had not been plowed for some time and were covered with wild grasses, with outcrops of goldenrod and chicory and other weeds. As he assessed the fields, thinking he could never cross them (it was too far, too exposed), a wind came down the hill. It pressed over the dry grasses and weeds, making their heads bend, until it reached him. This wind, to his amazement, was warm. The day was cool, but a warm wind was coursing over him, touching his face, wrapping him in warmth, moving the plants and branches around him. In his chest, something seemed to break.

He did not know what happened next. In his whole life, thinking of it, he never would understand. But the next time he was conscious, he was on the hilltop, two hundred yards from where he had just been standing. He had no idea how he had got there; it was as if he had crossed the fields in a dream or as if some power—the wind itself, perhaps—had picked him up and deposited him on the high bald hilltop, on the grassy edge of an old lane.

He realized he was weeping, gladly and without stint, sobbing like a child. He was sitting with his legs stretched out on the ground, like a child in a sandbox, amazed at everything he saw. Far down by the river, a few poplar leaves glittered. Clouds sailed overhead, a scattered fleet with emblazoned sails, swelling to the west. The erect white tail of a deer disappeared over the hill. Normally, he would have been surprised to see a deer, but just now, everything was a miracle equal to it. A flock of starlings pulsed by with a thrumming of wings he felt in his breastbone. A lone heron launched itself from the water's edge, its wings rowing the deep air as it labored above the town.

He was rocking, in some ancient vital movement of self-solace, though the comfort seemed to come not only from him. Looking down the slope to the river, he knew he was part of it all still. It held him still. He knew he would go on, whether he wanted to or not; he would be carried on, by whatever had carried him to this hill, by whatever it was that moved the clouds and the birds and the leaves swirling off a nearby tree. But also, he *wanted* to go on. It was in him again, the desire to go on, however weak or unhappy or afraid he still was, and it brought as much grief as joy, because he knew, now, where life was headed. Yet he wanted it anyway. He wanted it because he wanted it; there was no more reason than that. He was alive.

ACKNOWLEDGMENTS

The stanza from Johnny North's poem, on page 280, is taken from a poem by Bobby West, eccentric, river-man and entertainer of Paris, Ontario, who died in 1941. Originally published in the *Paris Star,* the poem was reproduced in D. A. Smith's superb local history, *At the Forks of the Grand*, privately printed in 1956.

Except for the characters of Johnny North, based on Bobby West, and Abraham Shade, partially based on Hiram Capron, the Vermont-born founder of Paris, Ontario, this is a work of fiction. Any resemblances between the novel's other characters and any persons living or dead are entirely coincidental.

I wish to thank the Ontario Arts Council for a Works in Progress grant, 2000.

John Bemrose is a contributing editor at *Maclean*'s magazine, where he writes features, profiles, and criticism. A native of Paris, Ontario, he lives in Toronto. *The Island Walkers* is his first novel.